# THE WHISKERS OF HOPE

# THE WHISKERS OF HOPE

LAURA NAPOLI

HCP
HEATING CATS
PAWBLISHING

The Whiskers of Hope



First Printing, 2023

Paperback ISBN: 9798987194942

EBook ISBN: 9798987194959

Heating Cats Pawblishing, LLC

https://heatingcats.com

# CONTENTS

As promised, this book is dedicated to my friend Machina, who has been with me from the beginning of this journey. One of my fondest memories of writing this series was watching you read through the ending of the very first draft. In case you haven't figured it out yet, I dare a great deal. I hope you enjoy this version and the ending as much as you did the original, and as always...

With all my love,
Boot to the head!

# CHAPTER 1

# Jeran: Senior Councilor

As he usually did, Jeran Chenzira woke long before his alarm went off, only today was the first day he'd ever woken as a member of the Senior Council, and, for perhaps the first time in his life, he had absolutely no desire to get out of bed and go to work. He lay there quietly purring, wrapped in his partner's strong embrace, thanking every Ancient God in the universe for the blessing of this glorious day. He could barely believe that he and Myra had both survived, and on far better terms than they'd had any right to expect.

He'd walked into the council chamber prepared to die, prepared to watch the love of his life die and his children and grandchildren punished for a crime they did not commit, and prepared to commit treason to save the Hue-mans from genocide. Instead, he'd walked away with a new daughter and the rank of Senior Councilor for her people, making him one of the six most powerful people in the universe. That thought downright terrified him. *His people,* he reminded himself. He was now, and would always be, counted as one of them.

Somehow, Little Flower had managed to take on the entire Senior Council without raising a single claw, changing his and Myra's convictions into a victory. He wasn't even sure if a Senior Council verdict had ever been changed before, certainly not within minutes of that verdict being read, and not without the majority support of the Full Council.

He chuckled at the memory of Tabor's stunned silence. Granted he'd been just as stunned. Not just by Little Flower's decisions, but also by her defense of him. He had absolutely no right to that, after everything that had been done to her under his care and jurisdiction.

The day hadn't been entirely celebratory though. He'd still had to oversee the execution of his daughter's rapist, and while he was glad the male was now dead, he was sure he'd hear the male's screams in his nightmares for years to come, and not just because they'd sounded like screams of a cub. He'd overseen several executions in his life, but they'd never been as drawn out. 2A326 had earned his death, and spent the last hour of his life regretting the horrible decisions he'd made before Jer had given the order for Myra to end it.

At the time, he'd been far more worried about Myra. She'd been so close to losing control during the trial. Both he and the Senior Honor Guard had attempted to convince her to let them perform the execution, but she'd given her word to Little Flower, and had insisted. To his absolute relief and astonishment, Myra had remained in full control of her instinct the entire time, and outside of being placed on the watch list by Kendra, which was both expected and the standard procedure, there had thankfully been no issues. If anything, Myra had calmed significantly.

He was honestly glad she'd turned down his offer, although he'd never admit it to anyone. He had never killed before, had always let the Senior Councilor or the Guard handle it when necessary, but now that horrible duty was his responsibility. That thought caused him to stop purring. *He* was the Senior Councilor now, and he didn't have a Guard to call in. He honestly wondered if he could go through with it, if, no when, he had to in the future. He just prayed that 2A326 was the only monster they'd rescued from Earth. *I wonder if I can borrow Kendra and her guards for a while, at least until the Hue-mans set up their own guard. I imagine Marcus wouldn't mind.*

Soft snores came from the other side of his room. He shifted his head slightly so he could see in that direction and smiled. His parents hadn't wanted to leave his side to return to his brother's suite, had stayed late celebrating the night before, and now slept soundly on the other bed in his room. He didn't mind and fully understood. They'd been expecting him to die the day before too. He didn't get to see them nearly often enough either. It had been good having them here, and he knew they'd be returning home as soon as transport could be arranged, now that they no longer had to worry about burying their children.

His alarm eventually went off, but rather than getting up, he hit his tablet with his tail to silence it, having absolutely no desire to move from Myra's arms, or face his new responsibilities.

"Good morning, Senior Councilor," Myra whispered softly in his ear.

Jer chuckled, squeezed the arm that was currently draped over him, and twined his tail around hers. "It is far better than good, my love," he replied just as softly. "Although for probably the first time in my life, I have absolutely no desire to get out of bed and go to work." The crushing weight of responsibility he'd accepted the day before was frankly just a tad overwhelming, although in many ways far less terrifying than what he thought his actions for the day were going to be. *At least it's not treason to protect the Hue-mans now.*

"Just because you get to make the law now, doesn't mean you get to lay in bed all day," his father teased from the other bed. "Senior Councilors don't get snooze buttons."

"Tell me where it says that in the Charter, Papa." He grinned realizing he sounded just like Marsee the day she tried convincing him to let her kick the hydroponics unit.

"Not the Charter, your oath," his father replied.

Jer snorted at his father. His father might be retired now, but he was still a councilor at heart. "Well, my oath can wait a few minutes. I thought I was going to die yesterday. I fully intend to enjoy the morning that I never thought I would live to see, wrapped securely in the arms of the partner that I was terrified I would have to kill."

His father chuckled, but otherwise didn't respond. Six minutes or so later, his alarm went off again. He hit his tablet with his tail to silence it, again, and still didn't move, outside of re-twining his tail around Myra's. Neither did anyone else, not until his alarm went off a third time. He hit it again, with perhaps far more frustration than was becoming of a Senior Councilor, but this time sat up with a heavy sigh to turn it off. Alarm off, he was now presented with all of the additional applications he had access to, and as he stared at the screen, he once again felt the crushing weight of responsibility settle on him.

He nearly crawled back into Myra's strong arms to hide, but he didn't. With another sigh, he squared his shoulders, and forced himself to climb out of the bed. He padded his way across the common room to use the waste room, but stopped midway, changing his mind, and turned to look out the large window and the world below, instead. The sun was just starting to rise on the horizon, with pastel hints of color lighting up the sky. He didn't think he'd ever seen a more beautiful morning, full of promise and hope for the future.

"You'll make a wonderful Senior Councilor, Kitten," his father said behind him.

"Thanks, Papa," he replied without turning around. "I just hope I don't mess it up too badly."

His father snorted. "Well, if you do, I'm sure my new granddaughter will be able to set you straight."

Jer shuddered at the idea of being front and center of Little Flower's wrath, after seeing what she'd done to Senior Councilor Tabor the day before. "Now I really don't want to go to work."

His father chuckled. "Well, you've already faced down the impossible. Everything else should be cub's play. All you have to do now is build a home for your people, teach them to be honorable and productive citizens of our world, *and* put up with your brother."

"Is that all?" He frowned at how much work that would entail, and then turned around with a raised brow at his father. "My brother? What do you mean by that?"

"You do realize just how insufferable Marcus is going to be, now that you outrank him?" His father's face was serious, but his tail curled with humor.

Jer raised his other brow. He'd not even remotely considered that, but his father was right, even if he was joking. He now had to negotiate with his brother, who was now the councilor for the district Jer's people lived in, and his big brother had always outranked him, both in authority in the Council, and as his mentor. He wondered just how his promotion would affect their relationship. He doubted it would change anything all that much. While he might have the authority of a Senior Councilor, he had far fewer people under his care, and didn't even have a planet to call his own. He snorted. He didn't even have a home to call his own anymore, now that it had been given to the Hue-mans as punishment for his partner's crimes. But that was a far easier price to pay than the one he'd expected. He didn't particularly care where he lived as long as his family was with him.

He shrugged. "I'm sure Marcus will get over it. I'm far more worried about Tabor." Neither Tabor or the rest of the Senior Council had said or sent anything to him since he was unexpectedly promoted, and he wondered just what they were all thinking.

His father snorted and turned to find something to eat in the refrigeration unit. "She's still licking her wounds, I'm sure. Besides, after the public tail lashing she took yesterday, she won't dare to say no to whatever you need, nor will the rest of the Senior Council."

Jer turned back to the window, not really seeing anything, his thoughts in a whirl with everything he now needed to do. He stayed there until Myra walked up behind him and wrapped him in a hug. He sighed with happiness and purred, relaxing into her strong arms. Whatever happened, he still had his family, and that was all that really mattered.

The others soon exited their rooms. He hugged his daughters and wished GrandFather a good morning before making his way over to the table and the meal his father had prepared. After breakfast, they all walked over to the Guild, to meet up with Ellie and continue discussing their plans on how to retrofit the compound to best house and care for the few remaining species of Earth.

He had originally been scheduled for a Local Council meeting to follow the full one, to deal with any ramifications coming from the trial, assuming any of them still had seats, or lives for that matter. But as he was no longer part of that council, and as the other Seniors had still not reached out to him, he found he suddenly had the day off, and happily joined his family. Granted, ensuring his people had a home where they felt welcome, safe, and fit their unique needs was paramount in his list of responsibilities anyway.

Before they started discussions on the compound, Little Flower insisted on a tour of the Guild, and took the time to meet and personally thank everyone who had helped in providing her and her people with clothing and supplies. She made a point of not only asking about what they had been working on for her, but what they were passionate about, and asked to see examples of the work they were the most proud of. They all wanted to see her drawings as well, but she hadn't brought her sketchbooks with her, so she promised that she would bring something by another day.

He watched his new daughter throughout the morning, silently observing from behind the mask he was trained to wear, marveling at how much she had changed in the past month. When she'd arrived at his home, she was nothing more than a broken and scared cub, but she was now interacting with the others like the councilor she now was, and he wondered again why she'd really chosen him to be Senior Councilor, when she was so very clearly capable of that position herself. A part of him wondered if it had just been a ploy to get his conviction overturned. He certainly didn't feel like a Senior Councilor, and he wondered how he could possibly manage to counsel a species and culture he barely understood.

The tour took a good portion of the morning, so they broke for an early lunch in Ellie's office, and began work on the plans for the compound afterwards. Nearly three dozen masters across all aspects of the Guild provided their assistance and guidance to help make his daughter's dreams come true. To his surprise and hers, they were all reasonably fluent in sign language, almost as well as Ellie, and it was rather surreal to be in a meeting with that many people and have it be so quiet. Only their laughter broke the silence, or the occasional need for Marsee to translate.

The conversation and designs further highlighted the vast differences between their species, and the way that they looked at the world. He wouldn't have come up with a fraction of the things Little Flower and GrandFather were requesting from the Guild Masters, ways to make their home more livable. The suggestions were all obvious once they made them, but he knew he would never have come up with them, and he'd never seen the Senior Guild Master so excited before. She was coming away from this conversation with dozens of new products, which would ultimately benefit his people, since they were Little Flower's and GrandFather's ideas, and they would get the credit for it. Even something as simple as a door knob, something he would never have given a second thought about, had a significant impact on just how easily they could interact with his world, and they had dozens of ideas on how to solve that problem for all of the species that would eventually be visiting or living in his home.

They spent the first few hours listing out everything Little Flower and GrandFather thought they would need or want, for their people and the other creatures, not just as they were now, but planning for the immediate future, and the expected size of the next generation. They were currently listing out what needed to go in each of the rooms for the nursing and expecting mothers, and Little Flower was madly sketching her ideas.

"Oh, and rocking chairs," Little Flower added, before returning to her sketching. When she looked up though, it was to see Ellie staring at her in shock, and Myra laughing so hard she nearly fell out of her seat. Jer was honestly worried she'd break her tail from how tightly it was curled.

"What's so funny?" Little Flower asked, looking between Myra and Ellie in confusion, as she turned her sketch around for the others to see.

Ellie lifted her paws to sign, but she stopped and blinked at the drawing for several long seconds before answering. "Are you serious? Rocking chairs?!"

"Yes, babies love the motion," Little Flower replied, and frowned at her mother. "Mama, what's so funny about a rocking chair?"

Myra couldn't stop laughing, just pointed at Ellie and lifted her tail dramatically kinked over. Marsee was having a hard time keeping a straight face too, but she was managing, that was, until Ellie lifted her paws at a complete loss for words, at which point it was too much and Marsee started laughing too. Everyone else in the room was completely baffled as to what was going on, but their humor was infectious, and tails were curling everywhere.

Finally, when Myra managed to gain a semblance of control over her laughter, she began telling the tale of how Ellie had once tried inventing rocking chairs for her master's project, only to roll over her tail the first time she tried it out, and had then fallen over backwards reacting from the pain, and in the process destroyed the chair she'd spent months working on. It took her a good ten minutes to get the story out though, as she kept doubling over with laughter.

The other Guild Masters in the room began laughing and teasing Ellie, and Ellie's expression shifted from amused to annoyed, which made everyone laugh even harder. "You'd think I'd never made a mistake before," Ellie muttered.

"Is that why your tail was in a splint for weeks?" one of the older masters asked. "I thought for sure someone had bitten it."

Ellie snorted. "That probably would have been far less painful. Little Flower, are you sure you want a rocking chair? They're dangerous."

"Absolutely," Little Flower replied with a wicked grin. "Last I checked, we don't have tails, so we should be safe. You might want to keep your distance though."

The glare Ellie gave Little Flower caused the room to burst out laughing again.

He was still chuckling when his tablet dinged with the tone he used for an urgent message, and he raised his brow as he unclipped his tablet and read.

"Well, as much as I would love to stay here and pick on Ellie, it looks like I need to go. Tabor has asked for my presence at her council meeting."

"What does she want?" Little Flower asked.

"I don't know. She didn't say," Jer replied, and left the others to continue on with their teasing and designs. As he walked, he wondered just what Tabor wanted him for. He was fully aware of everything on the docket, and none of it should have required his attendance.

He arrived only moments before the session started, and the moment he entered the Senior's conference room, where the others were all there and waiting for him, Tabor stood and walked out into the local chamber, not giving him a chance to ask what was going on.

"All rise as the Senior Council enters the chamber!" came the booming voice of the guard outside the door, Kendra, from the sounds of things, which made him raise a brow. Her presence at the Full Council was unusual enough, but she almost never attended local sessions. The others followed out after her, with nothing more than a nod to him. He shrugged and pulled on his mask before following them out, taking his seat next to Apakna, the Senior from the Ice Planet. Murmurs went through the Council at their attendance. While any Senior could attend the local meeting of another planet, they rarely did, except on special occasions, and that was usually known in advance.

"Please take your seat. This council is now in session," Tabor called out, and then walked out in front of her desk and turned to face him.

"Senior Councilor Chenzira, on behalf of your people, I formally submit my public apology for all of the harm I have caused them since their arrival on our world. I kept them in isolation for fear of what pathogens they might carry, even after being informed multiple times that they were suffering from their isolation. I chose not to further investigate the illness your partner claimed they were suffering from, because I did not believe that isolation could cause the kinds of problems she indicated. I also believed that they were not sentient, as we could not communicate with them, not taking into account that they might not even be able to hear us due to the injuries they received. I used that as an excuse to deny them the comforts and distractions they needed during quarantine, and then later felt so guilty about what I had done, that I chose to put them in stasis, risking their very lives, because I couldn't bear having them suffer more from their isolation. Yesterday your daughter came before the Full Council and blamed us all for a crime she considered to be far worse than the rape and beating that occurred under our care, and based on the Charter of this Consortium, we have broken the law, and caused her and her people significant harm in the process. I take full responsibility for that harm *and* the decisions made by this and the Full Council that led to that harm, as it was with my recommendation that the other Seniors did not call for ending isolation either. And as such, I am formally submitting my resignation as both Councilor and Senior Councilor, effective immediately."

With that, Tabor turned and walked out of the room, to the stunned silence of everyone there. No one spoke for several minutes, but finally, Clear Seas, the highest ranking member of the Senior Council, as he'd been a senior for over a hundred years, floated up from his seat. "Former Councilor Tabor's district position will remain open until elections are complete. Until then, her senior advocate will be the acting councilor for her district. Councilors, please submit your nominations for senior councilor."

No one moved. No one submitted a vote. For over an hour, no one even so much as requested to speak. Jer had witnessed several elections in his career, and he'd never seen anything like it. Most elections were highly contested. He glanced over at Marcus, who was sitting with his arms crossed looking back at him, and he wondered just what his brother was thinking.

Finally, Councilor Paxton Parner hit his light, requesting to speak.

"Councilor Parner. You have the floor," Clear Seas stated.

"Thank you, Senior Councilor." Paxton stood and turned to face the council. "Councilors, I would like to put forth the nomination of Marcus Surellis for Senior Councilor, as he is the only one among us who deserves this position. He has advocated for the rights of the Hue-mans long before any of us believed they were sentient, and he put his very life on the line for them to ensure they had a fair trial, because we weren't brave enough to give them the rights they deserved. Additionally, he has served as Councilor longer than any of us, and has historically had the highest ratings of any of us, by the people we represent. Our ratings have all dropped, but he has some of the highest ratings ever seen, in a district he has only represented for a day. As such, I believe we should follow the will of the people in this matter. I release the floor."

"Councilor Surellis, do you accept this nomination?" Clear Seas asked.

Marcus was silent for several moments before standing. "Councilor Parner, I thank you for your kind words, but I respectfully decline the nomination. Instead, I put forth the nomination for *you* as Senior Councilor. You alone called out that the plans proposed by the Agency were wrong, yet you alone, outside of myself and Former Councilor Tabor remained in isolation for the full day, as had been suggested. I only did so to prove a point, but you did so to fully understand what they were going through, something no one else in this room was willing to do, and you changed your mind in order to help the Hue-mans. Not only that but you faced your fears and personally came to meet Little Flower, the only one out of this entire Council who did so. You took over Councilor Chenzira's committee positions without hesitation, and from every report I've heard, did an excellent job, while still helping us prepare for the meeting, which you didn't have to do, and for which, I thank you. I release the floor."

"Councilor Parner, do *you* accept this nomination?"

Paxton stared at Marcus for several moments before standing. "Councilor Surellis, I thank you for your kind words, but I too respectfully decline the nomination. What I have learned over the past few weeks is that I am not ready for that level of responsibility, even though I knew full well going into that meeting that I might end up with it anyway."

This caused murmurs throughout the entire council, as it was incredibly rare for any councilor to admit they weren't fully capable of whatever was asked of them, and certainly not in public, or from Councilor Parner, who had walked into the chamber on his first day as if he owned the place.

The murmurs eventually quieted, and again they sat in silence for another hour before Clear Seas spoke again. "Well, this is certainly an exciting meeting." The council chuckled in response, and the tip of Jer's tail curled with suppressed humor. Clear Seas turned again to Marcus. "Councilor Surellis, as there are no further nominations being put forth, I ask again if you are willing to accept."

Marcus sat there for several minutes this time, before standing. "I will accept the nomination, as long as Councilor Parner *also* accepts the nomination."

"Councilor Parner?" Clear Seas asked.

"I accept," Parner replied, after only a few moments of hesitation.

"Then if there are no further nominations, Councilors, please submit your vote," Clear Seas ordered.

It was all Jer could do to keep from snorting at his big brother's reaction when the vote came in unanimous, and Marcus was sworn in as the Senior Councilor.

"It's about time you accepted the position," he told Marcus, as he shook his paw in congratulations. "Just don't spend all your time in the Ancient Archives. You still have requisition meetings to attend."

Marcus chuckled. "I'll see what I can do."

Jer left with the rest of the Seniors, excused by Marcus, as they were not needed for the rest of the local meeting, and found himself back in the Senior's conference room with Clear Seas, Apakna, Sammianna, and Wind Rider.

"Did you know she was going to do that?" Jer asked, once the door was shut.

"No," Clear Seas replied. "We only arrived moments before you did. I too am sorry for the harm my inaction caused your people."

The others all added their agreement and Jer tilted his head in acknowledgement.

"The real question is what to do next, now that Tabor has taken full responsibility. I'm not sure if a Senior Councilor has ever been found guilty of a crime before," Wind Rider stated.

"We didn't find anything in our research," Jer replied. "Councilors yes, but not seniors."

"Well, either way, we should wait for Marcus to discuss it," Sammi-anna stated. "Jeran, it would help if we knew what kind of reparations your daughter wants. I'd personally rather avoid another trial if we can come to an agreement."

Jer nodded. "I'll ask. Shall we meet after the evening meal? That should give Marcus plenty of time."

The others all nodded their agreement so he turned to leave.

He was nearly at the door when Clear Seas stopped him. "Jeran wait."

Jer turned back to the room, surprised at the formality from Clear Seas. He had known Clear Seas for years, long before either of them were on the Council, and had grown up with him while their parents ruled the universe. Clear Seas had taken his seat of power very early on though, just as Jer was starting his training, when Clear Seas' father unexpectedly died. The Water Sprites had a fairly feudal system, but even though a vote was required by law, and Clear Seas had little actual training, his people had voted him in, not just as councilor but as senior councilor too. They had spoken often about the challenges of their positions over the years. Jer couldn't remember the last time Clear Seas ever used his full name.

"For what it's worth, I am sorry for the decisions we had little choice but to make, as they were precedent and law, but I hope that we can still be friends, and find a way to work together."

Jer nodded. "I made the same decisions you all did. My partner and I took full responsibility knowing what that would mean for us. I thank you all for taking my suggestions on how to work around such an unjust precedent, although, I for one, am very thankful my daughter is far more inventive and forgiving than she has any right to be. My partner and I are alive because of her and the chance you gave us, and I thank you for that."

Clear Seas nodded in acknowledgement, but Jer wasn't done. Squaring his shoulders and pulling forth every ounce of authority he now had, he continued. "But know this too. I fully intend to honor my oath, with my very life if it comes to that. Little Flower came to us angry, scared, beaten, and alone. If she can bloom into the amazing person she has in just a month, I have no doubt the others will as well. As long as they remain safe, I see no reason why we can't continue to work together, as friends."

Jer knew from Marsee that they had been contemplating genocide to get rid of the threat the Hue-mans posed, after Little Flower's frank and rather terrifying testimony about the nature and history of her people, and he had been fully prepared to fight the Council if they had tried anything, not that he'd stood a chance. If the Guard hadn't stopped him, Clear Seas would have been able to kill him with a touch.

Clear Seas nodded. "I am sure your daughters told you of what was discussed here. Her people presented an unknown threat that we needed to take seriously, but we unanimously decided that they deserved a chance to prove themselves, and I have full confidence in your ability to lead them. I'm honestly glad she chose you. I can't think of anyone better to be their protector and mentor, and as long as they don't harm our people, they will be welcome members of this Consortium."

Jer gave a single nod, turned, and left the room and the other seniors behind. He walked slowly back to the Guild, taking a more scenic route as he tried to clear his mind of the racing thoughts in his brain, and failed miserably. While they had effectively declared peace, he wondered if they'd ever been as close to war before, and wondered what would happen if a single person was harmed, on either side. He had no way to keep his people safe. He had nothing, no land, no resources, no guard. His people could be wiped out with next to no effort, but could he turn the others into valued members of society, or would the darkness from their now destroyed world infect his own. He honestly had no idea. He wasn't even sure how he'd managed to win Little Flower's favor. After what had happened to them, would they even forgive him, or just vote him out the first chance they got?

When he finally returned, he sat down not saying anything at first. They all sat there watching him for several moments, before he snorted and shook his head. "Well, that was rather unexpected," he finally said.

"Oh?" Little Flower asked.

He explained, giving them a quick rundown of what had happened in the meeting. "Anyway, they voted and Marcus was unanimously sworn in as the new Senior Councilor."

"Unanimously?" Ellie asked. "Has that ever happened before?"

"Not as far as I know, at least for our planet anyway," Jer replied.

His father started chuckling, which turned into full on laughter, and he couldn't stop for several minutes.

Jer had rarely seen his father so amused and looked over at him with a raised brow, but otherwise blank expression. "Care to explain what you think is so funny, Papa?"

"You and Marcus. I came here thinking I was going to lose both of you, but instead, you both somehow managed to get yourselves elected to the Senior Council instead. I still can't believe what happened yesterday, but I'm honestly more surprised that your brother finally accepted his place as Senior. I thought for sure he'd never accept a nomination, after all the times he's turned it down, but I'm guessing the lure of the Ancient Archives finally won out. That, or he couldn't handle his baby brother one-upping him. But what made me laugh was the thought of Little Flower taking on Marcus next. I just hope you're prepared to protect him from her."

Jer snorted. "If my big brother is stupid enough to get in her way, he deserves it. She may be tiny but she bites."

Little Flower bared her teeth in a wicked grin, and signed 'this little flower has thorns too', causing everyone to laugh.

"So, what did the other Seniors have to say about Tabor's admission and Little Flower's accusation?" her mother asked.

"Not a whole lot. They were just as surprised as I was. We have a meeting scheduled for this evening to discuss it though," Jer replied. "We're waiting for Marcus to finish his meeting. Little Flower, we do need to know what you want for reparations."

His daughter nodded but didn't answer. "I'll think about it and let you know before your meeting," she said eventually.

They took a small break to watch the recording of Tabor's speech, which Marsee translated for Little Flower. After shaking her head in disbelief, and stating that she was unsure about how she felt about Tabor's apology, Little Flower shrugged and went back to work.

They were just about to take a break for the evening meal when Myra received a call from Brice and stepped out, but was back a few minutes later with a look of incredulity on her face.

"What's wrong, Myra," Jer asked.

"I'm honestly not sure I believe it," she said, scratching the back of her ears. "Brice says Tabor just showed up at the Agency, demanded to be handed a single puzzle box and shown to Little Flower's old cell, and then promptly locked herself in. She ordered Brice to give her the exact same care that had been given to Little Flower, no more, no less, and not to release her until she had spent the exact same amount of time that Little Flower had been stuck in that room. No one was to speak to her or let her out, no matter what she told them, and ordered that she was not allowed contact with her partner or four young cubs, or informed of their health or wellbeing, no matter what happened in their lives."

Little Flower sat there stunned by this announcement, a mix of both shock and horror on her face.

Jer saw her expression and pulled her out of Ellie's office and into an empty room, shutting the door behind them. "Are you okay?" he asked.

"Not really," Little Flower replied. "I am mad at her, but I got most of that out yesterday. Part of me wants her to experience even a little of what I went through, but I'm also horrified by the punishment. This will destroy her and affect her family, and it's against the Charter, even if it is self-imposed."

Jer nodded. "What would you like me to do?"

She shrugged. "I don't know. It is equal to what I went through, but I'm not the only one that was affected by her decisions. If it were just me, I think I would be fine with her apology and stepping down, and perhaps some form of additional monetary reparations or community service. But she nearly killed my people, and not just with our isolation. She could have killed us again when she ordered everyone thrown into stasis against Mama's recommendations. Part of me wonders if she wasn't hoping for that outcome. It will take us a long time to recover from what happened to us, and trust your people. This will help the others, I think, even if I feel icky about it." She was silent for another moment. "I'll abide by whatever you and the rest of the Seniors decide is fair and just."

Jer looked at her with a sad smile. "I'm proud of you daughter, and I think you would have made a wonderful senior councilor. If you change your mind, let me know."

"No thank you. Councilor is good enough for me," she replied. "Besides, I'm going to be on maternity leave soon."

"So you've decided then?"

She nodded. "I think so. I'm worried that I won't be a good mother, and that I won't be able to get past my trauma. I don't know what I'll do if the baby looks like him though. But, there aren't many of us left, and it's not the child's fault who their genetic donor is."

"Your mother and I will care for the cub if you can't," her father said. "But I have a feeling you will be an incredible mother, if the compassion you've shown for my family is any indication."
"Thanks," Little Flower replied with a nod, but her expression was haunted. Eventually, she just shook her head to clear her thoughts, and left to return to the others.

Jer let out a heavy sigh as he watched his daughter walk away. Everything had worked out far better than he could have possibly imagined, but he was still very worried about her. There was still the very real risk of death or complications from childbirth, and if she died, Myra could still be found complicit in that death. He had less than two months to build a new home for the people he represented, and get them to trust both him and Myra if something happened to Little Flower. If she died, he would have no choice but to bring Myra before his new people for an adjustment in sentencing, as Myra had been found complicit in his daughter's rape, and he had no idea how they would vote. Myra could appeal to the Senior Council, but he doubted they would find in her favor either. In this, they would go with the will of the people.

With another heavy sigh, Jer went to send the Seniors a message, but noticed Marcus's busy light was off. *The Council meeting must be over,* he thought and decided to call Marcus first to see if they could come to a decision without involving the others.

Marcus answered with a look of pure annoyance on his face. "What's wrong this time, Cub."

Jer grinned. "You know, I am a Senior Councilor now, and if I'm not mistaken, I've had that rank for an entire day longer than you. That gives me seniority. You could at least call me by my name."

Marcus chewed his lip and glared at him. "You may have seniority, but if you think for a second that I don't outrank you, you're sadly mistaken. I am still your mentor and older brother, and I can and will pin you to the ground, if I need to prove it."

Jer raised a brow. "Is that a threat? Are you declaring war? Shall I gather my forces?" He kept his expression neutral and hidden behind his mask, but his tail was spiraled.

His brother snorted. "What forces? You don't even have a guard."

"I don't need one. I have Little Flower. If she can take on Tabor and win, you don't stand a chance." Jer crossed his arms and leaned back in his chair, projecting all the confidence in the world, very curious to see how his brother would respond.

Marcus glared at him and let out a sigh. "What's wrong this time, *Senior* Councilor Chenzira," Marcus replied, with just the barest hint of a growl

Jer grinned with the victory. "Now see. Was that so hard?"

Marcus just continued to glare at him, waiting.

He let the silence linger for a moment, basking in his tiny victory, one of the few he'd ever had over his older brother, before answering. "Myra got a call from Brice a few minutes ago. Tabor showed up at the Agency and locked herself in Little Flower's old habitat."

Marcus snorted and flipped his ears back in surprise. "Seriously?"

"Would I lie about something like that?" Jer asked.

"Yes, especially if you're plotting with Wind Rider," Marcus replied.

Jer chuckled and filled Marcus in on the details and what Little Flower had said.

"I'm honestly not aware of a Senior Councilor ever being convicted of a crime," Marcus said. "We certainly didn't find anything on our search. So, I doubt there's precedent. Her self-imposed punishment is good enough for me, but we should talk with other Seniors first. Little Flower is right. It does go against the Charter, but it's also fair, equal, and just, for what happened to her people. Is there anything else?"

"No. That's it for now," Jer said. "But we do have a lot to talk about. That can all wait until tomorrow though."

"That we do. Let the other Seniors know, and we can discuss it in our meeting later. I have things to do before then," Marcus said, and hung up without so much as a goodbye.

Jer grinned at his blank screen. He had a pretty good feeling those things involved a trip to the Ancient Archives. *If he's not already there,* Jer thought. He fired off a message to the rest of the Seniors letting them know, and made his way back to Ellie's office, to see what plans his daughter had hatched in his absence.

His meeting with the Seniors ended up being fairly brief, seeing as Tabor had essentially solved their problem for them. They ultimately decided to leave it up to Little Flower, finding the self-imposed punishment fair, equal, and just. Frankly they were all relieved that they didn't have to schedule another trial, especially seeing as Little Flower had charged pretty much the entire Full Council with being complicit in that crime. Tabor had admitted her guilt, taken full responsibility, and done her own sentencing, and that was good enough for them. If Little Flower wished to shorten the duration or allow for visitation, then it was entirely up to her.

A statement was released shortly afterwards regarding Tabor's self-imposed punishment and admission of guilt, even though it was all over the news, along with formal acknowledgement that Jer's charges had been dropped, as had been implied with his promotion to Senior Councilor. Included in that statement was the approved aid, which had been quadrupled. While it wasn't stated officially, everyone knew that it had been the Senior Council's way of apologizing for not speaking up about the conditions at the Agency, as Myra had reached out to all of them for assistance when her pleas to the Local Council and Healer's Guild had gone unmet, and for not providing adequate living conditions during their time trapped there in the first place.

By the time he was done, the others had finalized the initial plans for the rebuild, scheduled to begin the very next morning. So, rather than waiting until morning to return home, they made their way over to the Ship's Guild to pick up the interplanetary ship he now qualified for as a Senior Councilor.

"I'm very sorry, sir. Your official ship isn't quite ready yet," the attendant at the reservation booth stated. "We weren't sure what the Hue-mans would need, and figured it would need to be reconfigured, but we can assign you another one."

"I figured as much. Any ship will do," he stated. "I'd like to make modifications of my official ship to better fit my family and people anyway."

"Of course, sir," the attendant stated, and began taking down Jer's requirements, while his parents spoke with another attendant about getting tickets on the next public transport home. From the sound of things, it wasn't going well.

"Running away so soon?" a voice called out behind him.

"Wind Rider, what are you doing here?" Jer asked, surprised as there was little need for the Flyer's senior to be at the Shipyard. The Council had their own shuttle bay.

"Running away," she replied with a grin. "I left my ship for mainte-nance while I was stuck here, trying to solve *your* little problem, and I was just informed that it was complete. I'm heading back to Flyer. You?"

"Picking up a loaner ship until mine is ready, and my parents are trying to arrange transportation back to Flyer."

"Well that's not needed. They're more than welcome to fly back with me, if they're ready to leave now. I have plenty of space on my ship," Wind Rider stated.

His father heard and turned towards them. "That's very kind of you, Senior Councilor, but it's not necessary."

"My pleasure. Besides, we can't have the parents of two of our Senior Council taking a public transport, which if my ears heard correctly, isn't available for another several weeks."

"Well then, thank you," his father replied.

Jer glared at Wind Rider. "Why do I have a feeling you're going to be asking them for embarrassing pictures and stories of me as a cub, the entire flight back?"

Wind Rider burst out laughing and fluttered her wings. "I wasn't, but that's an excellent idea. I've known your brother since I was a child, but I don't know all that much about you. Do you like fish as much as your brother does?"

Jer grinned and his tail curled in laughter. "Sadly no, I'm allergic as are most of my species. However the Hue-mans enjoy it quite a bit. Apparently, it's very tasty when cooked over a flame."

"I will have to give that a try sometime," Wind Rider stated. "Well, we should be off. I have been away from home for far too long, and I must admit, I'm starting to get a little uncomfortable." She turned to face Little Flower. "Councilor, It has been a pleasure meeting you, and I hope our next meeting is under better circumstances."

"As do I," Little Flower replied. "Safe flight."

They said goodbye to his parents, and he watched them follow Wind Rider to her ship, sad that they were leaving so soon. Once they were out of sight, he turned back to the attendant he was working with and finished documenting the changes he wanted. A few minutes later they were led to the ship he would be borrowing until his was complete.

He was a competent shuttle pilot. Living in the South District required it, but he'd never flown a ship before, or had the privilege of flying on one of the Senior's ships either. His new ship, he was informed, came with three full time pilots, ready to fly him anywhere at a moment's notice. The council transport ships he took to travel to the other planets for the Full Council meetings were nice, but nowhere near as nice as the ship he was on now, and he spent the majority of the trip back, absently watching the conversation of his family, and rubbing the soft material of the arm rest on his jump seat, as his mind drifted, yet again.

"Papa," Little Flower asked and waved to get his attention when he didn't respond right away. "What did Wind Rider mean about it getting a little uncomfortable? Was that a subtle reference to the trial?"

He raised a brow, not having made that association, and looked back at the conversation. "No, I don't think so. Based on her size, she has eggs to lay. She can choose when she lays them, give or take a week or so, but the longer she waits the more uncomfortable it gets as they grow and start to harden. Timing wise, she usually tries to lay them mid cycle between Full Council meetings. My guess is that she had her mating flight just before we found out about your rape, and the Senior Council deliberated for far longer than with any of the other sentience trials, so she's probably overdue. There aren't any hatcheries here for her to use either, although my understanding is they are considering adding one."

Little Flower nodded her understanding, and then slid out of her jump seat to make her way back to the waste room. Shortly after she returned, the pilots announced they would be landing. Jer looked out the window and watched as their compound came into view, knowing it was the last time he would see it look like this. The suns had set, but the sky was still riddled with the last hints of purple and pink. The first hints of stars were visible, while off in the distance, the first of the three moons started to crest the distant mountains. Still, it was dark enough that the compound's automatic lights turned on as the ship approached and landed just outside of the shuttle bay, as it was far too big to fit inside.

When he opened the door to the compound, Little Flower, Marsee, and GrandFather all went inside, but Myra didn't. Instead she turned and looked out at the moonlit valley with a heavy sigh.

"Are you okay?" he asked her. They hadn't had any privacy to talk about everything that had happened yet.

"Better than okay," she replied. "I never thought I'd see this view again, and I'm beyond grateful for what Little Flower managed, but I'm also a little sad too."

He walked over and wrapped his tail around her. "Why?" he asked quietly.

"Because I feel like I'm losing a little bit of my parents and history," she said eventually. "This compound has been here for thousands of years, handed down from one Chenzira to the next, mostly untouched, outside of the repairs and tech upgrades. I know it's always been far too big for us, especially since our first litter moved out and my parents died, but I couldn't bear giving it up for something that better fit us. This is all I have left of them, and tomorrow, most of it will be torn down."

Jer hugged her. "You have every right to feel sad about this change, but because of it, there will now be more Chenziras, and I think your parents would gladly have done the same. I know I would gladly tear down every brick and stone in the compound to have you with me, and to someday have half a dozen little Marsees pouncing on our tails."

Myra grinned over at him with love, but her smile did not reach her eyes. They glittered with suppressed tears in the moonlight. She turned, placing her paw on the ancient stone and began walking around the compound, never taking her paw off the wall. He followed, keeping her company as she said goodbye to their home. They made the loop in silence, only stopping once to look up at the lights coming from Marsee's tower room, and listen to the music Marsee was playing. He smiled, recognizing the song. It was one his older cubs had recorded, and one of his personal favorites as it reminded him of Marsee when she was a cub.

When they made it back around, Myra walked around the inside, stopping to look in every room. His thoughts were full of his own memories of this home and the family he'd raised here, and he prayed to the Ancient Gods that the rest of the Hue-mans would find this place as warm and loving as his newest daughter apparently did. He still couldn't believe she wanted him as her father after everything that had happened.

They eventually made their way into the garden and sat down under the bandala tree, watching the flicker flyers dance between the flowers, and listening to the gentle murmurs of the nearby stream, and the occasional drifting sounds of music coming from Marsee's room.

"Jer, how under the bright blessed full moons are we ever going to be able to care for all of them?" Myra asked him eventually.

"Not a moons' forsaken clue," Jer replied. "But you've managed admirably so far. Look at it this way. You've always wanted lots of cubs. Now's your chance."

Myra snorted. "Not five hundred of them! That's a bit of a stretch, even for me."

He chuckled. "Well, that's just the bi-peds. You're forgetting about all of the other creatures we rescued. I have a feeling they won't all fit in the nursery though."

"What nursery," Myra muttered. "That will be gone tomorrow too. I'm just surprised Marsee offered to give up the rest of the tower though."

"So am I, but we don't always have to stay there. Once everything's built up we can always move to another suite if you want. It might be more comfortable."

"No, I want to be close to Little Flower and her cub," Myra stated. "She'll need my help."

Jer nodded. That had been the argument Marsee had used earlier too, when she'd suggested it. He just hoped Marsee would manage with them that close, although she might want to move out, as was common for people her age.

"Well, come on. We'd better start packing," Myra said, and stood.

"It's late. It can wait until morning," Jer replied, but he stood and followed after her anyway. When they were back in their suite, he tossed his carry harness on the hook by the bed and turned to face Myra, only to find she wasn't in the room anymore. He followed her through the open door to the attached nursery, and found her curled up on the nest where they'd raised their children and grandchildren, holding a well loved, and slightly chewed stuffie. Leaning up against the door sill, he smiled at her, and started chuckling as a thought crossed his mind.

"What's so funny, Jer?" she asked, looking up at him.

"Oh nothing," he said with a sigh.

"That chuckle wasn't nothing," Myra glared at him. "Nor was that sigh."

"Well I was just thinking that the last time we had cubs was far more enjoyable, and I'll admit, there was a tiny piece of me that was hoping we'd get to experience *that* again before we were both executed."

Myra grinned at him and her tail spiraled. "That thought crossed my mind a time or two as well, but at least this way, the labor was far less painful, even if the pregnancy was *exhausting*."

Jer snorted, but wisely kept his mouth shut. The last month had been one of the hardest of his life, but Myra had nearly died with Marsee's birth, and had spent over a month in the trauma center because of it.

"You could go to a mating clinic, if you really want to feel that again. I wouldn't be upset," Myra said.

"I know you wouldn't, but I won't. It wouldn't be the same, not without you," Jer replied and then grinned. "And besides, if Senior Councilors don't get snooze buttons, just imagine the scandal if I took three days off to go play at a mating center after just being promoted."

"That didn't stop Tabor, and you wouldn't be on maternity leave for six months like she was," Myra replied.

"True," Jer replied. "But I'm not Tabor, and this is my first term, not my fourth, and besides, I would much rather spend my time with you, even if it's not the same as true heat."

Myra smiled up at him with an almost feral expression, and climbed out of the nest. "Well, in *that* case..." Myra purred and rubbed up against him as she walked past, flicking her tail up and to the side. He grinned and followed after.

# CHAPTER 2

# Readjusting Plans

The universe imploded and exploded again as his ship shifted into jump, but he barely noticed. All of his plans had gone awry, and he was furious. He turned off the news broadcast with a disgusted snort, as all they were talking about was Tabor's self-imposed punishment, and Surellis's ascension as King. *Why did it have to be him?*

Flashing his frustration, he swam over to grab something to eat, only to frown at the selection available. It was always so difficult to find good food off-world without having to pay a fortune. The foods the Sabers ate were disgusting. They had absolutely no sense of taste in his opinion.

*Saber. What a joke,* he thought, and flashed his disgust at the name the little rodent had given the pussycats. It hadn't even been a full day and already the press was using it. *Named after the fiercest cat that ever existed on the rodent's home world. How fierce could they be if tiny rodents like her could kill them all off? Then again, those rodents have awfully sharp fangs. I'll have to keep watch of them. If even half of what she said was true, they're far more dangerous than they look.*

Finally deciding on something somewhat remotely edible, he swam back to his seat, and looked out at the rainbow of the universe in jump. Feeling slightly queasy at the sight and the after effects of jump, he hit the switch that turned all the windows opaque. Most people found the sight beautiful, but he didn't. It meant days out of communication with the rest of the universe, and far too much could happen in the nearly four standard days it would take to return home.

*Standard,* he flashed with disgust. *Even time was measured by the pussycat's standards, even though they were the exception, not the rule.*

As he ate, he tried to figure out what to do about his latest setback.

*Parner I could have easily manipulated into doing what I wanted, but Surellis, no. No, I'll have to get rid of him. The question is how. His people like him far too much, and he's far too honorable to bend the rules. I've never been able to find anything on him. I thought for sure he'd never accept Senior Councilor after all the times he's turned it down. I wonder why he finally did. Was it just because no one else would run, or is something else going on? It's bad enough that little rodent picked Chenzira for Senior.*

He couldn't understand that decision at all. *Who gives control up to the very people that imprisoned them?* He could see possibly giving up control to one of her own people, like her grandfather, especially since she would be out on maternity leave soon, assuming she decided to keep the parasite that was forced on her, but to give up control to another species? *Ridiculous. What did Chenzira do to convince her to forgive them, or that he and his partner would be adequate parents, much less that Chenzira would be a good king for her species? I suppose anything would seem like luxury after those empty rooms they were locked in.*

The thought of spending even a minute in one of those cells made him shudder. *I'm honestly surprised she didn't go mad.*

His thoughts drifted to memories of his own dead parents, and as it often did, the abuses his father put him through under the pretext of making him a better councilor. That thought made his tentacles twitch with fury, but there wasn't anyone on the ship for him to take it out on. His father had claimed that understanding what it was like to live without the latest in modern comforts would make him more sympathetic to his people, and the test he'd forced upon him to become a Junior Councilor, which should have been his right by birth, made his insides boil with fury. His father had said it would make him understand what it was to be a victim, but it just made him loathe feeling weak and powerless instead, and the first chance he'd gotten, he'd made sure his father never had the opportunity to hurt him again. He threw his meal against the wall in anger at the memory, and then sighed at the waste of a perfectly good meal.

*At least that insufferable furball Tabor is gone. I do have to admit watching her flayed alive in front of the entire Consortium was rather entertaining. Still, Saber has far too much power now. Instead of having their power weakened by the addition of a new species, they now have a third of the Senior Council, and that can't stand unchallenged. The real question is how do I get rid of them both, or better yet, how do I destroy them and all of Saber at the same time?*

By the time his ship landed back on the Water World, he had the start of a plan, but first, he needed to let off some steam. It had been far too long since he'd heard the sounds of someone scream, and right now, he needed to feel powerful and in control. Pleasure rippled across his skin at the very thought.

*Enjoy your little fiefdom while you have the chance, Chenzira. When I'm done with you, you'll scream for me to take it from you, and be grateful when I do.*

# CHAPTER 3

# Little Flower: Packing

Jessica O'Neil sat out on the ancient tower's balcony, feet dangling over the edge, looking out at the moonlit landscape as she tried to come to grips with everything that had happened this past week. She had a new name, 'Little Flower Chenzira', a new title, 'Councilor', and a new family. Her rapist had been found guilty and executed, and her home for the past month was being transformed into a home for all of her people, starting first thing in the morning.

*Councilor Little Flower Chenzira, I wonder how long it will take me to get used to that? What would my parents think of me right now, a leader for what little remains of our people? Shocked? Proud? Councilor was never once on my radar. I just hope I don't make a mess of things. What do I know about leading people?*

As she sat there, movement caught her attention, and she watched as her new parents came around the outside of the compound, paws and tails entwined. *Mama looks sad. I hope she's not too upset about the changes that will be happening. At least she's alive and Marsee will be able to have cubs someday.*

When her parents disappeared out of sight again, she took a deep breath and mentally said goodbye to the old Jessica, and all of the O'Neils that had died the day of the Cataclysm. For better or worse, she was now Councilor Little Flower Chenzira.

Climbing to her feet, she walked over to the door and watched for a moment as her sister paced in their room, picking up objects and setting them back down. She waved her arms to get Marsee's attention. "What are you doing?"

Her sister looked over in her direction and let out a heavy sigh. "I'm trying to figure out what to keep, and how to fit everything I have in three rooms, into one, *and* still have room left over for everything else you need."

She frowned, confused, as the only thing she'd asked for was a proper toilet and toilet paper. "I don't need anything, and we can easily find room for the one bookcase we'll have to move for the hole of muck."

Marsee shook her head. "We need room for all the things you wanted for the baby, and you should really have your own desk, properly sized furniture, and space to store your clothing. This room isn't designed for you or your cub."

"Perhaps, but I love it anyway," Little Flower said. "And I've already caused you to have to give up far too much. I don't want you to have to give up anything else."

Marsee spun to face her full on, "You did no such thing! You saved my mother and all of our future descendants, and you deserve a home that fits you too. I know you didn't ask for it, but I intend to give it to you as my thanks. I..." Marsee paused, stopped, sat and looked down at her paws, almost as if trying to will them to form words, her conviction, turning to worry in an instant. Little Flower walked over and gave her sister a hug, not sure what was really bothering her, but offering her support anyway.

After the hug, Marsee took a deep breath and continued. "Little Flower, I knew there was a good chance the Council would order Mama's execution. She told me as much, but Papa told me not to tell you because he didn't want to worry you. I expected them to make her go through what you went through. It probably would have killed her, but there would have been a chance she'd survive. I never thought the rest of us would be harmed, certainly not my baby nephlings. When the Council gave their verdict, I was so mad and so...so...*disappointed* in them. What they did was wrong, even if it was precedent. And well, I know I've said several times that I don't want to give birth to cubs, but...really, I'm just afraid of going through it. I really want cubs of my own someday. I know they don't exist yet, but the moment that option was stripped away, it...it was like the Council had just killed them for no reason. What right did they have to take *my* children from me for someone else's crimes? To even suggest it... It goes against everything I was ever taught, and that's on top of what they were already considering doing to your people. I'm glad Uncle Marcus is Senior now, and Papa, but..." Marsee threw her paws up, unable to turn her jumbled thoughts into words and started pacing again.

"I'm proud of you," Little Flower signed when Marsee refocused her attention back on her.

Marsee flicked her ears back in surprise. "Thank you, but why?"

"From everything I've learned about your society and laws, it's far better than my world ever was, and your leaders appear to act with honor, for the most part anyway," Little Flower replied. "I can't fault your council for trying to protect your people from the risk of mine, but the Senior Council has absolute power, and what they say is law, with little anyone can do to change it. Yes, you could vote them out if they made a bad decision, but that's after the fact, and your culture reveres your leaders as if they could never make mistakes. You however, had the courage to speak up and stop Senior Councilor Tabor before she could even begin to make another mistake. I don't think anyone else in that room would have done so, or even considered speaking up, much less interrupting."

"You did," Marsee replied.

Little Flower grinned. "I was an Ambassador. Until I gave up my authority to Papa, I had as much rank as her, but I'm pretty sure even Papa would have gone with whatever Tabor finally decided, if you hadn't said something. I fully believe she would have gone through with the precedent just to get back at me for challenging and charging her in front of everyone. She's used to having everyone follow her decisions without question. You should have seen her that day in the conference room when you were asked to stay behind. She was absolutely shocked when I swore at her. She's been Senior Councilor for what, nearly fifty years? In all that time, has anyone ever told her no, stood up to her? I doubt it. Look how harshly she reacted that one time Paxton tried. She literally threatened the entire council with being kicked out if they didn't do what she wanted. Having absolute power corrupts absolutely, if you're not *very* careful. I've seen it far too many times. *You* saved your mother. *You* saved your own children, because you had the courage to break with ten thousand years of precedent, recognize that it was wrong, and speak up to your leaders, and tell them no. The Marsee I knew even a month ago, wouldn't have been brave enough to do that. She wouldn't have even questioned it, or their right to make that decision. Even your father and uncle didn't question it. They didn't even stand up to her over the leash, even though they both knew it was wrong, and there wasn't anyone here to witness it."

Marsee stared at her, blinking slowly, and eventually nodded, although her ears drooped. "I am sorry I wasn't then. I hurt you by following their orders."

"I forgive you. I could tell you didn't want to follow those orders, any more than Papa did, and you did your best to work around them and get them changed. You all did. But more importantly, you never once saw me as an animal. You treated me as a person and with respect from the day I arrived."

Marsee hugged her again. Little Flower hesitated about telling her about what else happened during deliberation, but decided it was better she knew. "Marsee, I'm not sure, but it's possible Tabor went with precedent *because* of you."

Marsee flicked her ears back in surprise again. "What do you mean?"

"The other day when the Seniors called me back without you, it wasn't just because they were trying to make sure that no one had forced me to change my statement. Tabor was trying to find out if you'd hunted and hurt me. She thought that's where my injuries from falling out of the tree came from. I did everything I could to protect you, going so far as asking Tabor if she wanted me to stick my head in your mouth to prove you were trustworthy, and I told her to stuff it where the moons don't shine. Clear Seas thought it was pretty funny and took your side, ordering Tabor to back down. I personally think she went with precedent, because of your psychosis, so that you couldn't have cubs and pass it on to them, and because she couldn't get rid of you before or during the trial without appearing to tamper with the proceedings. The guards still have you on a watch, according to Ellie, even if informally, likely for the next six months, and if something should happen and they arrest you, you should demand to have your case brought before the Full Council, and try to stay as calm as possible."

Her sister sagged. "I was afraid of that. I *am* afraid of that, of passing this illness onto my cubs. I talked to Mama after that night in the garden. They have no idea what causes psychosis, and she's never heard of anyone surviving before. They're right not to trust me. I still don't trust me, even though I feel so much better."

Marsee stood and turned away, tail shivering with emotion. Little Flower walked over and wrapped an arm around her and Marsee leaned in, wrapping her tail around her back. Eventually, Marsee gathered her thoughts, took a deep breath, and turned back to face her. "Please don't tell anyone, but for a moment, there in the council chamber, the beast and I both wanted to attack them for what they were doing to us. I only held it together because you'd been able to figure out how to save Papa already. I don't know what would have happened if they'd ultimately said no to your suggestion. You may think I was brave for speaking up, but I was terrified, and just trying to save my life. I knew full well, if I made even a single step towards the Senior Council, I would have been killed."

"Well, you can't be brave if you're not scared, and if it makes you feel any better, I was terrified and wanted to claw her throat out too," Little Flower replied.

That made Marsee snort and then square her shoulders. "Now, I'm not taking no for an answer. You're getting all of the same stuff you wanted for everyone else, and we're making room for it." Marsee turned and looked at her bookshelves again and drooped with a heavy sigh. "I just have no idea how."

"You know, your room is bigger than the entire house my family used to live in before," Little Flower stated. "I'm sure we can figure something out, but don't you dare get rid of anything you really want, or your hanging bed. You've already given up your tower to Mama and Papa. I know how much the privacy of this place meant to you."

Marsee flicked an ear back dismissively. "You're going to need help with that cub, and it's safer if they're close by. Besides, they'll need someplace to stay anyway, since their room is being destroyed to make way for everything else we want to add, and I did promise to share my home with your people."

"That may be, but I never intended for you to have to give up your rooms or anything in it. I was thinking we'd just rework all of the spare rooms into shared living spaces, at least to start. What we have planned is far more than I expected."

Marsee's fur rippled in a shrug. "It's not all that bad I suppose. My workshop is moving to the new guild hall, and I'll have access to far more tools and space than I have here. It won't be quite as convenient, but it'll be an upgrade. As for my library, I'll still have access to that too. It'll be a while before the others learn to read anyway. The hard part will be figuring out which books I want to keep here."

"Well, start with anything you've read more than once," Little Flower suggested.

Marsee snorted. "I've read them all more than once, some a dozen times or more. Books were my only friends, and reading was how I escaped when things got too bad."

"I get that. Drawing's the same way for me."

"That's the other thing we need to make room for. We'll need to move all your drawings from the family room to here, somewhere." Marsee looked around the room at the walls that were covered in floor to ceiling bookshelves and Marsee's own artwork. "Unless you want them hung up somewhere else."

"Maybe a few," Little Flower replied. "But others can go in our parent's room or the new family room, or we can send them off to your extended family, if you think they'd like them."

"They'd love them," Marsee replied, and with another heavy sigh, began pulling books off her shelf and stacking them on a nearby table.

Little Flower watched for a few moments, then pulled out the drawing tablet Marsee was letting her borrow, and went back to work on the children's book of now extinct Earth animals. She'd had very little time to work on it over the past few weeks, as preparing for the trial had taken just about every free second. When she looked up from her drawing, maybe an hour later, Marsee was just sitting in front of a bookshelf, and only a small stack of books had been pulled off.

She set the tablet down and walked over, giving her sister another hug. "That's enough for tonight. It might be easier to start with the books in the library below and pull out the ones you really want to keep instead. I'm guessing these are all in your room here because they're your favorites anyway."

Marsee nodded. "For the most part. Some I keep below to protect them from the storms. I'll probably have to build some protective bookcases now."

"Well, that can wait. Come on. We should get some sleep. Tomorrow's going to be a busy day."

"Don't remind me," Marsee muttered with drooping ears, but turned and leapt into the hanging basket.

She eventually followed, after a trip to the hole of muck, and once curled up safe in Marsee's warm embrace, she was soon fast asleep.

# CHAPTER 4

# Marsee: Armada

Marsee's alarm blared. Half asleep, she fumbled for her tablet to shut it off, but ended up dropping it off the bed with a loud thud. The motion was enough to cause it to shut off, but now she was worried she'd broken it with the fall. "Moons," she whispered, and flopped back down on the bed, not daring to look. She didn't have the credit to buy a new one, not of that caliber anyway. It had taken her a year to afford her drawing tablet, and this one was far nicer.

"Did you break it?" her sister asked, after tapping her on her shoulder to get her attention.

"I don't know. I'm afraid to look." She covered her eyes dramatically with the tip of her tail, and peered cautiously out from under it.

Her sister chuckled. "Well, Ellie should be here today, if you did. I bet she could bring a replacement with her."

Marsee sighed. "I can't afford a new one. A basic one sure, everyone gets one of those, but not one as good as that. It was a gift from my grandparents for my Name Day, and I don't have a mentor yet. They would help pay for whatever I needed for my craft."

"What do you have to do to get a mentor around here anyway?" Little Flower asked.

"Stick to a craft for one, and be really good for another. I bounce around too much and I don't stay focused on the finer details of any one craft. My work is solid but nothing special, and no one's offered yet." Marsee sighed at that long-standing frustration, wondering if she'd ever be considered good enough to earn a mentor. She'd failed miserably in both the Crafter's and Artist's Guilds, and she'd had to set aside most of her current classes in the Writer's Guild in order to help prepare for Little Flower's trial. Her progress had been sporadic, outside of learning Water Sprite, and she knew it would take a long time to get caught up. She just hoped that wouldn't hurt her prospects.

Shaking her head to clear her drifting thoughts, she refocused on the current problem. Holding her breath and gathering her courage, she peered over the edge of the bed and flicked her ears forward hopefully. *It doesn't look damaged.*

She hopped down off the bed, purposely sending it swinging wildly. Her sister screeched with laughter. She ducked under before it could hit her in the head on the way back, and carefully picked up her tablet. Just as she did, the snooze went off. It scared her so much, she jumped with a yelp, just as the bed came back again, and it thwacked her hard.

"Oof!" she grunted, and fumbled to not drop the tablet again, as the impact nearly knocked her over.

Climbing out from under the bed while rubbing the side of her head, she examined the tablet, flipping it over. *No cracks. Just the large one in my skull.* She cautiously turned it on, and let out a sigh of relief as it powered on with no visible signs of damage.

"Well?" her sister asked.

She grinned in response and held it up. "All good," she signed with her other paw.

"You should really put a case on it, or something. Once my cub is born and walking, they'll be throwing everything around," her sister said, and climbed down off the bed.

"A case?" Marsee asked, confused, as the sign her sister had used didn't fit with her definition of the sign. "What does something needing investigation have to do with my tablet?"

"No. Clothing for your tablet, like the container you put your hearing aids in. The words in my language are the same."

Marsee furrowed her brows. "The same? You have words that mean two different things?"

"You don't?" Little Flower asked in reply.

Marsee sat and considered, wondering if that was why she had such a hard time learning the Hue-man's written language. "No. Not in our language. The Flyer's language shifts meaning based on pitch, but I would consider those different words as they have different spellings. The overall meaning of a sentence can change based on inflection, emphasis, and body language, satire, jokes, that kind of thing, but the word always means what it means."

Little Flower looked surprised. "I suppose that's the same with our language, but words change meanings all the time. We borrow from other languages, use existing words when we don't have a word for something. Just about every word in our language has more than one meaning."

"How do you keep it all straight?" Marsee asked.

"We don't. It's a mess, and causes all sorts of problems," Little Flower replied. "Anyway, back to our earlier discussion. What I meant was that should put something on the corners of your tablet at least, to absorb the shock. I'm not sure how it would work with yours, since it folds up so much, but I think you could put some sort of coating on the outside. With our tiny paws, we drop things all the time. Cracked screens were common. We had clear covers we could put over them too, to keep the glass from getting scratched, and allow us to continue being able to use it, if the glass was broken, until we were able to repair it."

Marsee raised a brow. "You should talk to Ellie about that. She'd love those ideas. I'm an absolute klutz. If it can be broken, I will break it, and that includes me." She rubbed her still aching brow for emphasis.

Her sister chuckled as she walked over to dig through her clothing. When she was properly protected from the heat of their world's suns, they made their way down to find something to eat. Her mother was already preparing breakfast in the kitchen when they arrived.

"I thought we'd eat out in the garden this morning. Go on ahead, I'll be out in a minute," her mother said, so they turned around and made their way back out into the garden.

It was a beautiful morning, cool, with just enough of a breeze to make the leaves of the bandala tree rustle. Her father and Little Flower's grandfather were already there. *My grandfather now too,* Marsee thought. *Or is he now my nephew, since Little Flower is now his legal guardian? Both?* Marsee considered the question as Little Flower ran over and flopped down next to her grandfather and leaned up against him.

"Good morning," her father signed.

"Morning, Papa," Marsee replied. "Mama says she'll be out shortly with breakfast."

Her father nodded. "Did you sleep well?"

"Not really," Marsee replied. "Too much to think about."

"It has been rather eventful lately. Is there anything you'd like to talk about? You looked like you were lost in thought."

She nodded. "Yes, but later," she replied. "Most of it can wait. I was just trying to decide if GrandFather was now my grandfather or my nephew, or both."

"Legally neither," her father replied. "Guardianship doesn't imply a family relationship, simply a responsibility to care for that person and ensure they become productive members of society, as it is we don't have any paperwork from before to show he's Little Flower's grandfather anyway, outside of her word."

"You're welcome to call me GrandFather, Uncle James, or James," GrandFather replied. "I was Uncle James for years before I could legally partner with Little Flower's grandfather. As far as I'm concerned though, you're my granddaughter's sister now, which makes you my granddaughter, at least in my heart, regardless of what the law says."

"Then I consider you my grandfather too," Marsee grinned, but then tilted her head in confusion when Little Flower frowned, wondering if Little Flower didn't want to share her grandfather.

Little Flower replied before she could ask. "Is there anything I can do to make him legally my grandfather?"

Her father shook his head. "Not really." He paused and raised a brow. "Well, I suppose that's not entirely true. He could legally adopt Myra, if she wanted him to, since her parents are dead. It's not necessary though. Those titles are more for identifying legal responsibility of children than anything. If something happens to you and you want your cub to go to him, you can just put that in your will, and it will be honored, assuming he's willing or capable at the time. You can also indicate who you consider family for the purpose of deciding medical care, if your mother and I are not around, but other than that there's really no legal reason for it."

The rest of breakfast was a quiet affair, as they were each lost in their own thoughts, knowing this was likely the last private breakfast they'd ever have in the garden. Before they'd finished, Marsee heard the sounds of a ship approaching and looked up as the ship slowly circled low over the compound, the sides well marked with Saber's planetary logo and colors for the Senior Council. After a second pass around the compound, the ship landed outside their shuttle bay.

"Marcus is here early," her father said, but no one bothered to get up to greet him, although her father did send him a text letting him know where they were.

A few minutes later, Marcus walked in. "I see how it is, *little brother*," Marcus growled at her father. "Promoted for two whole days and now you can't even be bothered to welcome another Senior Councilor when they appear at your home." Marcus's face was blank behind his mask, but his tail was curled.

"If you think I'm going to treat you any differently than before, *big brother*, you're sadly mistaken," her father replied calmly, and popped a piece of fruit in his mouth.

"Impudent cub," Marcus muttered.

Her father shrugged. "It seems to work well for my newest daughter. So, now that I'm one of her people, I figured I'd give it a try for a bit." When the laughter died down, he continued. "So what brings you here this early? Construction isn't scheduled to begin for another couple of hours."

"Well, for one, you are building on *my* territory, and I've yet to see or approve the plans, and for another, this compound is listed as a family home, not rated for housing several hundred people, which in of itself, would rate village status."

"Oh, is that all?" her father asked, waving a paw dismissively. "Well, it turns out Myra and I had a lot of unexpected cubs the other day. We're redecorating. Our nursery isn't nearly big enough."

Marcus chuckled. "That you did. Still, we have some legal work to figure out, seeing as you don't actually have your own planet to govern, and Marsee, we're going to need your help again as a translator. We still need to finish translating the various charters into both sign language and the Hue-man's written language."

"Me?!" Marsee exclaimed with a frown.

"You are the only recognized sign language translator for the Council," her uncle replied. "Which means you're the only one qualified to do it."

"Ellie's recognized too," Little Flower stated. "They made her give the same oath as Marsee when they called me back the other day."

Marcus raised a brow and nodded. "I didn't realize, still, I doubt Ellie will have time to manage that. Besides, Marsee is far more fluent in sign than Ellie, especially with regards to the legal terms in the Charter."

Marsee sighed at the amount of work that would entail, but nodded. "How quickly does it need to be done? I still need to pack and clear out my rooms in the tower so Mama and Papa can move their stuff in."

"We've got a little time, but it would be good to at least have the Consortium Charter and the Local Charter translated into sign before the Hue-mans move from the Agency," he replied. "The others can wait, as I imagine it will be a while before anyone travels to the other planets."

Before she could respond, her ears picked up the sounds of another ship approaching.

"Well, I have a feeling breakfast is probably over," her mother stated when the Senior Guild Master's ship came into view and disappeared behind the wall to land next to the other two ships. "But I'm also thinking we need to add a much bigger shuttle bay to the designs."

"You're probably not wrong there," her father chuckled. "Although there's plenty of room for parking around the compound."

A few minutes later, Ellie joined them, along with several of the guild masters they'd worked with the day before.

"Oh wow, I can see why you wanted to keep this," one of the Master Builder's stated, staring up at the tree. "I had no idea they grew this big."

"Is this your first time to the South District?" her father asked.

"Yes sir," he replied. "I'm originally from the Jandolf Square District, so I have plenty of experience with desert construction, but our trees don't grow anywhere near this big."

"Well, this beauty has been in our family for thousands of years. I'm told the compound was built around it four or five thousand years ago," her mother replied.

"It's quite a bit older than that, Myra," her uncle stated. "I did some research yesterday, and it turns out your deed goes all the way back to the founding, two hundred and fifty square leagues, to one Grace Chenzira, locally known as 'The Wilds'"

"What?!" they all exclaimed.

"Leagues?" her mother asked. "Are you telling me, my deed is *that* big? I thought it was only the compound. That's all I've ever had on my annual council report."

"I am," Marcus replied. "Most of it was designated a wildlife refuge in the year four-thousand eight-hundred and sixty-three. I'm guessing that's the date you've always been told, but the Wilds still belong to you, even though you couldn't develop it without Council approval, which is why it's not on your council report."

"I had no idea. Well, I knew about the wildlife refuge, who doesn't around here, but I didn't know that it was mine. When my parents died, I was in the Trauma Center trying to stay alive with Marsee. I was so upset and out of it, that I never even looked at the deed, figuring it was just the compound and the immediate area around it. Am I even allowed to have that big of a deed?"

"You are, as it's inherited," Marcus replied. "Although I'm not aware of any other deeds this big. My understanding is that the Council bought up most of the deeds back when they formed the Consortium, and have slowly acquired the rest when there weren't heirs over the years in order to change how housing was managed, once it became a protected right. I have no idea why they didn't buy yours." He shrugged. "I suppose it could be nothing more than the fact that there's always been an heir, so there hasn't been an opportunity."

"I'm not sure how I feel about changing it then," the builder stated. "This place is a treasure and should be protected."

"My daughter's people need a home, and that's far more important than a few pieces of stone," Myra stated. "No matter how old it is."

"Still, I think we should make an effort to preserve as much as possible. At the very least we should record it for posterity. Come on, Gregory, let's go take a look around and see what we can do." The others all left to follow the Master Builder, with Ellie along to keep them in line. Marsee followed them with her ears as they left, and heard them marveling at the carvings in the ancient doors.

"So Marcus, what do we have to do to change the deed?" her mother asked.

"Well, that's where it gets complicated. If we're going to move all of the Hue-mans here, one of two things will need to happen, either the deed will need to be handed over to the Council so it can be reclassified as a village, and be broken up into separate deeds of residence for each of the Hue-mans, or as Jer mentioned, you will need to take official guardianship for all of them. Either way, as you are expanding the compound, the deed would have to be adjusted anyway to allow you to build, which would mean taking some of the land from the wildlife refuge."

"Isn't guardianship essentially what happened, by taking them into my home?" Myra asked.

"No, you all agreed to share your home and help them get back on their feet. That's no different than if you took in your neighbors.

We would change their location of legal residence to your compound, which we could do for the first twenty-six of them, based on the size of the existing compound, as we did for Little Flower and GrandFather. They will need a legal guardian before becoming an adult, just as Little Flower did for her grandfather, so that may be the easiest path, but that does come with significant risk, since you don't know the character of the others rescued. You'd be legally responsible for any crimes they commit until their adulthood and the first ten years afterwards, just as you would with any child you took guardianship for."

"That does add a bit of a complication," her father said. "The female population already needs a guardian for their oath of adulthood, since they are old enough to have cubs. I figured I would be doing that as their senior."

"No," her mother stated. "I will take guardianship for them. I already have a criminal record, I won't risk that happening to any of you, or risk them committing a crime just to get back at you."

"It doesn't work that way when someone is a ward of the Council," Jer replied. "The expectation is that it is a temporary guardianship until a new parent or guardian can be located. Often, if someone ends up a ward of the Council it's because there's already been a crime that occurred, or a good chance of one happening. As a ward though, if someone qualifies for adulthood before new parents or guardians can be found, we can swear them in without legal responsibility for them. That often happens if someone is close to their adulthood and would prefer to live on their own. At most, all I would need from you is proof they are physically mature. At the moment, Marcus has jurisdiction as everyone is currently a legal resident of the South District. I may be a Senior Councilor, but right now, all of my people, including myself, are designated off-world citizens. Which is something else we need to figure out. I'm legally required to live in my district or council city, but we have neither."

Marcus nodded. "We won't be able to change that until the next Full Council meeting, but in the meantime, if Myra transferred her deed, I could instate you as the advocate for the village, which would give you legal authority over the people who lived here. And, as no one currently lives in the Wilds, I'm hoping we can convince the rest of the Council to grant your people that deed. At the moment though, it would require a change to the Charter, since no other council is allowed to own the deed to land on a different planet. That's a protected right, so that's going to be a challenge as you'll need unanimous support. I don't think we'll have a problem convincing my Council of that. It's not like anyone actually wants to live here, but we will need to make sure there are provisions in place to protect the surrounding community and wildlife."

"What kind of compensation will Mama get if she transfers her deed?" Marsee asked. "That's a massive piece of land."

"That's the added complication," Marcus stated. "Normally when someone gives up a deed, we provide a matching equivalent deed wherever they move, or pay the difference if they don't want or need something as big as what they had before. At the current listed rate, that would be the equivalent to the annual budget of the South District, for ten years, and we can't afford it. Even split out over the rest of your life, Myra, it would put significant hardship on this district, which may also be why it was never bought up in the first place."

"Bright moons!" Myra stated.

"So exchange it for something else," Little Flower suggested. "As far as I'm concerned, if Mama gave up the deed, I would consider that more than adequate compensation for providing my people with a home, since it would outlive her, and it would get her out of having to spend the rest of her life here, if she ultimately wanted to move, or maybe a combination of the both. Our people could use the credit too. If you can't afford it all at once, a future trust could work too, that way we'd have credit to expand in the future."

Both her father and uncle flicked their ears back in surprise at those suggestions, and then her uncle's expression turned to one of consideration. "Those are really good ideas, Little Flower. That would account for most of the requirements. She would still be required to care for you and your cub as long as you wanted that help. What do you think, Myra?"

Her mother considered for several minutes. "I don't see caring for my daughter and her cub as punishment, but as a gift I never thought I would even live to see. I would do that willingly without a council edict, just as I would also care for anyone in my area as a healer. The Wilds, I don't mind transferring, as I didn't realize that was mine to begin with, but, I don't want to give it all up. This is all I have left of my parents. We'll be living in the Tower, so I'd want to keep that, and the garden. Nearly half of the plants in here came from our home world, or so I've been told. Several of them don't exist anywhere else, outside of the few that I've transplanted and given away. I don't have a problem sharing it with everyone, but I want to protect it, and have a say in what happens to it. Most of the rest of the compound has already been marked for destruction anyway, to make way for all of the new buildings we are going to add, unless the builders change their minds."

"The Tower is a given," Marcus stated. "You will need residency listed somewhere at the very least, and that could be listed as an apartment, or broken up into three if you wanted, as it's big enough. As for the garden, if there are indeed endangered species in there, then we could easily mark it as a communal protected space afterwards, much like the Wilds are now. That way when you die, it will remain protected, regardless of who owns the deed."

Her mother nodded. "That works for me, if the Council will go along with it."

"You have my vote," her father stated. "I have a feeling we can convince a majority, although Marsee is currently listed as your heir for this place if we both died. Marsee, what do you think?"

"I agreed to share my home too," Marsee replied. "If this pays off Mama's debt to the Hue-mans, then I'm all for it, but there's no need to break up the tower into separate apartments as long as I can keep my room."

"Of course, Sweetheart," her mother replied. "You'll always be welcome as long as you want to live here."

"Alright, we'll wait for the final designs from the builders to see what we need to change from wildlife habitat to village, and figure out what, if anything else, you want to keep before bringing it before the rest of the Seniors. It will need to be a continuous plot of land, so likely the outer courtyard as well," Marcus replied. "Or at least part of it."

Before her mother could reply, Marsee heard the sounds of another ship approaching. When this one flew over though, it was massive, on par with the public transport ships. She had to pin her ears back from the noise of the engines as they settled outside the compound. Her father frowned. "I wasn't expecting a ship *that* big," her father said. "I should probably go check that out."

Before he could leave though, another ship, equally as massive, flew over and landed next to it. "I think maybe we should all go check it out," Marcus stated, as a third appeared right behind it. Before they made it to the entrance of the garden, a fourth ship flew over, followed by half a dozen smaller ships. Ellie met them at the entrance.

"I see the builders have started to arrive," Ellie said with a grin.

"Started?" Marsee exclaimed. "Those ships are massive. How many builders are coming?"

"All of them," Ellie replied with a grin. "I called in support from every guild master on the planet, and every last one of them said they would be here. It's not just people on those ships, but the equipment and supplies needed to build with too. By time the new buildings are completed, we should have all of the furniture and other items requested, ready for delivery. I intend to get Little Flower's people out of the Agency as quickly as possible."

"Well then, we'd better get to work on finalizing those plans," her father stated, and they kept walking. Another ship appeared, but didn't land, and instead began flying slowly back and forth over the compound.

"What are they doing?" Marsee asked.

"Surveying, most likely," Ellie replied, as another massive transport ship arrived and landed.

By the time they made it outside the compound, the first of the ships were already being unloaded. Strange giant pieces of machinery were being driven off and parked outside of the ships. Marsee hadn't spent much time in the Builder's Guild, outside of the required classes as a new apprentice, designed to give people exposure into each of the guilds, but many of the classes were shared, enough that she'd been able to easily follow the blueprints as they'd designed them. Even still, she wasn't sure what half of the equipment was. Off in the distance, Marsee could now see a long line of ships and shuttles approaching from multiple directions.

"I've never seen so many ships in one place," Marsee marvaled.

"That's not surprising," Ellie replied. "We don't often have places to park this many. Oscar's likely having a fit right now, since I ran off with half of his ships without warning, but he can just deal with it."

Her father chuckled. "I'm sure I'll hear about it later."

"Sooner, rather than later, it looks like," Marcus stated, pointing over to one that was just landing. "Isn't that his ship?"

"Looks like it," Ellie replied.

Marsee kept her ears firmly pinned as the ships continued to land and they waited for people to unload. Eventually she pulled out her hearing aids and used those to block out some of the sound. Even with them in it was still loud.

Ellie noticed her put them in. "Does that help?" She signed, as there was little they could hear over the roar of the massive engines on the bigger ships.

"Some," Marsee stated. "It's bearable at least." Everyone else had their ears pinned back too, except for Little Flower and GrandFather. Little Flower didn't seem to notice, but GrandFather had his paws over his ears. Eventually as the area filled up, the sound became more bearable as the ships had to land further away.

Ellie raised a brow. "I'll need to look into that more then. I imagine the Ship's Guild would appreciate something like that.

"I wish I had some ear plugs too," GrandFather stated. "I didn't realize how loud the ships were. Our people used a compressible foam to block sound out when we needed to, or devices that covered our ears entirely. As you've realized, our hearing is rather delicate."

"Foam? That's all? That would be very inexpensive to produce," Ellie stated. "We'll talk more later."

"Welcome to my home, Commander," her father said when Oscar Rynhold appeared. "Sampson, it's good to see you as well. I wasn't expecting either of you today." Marsee began translating immediately for Little Flower and GrandFather.

Oscar snorted. "Thank you, Senior Councilor. I wasn't intending to come, but then I woke up and half of my transport ships were missing. I figured I should come and track them down."

Ellie shrugged. "You should be used to my shenanigans by now, Oscar."

"Fair," he chuckled. "You do tend to mess with my schedule on a regular basis."

Ellie snorted. "I account for more than half of your regular schedule, so that's only fair. You'll have them back as soon as they're unloaded. Most of them anyway, for now."

"That's what I figured. I'm leaving Sampson here to help you coordinate whatever else you need," Oscar replied.

"Much appreciated," her father stated, nodding his head in respect. "Now, where are my manners, let me introduce you to my family. This is my partner Myra, my daughters, Marsee and Little Flower, and Little Flower's grandfather, James. Everyone, this is Senior Commander Oscar Rynhold. He's the senior for the Ship's Guild, and this is his protege, Commander Nichola Sampson. Sampson was instrumental in helping us set up the Agency in time for your arrival."

"Thank you very much for your assistance, Commanders," Little Flower replied. "Both in the extreme risk your people took in rescuing mine, and in caring for us afterwards. My condolences for the people you lost in that effort."

"Thank you," Oscar said. "It was our honor and I will be sure to pass your condolences along to their families. I just wish we'd arrived sooner."

Her sister nodded. "I'm just thankful you were there at all."

Oscar nodded the point. "Well, I should probably get out of here, before Ellie puts me to work too. Councilors." He nodded, turned, and left without another word.

"That was a short visit," Little Flower replied.

"That's Oscar for you," Marcus stated. "I've known him since I was a cub. He wasn't any different then either. He started out as a guard, but decided he liked flying better than fighting. Both guilds require much the same amount of discipline, which was perfect for Oscar. I couldn't think of anyone better suited to run the Ship's Guild though."

Her father chuckled and they all turned to look at him. "The day of the Cataclysm, I called Command to coordinate the rescue effort. He answered...and yelled at me for interrupting."

Marcus laughed, tail spiraling. "That sounds about right."

Sampson's tail curled in amusement too, although his face was fairly neutral. "I've seen him take on Kendra a time or two."

"Now that I would have liked to have seen," Marcus replied. "What did she do to get on his bad side?"

"Oh nothing. We were playing Rando-tat. Never ever play Rando-tat with the Senior Honor Guard," Sampson explained.

"I didn't know she was a fan of that game," her uncle said, with a gleam in his eye. Rando-tat was one of his favorite games, and one she played regularly with him.

"It's apparently a favorite among the guards, but trust me, you do not want to play with her, or them," Sampson replied. "I've yet to win a single game against any of her senior guards. And I don't think Oscar has either. I don't know how they do it, but no matter what I do to try to hide it, they always seem to know when I'm lying."

Marcus raised a brow at that, but the conversation stopped as a group of people started heading their way. They were soon deep into conversation about the changes the master builders wanted to make with their designs. An hour or so later, those plans were finalized and the builders got to work. In the time they were in her father's office reviewing the plans, hundreds of ships, shuttles, and ground crawlers had appeared and parked outside of the compound, not just just the builders, but volunteers from the neighboring community, the techs Marcus had requested to record the various charters in sign, and moving crews, to help them pack up and store their belongings until the new buildings could be finished. Others had brought food and shelter for everyone.

To Marsee's utter embarrassment, Ellie followed her back to the tower to see just what she had in her workshop and library, since most of that was being moved to the new guild hall for use by everyone, trailed by several of the movers. A good portion of Marsee's training included learning how to make the tools they use for their crafts, and she had made modifications to better fit her size and preferences over the years. Ellie examined everything closely, and grilled her on why she'd made certain modifications, even going so far as to try out a few of her tools. She was practically a blubbering mess by the time Ellie was done and walked over.

"Relax, Marsee. I'm not going to bite," Ellie said. "I'm merely curious. I'm not used to seeing journeymen making their own modifications, but I can see how these would better fit you, and quite likely the smaller sizes of the Hue-mans. Now, let's see this library of yours."

Marsee led her up to the next level and swung open the ancient door. Ellie peered over her shoulder and flicked her ears back in surprise. "Moons! Did you raid the archives?"

Marsee chuckled. "No, just my uncle's public library. I'd say about half are gifts from him, the other half I've purchased over the years. It's pretty much where all of my spare credit goes."

"Well, you've been good for the Guild, I'll say that much. Did you make the bookcases as well?"

"Yes, ma'am," she replied, causing Ellie to glare at her. Ellie tended to get very grumpy when Marsee went all formal on her, but outside of the glare, Ellie didn't comment, likely realizing just how overwhelmed she was feeling right now. It was one thing to examine tools and workbenches, but watching Ellie examine her collection of books was like having her examine her soul. She'd been picked on for years by her classmates for the types of books she like to read, so much so that she'd stopped even discussing them with anyone outside of her uncle.

Ellie squeezed her way through the stacks of the nearly full room. There was barely enough space for Ellie to fit, as Marsee had spaced the stacks for her own size, so she could fit as many bookshelves as possible. She waited by the door for the Senior Guild Master to finish perusing. Ellie stopped several times, pulling out random books.

"You have an incredible collection, and it's far more diverse than I was expecting. I will reimburse you for whatever you donate to the library, so you can download replacements if you'd like. The same goes for whatever bookcases, workbenches, and tools that you make available for public use. They're all well made, and it'll save me the effort and expense of transporting it. Tag what you want to keep and my movers will take care of the rest."

Marsee flicked her ears back in surprise. She was not expecting the Senior Guild Master to buy *her* workbenches, much less hear that they were well made. She'd made them for her own use, not for sale, and hadn't put all that much effort into them. Ellie seemed to misunderstand. "You offered to share your home, not give up all of your personal belongings, and you should be reimbursed for that. And I meant what I said. They are well made."

"Thank you, Senior Guild Master," Marsee replied, but grinned and curled her tail to purposely show she was joking with the use of her title, in an effort to deflect the discomfort she felt at being praised by Ellie.

Ellie growled at that. "I can change my mind, you know," she replied, but her tail was curled, so Marsee knew she was joking. "When you're done here, come find me and we'll get you set up with the techs to start recording the translations for the Charters."

"Yes, ma'am," Marsee replied.

Ellie glared at her again and walked out, thwapping her hard with her tail on the way by, leaving Marsee chuckling from both humor at Ellie's reaction and her frayed nerves. Then, with a heavy sigh, she made her way down the ramp to clear out her workshop. That would need to be done first so her parents' belongings could be moved in.

# CHAPTER 5

# Little Flower: Councilor

"I get what you're saying, Papa, but no. We're not having a guard, at least not to start," Little Flower stated. "My people have been locked up for what to us has felt like more than two years. The sight of a guard will be triggering, not just because of their isolation, but because the guards we had on Earth were not always honorable. People are going to be dealing with their trauma, and I don't want someone arrested because they're having a panic attack, or because your people don't understand our culture. They need time to recover. If we need guards, we'll call them in from Sand Dune, but it has to be their choice *if and when* we have a permanent guard."

Both her father and uncle frowned at her.

"In all my time as Councilor, I've not had a single complaint against any guard," Marcus stated. "You can trust them."

"I'm not trying to imply that your guard isn't trustworthy. On the contrary, at least the few I've interacted with were exceptional. I have no doubt the guards with me the other day were prepared to commit treason to save my life. But my people won't trust them. They're not even going to trust you to start. This place needs to feel like a home, not just a fancier prison, and if there are guards walking around glaring at them all the time, that won't happen. Besides, we have you, Papa. If you can't arrest a single Hue-man, if necessary, then perhaps you should spend some time sharpening your claws."

Her father glared at her.

Marcus chuckled at his expression. "She's got a point, cub," Marcus replied. "You *should* be able to take on a single Hue-man, after all the time and training I've put into you over the decades."

Her father turned his glare to Marcus before looking back at her. "Little Flower, I'm not worried that your people are going to commit crimes, or that the guard will arrest them without just cause. They're too well trained for that. I'm far more worried about someone else trying to hurt your people, and if someone does, I'm not going to be able to stop that," her father stated.

She frowned at him with concern. "Do you believe someone will?"

"I honestly don't know. I'd like to think not, but I can't guarantee it," her father replied. "I don't believe the Seniors will, not now that they've welcomed you into the Consortium, and directed so much in the way of resources here. Clear Seas said as much, but someone else might decide you're too much of a risk. The vote for inclusion into the Consortium was not unanimous, and that hasn't happened before."

"We're going to have to learn to start trusting each other eventually, but if we start by reacting with suspicion, it'll just breed more suspicion," Little Flower replied.

"My granddaughter is right. I've seen it far too often in my lifetime. It might be putting us at risk, but you can't protect us from everyone. And every single one of your species could hurt us without trying. We need to move forward with the idea that crime, war, and racism is a thing of the past, and the only way to do that is to move forward as if both sides are trustworthy, and punish harshly when or if something happens. When presenting the concept of the guard to my people to vote on, their other responsibilities, such as search and rescue and predator control, should be highly emphasized and reinforced as being their primary role, and you should probably bring up that they were the ones with the most casualties saving our people, and who kept us alive on the trip here."

Her father was silent for a long time but finally nodded. "Fine, we'll bring it before the Council. However, Marcus, I would prefer it if we had guards closer than Sand Dune. I know there were guards at the Agency, although I don't know if they're still there, and I'd like permission to borrow Kendra if I need to."

"Of course. Until we figure out the legal framework for how all of this is going to work, you'll be under her watch anyway."

"That's the other reason I don't want guards snooping around. I'm worried that they'll mistake Marsee being flustered as having issues with her psychosis again," Little Flower stated.

"I can't keep the guard from watching her," her father stated. "Or your mother. They're allowed to come here any time they want and check on them."

"No, but it doesn't have to be obvious and right under their noses all the time either. You and Marcus are perfectly capable of determining if they're a risk or not."

Her father pursed his lips. "Once we've grown from village to town, we'll be expected to have a guard hall, especially as this will be our council city."

"That's fine," Little Flower replied. "By then my people will have had a chance to adjust, and guards won't stick out as much with more people around."

"Alright, next topic," Marcus said. "We've already established that the age of adulthood is whenever the females of your species have their first heat or turn seven, unless someone sponsors them, but we don't have any paperwork for any of them, except for the two that were born after arriving. My thought was that we could either set everyone's birthday to the date of the Cataclysm, which would put everyone on equal footing, or use an honor system and have people tell us when they were born and convert it to our dates."

"The date of the Cataclysm works for me," Little Flower replied. "A few years to adjust to this new society, prove their worth, and learn a new skill or craft, seems reasonable."

GrandFather looked over at her and grinned. "That works for me too."

Her father nodded his agreement as well.

"Alright, that was easy," Marcus stated, and tapped away on his tablet for a moment. "Next, education. Ellie has already stated she'll be providing masters from the various guilds to teach those interested. We'll need to get the other guilds to send instructors as well, and educate people on the Charter, continue with sign language classes, and provide primary education to your cubs."

"And quite likely everyone else," Little Flower added. "We can't assume that anyone rescued has a solid primary or secondary education, or can even read, write, or speak the same language. The cost of an education was becoming prohibitive. We'll certainly need to know your history and sciences, and learn to read and write in Saber."

Her grandfather nodded. "Based on the images you showed me, you picked up a rather diverse group of people, which considering where you rescued us from, is rather surprising. That'll mean different languages, cultures, religions, and education levels."

"And possibly learning disabilities, like I have flipping letters around, that have gone untreated for years," Little Flower replied.

"That will make things more challenging," Marcus stated. "We have assessments, but it would be difficult to assess someone's education level when they can't read or write in our language."

"So don't, at least not to start," GrandFather suggested. "Our higher education system would offer classes and allow people to choose what they wanted to take. We could have some be mandatory, such as reading, writing, and the Charter, but allow others to take the classes that interest them."

"That could work," her father stated. "Mattis Lawson is the head of the primary school guild. I'll put a meeting on his calendar so we can see about borrowing some instructors. That may be slow to start, as I don't know how fluent any of his instructors will be in sign language yet."

"Marsee and I can help translate, at least for the required classes," Little Flower stated. "And Lawson can send his instructors to our sign language classes, if that helps."

"Alright. I have a meeting scheduled for tomorrow morning with Mattis," Jer replied a few moments later.

"We'll come back to that item tomorrow then," Marcus stated. "Next, official holidays?"

"That should be a Council decision as well, as I don't know what religions are represented," Little Flower stated. "But there were a few non-secular holidays that focused around the start of the year and the formation of our district. We could have a remembrance day celebration on the date of the Cataclysm, to remember those we lost, and honor those who died saving us."

"I like that," GrandFather replied. "What holidays do you have?"

"Founders Day is our biggest holiday, for our species anyway," Marcus replied. "That's essentially the start of our new year, and commemorates when we arrived on this planet. We also celebrate the anniversaries on which all of the species joined the Consortium. The rest of the holidays are usually district specific, and often seasonal. In the southern districts we celebrate the first of the rains each spring, while the mountain districts have winter festivals after the first big snow storm of the season. We'll also have local memorial celebrations in honor of people who died, but those obviously aren't scheduled. Very few of our people celebrate the old religions anymore, even though we still pray to the Ancient Gods. Some of the other species do however. The Ice Giants and Water Sprites have a fairly detailed religious practice and belief structure. The Diggers never did, and while the Flyers say they don't, I'm pretty sure they follow the religion of the Ancient Trickster God."

GrandFather chuckled. "We had a god like that too, in one of our ancient regions. We didn't celebrate them directly, but we did have a holiday called April Fools, where the entire point of the day was to play practical jokes on each other. The more elaborate the better."

"Oh Gods, don't let Wind Rider find out about that," Marcus groaned. "She would be liable to make it a holiday for her people as well, and then none of us would be safe."

Little Flower grinned at his expression. "Oh I think that's perfect. It would be good to show how we have similar holidays and culture where possible. My personal favorite holiday was Halloween, which I suppose could translate into Hallowed Eve. It was fairly nonsecular in my district, although other cultures had more religious practices around it. My understanding was it was a day in which we were closest to the spirit world and could communicate with our ancestors, but don't quote me as I didn't practice those beliefs. We would dress up in costumes, pretending to be monsters, ghosts, animals, or popular characters from our entertainment programs, and go from door to door collecting sweet food." She didn't have a sign for candy. "We'd play games, and find our way through mazes and haunted houses where people would try to scare us." She let out a heavy sigh. "I miss chocolate."

"And peanut butter," GrandFather added.

"Peanut butter cups..." Little Flower whimpered. "One of the greatest losses to the universe." Her stomach took that moment to rumble. "I'm honestly not sure what I miss more. That or bacon double cheeseburgers and fries. I had a dream about finding a McDonald's in Council City last night. I honestly cried when I woke up."

"Did you have to mention burgers?" GrandFather asked, a look of pure misery on his face. "The fried fish is better than what we had at the Agency, but I'm getting sick of it already. What I wouldn't give for a steak. I think maybe we'd better break for lunch, or I'm liable to go hunt one of the neighbor's chenzies."

She groaned in response. "I wonder what grilled chenzie would taste like."

Both Marcus and her father were staring at them in ears back surprise.

"What?" she asked them.

"I know your species is omnivorous, but you've never mentioned hunting before, or food cravings. Did your species hunt, or is this because of your pregnancy?" Marcus asked.

"Yes and yes," Grandfather explained, before she could answer. "We hunted, but beef came from one of our domestic animals which sadly you didn't rescue, and food cravings are very common with pregnancy. We're all likely anemic at this point from not getting enough metal in our diet."

"Metal?" her father exclaimed. "You ate metal?"

"No, not directly. I don't have a sign for the specific metal, but it's something we got from the blood of our land based creatures," he explained. "It's necessary for the formation of red blood cells."

"You should talk with Myra. She's worried because your species is still losing weight," her father replied.

"Well, we eat far healthier here, so weight loss isn't surprising," he replied. "But anemia is common especially in our female population due to their cycles and blood loss each month."

"Figure out what species gives you what you need and I'll make sure we get it imported," her father said. "If we can find something that tastes even remotely good to you, and we can't find a way to get you a supplement for it."

"Well, on that note, I either need to find something to eat or I'm going to be sick," Little Flower stated and left without a further word. Unfortunately though, when she found her way to the kitchen, she found nothing, literally. The kitchen was completely missing. There was nothing left to the room but the doorway and a large gaping hole where the room used to be.

"Well that's going to make things a bit more challenging," she said to the others, who had followed her out.

"That it will. There's food on my ship," her father replied, tail curled in amusement at the understatement, so they turned and made their way across the courtyard to the ship. The outer courtyard was now full of containers stacked up and labeled containing the objects pulled out of the various rooms, making it impossible for her to see.

"It looks like there are people in the garden," her father said, so they made their way in and found a buffet set up under the bandala tree. The table was too high for her to reach, so her father helped her and GrandFather with a meal, and then they wandered over to where Ellie and her mother were sitting.

"Where's Marsee?" she asked awkwardly, after popping a piece of fruit in her mouth.

"Last I saw her, she was banging her head against her bookcases," Ellie replied.

"I should probably bring her something to eat then," Little Flower said, and popped another piece of fruit in her mouth.

"No doubt. She'll forget to eat if you don't remind her," her father replied. "Oh before I forget, Myra, GrandFather was saying that they need some form of metal in their diet that comes from the blood of other animals. Could this be your missing nutrient?"

Her mother's ears flicked up in interest and began a conversation with GrandFather trying to figure out which one it was. Little Flower's eyes quickly glazed over at the conversation, as she'd never been good at science. She quickly finished her meal and brought her dishes back, and her father handed her a plate for Marsee.

She left making her way back to the tower, figuring that's where Marsee would be, and found the first two rooms open and empty. As she took the ramp around the outside of the tower, she marveled at the sheer number of ships now surrounding the compound and the changes that had occurred in only a few hours. Giant holes were being dug where the foundations of the new buildings would go, and several sections of the compound were missing, where the entrances to the expanded kitchen and cafeteria, the new healers clinic, and the council chamber would go.

She found Marsee in their room surrounded by a tall stack of boxes, just staring at one of her bookcases. She set the food down on a nearby table and walked over. Marsee's back was to her, and as her ears didn't twitch, she guessed that she still had her hearing aids in. When she tapped on Marsee's shoulder, Marsee jumped and flipped around, eyes glaring and tail lashing, for scaring her.

"Hey, Chenzie Butt. I figured you'd rather eat up here. The garden is packed right now," Little Flower said, grinning, and pointed to the table where the food was.

"Thanks, Fish Breath." After a lengthy stretch, her sister padded over to the table to eat, thwacking her in the head with her tail on the way by.

Laughing, Little Flower joined her and pointed to the boxes. "I see you're making progress."

"Not really. Ellie gave me credit to download copies of books any I donate, and whatever tools and workbenches I move over to the guild hall, but I was only a fraction of the way through the books when the moves arrived, and now I have to go through all of *that!*" Marsee pointed to the piles of boxes. "And still get rid of a bookcase or two in here." She let out a heavy sigh.

"We'll find room for it," Little Flower said. "At least you managed to get the other rooms cleared out so Mama and Papa can move in."

"Yeah. That was painful. My workshop wasn't so bad as I just kept my favorite tools and what I'm using right now, but the books..." Marsee let out another anguished sigh.

"Well, it's not like you can't check them out or download them again. They won't be far," her sister said.

"I know. That helps, but digital copies aren't the same," she replied.

"How are you doing with all of this?" Little Flower pointed to the hearing aids in Marsee's ears.

Marsee let out a deep sigh. "I honestly envy you and your deafness right now. I have everything turned off and the noise still makes me want to pull my fur out."

"I'm sure it does," Little Flower replied. "I can hear it a little bit, which must mean it's really loud. I suppose you could go hide in Papa's ship. It might be quieter in there."

"That's not a bad idea, but after I finish here, I really should go find Ellie and start translating the Charter. The rest of this can probably wait. I'll just have the movers pack everything up and go through it later."

Little Flower nodded. "That's probably the easiest, that way you can take your time. Oh, just so you know, the kitchen and family room is already gone. I'm really going to miss that window seat."

"Me too," Marsee replied with drooping ears. "Maybe we can put one in the new family room."

Marsee was halfway through her meal when people they didn't know appeared. "We're here to begin work on installing the new waste rooms," one of them stated.

Marsee sighed. "I'll go find the movers and have them pack up whatever you need moved. Do you know where it's going yet?"

"Yes, we're going to put it against this wall, as it's closest to the existing plumbing," the builder replied. Marsee nodded and left.

She watched her sister leave, feeling guilty about the changes she'd caused her new family, even if it had been to save their lives.

"Councilor, the design states you want the waste hole raised to be able to sit on it?" the builder asked, radiating both surprise and confusion, as if not believing their orders.

"Yes, as my pregnancy increases it will be difficult for me to squat," she replied.

The female builder nodded. "I remember how difficult it was to get around in the last few weeks of my pregnancy. What height do you want it at?"

"The chair the Guild built for me for the council meeting was just about perfect," she replied.

The builder nodded and took out a device and asked her to stand, scanning her backside.

*Custom fitted toilets,* Little Flower chuckled. *Can this world get any better?*

Marsee returned with several other people carrying a load of boxes "Pack up this bookcase and this one, and place everything in this pile," Marsee instructed, and then with another sigh, left again.

As she watched her sister leave again, her own words came back to haunt her. *Every decision you make has unintended consequences, Councilor.*

"Councilor?" one the movers signed, waving their arms to get her attention.

"Yes?" she asked.

"I want thank you," the mover signed hesitantly in broken and halting sign language.

"Why?" she asked.

"For you forgive. Save us hard time," he replied.

"You're welcome. Thank you for taking us in and all your help today," she replied.

The mover grinned and went back to work. She watched them for a moment, and left to return to her own work, and to hunt down a working hole of muck, as the one she normally used was now also missing.

# CHAPTER 6

# Marsee: Lost Trust

Marsee left her room feeling jagged and overwhelmed by the changes taking place to her home, and the sheer number of people that were there. She was sure there were thousands of people in and around the compound, and the noise of construction was deafening. Taking her sister's suggestion, she made her way over to her father's ship and climbed inside. The quiet, the moment the door slid shut, was profound, and she sighed with relief as she took the hearing aids out of her ears and stored them. She rubbed her ears a bit as they were sore from wearing them so long, and she made her way over to the small kitchenette to see what was available. She'd left her meal half unfinished in her room and was thirsty, even if her stomach was in knots. She was just putting the pitcher of juice back in the refrigeration unit when she heard the door to the ship slide open, and looked over to see her father enter.

"Are you okay, Kitten?" he asked.

"Not really, but I'll manage," she replied. "I needed a few minutes of peace and quiet. I have a headache and it's just too loud out there, even with my hearing aids in, and I just got kicked out of my room."

He came over and looked into her eyes before taking the drink out of her paws with a frown. He set the drink down on the counter, wrapped her in a hug, and gently pulled on her scruff. She sagged against him, and took strength from him, just as she did that day in the garden, and after a few moments felt everything quiet and calm. When she felt calmer she pulled away. "Thanks Papa. I needed that."

"Your instinct was on," he said, after looking at her face again. "Were you aware of that?"

"No, but I didn't feel any different, or out of control either," she replied. "Just on edge. Am I in trouble?"

He shook his head. "No. That can occur when you're under stress. You weren't acting out of control, but you'll need to watch out for it."

She sighed and nodded. "I'm sorry, Papa. I'll do better."

"You *are* doing better. The Marsee I knew a few weeks ago would have gone and hid the moment the first ship appeared." He handed her back her glass and motioned over to the seats. "You said you wanted to talk to me about something? Do you want to talk now?"

She nodded and sat, taking a sip of her drink to give herself a moment to focus her thoughts. As she did, he rummaged through the first aid kit and handed her something for her headache, before sitting acros from her. "Thanks. I'm worried, Papa. The other day at the Council meeting when Tabor...when she announced the punishment for Mama...I was so mad I nearly lost control. Both me and the beast inside me wanted to claw Tabor's throat out for taking our cubs away."

He sighed, but didn't answer for several long moments. "You had every right to be mad at Tabor, and at your uncle and I too. We suggested the adjustment. It was the best we could come up with to counter the existing precedent. Neither of us could figure out a way around it that we thought the Seniors would accept as equal."

Marsee scowled, Little Flower had hinted that they were involved in that decision, but she hadn't wanted to believe it. "But it was wrong, Papa! I didn't hurt Little Flower. Why should I have been punished for what Mama did?"

"Yes, it was wrong. As for why..." He paused as he considered his words. "Tabor greatly simplified what was done to that last victim's children. Without the hormone blockers we have now, I'm told we would go into heat once our cubs were weaned. He apparently killed them to bring her back into heat, but not before doing unspeakable things to them. The mother wanted him to feel the pain she did, and wanted to ensure that his line didn't survive to pass on his violent tendencies. If they had gone with the real precedent, you wouldn't have just been killed. Your mother would have had to watch you tortured and killed in front of her. We were trying to save your life. With my vote, and with Marcus's encouragement, I pressed hard to focus on the victim's choice as to what would happen, rather than the actual punishment, in the hopes that your sister would be able to figure out another solution. I am very grateful she did, but I know you're still suffering because of it. If you want to move out, you're more than welcome to, or if you want us to move out, so you can have your tower back, we'll move just as soon as there's a space."

She shook her head. "No, Little Flower needs my help and yours, and so do her people. But...but why didn't the Seniors just change the law if it was so unjust? Was it because of me?"

Her father frowned at the question, and looked away as he considered, and then let out a sigh that told her everything she didn't want to know. Her father rarely let slip what he was feeling when he was wearing his Councilor's Mask, as he was now. "I honestly don't know, Kitten. Possibly. More than likely, if I'm being honest with myself. They haven't said, and I haven't looked to see who voted for it. I don't really want to know, because I'm worried that knowledge would affect my ability to work with them. I did speak with the Senior Honor Guard about you. Even though your uncle took you off the watch list, you *are* still being watched."

At her frown, he continued. "The watch is because we need to better understand what happened to you, to be sure this isn't just a reprieve. Kitten, I've seen far too many children lost to psychosis over the decades, your uncle, even more. They never came back, not like you did. I cried myself to sleep for a week after I had to call the Guard in, that first time. We're both very hopeful that sign language will help the others, but until we know more, we're all being cautious. Kendra says they're planning to bring anyone close to adulthood with issues in, to try what we did with you. On the plus side, she said she saw nothing concerning about your behavior during the trial. I've worked with her enough to know that if there was even the slightest concern, she would have brought you in to be tested, even at the detriment of your sister and her trial."

She nodded. "I understand everyone's concern. It just doesn't help being on the receiving end of it."

"No, I imagine it wouldn't," he replied.

She looked down and sighed again.

"What is it, Kitten?" he asked.

"Papa, what if I give it to my cubs?" she asked eventually, barely above a whisper.

"I suppose that's possible, too. We don't know what causes it, but I'm hopeful that what we did with you will help others like you. I was worried about the same when I had you and your siblings. Your siblings didn't have any issues, so it's more likely related to being an only cub than hereditary. My loss of control was caused by hunting, not because I was an only cub. Then again, perhaps that's why I had difficulty with my hunt, and afterwards. If it weren't for Marcus and everything he did to ensure I was safe, I probably would have been put down too. Perhaps I should have been."

"What did you do? To stop it, that is," she added.

"Much like you I guess. We went on hunts, but I never killed after that first time, and Marcus pushed me to try and make me mad and lose control. We fought often, and we didn't stop until he had me pinned to establish dominance over my instinct. I came close to killing him a few times before my instinct gave up fighting him. I've only really had issues once since. That was the day we found out about the precedent. I threatened to kill the entire Senior Council if they did that to you. Your uncle grabbed me by my scruff and threw me across the room before I completely lost control. I didn't want to fight it. I wanted to protect you as much as my instinct did. And I'll be honest, it took everything I had not to lose control the other day too. I thought your mother had when I heard you call out her name. Her instinct was fully on, and I thought the guards had killed her before I realized she'd just passed out. I think if the Seniors had gone with precedent, she would have lost control."

Marsee's eyes widened as her father spoke. "How did you know her instinct was fully on? You weren't close to her, like you are when you check me."

"Most of the time we're looking to see how your eyes react. When your instinct is on, your pupils will fully dilate, but there are other signs, your nose will flare, and your claws will come out," he replied.

"But that can happen when you're angry or upset," she said with a frown.

He nodded. "It can and it does. Which is what makes it hard to tell if there's an issue or not. As long as you're not pouncing as an adult, or going non-verbal, it's fine, and perfectly normal in a stressful or life threatening situation. It's your ability to turn it off that matters."

"Uncle Marcus said I would have been tested. Is it what you've been doing? Having me turn it on and off?"

"No, and I can't go into details either," he replied.

She understood and nodded. She might still have to be tested one day. "Papa, can the other Seniors be trusted?"

"What makes you think they can't?" he asked instead.

"They were considering genocide of Little Flower's people," she replied.

"They were, and they had every right to, after her testimony. It's our job as Seniors to protect our people from all threats, with our very lives, if it comes to that. And no, we don't always make the right decisions. But they did tell me that they won't harm them as long as they don't harm any of their people. And frankly, they're now members of the Consortium and subject to the same laws and punishments as the rest of us. I've known Clear Seas since I was a cub, and I've found no reason not to trust him. I don't know the others as well, but Marcus does, and between us, we have significant sway in the Council now, which should hopefully be enough to protect them."

Marsee nodded, feeling slightly better. Her faith in the Council had been severely shaken. "I'm glad you and Uncle Marcus are both Seniors now. I know you'd never do anything like that."

He was silent for a long time, and she tilted her head in confusion at his lack of response.

"Marsee, I was prepared to commit treason to protect them, and I *would* commit treason, to protect the other planets if there was need. As a member of the Senior Council, my oath is not just to my people, but to everyone."

She smiled at him. "There's a difference between protecting people from those who intend and plan harm, and killing people because of the threat they *might* someday pose. I believe you would make the right decision if faced with it, even if that meant killing your own family."

He tilted his head acknowledging her statement. "I pray I never have to make that decision."

"If I do lose control, know that I won't hold it against you," she said.

He sighed. "I pray that never happens too. Speaking of which, now that you've had time to calm down, turn your instinct on."

She did, and waited for him to tell her to turn it off. He walked over and lifted her head, staring into her eyes for a long time, and then to her surprise swung at her. She blocked instantly, before she could even recognize what he was doing.

"Now turn it off," he ordered. She did immediately, although her heart was racing. He nodded and gave a sigh of relief.

"What was that for?" she asked.

"If you weren't fully in control, you would have had a much harder time shutting it off," he replied. "I needed to be sure."

She nodded her understanding.

"Now, feel free to spend as much time in here as you need, or come find me if you need another hug. If it makes you feel any better, I'm feeling a little overwhelmed myself."

"Thanks, Papa. And thanks for listening," she replied.

"Any time, Kitten." He gave her another hug, and left.

# CHAPTER 7

# Little Flower: Guild Hall

Little Flower sat perched on the back of a chair in Ellie's office in the newly built guild hall reviewing all of the new apps that had been translated for her people. These would come pre-installed on the new tablets they would receive when her people arrived from the Agency in a few days. Marsee was busy, so Ellie was helping to translate where she could, as she was far more fluent in sign than the tech working with her.

"I don't understand. Why do you want the keyboard in that layout?" Ellie translated. "It doesn't follow the order you gave us, or follow the most commonly used letters in your language."

"No, it doesn't, but it's the order my people will expect and have been trained to use. It's muscle memory at this point. I was once told it was designed to actually slow people down when typing because the mechanical machines we used before we had computers would jam up. There are other layouts, but I couldn't tell you what the order should be for those, and I don't know if anyone else rescued used those layouts either, as it was far less common."

The tech shrugged. "We can easily add those as options later. In any event, that covers all of the standard programs. We'll still need to review the optional programs, but those can wait as they don't come pre-loaded. Thank you for your time, Councilor."

"You're very welcome," Little Flower replied.

After the tech left, Little Flower turned to Ellie. "Well, I should probably rescue Marsee. The last time I saw her, she was pulling her fur out trying to decide which books to keep. At this point she might not have much fur left."

Ellie chuckled, "I don't think you'll have to look far, I saw her walk by a few minutes ago with the movers, fur still attached. Come on, I'm guessing she's probably still in the new library."

Little Flower followed Ellie out, and sure enough, Marsee was there, helping to unpack her books, looking decidedly dejected. Little Flower walked over and gave her a hug, while Ellie grabbed a box and started to help unpack. "Thank you," Little Flower signed.

"For what?" Marsee asked.

"For sharing your knowledge with my people," Little Flower replied, and grabbed a book with a very intriguing cover. "This looks interesting."

"It's one of my favorite fantasy novels. I think you'd like it. I already have another copy though," Marsee said. "I'll help you read it if you want."

"I'd like that," Little Flower said, but sighed. "I really wish there had been time to save some of our books."

"You should try to write one," Ellie commented.

"She is. How is your cub's book going?" Marsee asked. "I saw you were working on it the other night."

Ellie's ears perked up with interest. "You're working on a cub's book?"

"The Lost Creatures of Earth," Little Flower replied. "I'm drawing them, and GrandFather said he'd add what he knew about them afterwards. Marsee said she'd help translate it too. I have quite a bit done already, but there are a lot I still want to add."

Ellie grinned. "That sounds wonderful! Have you given any thought about joining the Guild yet? I'd really love a copy. I'm sure it will be very popular."

"I've been thinking about it, but right now I don't have a lot of time to draw, much less commit to the needs of the Guild. My role as a councilor will probably take up most of my time between now and when I go on maternity leave, and I don't want to commit to anything until after," Little Flower replied.

"Well, we do have provisional accounts," Ellie stated. "It would allow you to trade your craft and take consignments without commitments."

"I'll consider it," Little Flower said again, and grabbed another book, placing it on a shelf.

Ellie glared at her. "What's your real hesitation?"

She snorted at the Guild Master for sniffing her out. "Honestly, I know you said I was a master, but after seeing all the artwork people sent for the apartments last night, it's hard to see myself that way. They've taken centuries to perfect their crafts, and I know I couldn't do a fraction of what they do, and personally, I think Marsee's artwork is just as good as mine, if not better, yet she's only a journeyman."

Ellie raised a brow at Marsee. "How come I haven't seen any of your artwork yet?"

Marsee shrugged. "You probably have. Some of my best work was in Mama's office. I haven't had the opportunity to work on my own arts and crafts since I switched guilds, and I paused most of my book restoration classes in the Writer's Guild to have time to help Little Flower prepare for the trial. I just kept up with language studies classes. Did you know Little Flower's Papa didn't want her to be an artist?"

Ellie shifted to look at her with a raised brow. "Seriously?"

"That's not entirely true. He felt I wouldn't be able to support myself as an artist, and that was probably the case. We actually had the phrase 'starving artist' because it was so hard to make a living in the arts," she replied, and then turned back to Marsee. "When did you find time to take classes?"

"Usually when you were napping, or drawing at night," Marsee replied. "But my lessons with Rainbow Scales counted too."

"Ah," Little Flower replied, and turned her attention back to Ellie, who was now glaring at her. "What?"

"No offense, but your father was an idiot, Little Flower. Your people too. You are exceptional. Your art is unique and you have a way of distilling a scene down to its essence that it can take others centuries to learn. I've had thousands of people reaching out wanting to know if the artwork we showed at the trial was available for purchase."

"Really?" Little Flower asked, surprised.

"Really," Ellie replied. "I'll be honest, I've not had this much demand for any particular artist's work in a very long time. Please, join the Guild. Not only will it give you access to supplies, but it will help your people. A good portion of what you earn will go back to the community too."

"I still have plenty of supplies," Little Flower replied.

Marsee rolled her eyes and Ellie sighed with frustration, which confused her. She hadn't been expecting that reaction.

"Come with me," Ellie demanded. "You too, Marsee. Maybe you can knock some sense into that skull of hers."

Marsee's tail curled with amusement, but she said nothing as they followed Ellie out and down to a section of the massive building that Little Flower hadn't seen yet. People were moving large floating shipping containers in and out of the space, and they had to dodge around several people to get inside. She quickly realized they were in a large warehouse that put the biggest craft or hardware store she'd ever been in to shame. Ellie led them to a section that was full of drawing supplies, canvases of every size, paints, pencils, brushes, and far more. It made what Ellie had brought her before seem like second-hand discards, and she just stood there in awe. Even Marsee seemed a little overwhelmed, and started drifting towards supplies and checking things out.

Ellie waved to get her attention again. "As a member of the Guild, whatever supplies you need are factored into any commissions you take. You would only have to pay for those supplies if they ultimately go into a gift. I never want an artist to be hampered by lack of materials. The same goes for tools and equipment. As a full member, you would be expected to complete a set number of hours towards your craft, but you'd also earn far more per commission, especially at your rank, and personal supplies would be significantly less expensive."

She couldn't speak for several long moments as she just took everything in, and visions of projects she'd always wanted to try popped into her head. She shook her head to clear her thoughts. "I've had dreams less well stocked than this room. The nearest craft store was over an hour away from where I lived, and I could rarely get my parents to take me there, assuming I could even afford anything. My art teacher would save broken supplies for me, rather than throwing them out, and I often had to scavenge paper from the recycling."

"What a waste of your talent," Ellie sighed. "I promise, you will never lack for supplies if you join the Guild."

"You really should," Marsee said. "Especially if you want to publish that book you're working on. I'll gladly help bind it up, but everyone should see it. What I've seen so far is really good."

"You should listen to her, child," Ellie said. "And I really want to see that book."

Little Flower rolled her eyes, but unclipped her tablet. It wasn't as good as the drawing tablet she shared with Marsee, but she opened up the drawing app, pulled up the project, and handed it over.

Ellie took the tablet and began scrolling, at first pleased, but then frowned, and her tail twitched.

"You don't like it?" Little Flower asked.

"I absolutely love it. What I don't like is this tablet. Where did you get this ancient thing?" Ellie asked, wrinkling her nose and holding it up like it smelled.

"That's my old tablet," Marsee replied. "It originally belonged to my brother, Thomas. My grandparents gave me a new one for my Name Day. Little Flower has been borrowing the drawing tablet I saved up to buy, about three years ago. It's a lot better than that one, but nowhere near as nice as the one my grandparents just got me."

Ellie placed her hand out and said something to Marsee. Marsee handed over her tablet, and a few moments later, Ellie handed it back and took off at a fast walk. They trotted after her to an aisle full of tablets, where the tech she'd been working with before, was now busy configuring them. Ellie picked up one the tech had just set down and fiddled with it for a moment.

"These are the tablets that are going to be handed out to the Huemans?," Ellie asked the tech for confirmation.

"Yes, ma'am," he replied. "I should be done in an hour or two."

Ellie frowned, looked back at Little Flower, and set the tablet back down on the stack. "No, this one isn't good enough either," she muttered. Marsee translated for her while Ellie turned and examined the shelves. After a moment she pulled one down and checked it. "This will do for now. Configure this one next," Ellie ordered, handing the tablet to the tech.

"Yes, ma'am," the tech replied.

While the tech went to work, Ellie turned back to look at her. "The tablet you'll get as a citizen is better than what you have now. That piece of junk was designed for cubs and was recalled decades ago. Marsee, I'm sorry you had to deal with that. You should have been given a better one when you joined the Guild. I'll look into why you didn't, and make sure you're compensated for whatever you paid for that drawing tablet."

Marsee raised her brows in surprise. "Thank you!"

Ellie nodded once, and turned back to Little Flower. "As for you, what the tech is configuring is equivalent to what Marsee has. If you join the Guild at least provisionally, I'll give it to you. It normally costs about a year's worth of credits."

Little Flower raised a brow, and then crossed her arms. "Is that the best you've got?"

Ellie flicked her ears back in surprise and glared at her suspiciously, but her tail curled in amusement. "No, there are better available, but this is the best we have here. Join the Guild as a full member and I'll make sure you get the best drawing tablet we have. It would make whatever drawing tablet Marsee has now look as ancient as your tablet in comparison."

Marsee's ears perked up and she motioned for Little Flower to accept.

"I said I would consider it. I'm worried about what's going to happen with my pregnancy. I really don't feel comfortable committing to anything until afterwards," Little Flower replied.

Marsee's ears and whiskers drooped.

Little Flower looked over at Marsee with a frown. "What? You know my pregnancy is high risk."

"I know. I was just hoping you'd join, so we could get that drawing tablet," Marsee signed back.

She grinned with understanding and turned to Ellie. "I don't need a personal tablet that's any better than what the rest of my people will have, but if you send us the best drawing tablet you have instead, I'll join provisionally."

Ellie grinned at her with her victory. "Deal, and you're getting this tablet regardless. I don't want you limited if inspiration should hit." At that, Ellie pulled off her own tablet and fiddled with it for a moment. "Your account has been created, *Master* Chenzira," Ellie replied. "Now, what drawings can I have now, to scan in for prints?"

Little Flower shrugged. "I don't know what would sell. I haven't really given any thought to it either. You're welcome to look through my sketchbooks if you want."

Ellie snorted. "Of course I want," she replied, and then turned back to the tech with a growl. "Is that tablet done yet?"

The tech handed it over. "Yes, ma'am."

Ellie passed it over to her, and started walking away. Little Flower looked over at Marsee who grinned back at her, tail spiraled.

"You can fiddle with that tablet later. Come on. I want to see those drawings," Ellie growled at them.

Laughing they followed her back over to the tower. "Most of my framed work is still stacked in the family room. We haven't hung it up yet," she told Ellie. "I'll grab my sketch books while you drool over those."

"I don't drool," Ellie replied with a glare. "I browse with enthusiasm, and Marsee, I want to see some of your artwork too."

Little Flower smirked and Marsee groaned, but they continued making their way up to their room, leaving Ellie behind. Marsee started to pull down some of the drawings they'd already hung back up, including a few Marsee's pieces. Marsee's tail was curled and she looked far more enthusiastic than she'd seen her sister since they'd returned home, which surprised her. She'd been expecting Marsee to be pulling her fur out at having to pick which artwork she was going to show Ellie.

"I'm guessing from your reaction, that tablet's really good?" Little Flower asked.

"If it's the one I think it is, it would take me years to earn enough to buy it at my rank," Marsee replied. "Thank you."

"Huh. I should have asked for more then," Little Flower replied. "Ellie gave in far too easily, which means there are far more people asking for those prints than she indicated."

"I wouldn't be surprised. Your drawings are really good."

"So are yours," Little Flower replied.

Marsee just shrugged. "I'm sure yours will be far more popular. I've put a few pieces up for sale before, but they've never sold much. Your artwork is unique, so I'm sure it will be very popular."

"I bet yours will be too, now that people know about you," Little Flower replied.

Marsee just shrugged again and pulled another painting down. When they arrived back in the family room, their parents were also there, unpacking, or her father was anyway. Her mother was peering over Ellie's shoulder.

"You can't have that one," Myra said, and grabbed a frame out of Ellie's paws. Ellie resisted handing it over and Myra actually growled at her. "That's mine and I'm not sharing. It's going up in my office." Ellie huffed but let go.

She chuckled when she saw it. It was the one she'd done of Marsee sticking her hand up the chenzie's butt to turn the breeched calf.

Marsee groaned. "Do you have to, Mother? It was bad enough in your office before."

"Well it's that or the waiting room," her mother teased, "but it's going up in my clinic and nowhere else."

Marsee flopped down on a pillow and buried her head. "Mother!"

"It would be very popular," Ellie replied. "I'm sure I'd sell a lot of prints."

"I'm not sharing," Myra insisted. "I'm perfectly happy embarrassing my daughter in front of the people who actually understand how important that moment was, but I am not sharing it with the general public."

Ellie glared at Myra, but to Marsee's evident relief their mother didn't back down. Ellie shrugged and went back to digging through the artwork. "That's okay, this one works just as well. I know I want a copy for my office." It was the updated drawing of the water fight she'd had with Marsee in the sink that first day.

Marsee looked up, saw which one it was, and groaned again, burying her face under a pillow. Whatever she said made the others laugh.

"You will not die from embarrassment," her mother replied in sign. "I'm pretty sure that's medically impossible. And no, I'm not sedating you for the next three years either. You'll just have to deal with it."

Laughing, Ellie went back to browsing and stopped at one of Marsee's. "You drew this one Marsee?"

Marsee peered out from under her pillow and sighed. "Yes, ma'am."

Ellie glared at Marsee and returned to examining the painting. Little Flower watched her sister, who practically vibrated with tension as Ellie looked at it, and then her ears went back in shock as Ellie placed on the pile she was taking to scan in.

Half an hour later, Ellie left with her arms full of her sketchbooks and dozens of their framed drawings, both hers and Marsees, indicating they'd be returned in a day or two. Marsee didn't come out from under her pillow for a good hour.

"Still worth the tablet?" Little Flower asked when she finally surfaced.

Marsee just growled, and threw the pillow at her.

# CHAPTER 8

# Damon: Hopes and Dreams

Damon Minor grabbed his tiny box of belongings and followed his warden out of his prison cell for what he hoped was the last time. The two years of confinement, while the strange cat-like aliens had studied them, to determine if they were safe to interact with, was finally over. He'd been in prison before and was used to the boredom, isolation, and confinement, but then those times he'd deserved it. *Be fair, we could have killed each other with a sneeze.* Conditions had improved as they finally started to learn how to talk to each other, but he was still grieving the loss of his wife and daughter, and like everyone, angry about their long confinement and mistreatment.

Word had it they were moving to their new home, and he wondered if it would be any better furnished than the empty rooms they'd had here, or if the cats didn't believe in that kind of thing. He smiled at Paul, his one friend, as they made their way out of their dorm and onto the waiting shuttle.

The others in his dorm looked at him with suspicion, but he didn't blame them. He'd been thrown stark naked into another cell before they'd started providing them with clothes, and he was covered in tattoos that the clothing still didn't fully cover. He had no way of covering them up with makeup like he used to either. His clothes covered the worst of his tattoos now, but he feared the damage had already been done.

Cats he now knew were guards, based on the badges and equipment they wore, were helping to load the shuttles. They waited in line while the guards took their boxes from them, and stored them. Another guard unclipped the bracelet that had been on his wrist for the past two years, and motioned for him to hop on. He found an available window seat that looked out at the desert around him, climbed up into the overly large seat, and just stared out the window. He'd grown up in a city, so the vast empty space was still a little unsettling. It didn't take long for everyone to be loaded. The guards came around and showed everyone how to use and adjust the strange safety harnesses, and checked to make sure everyone was secure before they took off.

He'd never traveled in a plane before, although he'd watched them often from his tiny apartment near the airport, and he'd always wondered what it would be like to fly. Unlike the planes back home, these shuttles hovered to take off, before flying off at a much lower altitude than he expected. Even still, the view from the window of the vast desert and mountains in the distance was astounding. Strange herds of creatures ambled along, causing dust to billow in their wake, and as they flew it was like every care in the world just vanished. He was hopeful he could build a new life here, a life his Amanda would have been proud of.

Before long, they were approaching a new collection of buildings, which the pilot circled around, giving them a chance to see their new home. Like everything else on this world, it was massive, and surrounded a tree that made the giant one back at the Agency look scrawny. He could barely grasp its size. As they circled around the tree, the sun glittered off of a large glass dome. *Is that a pool?* he wondered. *Looks like one.* He grinned at the thought of going for a swim, but then frowned when he remembered his tattoos.

"Welcome to your new home," his doctor/warden signed when they landed. "Please follow me. Your belongings will be brought to your new rooms."

They were led down a long hallway into a massive amphitheater, where others were already gathering. He followed the others from his group down the long ramp to the next unfilled row and found an empty seat. *High quality,* he thought as he examined it. Everything about this room seemed brand new. It even had the strong smell of fresh paint. It didn't take long for what remained of the human species to find their seats, as it was a depressingly small number. *Five, six-hundred, maybe,* he thought.

Conversation stopped as two humans and three of the cats took the stage. "Good morning and welcome! My name is Little Flower Chenzira, although you can also call me Jessica. It's my pleasure to introduce you to my family. My father, Senior Councilor Jeran Chenzira, my mother, Senior Healer Myra Chenzira, my sister Journeyman Crafter Marsee Chenzira, and my grandfather, James O'Neil." She gave both the spelling and the name signs for everyone.

Damon listened and watched quietly as Jessica told them about their new home, their newly won freedom and inclusion into the Consortium, and their new rights and responsibilities, along with the consequences for any crimes they might commit. As part of that she explained what had happened to her at the Agency, and what had happened to the person who had harmed her.

He did give a little snort when realized they were all on probation, well, the guys anyway. *I suppose that's fair. We did make a mess of our old world, and that idiot messed things up for everyone.* They all knew about Mitch, and the fact that he was being guarded, but no one had known for sure what he'd done, as none of their wardens would say, but there had been rumors. Ezra had claimed he'd been brought into a room with a badly beaten girl, who had been terrified of him, and implied that she'd been raped. Unable to do anything else against the cats, he'd kicked his warden and run away, refusing to have any part of that, but no one had seen her since, and their wardens wouldn't say what had happened to her. Everyone had been uncomfortable wondering if they were being kept for breeding, as it had appeared, and everyone thought she'd been killed. The woman Damon had been thrown in with had tolerated him, simply because she was lonely, and talking to someone was better than nothing, but they'd never become close. They'd both assumed the cats were trying to get them to procreate, and neither of them had any desire to bring a child into captivity.

Now they all knew what really happened. *She can't be more than what sixteen, seventeen maybe?* he thought with a horrified sigh. *I'm impressed she stood up for us at all after that.* As small of a number as they had left, they'd still killed him, which told him just how serious consequences were on this planet.

Jessica switched to talking about the education they were going to be given, free of charge, and a quick overview of the different organizations on the planet and the guild system that they had.

He was excited about the possibility of learning new skills. *Maybe I'll learn how to fly. Wouldn't that be wonderful!*

After the presentation and ceremony to make all of the women legal adults, and also apparently this world's equivalent to leaders, they waited for their turn to be taken on a tour of their new home. While they were waiting, Paul turned to him. "What gives them the right to take our adulthood from us?"

Damon snorted. "Every woman here has likely been harmed by a man at some point in her life. If the first thing Mitch did was to rape and beat that poor child, we're lucky they let any of us live."

Paul looked at him and rolled his eyes. "So are you just going to allow them to do this?"

Damon shrugged. "I've been on probation before. If you want early release, prove to them you deserve it. I doubt any of the women will sponsor us, so we'll have to convince the cats, and the only way to do that is with hard work and by staying out of trouble."

His friend shook his head. "A year or two, I could see, but she's talking eighteen years before we're legal adults again with the right to vote, and by then everything will be decided."

"No doubt, but then all we ever decided to do when we had power was fight each other and kill. Maybe they'll do a better job." Damon stood as his warden motioned them up. He'd killed before, many times, when he'd been in a gang in his youth. Thankfully the police had never found out about that, and he'd only been arrested for car theft and drug trafficking. He'd been lucky though. Due to his age at the time, he'd been placed on probation after a few years, and moved to a half-way house where they'd taught him carpentry, helped him to earn his G.E.D., and found him an honest job, but it had been Amanda that had saved his life. He'd fallen in love with her the moment he saw her, and the desire to be good enough to earn her love had been what he'd needed to put his troubled youth behind him.

It didn't take him long to realize this place was far nicer than any-where he'd ever lived before, and it had all been built and designed for them. The garden was spectacular, and the pool practically a resort. The only thing missing was a water slide. The guild hall where they would be taught many of their classes was incredibly well equipped, far better than the school he'd attended as a child.

He did chuckle when he learned that the ruling family lived in what looked like nothing more than the stone tower of an ancient castle. His warden informed them how the original compound was over ten thousand years old, going all the way back to when they first arrived on this world, and that significant effort was made to preserve as much of the original structure as possible. He was impressed at how seamless the old and new construction was. If his warden hadn't pointed out what was new, he'd have never been able to tell.

The last place they were shown was to their new apartments. They'd been asked to write their names several days prior, and these were now outside of their doors, above large mailboxes. They were led up to the fourth floor of one of the massive apartment buildings, and down one wing until they came to their rooms. Damon found his room and put his hand on the scanner as indicated, and when the door slid open, he just stood there in shock. *This is all for me?*

He shook his head in disbelief and wandered the apartment exam-ining everything. The main room had more furniture than he'd ever owned in his life and was incredibly well made. Far better than he could build for sure. Stunning artwork hung on the walls and decorated the tables and bookshelves, mixed with strange flowering plants that gave the space a floral scent, although he could still smell hints of fresh paint. The small kitchen had a stove, sink, dishwasher of sorts, and a refrigerator, with instructions on how to use everything. The cupboards were full of dishes and silverware, enough for a dozen people. On the wall was a TV bigger than anything he'd ever been able to afford.

Attached to the main room were two bedrooms. His entire apartment had been half the size of one of the bedrooms alone. The bed was massive, with built in storage, containing additional bedding. A note on the bed provided instructions on how to split it into two beds if he wanted. Additional furniture filled up the room with tables, chairs, desks, and bookcases. An equally massive walk-in closet was full of his belongings, everything he'd ordered, and then some. A window took up most of one wall with a built-in padded bench, surrounded by more bookcases and when he examined the bench he realized there was even more storage, but this was filled with boxes. He pulled out one and realized it was a board game of some sort. Checking out the desks, he found them full of stationary and drawing supplies. Some sort of strange device sat on the top, which he picked up, and after examining the note left behind, realized it was the cats equivalent to a tablet or phone. Once he figured out how to work it, he realized everything had already been translated into English, and their personal contacts updated to include everyone rescued, along with dozens of others. He set that back down on the desk and kept exploring.

The second bedroom was set up the same way, but was empty of belongings. Grief hit him when he saw the empty closet in that room, and he wished his family was here to share it with him. This was far more than he'd ever been able to provide them before, and they deserved it far more than he did. *If only they'd been with him,* he thought for the hundredth time, wondering if they'd died instantly, or had suffered for hours before the planet was no longer habitable. He sighed and prayed it had been instant, and then shoved that thought down and returned to examining the suite.

He eventually made it around to the bathroom and read the instructions that had been printed out and left on how to use everything. *Oh thank god, a real toilet!* he thought, but peered dubiously at the stack of 'toilet fabric' that had been left next to a small cleaning unit beside the toilet. *Better than nothing I suppose.* To his immense surprise, the cleaning unit sanitized the fabric in less than a minute, and he couldn't find any hint that it had been used before. Well, *that's a definite improvement,* he thought, and then tried out the shower.

They'd provided water for bathing recently, which had been a huge upgrade, but knowing now that this place was a desert, he understood why water hadn't been provided before. The sonic shower was strange, but he left feeling clean, which was a wonderful change. Whatever it was they'd sprayed them down with had always made him feel sticky for several hours afterwards and with this heat, he knew he'd be a sweaty mess fairly quickly. He'd never done well with heat.

After he exited the shower, he took a moment to look at himself in the full length mirror that had also been provided. He'd spent his time working out, for lack of anything better to do, in the hopes that he might one day find a way to escape, and he was probably the fittest he'd ever been. Between that and the food, he'd lost every ounce of fat that had been on him, and injuries that had plagued him since he was a kid had been treated. Even his vision was better. Only his partial hearing loss remained, although they were apparently trying to figure out how to repair it as he'd been brought in to be examined by a healer the day before.

He let out a sigh as he examined the tattoos that covered most of his body. He'd been young and stupid when he'd gotten them, and grown up in a very racist household. His beliefs had changed over the years, but his finances hadn't, and he'd not had the money to have the tattoos removed, although some he'd been able to alter. *I wonder if the cats can do that? It's worth asking, I suppose.*

The cabinets in the bathroom held all the grooming equipment he could possibly want and once he figured out how to use it, went to work on the rats nest that was his hair and beard. It wasn't exactly a professional job, but it was far better than what it had been before. Properly groomed for the first time in years, he put on a clean change of clothing, by far the nicest he'd ever owned, and tossed the rest in the larger cleaning unit, giving that a try. Then, after looking out the view from his balcony for a few minutes, he made his way back over to the clinic they'd been shown. He got himself turned around once, but eventually found his way there.

"Good morning, is there a problem?" Myra, the gold colored cat they'd been introduced to earlier, asked at the entrance.

"Not really. I was just wondering if there was any way you could remove my tattoos?" He pointed to the drawings on his arm as he didn't know the sign for tattoo.

"Why? They're very pretty," she asked. "Do they have meaning?"

"Thank you, but yeah they do. Many of them aren't very nice. I got them when I was young and stupid, and I'd like to have a clean start," he replied.

"Do you want them all removed?" she asked.

"No, not all of them. This one here is a picture of my partner and daughter. The rest I'd like to get rid of though."

"I am sorry for your loss," she signed, motioned for him to follow her back, and then helped him up onto an examination bed. While much of their new home had been designed for his species, apparently the clinic was designed for the healer's convenience, as the bed was far above his head.

"Yes, I think we should be able to get rid of these," she stated after a few minutes. "Please take off your clothing. I will be right back."

He stripped down to his underwear and waited. When she returned a few minutes later, she had an odd device with her. He watched as she ran the device over a tattoo on his leg and the ink just vanished painlessly where the blue beam struck it. He'd had one tattoo removed before. It had been painful, and hadn't done all that good of a job either. It took about an hour before she was done, taking extra care around the ones he wanted to keep, but to his amazement there was no sign they'd ever been there before. "Your pee may be a different color for a day or two, as the ink washes out of your system. I'll give you some nano cream to use if your skin should hurt at all. It might get irritated. If that doesn't help, come back."

He nodded his understanding and began dressing again. "Thank you," he said. "I could never afford to have this done back home."

"Of course," she replied. "If you need anything, please let me know. I want you to be happy here, and I'm sorry I couldn't provide you with better before."

He raised a brow. "Couldn't?" he asked.

She nodded. "I was the healer in charge of the Agency. When we were unable to communicate with you, many in our Council believed you were not sentient. I only had enough budget to provide the bare minimum. Much of what you were given was donated by friends and family, but I tried hard to improve your living conditions. I am sorry for the harm your isolation caused you. I hope that what we have provided for you here helps to make up for that."

He nodded. "My entire apartment on Earth would have fit into half of one of the bedrooms in my suite. I could have never afforded what you've given me before." He sighed and jumped down.

"What is it?" she asked.

"I just wish my family was here too," he replied, and made his way over to examine his new appearance in a mirror, shocked at what he was seeing.

"Is everything okay?" Myra asked, waiting for him, and looking at him with sympathy and concern.

"I don't recognize myself," he replied. For perhaps the first time in his life he felt respectable. Even the suit he'd rented for his wedding hadn't been as nice as the clothing he was wearing now. *I wonder what Amanda would think.* He swallowed hard to control his grief, and turned to follow Myra back out.

He spent the rest of the day wandering the compound, swimming in the pool, and trying to make friends. It had been years since he'd been to a pool or felt comfortable even wearing shorts to go swimming, but he sighed when the others still looked at him with suspicion. Most wouldn't even talk to him. He shrugged. It would take time to earn their trust and he didn't blame them for their suspicions.

On the way back he took a look at the board outside of his apartment building to see what classes were being offered, and frowned when he didn't see anything about learning how to fly one of the shuttles. Most of the classes were introductory level though. *Maybe that will come later,* he thought. Many of the mandatory classes made sense, government and law, reading and writing in Saber, and sign language. As for the optional classes, he found many that sounded interesting. Next to the class schedule was a list of jobs that needed to be done to support the compound, and found that many of the more interesting ones had already been taken. Shrugging, he signed up for groundskeeper, figuring no one else would. That section was completely blank. *Maybe that will win me some bonus points with the parole board,* he thought.

That afternoon Damon returned to his room and sat out on his surprisingly air-conditioned balcony and dug through all of the apps on the tablet they'd given him. Eventually he came across the recording of the trial Jessica had mentioned, and decided to watch, even though she'd said that they'd go over it in one of their required courses. Between what he'd learned of sign language and the rough translation that his tablet did, he was able to follow along reasonably well. When he was done, he set the tablet aside and thought for a long time. He certainly hadn't been expecting what he saw. *This place is very different,* he finally decided with a yawn.

The days were exceptionally long here and he hadn't taken a nap yet, so he fiddled with his tablet until he figured out how to set an alarm, not wanting to miss the first scheduled council meeting that evening, and went to bed. As comfortable as the bed was, it was a long time before he fell asleep. Curling around a pillow, in the overly large and nearly empty bed, he eventually cried himself to sleep, and dreamed,  as he always did, of the family he'd lost.

# CHAPTER 9

# Jeran: First Council

Jer stared at the clock above the entrance to the council chamber, trying to gather the courage to run his very first council meeting, and wondering if it would be his last. He wouldn't put it past any of his new people to vote him out as their first action, if what he'd seen and heard so far was any indication. The anger his new people had for him had been palpable that morning, although surprisingly few people had come to his office afterwards. Most had sought out Little Flower or GrandFather. He'd spent the last hour preparing with them and Marcus, but Marcus had signed off, and Little Flower and GrandFather had left to help everyone learn how to use their desks and log into the meeting. Finally when it was time, he took a deep breath to steady his nerves, and hit the switch to open the door.

"All rise as the Senior Council enters the chamber," he heard Kendra call out.

While Little Flower hadn't wanted a guard stationed at the compound permanently, he had a feeling tonight's meeting might get out of control, and had asked Kendra if he could borrow guards for the meeting, since they would already be there to help with the transfer from the Agency. He hadn't expected Kendra to show up too, but he probably should have.

He made his way up onto the podium and started the meeting. "Please take your seats. This council is now in session," he signed, and waited for everyone to settle before beginning. "I hope everyone has found their new homes to their liking. Before we get started with the planned agenda, has everyone been able to successfully log into the meeting? If not, please raise your paw."

He waited for a moment for GrandFather to translate his words into their spoken language, for those who were not fluent in sign language yet. No one raised their paw, so he gave a quick rundown of the application. "Please be aware that every council session is recorded, as is the law. From here, you can watch any council meeting already in session, even if you're not in this room, or pull up past meetings. However, you can only participate in a meeting if you're in the room itself, a member of the Council, or directly invited by a member of the Council. When you're logged into an active meeting, you can message someone individually by clicking on their image, or indicate you wish to speak by touching the big blue button in the lower right hand corner. People will be called upon in the order they request to speak. For those of you who are now listed as councilors, you will have additional options that will allow you to submit new agenda items to the docket and vote. For everyone else, please come talk to me, or one of the other councilors to get your items on the docket. As you are all new here though, I want to open the floor up to everyone, for any questions you might have so far."

Dozens of lights activated. "Damon Minor, you have the floor."

"Thank you. I was looking at the list of classes, and I noticed that there weren't any on learning how to fly. Is that planned for later?"

"Yes. However there are requirements. There are a number of classes you'll need to take first, including learning how to read in Saber, and you'll need to be an adult before you'll be allowed to fly. Many of the guilds, such as the Ship's Guild, Council, Healers, and the Guard, require that you are an adult before taking classes or joining those guilds, because of the life or death decisions you will face in those roles."

"I can understand that," Damon replied. "However, most of us were adults before. Could an exception be made?"

"At this time no. Those rules are in the charters for the specific guilds, but I will talk with the Seniors of those guilds to see if they would be willing to make exceptions for your unique situation," he replied.

Damon frowned, but nodded and sat down, so Jer called the next person. "Danny Shuto, you have the floor."

"What gives you the right to take our adulthood from us?" he asked, and many of the men grumbled their agreement.

"We wanted to put everyone on equal footing and give you time to learn our culture, laws, and skills. This is not meant to be a punishment, but an opportunity for you to learn without the requirements of being an adult in our society," Jer replied.

"Yeah, but if the women get to be adults when they hit puberty, why don't the men?" he asked.

"That is a fair question. Your requirements for adulthood are the same as any of the species, although they have been adjusted for your lifespan and biological differences. The females of all the species gain their adulthood when they're capable of bearing young, because they will be responsible for caring for another person, should they become pregnant. We do not hold the male responsible for caring for the young in that pairing. It's entirely up to the mother to decide who has parental rights to their children, regardless of a person's sex or who they mated with. In my species, for example, everyone earns their adulthood at the age of twenty, but our females don't have their first heat until they're around forty."

"Are you saying, I don't have any rights to my son when he's born?" another male called, out of turn this time.

"Not unless the person you mated with gave you those parental rights. That's what we call a partnership. Now, please, wait your turn," Jer replied. The male who had spoken glared at him but sat down, hitting the button on his desk hard. Jer called the next person on the list.

"I get that you don't have birth certificates for us, and that we've messed things up in the past, but the males of my species become fertile around the age of twelve on Earth, give or take. That's around four years here. Could we shorten the age of adulthood with the assumption that we are at least that old?"

Jer raised a brow. That seemed more than reasonable to him, so he opened it up for discussion. "Does anyone have anything to say for or against that suggestion?" he asked.

"Just because they're fertile doesn't mean they're responsible or can be trusted," one woman stated. "I vote we keep it as it is."

Several others spoke both for and against the suggestion, but to Jer's surprise when he put it to a vote, they voted it down. He'd thought it was a valid compromise, still he went with the majority's decision, and moved on to the next question.

With each vote, the order in which people requested to speak reset. When he called the next person it was the male who had interrupted earlier. "Aaron Delaney you have the floor."

"I watched the trial your daughter mentioned this morning. Let me see if I get this straight. Your people locked us up for two of our years without contact with another person, and then stuck us naked in a room with a member of the opposite sex in the hopes that we would mate to repopulate our species. It seems to me you thought we were mature adults at that point. I had what I thought was consensual sex with the woman I was paired up with, but if she was an adult and I wasn't, then that means I was raped, at least according our old laws, where sex with a child was considered rape, even if it was consensual. So which was it? Was I an adult or a child, and do I need to bring charges against the mother of my child?"

Jer blinked in surprise, not even remotely expecting the question, and frantically tried to figure out how to respond as the male had a valid point, but as he considered his answer, the room erupted in anger from both sides. GrandFather was unable to keep up with the translation. Jer tried calling for order but no one listened, so he roared and flashed the lights, and finally managed to get people to calm down.

"As we have not had the opportunity to teach you our laws yet, let me clarify the definition of rape, so there is no misunderstanding. We consider rape to be forcing another with the intent to impregnate them, regardless of whether it was successful or not. Rape is entirely based on the physical maturity of both people involved, not their current legal status. If it's not possible for the victim to become pregnant, such as in your case, we consider that sexual assault. The consequences are nearly as severe, but follow the same laws we have for any other form of assault, which can go as high as a death sentence depending on the severity of the assault and victims choice of punishment. Our laws around mating are entirely based on consent. Should either party feel they were forced into that act, it would be considered a crime, as would taking advantage of someone in an impaired status, as they would not be able to give consent."

"So you have no laws preventing an adult from having sex with a child?" someone called out.

"Each species has a set age of consent," he replied. "At this age, the child is legally old enough to answer questions about their own person, such as who they want for parents or guardians, give legally binding statements, or in this case give their consent. For your species this was set at the age of two, which we are informed was the earliest known age at which your species could become fertile." There was a great deal of anger at this, and dozens of lights hit up to speak.

Myra, who was in the chamber as well, requested to speak first. "Healer Chenzira, you have the floor."

"It should also be known that any signs of abuse, sexual or otherwise are flagged by healers if the person is not legally an adult. These flags would be investigated by the guard to ensure that no form of abuse or rape actually occurred. We understand that children may not have the knowledge to recognize physical or sexual abuse, or even know what do if it should happen, and protect against that. We also now have samples of your species sperm which our scanners are now programmed to pick up. If found, the child's medical record would automatically be flagged for investigation." When Myra finished, she sat down. Several lights turned off at her statement.

"If the age of consent is based on when I could potentially become physically mature, that should indicate that I'm at least two years old.

Yet I'm not even legally a year old based on what we were told earlier. Does that mean I was not legally able to give consent, and was sexually assaulted?" Aaron asked. "I ask again, should I bring the mother of my genetic offspring forward for trial?"

Jer frowned at the conundrum. "Do you believe you were sexually assaulted?" he asked instead.

"I can't say," Aaron replied, "until you first determine my legal age."

Jer actually snorted at the trap he'd fallen into, and nodded the point. *These Hue-mans are quick thinking.* "That is a valid point, and you are correct. Healer Chenzira, can you provide me with a list of the males who were physically mature at the date of the cataclysm or have become mature since?"

"Yes, sir," she replied, and a moment later, Jer's account dinged with that information. He confirmed that Aaron's name was on the list.

"By my authority as Senior Council, I am adjusting the birth date of every male on this list to be two years prior to the Cataclysm or the date at which they were determined to be physically mature. That decision is final. Aaron, as you are now legally at the age of consent, I ask you again, do you believe you were sexually assaulted?"

"I don't know," Aaron replied and Jer raised a brow in surprise, but Aaron continued before he could ask for clarification. "I willingly had sex. However that was under false pretenses, and under our old laws, that would have been considered rape. I not only wanted her companionship, but I wanted a family, and I expected that I would have legal rights to my son. That has been taken from me," he replied.

"You could still partner with the mother of that child," Jer replied.

"Not if she doesn't want me to. By my species laws I would have had at least visitation rights once it was genetically proven that I was the father and willing to support the child, and at this point, I can't even ensure that my child is protected, because I'm not listed as an adult, something that has also been taken from me. I get that we now live under your laws, but if she believed I was an adult at the time we had sex, then that means I should be an adult now, and if she didn't, then I believe that I was sexually assaulted and taken advantage of."

Jer stared at GrandFather as he watched the translation come in, and considered Aaron's points. "Who did you partner with?" Jer finally asked.

"Rachael Hoffsteader," the male replied.

"Councilor Hoffsteader, please rise." Rachael looked both scared and angry, and he didn't blame her. He had no doubt that the male had been an adult before, and he didn't want to see Rachael killed because of an oversight and technicality on their part. "Councilor. Did you consider Aaron to be an adult when you mated with him, or have any indication that he was a child at that time?"

Rachael didn't answer.

"You need to answer the question, Councilor Hoffsteader," he insisted after several minutes had passed.

"I plead the fifth," she replied.

"I don't know what that means," Jer said.

"It means that if I answer I would get myself in trouble either way," she replied.

"We do not have a law like that. If asked a question by the Council, you're required to answer. Are you saying you believe he was a child when you mated with him?" he asked.

"I am not," she frowned. "Based on what you told us earlier, if I say he was a child, then I'll be executed for rape, but if I say he's an adult then I'm worried you'll make me partner with him, or claim guardianship for him. I don't know him well enough to do that, and I don't want that responsibility or risk. Not until I know him better anyway. I'm also worried that he'll just turn around and offer guardianship to everyone else, and take control of the Council by systematically voting us all out, and voting the men back into power. The men far outnumber the women, and we've been denied our rights and freedoms for centuries. I'd rather be executed than allow that to happen again. So no matter what I decide, I'm risking my death or at the very least, my freedom."

Jer considered for several minutes before replying as he'd not expected her response at all. "Those are all valid concerns. There is nothing in our laws that would force anyone into a partnership, or force them to take guardianship for another. As far as sponsoring someone for guardianship, that oath must be given by another councilor or advocate, and if there is reason why someone shouldn't be granted adulthood, it can be argued at that time. The same goes with your oath as a Councilor. The final decision resides entirely with me as your Senior Councilor. While I'm not aware of an instance where the people's vote has not been honored, if there was just cause, I could decide not to swear someone in, or stop a revote if I even suspected the systematic type of coup you're suggesting. That decision would automatically go before the entire Full Council for review. You should also be aware that anyone found guilty of attempting or participating in a coup would be put to death. Also, unlike what happened to you on Earth, your rights and freedoms are protected. In order to change a locally protected right, it would require a unanimous vote by this Council, and be ratified by the Senior Council to ensure it does not conflict with the protected rights of the Consortium. For anything that is a protected right of the Consortium, it would require a unanimous vote by the Full Council or Senior Council to remove. So I ask you again. Did you consider Aaron an adult when you mated with him?"

She didn't answer right away, but he could tell she was trying to decide, and gave her time to consider.

"If I say yes, what will happen," she finally asked.

"I would consider your testimony as Councilor proof that he was an adult at that time, which means there is no need for guardianship, and as we have not yet filled the available seats on the council, which will go to the first four hundred legal adults, he would be sworn in as a councilor, unless someone brings forth proof that he has committed a crime since his arrival on our world, or he turns down that position," Jer answered. "Did you consider Aaron an adult when you mated with him?" he asked again.

"I did," she replied after several additional minutes of consideration.

"Then I consider your testimony as Councilor adequate proof that he was an adult at that time. Aaron, please come forward. For anyone else in the same situation, please come forward with the person you mated with, to vouch for their status as an adult prior to joining the Consortium."

Several people came forward and he went down the line, asking each under oath to confirm that they were not raped or sexually assaulted, and that they considered the other person to be an adult at the time. Once they were marked as legal adults, he asked if anyone had any reason to deny their membership onto the Council. When no one did, he swore the males in as councilors, and had them all sit back down, while he finished updating their accounts.

When he looked up from finishing that work, several people had indicated their desire to speak. "Damon Minor, you have the floor."

"First off, I would like to thank you for making the adjustment you just did, however, I for one respected the wishes of the person I was paired with at the Agency, and it's clear from the trial that we were being...encouraged to mate in order to save our species. It seems to me if those who chose to mate were considered adults, then those who chose not to breed in captivity and respected the wishes of their partners should also be considered adults, especially considering the fact that none of us knew if refusing to do so would be a death sentence."

It was all Jer could do to keep from letting his emotions out through his mask as he considered *that* statement, and the angry response from the rest of the Council. It was clear to him that none of the females wanted the males to have adulthood, and after learning what had happened to them prior, he didn't blame them. He was just as concerned as they were. They needed to learn a new way if they were to become welcome members of his society. "Councilors, please come forward with the person you were paired with if you believe that they were an adult at the time you were brought together," he finally ordered.

None of the women stood. He gave them several minutes to decide before calling it.

"I'm sorry, Damon. I believe the Council has spoken. I am aware of what your society was like before, and based on the testimony of Little Flower Chenzira before the Full Council, I agree with their decision. The society and laws you had before are not compatible with our society.

As a species, you pose a significant risk due to your violent nature and past history, a history that was dominated by the males of your species, and proven to be true by the violence that was done towards my daughter. Your inclusion into the Consortium was not unanimous because of it. You need to prove yourself to be trustworthy and honorable, not just to the females of your species but to the entire Consortium. That being said, that you did *not* force yourself on the person you were paired with has significant weight with me, and goes a long way towards proving your honor. I am sure if you continue to act with honor and work hard in your studies, that you will be sponsored for adulthood."

Damon frowned but sat down and the other lights turned off. When there weren't further questions, he sighed with relief, although he kept his expression neutral, and moved on with the planned agenda. "Now that you've had a chance to look around, we need to know what your goals are for the future. We've expanded my partner's family home to welcome all of you, and she has transferred her deed, which encompasses two hundred and fifty leagues of the nearby wildlife habitat, to Saber's Council. Senior Councilor Marcus Surellis of Saber and I are already working through the proposal for having that land transferred to your people. But it's very clear to us that this part of our world is not all that suited for your species. Those areas of this world are already fairly heavily populated, and while you are welcome to move there individually, there is little land available that could be given to you as a whole, as there is here. It would also make repopulating your species more difficult if you're spread out across the planet. There are other places on the other planets, such as the island chains on the Water World that might be better suited for your species, at least in the short term. Alternatively we could ask the Ship's Guild to find a suitable planet for you to repopulate. Before we do any further development, we should decide if you actually want to remain here."

Dozens of people indicated they wanted to speak.

"Jordan Ross," you have the floor.

"What does the weather the rest of the year look like around here?" she asked.

"What you are experiencing now is what we call high summer. This occurs for about half of our year. For the other half, we get fairly substantial monsoon rains, and it is significantly cooler in what we call spring. That should start in another month or so. The heaviest rains last for about three months. Drinking water for the compound comes from a large underground aquifer, so you need not worry about that."

"Well, it's ridiculously hot here, but inside it's kept comfortable, and I must say the apartment is far nicer than anything I've ever had. I was homeless before the asteroid hit, so I'm good with staying here for now," she replied, and sat down.

"Why would your partner give up so much land?" the next person asked, after asking to see what land was included in the transfer.

Jer pursed his lips and gave what could almost be considered a sigh, but once again managed to keep his expression calm. "My partner, who was once the Senior Healer for the Agency, took responsibility for the crime that happened under her care, and was found complicit in my daughter's rape by putting the two of them together, and for stopping the hormone blockers that allowed her to be impregnated. In punishment for that crime, she was sentenced to care for all of you in her home for as long as you would like to remain here. By giving up her deed, the Senior Council considered that adequate compensation to fulfill those requirements."

"And what about the crime of locking us up in isolation for two years?" someone yelled out, out of turn, followed by the angry grumbles of everyone in the room.

Jer nodded in acknowledgement of that statement, once the translation came in, fully expecting it to come up at some point. "Senior Councilor Jennette Tabor publicly took responsibility for that crime, and as punishment locked herself in my daughter's old cell, for the same length of time my daughter had been held. Additionally, the compensation earmarked for your people was quadrupled by the Senior Council, to make up for the lack of care we gave in providing you with adequate entertainment during your isolation. I know I can't change the past, or the horror and trauma you went through under our care, but we hope to make up for it in the future."

Thankfully, that caused everyone to settle down. After some rather lively banter and further questions, the Council voted to stay.

"Excellent. Next on the docket is deciding what you want to call your new home. My family just called it the compound, but that's not a particularly good name for a village, or the town I expect we will quickly grow to become. Does anyone have any suggestions?" Multiple names were called out, but ultimately no decisions were made. So that was tabled for discussion later in order to give people time to decide, and to see if anything naturally occurred.

"Next. When we reach town size, it will be expected that we have a guard hall, although as the location of our Council we qualify for one now. The primary purpose of the guard is to protect the citizens from natural predators, search and rescue, assist the fire brigade, and ceremonial purposes, such as guarding the council chamber while in session, and in the case of funerals, provide an honor guard for anyone who has shown great honor in their lives. For now, we are being covered by the guard still stationed at the Agency. Most of which came from the ships that rescued you. You should know that they lost several members of their own in that attempt. Going forward, do you want to provision your own guard, or continue to use Saber's when needed?"

Nearly everyone hit their light to speak, and most were yelling. He noticed his daughter was leaning back in her seat with her arms crossed and an 'I told you so' expression plastered firmly on her face, which almost caused him to drop his mask and snort with laughter, but Jer kept his face calm, recognizing that amusement when his people were so angry would not be appreciated. He eventually managed to bring things back to order and called the first person.

"If there's no war or crime on this planet how come you have guards?" they asked.

He tilted his head in acknowledgement of the point. "From what I understand of your history, the types of crime you experienced, such as premeditated murder, theft, and rape are exceptionally rare, but we are an emotional people and sometimes people do get hurt or property gets damaged, and the Guard can be called in to control a situation. Most of the time though our guards are here to protect and serve in whatever capacity is needed. As already mentioned, the primary purpose is to help when there are fires or other natural disasters, protect from predators, or assist with search and rescue."

"Well, I for one, don't trust any guard," the next person said. "I don't know what yours are like, but our guard had issues." That person had dark skin like GrandFather, so that comment didn't surprise him at all.

"I understand your concern, and have had lengthy conversations with my daughter and her grandfather, about the issues you've had with your guard. I promise, our guard is not that way."

"I doubt that!" someone yelled out.

Jer turned to face Kendra. "Senior Honor Guard Kendra Hunt, would you care to speak on behalf of your guards?"

"Yes, sir," Kendra replied, and came forward slightly. "You do not need to worry about the Honor Guard. Every member of my guard takes an oath to protect the rights of the people above self, family, and council. As part of that oath is the understanding that if they are caught committing any crime, no matter how small or large, they will be executed for that crime. We take our responsibility seriously. Every member of the guard is trained in the charters for all of the species, as well if not better than the Council, and every member of the guard is given medical training equivalent to the journeyman rank in the Healer's Guild. My guards are taught how to de-escalate situations, and only use force when absolutely necessary to protect another."

"We've been locked up for two years. The last thing I want to see is another guard, ours or yours, no matter how honorable they might be," another person called out, and many people agreed with her.

"I fully understand your concerns. Mistakes were made in ensuring that your rights were protected. I was not aware of the conditions of your habitats until harm had already been done as the guards at the Agency were kept out of the habitats to protect both them and you from illness, and I have made sure that that oversight will not happen again. I hope that with time we will earn your trust back," Kendra said, nodded to him, and returned to her post.

Jer tilted his head in acknowledgement and called the next person.

"What kind of predators do we need to watch out for?" they asked.

"One of the required classes is on identifying dangerous plants and creatures. Inside the compound you should be fine," he replied. "Shields are being built and will be delivered by the end of the week. They will protect from all of the bigger predators. There are still crawlies that you'll need to watch out for. Many of which are venomous. If you are bitten or stung, go to the clinic as soon as possible for treatment, as we have no idea how they might affect you, and if you don't know what it is, avoid it."

"Well, once the shields are up, I don't see a need for the guard stationed here, and if there is we can call someone in," another person stated.

After significant additional heated discussion, votes were taken, and as expected from the murmurs and comments he was able to both see and hear, they voted to use Saber's guard, but not have them stationed at the compound until they reached town size, when it was expected. At that point, it was late, so he called an end to the session, even though there were still dozens of items on the docket.

"All rise as the Senior Council leaves the chamber," Kendra called out.

Jer stood and made his way out. Once the door was shut he collapsed into his seat and pinched his nose where a headache was already throbbing. The session had been far harder than he'd expected. He was still sitting there several minutes later when Marcus called him. He almost didn't answer it, even though they'd planned to speak after the meeting. When he did, he just growled at his brother.

"I'm sorry Jer, I should have caught that little oversight when we set everyone's date of birth."

Jer snorted. It was rare that Marcus admitted he was wrong, about anything. "Well, to be fair, I didn't catch it either, and neither did Little Flower or GrandFather."

"True. Still you handled it well. That was quick thinking," Marcus replied. "I'm not sure I would have come up with solutions that quickly, or as elegantly."

"Thanks," Jer replied. It was rare Marcus complimented him either. "Do you think we can review tomorrow though? I know we planned to talk tonight, but I have a headache, and I really don't think I could listen to Layton right now."

Marcus chuckled. "Oh, he's in full form tonight, but it's nothing I'm sure you're not already expecting to hear. You still have a job, and you managed to avoid needing to execute several of your people tonight, so I think you've earned yourself the night off. You did pretty good for your first council meeting, cub. I've seen far worse. You'd be surprised how many people freeze running their first meeting, and they rarely have to deal with situations as severe and unexpected to begin with. If I remember correctly, Apakna accidentally kicked everyone out of her first Full Council meeting."

"Thanks, Marcus," Jer replied with a snort as he'd been there for that meeting. "Go have fun in the Archives. I'm going to go find a pillow to hide under."

"You know me far too well," Marcus said with a laugh, and hung up.

# CHAPTER 10

# Little Flower: Lessons

Little Flower and Marsee were relaxing in the cool safety of their room during the worst of the afternoon heat a few days after her people arrived. The overhaul to the tower was finally complete, although several boxes of books still remained to be unpacked. A small room, using the same stone repurposed from the rest of the compound, had been added to each floor, which now contained the latest and greatest in indoor plumbing. A second wall of bookcases had been removed and replaced with storage facilities for her clothing, and a desk and workbench better suited for her size. Most of the books and artwork that had been displayed there, had been relocated to brand-new stand-alone bookshelves with glass doors and display lighting to protect them from future storms, which had all shown up unexpectedly one day. Supplies for her child were available for them to pick up at the Guild when Marsee finished unpacking, including a new crib and playpen.

The first floor had been retrofitted for their parent's use, and the second floor reserved as a private family room or space for family and friends to stay when they visited. A brand new and massive couch had been placed under one of the windows, which could be folded out into one of the softest beds she'd ever laid on. Those items that were of sentimental value were kept and transferred to their new rooms, while everything else had been moved to its appropriate place in the rest of the compound, for use by all of the inhabitants.

GrandFather requested that he be moved in with the others from his group at the Agency, so his belongings had been moved to the room of his choice, although they'd offered to give him the middle floor in the tower.

The shower room and hole of muck on either side of the tower had been carefully removed, and were now beautiful arched exits out of the compound that matched the style and carvings of the other doors, which had all been cleaned, refurbished, and upgraded to make them easier for her people to use.

The land in front of the tower, that faced the wilds, was planned for pasture, and was being dug out to support irrigation, and carefully planted with native grains and grasses that were safe for the various creatures to graze on.

Ellie had returned with their sketchbooks, drawings, and the new tablet, and informed them that both of their prints were already flying off shelves. Little Flower had been surprised at how much demand there was, even though she'd guessed it had been more than Ellie had indicated, but it was nothing compared to how Marsee reacted.

Several of Marsee's drawings were doing better than hers. Marsee had been so surprised that anyone had purchased her artwork that she had just stared at the purchase record for over an hour, completely unable to form words or even move. It was almost bad enough that their father had started to worry she was having trouble with her instinct again. That had finally caused her to blink her way out of her shock, but Little Flower had caught her checking her balance several times over the past few days, and bouncing a little every time another purchase was made. She understood completely and was honestly doing the same. She was surprised at how much attention her own drawings were getting, but it was good to see Marsee so excited.

Ellie had also surprised her with a brand new rocking chair that she had personally crafted. It was one of the most beautiful chairs Little Flower had ever seen, and it fit her perfectly. She'd brought ones for the two other nursing mothers as well, and promised more for the others before they were due to give birth. How Ellie had completed that with everything else she'd been managing, Little Flower had no idea, but her fairy godmother had delivered once again.

That morning, she had raided the guild hall for the biggest canvas she could find, which Marsee had helped her to carry back to their room and set up. She'd never had the opportunity to work on a canvas that big before, and was a little intimidated, but she intended for this painting to be her 'thank you' gift to Ellie and the Guild for all of their support.

While she worked on it, Marsee swung on her bed and played with the new drawing tablet. After a couple of hours, Little Flower put her brushes down, stretched, and stood up, looking at Marsee. "I think I'm going to go take a swim. Do you want to join me?" she asked. To her utter astonishment, Marsee said she did.

"You do? Really?" Little Flower asked in amazement.

"I want to learn how to swim. Will you teach me?" Marsee asked.

"I would love to!" Little Flower replied. As she expected, the place was packed, but there was plenty of space for everyone. Unlike their pools back home, rectangular and sterile, significant effort had been made to make this place into a welcoming resort. The pool was enormous and irregularly shaped, more like a medium sized pond than a pool. There was even a small tree-covered island in the middle, and a sandy beach and fountains for the children. Flowering plants and small trees had been brought in to decorate the rest of the place, and furniture to fit both species were scattered about.

The main pool was kept at a comfortable temperature and was deep enough for even the biggest of the cats to safely dive into on one end, while several smaller hot tubs had been added for those wishing to soak their aches away. Newly invented pool toys and floats had also been provided for everyone to share.

As with the other buildings, the groundwork to connect the pool to the tunnels the Water Sprites would use had been added, although they were not yet hooked up. Attached changing rooms, with actual freshwater showers and bathrooms were connected, as well as a small communal kitchen fully stocked with various drinks and fruits, and the dishes and implements needed to prepare and serve them. The entire pool was covered in a protective glass dome that filtered out the harsh glare of the suns, which she had been assured was strong enough to withstand the worst of the summer sandstorms, so that people could look out at the world around them while they relaxed. The room was kept at a warm, but comfortable temperature for both swimming and lounging, for most of the species, although it would be far too warm and humid for the Ice Giants, who preferred temperatures below freezing.

The moment she arrived, she ran and cannonballed into the water in the deep end of the pool, and then swam towards the shallows where Marsee was waiting for her, tail fully poofed out with fear.

"You do know you need to enter the pool if you want to learn how to swim," Little Flower teased after several minutes had passed and Marsee still hadn't entered.

Marsee just growled at her and forced herself to put a paw in the water, but her ears flattened with disgust. It took the better part of an hour before Marsee gained enough courage to enter the pool deep enough to actually swim, but she eventually made her way out to where Little Flower was waiting for her.

"This is far enough for now. Have a seat and get used to the feel of the water. I'm standing and it's not over my head, so you should be able to sit without issue," Little Flower signed.

Holding on to the side of the pool, her tail still poofed and held up as high as she could get it out of the water, Marsee slowly sat down until she was sitting with the water up to her chest, although the furry white tip of her tail was still sticking out. "Okay...I guess this isn't too bad, but my fur feels really weird with the motion of the water," Marsee told her.

"You'll get used to it. Just try to relax and enjoy it," Little Flower signed, and then let herself float on the water for a few minutes before checking on her sister. When she looked up, Marsee squinted at her with a mischievous expression and splashed her square in the face. Spluttering, she returned fire and madness ensued for several minutes until she called for a truce. When they were done, Marsee was thoroughly soaked and looked like a drowned rat. *More like a drowned horse,* Little Flower thought with a snicker. "Are you ready to try swimming?" she asked her sister.

"I guess so," Marsee replied hesitantly.

"Okay, stand on all fours and walk forward. As you get deeper, the water should start to support you. If you get scared just put your back feet down and stand up."

Marsee walked forward until she was standing on her tippy toes, tail sticking straight out, and ears flattened down and pinned to the side of her head. She snorted as water went up her nose, shook her head, and stood up to rub at her face.

Little Flower snickered. "You're not supposed to breathe the water, Chenzie Butt."

Marsee growled and splashed her, but after another snort and shake of her head, tried again.

"Good, now try picking your feet up one at a time and let the water support your weight." Marsee did as instructed and suddenly she was bobbing in the water.

After a few moments she stood up and bounced excitedly. "I did it!"

"You did! And you didn't breathe in any water that time either! That was the worst bit. Let's try it again, a little longer this time." Once Marsee had splashed her again and returned to floating, Little Flower continued. "Good. Now try moving your paws like you're walking. I cup my paws, but yours are webbed, so try spreading your fingers out so you have more resistance as you push against the water."

Marsee did and she started slowly paddling forward.

"Yes! That's it!" Little Flower encouraged. When Marsee finished making her slow way across the shallow end of the pool and stood up, Little Flower noticed a boy, maybe ten years old, watching them. "Hello!" she signed.

"Hello, Little Flower, Marsee" he signed shyly back. "I was wondering... Well, we were wondering..." he said hesitantly, turning to look at a small group of boys. "We were wondering if you would teach us to swim too."

"What's your name?" she asked him.

"Ben," he replied, slowly spelling out the word, and she gasped.

He frowned and looked at her in confusion.

"Ben was the name of my other grandfather who died in the Cataclysm," she explained.

He nodded his understanding, looking sad as he remembered his own family.

She smiled softly at him. "I would be very happy to teach you how to swim, all of you!"

He brightened immediately and waved the others over. The rest of his small gang came running over with a splash. She spent the next hour working with them and the two healers that were watching them, who asked if they could join in as well. After that, she had to leave to prepare for that evening's council meeting as they were having one every night until all of the immediate issues could be resolved. Along the way, she stopped and added swimming lessons to the class roster.

<div style="text-align:center">~~~~~</div>

That evening, she was in an animated conversation with Marsee as they made their way into the council chamber, and quite literally ran into someone. "Oh, sorry!" she signed, and gasped as she recognized the person she'd just run into.

"I take it you remember me," he signed.

She blinked out of her memories and nodded. "I do," she replied, trying hard not to let her panic rise, and keep the fear she was feeling off her face. *It's not his fault. He didn't do it,* she reminded herself.

He frowned at her expression anyway. "I'm sorry I couldn't do anything to protect you. I thought for sure they'd killed you when you weren't anywhere to be found later, but I did look. They wouldn't tell us what happened to you."

Marsee looked at them both with confusion. "What's going on?" she asked.

She sighed and finally managed to pull her emotions and memories back under a semblance of control. "This is the man they tried pairing me up with afterwards," Little Flower told her sister.

Marsee gasped. "The one who kicked Healer Morningstar?"

Little Flower grinned. "The one in the same." She turned back to the man. "There was nothing any of us could do, but I appreciate the effort and risk you took, and your refusal to hurt me further. It got me out of there, and watching you kick Brice was the one good thing that happened that day. I'll be honest, it got me through a lot of bad moments. What's your name?"

"Ezra Borovik," he replied.

"It's nice to meet you Ezra," she said, and held out her hand to shake. "I look forward to getting to know you, hopefully under better circumstances than before."

"I'd like that," he said with a nod.

"All rise as the Senior Council enters the chamber!" a guard called out.

She nodded to Ezra, and made her way to her seat as Marsee quickly made her way forward to translate.

She barely paid attention to the start of the meeting as her thoughts were dragged back to that horrible day. It didn't help that the planned agenda was almost immediately derailed to deal with the men's continued frustration with having to earn their adulthood. Finally she'd had enough and slammed the button to speak.

"Councilor Chenzira, you wish to speak?"

"I have had it up to here with all of you," she growled at the men in the visitors section. "You're acting like spoiled children throwing a temper tantrum, and proving me right in the process. You aren't adult enough to take on the responsibility of leading what's left of our people if you can't understand why you've been put on probation in the first place, and if you think I'm going to allow you to ruin the one chance we have, you're sadly mistaken."

"You had no right to strip us of our rights!" someone called out.

"I had every right!" she yelled back. "I had to go before the Full Council to prove our species was even sentient. We have one and only one chance to prove ourselves to the rest of the Consortium, because that idiot decided to act like men have acted for our entire history. "

"So you say!" someone else yelled out. "I watched the trial. They didn't show any evidence of you being raped. I bet you led him on and faked the beating just so you could gain sympathy and take control."

The chamber broke into pandemonium that was so loud even she could hear it. She growled and curled her fists, doing everything she could to keep from marching back and beating the man to a pulp.

"That's enough!" her father yelled out, and started flicking the lights, before she could control her anger enough to speak. "Quiet!" When the room settled to angry glares, he continued. "Paul Markson, those kinds of accusations are considered libel, and a crime without proof. In the case of rape, it's the female's word that matters, because we expect there would be little proof. If she believes she was raped, then she was raped. That being said, there was more than enough evidence to prove she was raped. The footage of the actual rape was not shown to the public to protect her from the emotional trauma of having to witness it again. Little Flower Chenzira, do you wish to bring forth charges against Paul for his libel against you?"

"Charges, for what?!" the male yelled before she could answer. "For demanding evidence of why our rights have been stripped away? None of the rest of us here have committed a crime, yet we're the ones paying for his *supposed* actions."

Little Flower turned to her father. "Play the video."

He looked at her hard. "Are you sure? It will become public record if I do."

"Play it!" she growled.

He sighed and brought up the recording. She was shaking from embarrassment at being naked in front of everyone, and rage from her remembered trauma by the time the initial rape was done. When Mitch switched to beating her, she motioned for her father to stop the recording, and it froze with an image of Mitch's face full of glee, fist raised to strike.

She closed her eyes, took a deep breath, stood, turned to face the man who had accused her of lying, and with a glare pointed hard at the monitor. "Is *that* enough proof for you? Or do you need to continue watching as he beat me for almost an hour to hide that he'd raped me? Can you understand now why the Senior Council deliberated for days? Why the decision wasn't unanimous? Why they didn't believe we were people, and why I was forced to wear a harness and leash like a wild animal? *That's* the legacy you have to overcome, and *that's* why not a single woman here will let you have adulthood until you prove yourself to be trustworthy, because I can guarantee just about every single woman in this chamber has experience some form of sexual harassment, assault, or rape in their lives."

"My step dad when I was ten," one of the women called out and stood up.

"My boss," another called out and stood.

"My first boyfriend," called out a third.

Moments later every single woman and even several of the men stood. With that, she turned and stormed out of the council chamber. She made it as far as the public waste room just outside before throwing up. Her mother appeared a minute later.

"Are you all right?" her mother asked, as she pulled out her scanner.

"Not really," Little Flower groaned from the floor of the waste room, and then blanched before throwing up again.

Her mother waited until she stopped. "Come on, I'll get you something to calm your stomach," she said, and carefully picked her up and carried her down to the clinic, purring the entire way. She leaned against her mother's side, trying hard not to throw up on her. Her mother placed her on an examination bed and left, returning a moment later with the drink she was used to. "You're exhausted and dehydrated as well," her mother said. "Drink all of it." Like always it quickly calmed her stomach, but it did nothing for her nerves. Once she was done with the drink, her mother scooped her back up, carried her over to a chair, and held her until she finally stopped shaking.

They were still sitting there when her father arrived, looking worried. "Are you okay?" he asked.

"No, but I'll manage," she replied, and motioned for her mother to set her down, so she could talk easier. Her mother placed her back on the bed.

He frowned. "I'm sorry you had to go through that, or that it had to become public to prove your innocence. As you are an adult now, I can't hide it like I could before, but I did order the press to blur out the images in the recording, like we did for the trial."

She shrugged, unsure how to respond, and finally sighed. "It's not like the entire Consortium didn't already know, and maybe this will get them to stop complaining for a while. I'm honestly more embarrassed knowing that everyone has now seen me naked."

He sighed and seemed unsure about what to say. "You didn't answer my question before you left the council chamber," he eventually said. "Do you want to bring charges forward for his libel against you?"

She shook her head. "No, we haven't covered that yet, so he would have no way to know it wasn't legal, but I do want him on the watch list for that comment. That was a common excuse men used to deny they'd raped someone."

Her father nodded and then frowned as Myra's attention shifted to the monitor.

"Is there a problem?" her father asked.

"No. She was dehydrated before, but Little Flower and her daughter are doing just fine," Myra replied.

"Daughter?" Little Flower asked. "She's a girl?"

Her mother looked down at her and nodded.

Little Flower sagged with relief. "Thank god! I was praying she would be."

"You wanted a daughter?" Myra asked.

"Yes. I was worried that a son would remind me too much of him," Little Flower replied.

"No matter what she looks like, your daughter will be nothing like him, not with a mother as wonderful as you," Myra replied, and gently caressed the side of her face. "Although I expect she'll grow up to be just as stubborn as you."

"No doubt. It tends to run in my family. Besides, someone needs to keep the Council in line, and I can't do it all myself," she replied.

Her father's tail curled, and his eyes twinkled with amusement, although he kept his face fairly neutral behind his mask. "Well I don't know about your birth family, but you're just like your adopted mother," he said, breaking into a wicked grin. "And I wouldn't have you any other way."

Her mother snorted and rolled her eyes at him. "Come on, let's get you back to your room so you can get some sleep."

"I can walk, Mama," Little Flower said with an annoyed huff when her mother reached over and picked her up.

"I know," her mother replied, but still didn't put her down.

Deciding it wasn't worth the effort to fight over it, she leaned up against her mother again, who started purring in response. She must have been more tired than she thought, because she was asleep before they made it back to her room.

Sometime in the middle of the night, she woke up screaming from a nightmare. Marsee flicked on the lights and said nothing, just held her until she'd cried herself out, and eventually fell back to sleep.

~~~~~

The next day, she was feeling much better, and while she took the morning off to recover, Marsee joined her for the swimming lessons again that afternoon. To Little Flower's shock the group waiting for the lesson was entirely Saber, including her mother, father, Ammond, and Ellie.

"I take it that swimming is not common for your species?" Little Flower asked her mother.

"It's certainly not a common skill one learns in the middle of the desert," her mother teased, with curled tail.
~~~~~

"Ellie and I know how to swim as we've both been to the Water World, but we figured you might need some help," her father added.

"That's fair," Little Flower replied. "And this was more than I expected to show up, but we'll make it work. Everyone in the pool."

To her amusement the adults were just as hesitant about entering the water as Marsee had been, if not more so. It took most of the lesson just to get everyone in and sitting down. Marsee however had gotten over her fear the day before, and purposely splashed her on the way in. While the others slowly worked their way in and got used to the feel of the water, she used Marsee to demonstrate what they would be learning to do first. By the end of the scheduled time, they had most everyone paddling around, if slowly, or at the very least walking in water up to their chest. It was a start.

Most everyone left afterwards, but her mother and Ammond stuck around, while her father stopped to talk with people around the pool, rather than returning to his office. She grabbed one of the spare floats and swam it over to where her mother and Ammond were sitting and talking, as it was well above her head, and it made it easier for her to sign back.

"So what did you think?" she asked.

"That was surprisingly fun," her mother replied. "I didn't realize just how buoyant the water was."

"I'm not sure I ever want to leave," Ammond replied. "This is far too relaxing, and I don't think I've been able to move around as easily in decades."

"You should try the hot tub," Little Flower suggested. "It's even better. The heat is wonderful for relaxing sore muscles, and the jets are great for working out knots in them. I'd use it myself, but I'm not sure if it's good for the baby. We had warnings on ours back home."

"Better than this?" Ammond asked. "I don't think that's possible."

She nodded. "Much better, if you like the heat anyway. Come on. I suppose I can probably put my feet in for a few minutes without issue."

Ammond didn't need any further encouragement, and immediately started paddling his way back to shore. Laughing, she followed, while her mother chose to remain in the pool. Ammond groaned as he walked out.

"The only downside to swimming is that gravity is twice as strong when you get out," she signed. He chuckled but didn't answer as he was walking on all fours. They made their way over to one of the empty hot tubs, and she carefully stuck her toe in. "Oh, this is perfect! Let me see if I can figure out how to turn the jets on for you," she told him, and made her way over to a nearby pole. Sure enough there was a timer in both Hue-man and Saber. She turned it on and made her way over, sitting on the outside with just her feet in, up against one of the jets.

Ammond was sitting on the outside of the hot tub with just the tip of his tail in. "This is much hotter than I expected," Ammond replied.

She chuckled. "That's why it's called a hot tub," she teased.

"Impudent cub," Ammond teased back. He eventually made his way in and groaned as he shifted to take advantage of a jet. "Oh, I see what you mean," he said, and closed his eyes to lean back in evident relief. When he opened them again he grinned at her. "I think this may be worth every hour I've spent trying to fix your people's hearing," he signed, as his ear drooped with relaxation.

She grinned. "I'm glad I could be of service, but it does have medical uses as well. We used water for physical therapy. It's low impact but provides resistance. I expect you may be sore tomorrow. You should talk to GrandFather about it," she replied.

Ammond raised a brow. "I certainly will," he signed, shifted, and closed his eyes again with a groan.

She only stayed for a few minutes, not wanting to risk overheating, and left Ammond and several others who came over to try it out, when they saw him enjoying it so much. She turned and saw her mother still leaning up against the side of the pool. So, with a wicked grin, she cannonballed off the edge with a large splash.

Her mother glared at her when she resurfaced. "Was that necessary?" her mother asked, wiping water off of her face.

"Yes," she replied with a wicked grin. "That's half the fun of playing in the water, and I won't be able to do that for much longer anyway.

Before long, I'll be moving slower than Ammond. Although I might just move here as my pregnancy progresses. My back is already starting to bother me at times, and this feels wonderful."

Her mother frowned. "Why haven't you said anything?"

She shrugged. "It's not that bad yet."

"You shouldn't be hurting at all," her mother replied.

She just snorted. "I'm going to be hurting a lot worse before this is over. If everything I've ever heard about pregnancy is true."

"Not if I have anything to say about it. Come on, let's get you checked out."

"I'm fine, *Mother*, and it can wait. I'm not ready to leave the pool." With that she flipped over on her back to float and closed her eyes. Some time later she felt the water shift and looked up again to see her mother standing up and looking in the direction of the hot tub with a frown. "What is it?" she asked.

"I think Ammond has melted. I'd better go check on him. Come by the clinic when you're done."

Little Flower followed her mother out instead, as she was starting to get hungry anyway.

"I'm fine," Ammond grumbled to her mother a minute later. "This is far better than I have felt in years."

Her mother had grabbed her scanner from her harness on the way over and was currently scanning Ammond. "You're not. You're over heating and need to get out and cool down. Don't make me pull rank."

"You don't have the authority to pull rank," Ammond growled. "I'm your mentor, and I'm perfectly fine. Go away."

"I am the Senior Healer at the clinic you are currently employed at, which makes me your Senior. Out, or I will call Jer over and have you arrested for disobeying my orders."

Ammond snorted. "I'm not on the clock or in the clinic. You have no jurisdiction," Ammond replied.

"I have every jurisdiction, when it comes to the health and safety of the people I serve," her mother replied, and then turned and apparently called out for her father.

Deciding to try and save Ammond from arrest, although she was mostly sure her mother was joking about that, Little Flower spoke up. "We usually go back and forth between the pool and hot tub every fifteen minutes or so, to cool down. It keeps us from overheating, and allows us to spend more time in the hot tub."

"*That* is an excellent idea," her mother said, as her father and Marsee joined them.

"Jer, Ammond is overheating and refusing to leave the hot tub. We need to cool him down. Help me get him out."

"I'm perfectly fine," Ammond reiterated with a scowl, but neither of her parents paid any attention to him, and each grabbed an arm, lifting him right out of the hot tub.

"Let me go," he growled, but while her father did, once Ammond was out, her mother didn't. To Little Flower's utter amusement, Myra grabbed the back of his scruff and dragged him spluttering and swearing at her over to the pool and tossed him in. Her mother flipped out her scanner again and observed, perfectly calmly, as he resurfaced growling at her. "Was that necessary? You could have drowned me!"

"Yes," she replied. "And I have the scans to prove it. Thankfully, your temperature is coming back down. Feel free to report me to Nerissa if you want, but I have a feeling she'll decide in my favor, and you will too, once you look at the scans and realize I'm right. We'll need to figure out how long our species can safely stay in the hot tub, but for now, stick to no more than fifteen minutes like the Hue-mans. As for drowning, all you had to do was stand up on your feet, so that was never a risk."

Ammond snorted at her and started paddling his way back to the shallow end. Tail lashing, he walked back over, he yanked the scanner roughly out of Myra's paws, looked at it, growled, and without warning shoved her mother in the pool. Ammond then stormed off without another word, tail lashing behind him.

Her mother resurfaced, spluttering, and glared at her father, who was struggling to keep from laughing. "Are you going to just stand there and let him do that to me?"

Her father shrugged. "It was equal, fair, and just for what you just did to him," he replied, failing to keep a smile off his face, or his tail from curling. Everyone else burst out laughing, if they hadn't been already. Her mother snorted at him, reached up for a paw's assistance in climbing out of the pool, which her father gave her, but rather than climbing out, she yanked hard, and pulled her father in instead.

Laughing he resurfaced and splashed her back. Little Flower grinned, as it devolved into a full blown water fight, knowing full well she would draw this moment later.

# CHAPTER 11

# Marsee: Practice

Marsee waited until her sister was sound asleep and snoring lightly before carefully unwinding herself from her sister and climbing off the bed. She waited to make sure she hadn't woken her sister, before padding over her desk and grabbing an empty sketchbook and the various drawings supplies she'd set aside that evening, and then quietly snuck her way out of the room and down the ramp. She sighed with relief when she saw her parent's room was dark, and quickly made her way across the courtyard.

"Where are you sneaking off too?" her father asked, just as she was about to enter the garden.

She jumped and yelped, dropping her supplies in surprise, not having seen or heard him approach behind her. "Papa! Don't do that!" she growled at him.

He chuckled. "Sorry, I didn't mean to scare you, but you're up late, and I wasn't expecting to see you out and sneaking past my window."

Marsee shrugged. "I wasn't sneaking, I was being quiet to not wake you. Besides, you're out late too," she replied, and reached down to pick up the dropped items.

"True. I had a meeting with Marcus that ran over. I haven't seen you with a sketchbook in a while," he said, as he helped her pick up several items that had rolled away.

"Yeah. Those other paintings I did are doing well, so I thought I'd see if something inspired me tonight. I'm not the least bit tired yet, but Little Flower's already asleep, and I didn't want to keep her awake."

He nodded. "It is a beautiful night. Have fun."

She grinned at him, and made her way into the garden. The moment she was out of sight of him though, she sighed with relief. While she planned to draw, she knew he wouldn't approve of what she really intended to do. Practice.

She made her way deep into the garden, until she came to the secluded cove where grandparents were buried, and where she had only recently learned her baby sister was also buried, although there wasn't a marker. It was the one area of the garden that she'd realized the Hue-mans avoided, whether out of respect or superstition, Marsee couldn't tell.

She sat and waited, making sure no one followed her, and then turned on her instinct. The world bloomed into a riot of glowing colors, and she just sat and observed for a long time, marveling at her surroundings, and trying to make sense of it all. That day in the garden, everything had just seemed more vibrant and intense, but things were changing, and she didn't really understand what she was seeing, and she was both worried and curious, but she didn't dare talk to anyone for fear they would think she was losing control again. She felt in control, but every time she used it, it seemed just a little stronger. She made sure she could turn it on and off again a few times, and then, pulling out the sketchbook, she began to draw.

As she did, the stress of the past few weeks faded, which surprised her, but she was relieved. While she'd tried turning her instinct on and off a few times during the few moments when she was alone, she'd been itching to draw what she'd seen that night in the garden, yet hadn't dared to return for fear that her instinct would pick up on the scents of the other Hue-mans. After a few careful tests from the balcony, she'd decided to risk it. Thankfully her instinct no longer seemed to see any of the Hue-mans as prey.

It was quiet now, the daily noise of construction had ceased, and the few people about, that she could hear in the garden, were being quiet too. Most everyone had gone to bed, but a few were still out enjoying the beautiful night, and she could hear the sounds of quiet conversations around her.

A light breeze ran through the garden, making the wind chimes dance and sing, and brought with it dozens of interesting scents. Oddly enough her enhanced hearing when she had her instinct on didn't bother her the way it did the rest of the time. It wasn't that she could hear additional frequencies, but that it was easier to hone in on distant sounds, which was oddly more comforting, as she didn't have to worry so much about someone sneaking up on her.

She drew for a good hour, trying hard to capture the beauty she could see, but it was frustrating too, because there were colors she'd never seen before, and had no way to reproduce. She didn't stop until the smell of something glorious drifted into the garden.

*What is that?* she wondered, sniffing hard to try and identify it.

**I don't know,** her instinct replied. **But I think we should find out, and hunt down whatever it is. It smells wonderful!**

Scared by the thought, Marsee immediately shut her instinct down, but even with it off, she could still smell whatever it was, and her stomach rumbled with hunger. *I'd better get something to eat anyway,* she decided. *Before I do hunt something or someone.* She closed her sketchbook and picked up her supplies before following her nose to the kitchen.

She cautiously opened the door and walked in, to find one of the Hue-mans alone in the kitchen, cooking something on the newly invented device her sister called a stove.

"Jordan?" she asked, not sure if she remembered the Hue-man's name correctly.

"Hey Marsee," Jordan replied.

"What *are* you making? It smells devine."

"Candy," Jordan replied. "Or trying to anyway. It's hard without all the right ingredients, so I'm improvising. I'm not sure it's quite right yet. It's not setting the way I'd like but here, tell me what you think."

Jordan handed her a small bowl. Marsee sniffed deeply and both her stomach and instinct rumbled with appreciation. "What is it?" she asked, not recognizing it, and wanting to make sure it wasn't one of the strange protein sources they ate.

"It's mostly dried star fruit, but it's coated in a few other things," she replied. "I know your people are vegetarian. It's perfectly safe and made entirely from the foods you eat."

Marsee raised a brow, as she loved fried star fuit, and cautiously pulled a small piece out of the bowl and tried it. Flavor like she'd never tasted before exploded in her mouth. The sweet, slightly sticky and tart outer coating melted away, leaving her with a chewy center that tasted like star fruit, but far sweeter. She groaned. "Oh wow! This is incredible! Papa has to try this," she said, handed the bowl back, and bolted out of the kitchen.

She ran up to her room, dropped off her other stuff, considered waking Little Flower, but decided her sister needed her sleep more, and then ran back down, banging on her parent's door. The light flicked on a moment later.

"What's wrong?" he asked, opening the door.

"It's what's right," she replied. "Jordan's made something in the kitchen. You just *have* to try it. It's better than fried star fruit." She grabbed his arm and started pulling.

"Alright, I'm coming," he said with a chuckle and followed after her.

Jordan looked up when they entered and just handed her father a bowl with a grin. He sniffed at it, raised a brow, and gingerly took a piece. Marsee watched as his expression changed from surprise to a groan of delight that matched hers from before.

"Oh wow," he both said and signed, and grabbed another piece. "I thought fried star fruit was good, but this is incredible. What is it?"

"Star fruit," Jordan replied with a grin, and then attempted to explain how she'd made it, but they were missing dozens of signs. Giving up, Jordan just demonstrated. They were still there when her mother and Little Flower suddenly appeared.

"Oh, sorry. I didn't mean to wake you," she told Little Flower.

"You didn't. Mama came and woke me up," Little Flower replied.

"I figured if it was something worth dragging your father out of his room to try, that Little Flower would want to try it too," her mother said.

"That I do," Little Flower replied. "It smells wonderful in here!"

Jordan handed over samples and waited anxiously.

"Marry me, Jordan," Little Flower said with a groan, after popping hers in her mouth.

Jordan laughed. "I'll take it you like it?"

"You have no idea. My mother used to run a bakery, and this is as good, if not better than anything she ever made, and this is exactly what I've been craving," her sister replied.

"What does 'marry' mean?" Marsee asked.

"It's the Hue-man word for partnering with someone," Little Flower replied.

"You want to partner with Jordan?" Marsee asked with surprise.

"No, Chenzie Butt. It's an expression of deep appreciation and perhaps just a touch of greed," her sister replied, and held out her empty bowl for more.

Jordan grinned and refilled their bowls with the latest batch as soon as she determined they were cool enough to safely eat. They were even better warm.

"Jordan, we'll talk in the morning about how to package and ship this, as I have a feeling it's going to be very popular," her father said.

"That's assuming Little Flower doesn't eat it all," Marsee replied, tail curled, as her sister refilled her bowl a third time.

Little Flower just glared at her and popped another piece in her mouth. "I'm *eating* for two, which means I need twice as much."

Laughing, Jordan refilled her bowl a fourth time.

# CHAPTER 12

# Nazari: Lost Cub

Nazari carefully set a crate containing the family of feline cubs down in their new habitat, which was full of climbing surfaces and places to hide and nest. She was curious what the tiny felines, which the Hue-man's called mountain lions, would think of their new home. Setting the crate down, she opened it to see the sedated felines inside, and smiled at how much they reminded her of her own cubs, even if they were far smaller.

After giving them a careful pat, she lifted them out and transferred them over to one of the soft padded nests, and applied the anti-sedative to wake them. She waited and watched for a while to make sure they recovered and woke without issue, and then observed as they began exploring their new habitat for a few moments, before grabbing the empty crate and walking back out. After cleaning and storing the crate, she checked the time with a frown. It was taking far too long to unload all the creatures, and she didn't want to be late for the council meeting, not tonight.

Saska, one of the other healers from her pod, saw her frown. "Go on, Nazari. We've got this. There's only one transport left tonight."

"Are you sure, Saska? Most of those are my patients," Nazari replied.

"I'm sure. Go fight for your cub, and good luck."

Nazari took a deep breath and bolted, stopping first for a quick shower, and then made her way over to the nursery. She only had a few minutes to spend with him before the meeting, and if tonight didn't go well, it might be her last opportunity to spend any significant length of time with him until he was older.

When she arrived, she found he was sleeping, so she just sat there watching him. She had fallen in love with the tiny cub over the past year, and had done everything she could to protect him, going so far as to break council orders and spend every night in his habitat. The other healers in her pod had known, but hadn't told on her.

With a heavy sigh, she gently stroked his head fur, and picked him up. He woke briefly, snuggled into her fur, and quickly went back to sleep.

"Bright moons, Nazari," the healer on duty said as she walked out.

Nazari nodded at the blessing, and offered up a prayer to the Ancient Gods herself, that tonight would go well. She had no idea how the Hue-man Council would vote. The Senior Councilor had stated he was more than willing to let her have custody, but that it had to go before the Council to decide, as she was not a citizen, and he'd warned her that they probably wouldn't vote in her favor. Still, she had to try. He needed a home, and it had been over a month since they'd arrived, and none of the cubs had been claimed yet.

She was one of the first to arrive and found herself a seat in the visitor's section to wait. The rest of the Council soon arrived, and she observed how different they were from her own council. Laughing and joking as they entered, they seemed more like cubs in school than councilors. Even the ceremony was different. Guards no longer attend the session now that the shields were up and they weren't stationed here anymore. There was no one to tell them to stand when the Senior Councilor entered, so he just walked in and up to his desk, unannounced, and from what she could tell, unobserved. She and the other visitors stood, but most of the Hue-mans did not.

"This Council is now in session," Chenzira called out, and signed, flashing the lights to get everyone's attention. "Please be seated."

GrandFather and Marsee both walked up to begin translating for those that weren't fluent in sign language.

As she sat, the cub woke from the motion, but still snuggled, shifting to stick his thumb in his mouth.

"The first item on the docket tonight is a petition by Master Animal Healer Nazari Jabri to adopt the young Hue-man cub currently known as 2A84. Healer Jabri, please come forward."

Nazari stood, took a deep breath to calm her nerves, and walked down to the witness stand.

"I have reviewed your application and have found everything to be in order, including the references you provided. Does anyone have anything to say for or against this adoption?"

Several lights lit up and Nazari held her breath.

"It says here, that you were his primary healer at the Agency?" the councilor asked.

"Yes ma'am," Nazari replied, letting Marsee translate for her as her hands were full holding the cub. "I also take the night shift in the nursery to be with him."

"In all that time, you still haven't given him a name?" the councilor asked.

"It was not my place to give him a name, but I have one picked out, if the adoption is approved."

"And what would that be?" she asked.

"Sari. It was my grandfather's name," Nazari replied.

"I figured as much," the councilor muttered, and then turned to face the Senior Councilor. "I object to this adoption because I believe that the *child*, not cub, should be raised by a member of his own species, be taught our culture, and be given a Hue-man name. I don't see how she can be an adequate parent if she can't even hear him cry or speak his language."

Nazari's heart sank as many of the others nodded their agreement. "I am more than willing to give him another name, if that is a concern, and I fully intend to stay here, so he can be raised among his people," she countered. "I am fully fluent in sign language, and I'm learning your written language. While I can't hear him, I can tell when he's crying, and it would be no different if I were deaf like most of you. He cries if I am not there at night, and wants little to do with the other healers. We tried on several occasions at the Agency to pair him up with others, but he did not want anything to do with them, and as several weeks have passed, and none of you even come to the nursery, I believe I am the best choice of a parent for him. I have raised four children of my own, and care for him deeply, and promise to give him a good and loving home."

"Did you seriously think keeping a child locked in isolation was the best care he could have?" the next councilor asked.

"Absolutely not! I sent multiple letters to the Council requesting that his habitat be improved, and that our visitation time extended."

"Letters? Is that all?" someone called out.

Nazari frowned and looked up at the Senior Councilor, not sure if she should admit what she'd done or not, but then squared her shoulders. "No. I disobeyed the Council's direct orders and spent every night in his habitat. If I didn't he would cry for hours. If I had been found out, I knew I was facing a possible death sentence for my crime. Children as young as he is, should not be left alone, and what we were being ordered to do was wrong. I did what I could to protect him and the others under my care."

Murmurs ran through the chamber and Chenzira raised a paw, looking at her hard. She returned his gaze, not backing down. She believed she'd done the right thing in disobeying those orders. No child should ever be left in isolation, and if that meant her death, so be it.

Eventually he nodded. "I was aware of this act of disobedience," Chenzira replied. "And as it has been determined that the rights of the Hue-mans were infringed upon during their time at the agency, and Nazari was in the right, no charges were brought forth. Councilor Little Flower Chenzira you wish to speak?"

"Anyone willing to risk their life to protect a child has my vote," Little Flower signed. "Healer Jabri has been the closest thing to a mother he's known since he was rescued. Taking him from her would be cruel, and she's right, none of you have shown interest before. Look at him. He's obviously comfortable with her. That's the most important thing."

"I didn't know any of the children were up for adoption. I'll adopt him," a voice rang out before the Senior Councilor could call the next person.

"I'm sorry, Damon, but you are not registered as an adult, so you would not qualify," Chenzira stated calmly.

"Someone could sponsor me," he countered. "I had a child before, about the same age as him, and I can prove it. I have a tattoo of her and her mother."

"Does anyone wish to sponsor Damon Minor for adulthood, so he can put forth a claim to adopt the child?" Chenzira asked.

"There's no way in hell, I'm allowing him to adopt," someone else called out. "I'd rather see one of the cats have him."

Several people started yelling or waving their hands in anger, but Nazari had a hard time following the arguments, and GrandFather couldn't keep up with the translations.

The Senior Councilor raised his paw for silence, but when that didn't work, roared. This caused everyone to quiet, except for the cub who started crying. Nazari shifted him in her arms and began purring to try and comfort him.

"Be seated," Chenzira ordered, and the others calmed and took their seats. "Now, is there anyone who wishes to sponsor Damon Minor for adulthood. If there is, please hit your light."

They waited for several minutes in absolute silence, but when no one did, Chenzira nodded. "I'm sorry Damon, your petition has been denied. Is there anyone else who wishes to adopt the child? If so, please indicate your desire to do so by hitting your light now."

Nazari held her breath, waiting, and prayed that no one would. When no one did, she started to hope.

"Then as no one else has..."

"I'll adopt him," someone called out and hit her light.

"Councilor Harding, your claim to adopt has been recognized. Is there anyone else?" When no one else came forward, Chenzira had them cast their votes.

Nazari's tail sagged as the votes came in. She had lost by a wide margin.

"I'm sorry Healer Jabri, your request has been denied. Councilor Harding, please come forward to take the oath of adoption."

Nazari pinned her ears back, trying hard to control her emotions, and hugged the cub tightly, before trying to hand him over to his new mother. He gripped her fur just as tightly, as if he knew what was going on, and it took everything she had not to run out of the council chamber with him, but she carefully pulled him away, and handed him over, as he began to cry. Without a further look back, she turned and ran out of the chamber.

# CHAPTER 13

# Jeran: Rules and Precedent

Jer left the council chamber at the end of yet another difficult session, and made his way back to his office to deal with the fallout from the meeting. It was late and the suns had long since set as he took his seat, but he didn't begin working right away. Instead, he turned and looked out his window at the moonlit horizon, and realized someone was sitting outside near the animal pastures, and from their body posture, he guessed who it was.

He sighed, hating the decisions he had to make at times, decisions that hurt good people, and made his way outside to where he found Nazari sitting, tears still streaming down her face. "I'm sorry, Nazari."

Nazari looked over at him and wiped the tears from her face. "You warned me. I just didn't want to believe it."

"It's possible the adoption won't work out. He didn't stop crying the entire session. If it doesn't, I'll let you know."

"I just want him to be happy," she replied. "He deserves a home."

"Do you intend to change your residency?" he asked after a while. "I know you were staying here because of him."

"No. I have others to care for, and as long as I'm here, I'll still get a chance to see him. Perhaps someday he'll want to be a healer, and if he does, I'll offer to mentor him." She let out a heartbroken sigh and didn't speak for several minutes.

He wasn't sure what to say to ease her pain, so he just kept her company.

"I should probably go. I have the night shift in the nursery." Without another word, she stood and walked away, leaving him there to watch the moons in silence. Clouds were starting to roll in, and far off in the distance he heard the low rumble of thunder, and saw the faint flicker of lightning.

Eventually, he shook his head and made his way back to the tower, where Myra was waiting up for him. She gave him a hug, but otherwise said nothing. She'd been there as one of Nazari's references, in addition to being the representative from the Healer's Guild, and had seen the whole thing. She was used to seeing him in these moods. She was the only one he really let his mask drop around, but most of the time he couldn't talk about what was bothering him, much like she couldn't talk about her patients. He sat in his favorite chair and tried to work, but he couldn't focus, and eventually just set his tablet aside, with a heavy sigh.

Myra looked up from her own tablet. "They're not going to vote in my favor, are they?"

He shook his head with a heavy sigh. "Probably not. They're still so very angry at us."

"They have every right to be," Myra replied, as another rumble of thunder sounded in the distance. "Sounds like the rains are coming." She stood and walked over to the window to look out.

"So it does," he replied, looking past her, out the window at the flickering sky. "Myra..." She turned to face him when he didn't continue. "Myra, if things go badly with Little Flower, I'll have no choice but to bring you before the Council again for a change in sentencing."

"I know that," she replied.

"If the Hue-mans don't vote in your favor, appeal it."

"If Little Flower dies, I will deserve whatever punishment they see is fit," Myra replied.

"Please, Myra. For me?"

Myra sighed, but didn't answer, and instead turned around to look back out at the window. He stood and walked over, wrapping an arm and tail around her. She wrapped her own tail back around him. "Jer, whatever happens to me doesn't matter, but if Little Flower dies, her daughter will need to go to another nursing mother. I won't be able to care for her."

They were silent for a while, before she continued. "Do you think the Senior Council would vote in my favor?"

"Honestly, I don't know. By precedent, no, but they might take Little Flower's preferences in mind. We have a third of the Senior Council. I would only need to convince two others for a majority."

"You honestly think Marcus would go against precedent?" Myra asked.

"Little Flower has already stated what she wants to happen in the event of her death. I believe he would follow her wishes," Jer said, although part of him wondered what his brother would do. *Myra's right. He would follow precedent. To do otherwise would put us above the law.* Technically they should both recuse themselves from the vote, if it came to that, which would mean that three of the four others would have to vote in her favor, and he didn't know the others well enough to know how they would vote. He sighed and squeezed Myra in a hug and turned to prepare for bed. She followed him shortly afterwards, and while they curled up in their normal position, they didn't sleep. Instead they waited up for the first of the spring rains, but the storm and the rains never came. Eventually he fell asleep, but he was woken long before his alarm was scheduled to go off by the sounds of banging in the tower above.

Both curious and worried something was going on, he climbed out of bed and padded his way up to find Little Flower stomping around the room, clothes, pillows, and even some small objects were scattered everywhere. Marsee watched the whole thing with a perplexed expression.

"She's in a bad mood this morning," Marsee said quietly.

"I see that," Jer replied, and walked in to try and get his daughter's attention. She yelped when she saw him. "Sorry, I didn't mean to scare you. What's wrong?"

"Everything!" she signed, and stormed out past him.

He watched her leave and then turned back to Marsee who just shrugged. "She came back from the council meeting thoroughly annoyed, but wouldn't talk to me about it, had a restless night's sleep, and woke up in a bad mood after another night terror. She's been stomping around for the last half hour, tried on half a dozen different outfits, claiming none of them fit, or the fabric was too rough, threw a few random items, and still won't tell me what's bothering her, and..." Marsee threw up her paws and motioned towards the door. "I figured it was safer to just stay out of her way."

"You're not wrong there. Your mother was just as grumpy for absolutely no reason during her pregnancies," Jer replied. "It's probably just that, but I'll check on her, once she's had something to eat. That usually helped with your mother."

Marsee jumped down and began picking up the mess Little Flower had made of the room, while Jer followed Little Flower back down. Myra was standing in their doorway, looking down the long hallway.

"Did she say what was bothering her?" Jer asked Myra.

"No, she just growled at me and stormed past," Myra replied. "I tried to stop her to check her over, but she just hissed at me and kept walking."

Jer grinned. "She's just like her mother then," he teased, with a curl of his tail.

Myra glared at him, tail lashing. "What's that supposed to mean?"

"I don't think you said three words to me during the last two weeks of either of your pregnancies that weren't laced with a growl or a hiss," he explained.

Myra's anger turned to a chuckle and she tilted her head. "Fair. She must be uncomfortable. Proportionally her cub is nearly as big as Margaret's cub was, and Little Flower's cub isn't big enough to be born yet. I'm honestly worried she'll have enough room for it. She's just so small compared to the other females."

Jer frowned at that information. "Should she be moved to the clinic?"

"I've already tried. She's refusing, saying she's not even close to being ready, and I know she's in pain, but she won't let me treat her. GrandFather says she has another several weeks for a normal delivery. I just don't see how," Myra replied, and then let a sigh of worry slip through her mask. "If she's starting to have mood swings like this then she's probably closer than we think."

He heard the sounds of Marsee padding down the ramp and looked up to wait for her to appear. Myra smiled at her daughter. "Oh good, you're here. Marsee, I want to make sure someone is with Little Flower at all times going forward, just in case. I know you've got a lot going on with the Guild right now, but any help you can give would be appreciated."

"Of course," Marsee said. "Do you know where she went?"

"She was heading in the direction of the cafeteria," Myra stated. Marsee nodded and trotted off after her sister. A few minutes later, they both returned, with Marsee carrying a large tray of food, while her sister carried a bowl of star fruit and ate as she walked.

Jer took the tray from Marsee and carried it over to his table, while Myra grabbed glasses for the juice Marsee had brought with her. Little Flower set her dish on the table, and then just sighed at the height of the chair, radiating frustration. Jer carefully picked her up and placed her in the chair.

"Thanks," she said, once she was situated. "It's getting almost impossible to climb anything these days."

"I'll pick up some furniture from the Guild later to better suit you," he replied.

"What I really need is a railing on the ramp," she said. "I'm worried I'll slip once it starts to rain, and having something to hold onto on the way up would be helpful."

"Of course," he replied. "I'll talk to the Master Builder this morning. Feeling better?"

"Not really," she replied. "I'm pretty sure this little parasite was trying to crawl out through my lungs last night. I had no idea they moved that much."

"Try with five," Myra stated, but then frowned and looked over at Marsee. "But it's when they stop moving that it's worse."

Little Flower frowned, popped another piece of fruit in her mouth, chewed twice, frowned again, slid down off the chair, and ran over to their waste room, hitting the door switch behind her.

Myra frowned and walked over to grab the med scanner off of her carry harness. "Are you still having morning sickness?" Myra asked when Little Flower returned, looking decidedly uncomfortable.

"Morning, afternoon, evening, and sometimes midnight snacks," Little Flower replied. "If the little monster isn't kicking my bladder, she's using my stomach for a pillow."

Myra frowned and started scanning her, but Little Flower growled at her and motioned her away. "I'm fine, Mama."

"I'll be the judge of that," Myra said, and continued scanning her. Little Flower growled at her and stormed out, leaving Myra standing there in both surprise and confusion.

"I warned Papa she was in a bad mood this morning," Marsee said, and took a sip of her drink.

"So you did. I suppose I'd better warn the rest of the Senior Council," Jer replied, nearly causing Marsee to spew her drink out in laughter, although Myra just glared at him.

Chuckling, he quickly finished his breakfast and made his way to his office for the early morning meeting he had scheduled with Marcus, to review the latest plans for the upcoming Full Council meeting. When he arrived in his office, he took a few minutes to watch the news, but within minutes was frowning, and shut off the broadcast with disgust. Layton was on a rampage again. *When isn't he though?* he wondered.

Moments later the call from Marcus came in. Marcus took one look at him and frowned. "Why do I have a feeling I'm not going to like what you've got to tell me?"

"Do you ever like what I've got to tell you?" Jer asked with a snort.

"Lately, no. What is it this time?" Marcus growled.

"Oh nothing much, just that Little Flower woke up in a bad mood," Jer replied dismissively.

"Ancient Gods protect us. I'd better let Kendra know to prepare for war. What did you do to upset her?" Marcus growled.

"Me?! I'm not that stupid. Honestly though, I have no idea. Could just be pregnancy hormones, but I have a feeling something is bothering her. She's just not ready to talk about it yet. Plus, the council meeting didn't go well last night. They denied Nazari's petition to adopt."

Marcus frowned and crossed his arms as he leaned back in his chair. "I was afraid of that. What was their reasoning?"

"A combination of anger over us holding the cubs in isolation, and stating that Nazari wouldn't be able to raise the cub appropriately, because she doesn't know their culture or language, among a dozen others. One of the councilors even went so far as stating this was just another form of genocide."

"Genocide?! How could they think that?" Marcus asked, surprised.

"I have no idea. I have a meeting later with GrandFather. I'm hoping he can explain it," Jer replied.

Marcus sighed. "Well, the rest are valid points, and cross species adoptions are rare."

Jer looked away with a frown.

"What's really bothering you, Jer?" Marcus asked.

"Honestly?"

"Honesty is usually best," Marcus teased.

Jer rolled his eyes at his brother's use of their father's favorite saying, causing his brother to chuckle. Shaking his head he frowned with concern. "Honestly, I'm worried what will happen if Little Flower doesn't survive the birth. She was sick again this morning, and Myra says the cub is already proportionally as big as the others were, but she still has weeks left to go. If I have to bring Myra before the Council for resentencing, it's not going to go well. The Council was angry last night, probably the angriest I've ever seen them. For a moment, I thought I was going to have to break up a fight between a few of them. I don't have any proof, but I'm pretty sure they were taking all of their anger out on Nazari, rather than thinking of the cub's best interest, and frankly the rest of the meeting wasn't much better."

Marcus frowned, considering the implications. "You could always override their vote."

Jer raised a brow. "You're seriously suggesting that? You? The Honorable Marcus Surellis, memorizer of the Charter and strict follower of the rules?"

Marcus snorted at him. "You are a Senior Councilor now. You make the rules, and have the authority to go against whatever the rest of the Council decides."

"You know I can't do that. Have you even bothered watching the news since the trial? Half the Consortium is livid with us right now. If I start overriding my Council's votes, I'll have a mob at my door, and not just the Hue-mans. You saw what happened after that first day."

"That depends on what you're overriding and why. You had the right of it that first day, which is clear since you still have full support of your council, which is what matters. The press is still clawing me to shreds, far more than you about that decision, as it was my idea in the first place. As far as Myra is concerned, I intend to honor Little Flower's preferences in the matter," Marcus replied.

"You're not going to recuse yourself?" Jer asked, thoroughly surprised.

"If I did, the entire Senior Council would have to, and frankly, I'm not willing to leave it to the rest of the Council to decide," Marcus replied.

Jer sat there in shock. "Seriously? You? You're going to go against precedent?"

"Jer, the entire Council let Myra take the fall for our crimes. I'm *not* letting that happen again. I've watched Little Flower's testimony a dozen times since the trial. She had the right of it. No matter what Myra had done, the result would have been the same, if not for Little Flower, then for someone else. As far as I'm concerned, Myra has paid for her part in that crime, and then some, and I will do everything I can to protect her, and so should you."

Jer closed his eyes and took a deep breath. "Thank you, brother. I take back half the mean things I've said about you in the past."

"Only half?" Marcus glared at him with mock indignation.

"I reserve the other half until after," Jer replied with a grin.

Marcus chuckled. "That's fair. Now, where do we stand on the land survey?"

Jer groaned. "Did you have to bring that up?"

"That *was* the whole point of this meeting, wasn't it?" Marcus replied with a glare.

Jer just grunted and rolled his eyes, and dug into the results of the survey with Marcus. Several hours later, he hung up and leaned back in his chair, feeling overwhelmed with the amount of work he still had before him. With a sigh, he turned off his busy light. Moments later there was a knock at the door.

He hit the switch they'd added, that let those who couldn't hear know they could enter, and to his surprise, Little Flower waddled in, rubbing at her back.

"I thought for sure you would never get off that meeting," Little Flower said, eyed the furniture in his office, and then made her way over to a pillow in the corner, flopping down with a groan.

"You and me, both," Jer replied. "So, am I correct in assuming that this is not a social visit?"

His daughter sighed. "You are. I figured I'd better come talk to you before I bit someone's head off."

His tail curled, although he kept his face neutral. "Well, I told Marcus you were grumpy this morning, and he said he was letting Kendra know to prepare for war. I'm personally hoping you save it all for the Full Council meeting, just as long as it's not directed at me."

Little Flower chuckled, and then winced as the cub visibly shifted inside of her. "I'll see what I can do. I'm not sure I'm going to make it to the council meeting though."

Jer frowned with worry. "Please let your mother care for you. She's only trying to help."

She sighed. "I know, but I'm fine. I feel like I'm going to explode, but I'm fine."

"So what has you so grumpy today?" he asked.

"A number of things. I don't like what happened last night, with Nazari, and I don't want that to happen to my daughter. If something happens to me, I want her raised by you and Mama, or Marsee, not any of the other Hue-mans except for GrandFather, if for some reason you can't."

"Your preferences are well marked, but if something happens to you, your mother may not be able to care for the cub. We still don't have a supplement to replace your milk."

"I know that. Do what you have to to get food for her, but I want her to grow up with your morals, not ours. She needs to learn a better way. I understand why the Council voted the way they did last night. It was considered a form of genocide to take children from their parents and give them to someone else to kill off a culture, and it happend far too often."

"I wanted to ask you about that," Jer interrupted. "I didn't understand that complaint last night. How is Nazari adopting the child a form of genocide?"

Little Flower pursed her lips. "You should talk with Kai and hear her story first hand. She's Navajo and was born on a reservation. It's kind of the opposite of what happened here. We took their most fertile land and forced them onto land that we didn't want, that was poor for growing crops, and then killed off the buffalo which was one of the primary sources for, well, just about everything, and then left them to starve. Then when the government decided that they were too poor to raise their own children, they took them from their parents and had white Christian families raise them, or made them send their children to residential schools, where all sorts of atrocities happened. Children were killed, raped, and abused. Many tribes weren't allowed to practice their religions or even speak their own language. The children grew up not knowing their culture, if they even survived, and languages, histories, and skills were all lost when the older generations died, and there was no one left to remember."

Jer flicked his ears back in horror as Little Flower continued to explain.

"But I know Nazari wouldn't have done that, nor would you," she continued. "You've been doing everything you can to help us preserve our history, and frankly, what they did last night wasn't in the best interest of that child. Nazari's been his mother for most of his life. He should have stayed with her, and she was right. None of the others of my species have come forward to care for those children. If their only reason to adopt is to get back at your people, then it's not a good enough reason to be a parent."

"Well, Nazari could bring it to the Full Council if she wants to fight it," Jer replied. "If you think she has a case."

"Do you think it would make any difference?" Little Flower asked instead.

He considered, and then shook his head with a sigh. "Honestly, the way things are right now, I don't know. If she did, she'd need an advocate. Someone like you to fight for her."

Little Flower sighed and nodded. "I would, but I have no idea when this baby is going to pop, or whether or not I'll be ready to travel by then. I'll talk to GrandFather."

"What else did you want to talk about?" he asked, sensing that she hadn't brought up the real reason she was there.

"Tabor," she replied.

"Tabor?" he asked, both confused and surprised, "What about her?"

"According to the information we had last night, Tabor's the only one left at the Agency."

"Pretty much. There are a few guards there to care for her, and a handful of builders who are taking the remaining structures down," he replied, "but that should be done by the end of the week."

She sighed and didn't speak for a while. "It's not right that the guards will have to remain in nearly as much isolation as her, and we've voted that that kind of isolation isn't allowed anymore."

"I had wondered what you wanted to do about her. I figured we could move her to Sand Dune, since that's the closest community with a guard hall," Jer replied. "We don't have anywhere here to put her, or guards to watch her."

His daughter made a face he couldn't quite decipher, and then shook her head. "If last night showed me anything, it's that my people still need to learn to trust yours. I was thinking about moving her here, but rather than putting her back in isolation, have her serve out the rest of her sentence with community service. That way she can get to know us, and we can get to know her."

Jer smiled at his daughter. "Your ability to forgive astounds me, daughter."

"I didn't say I was forgiving her," Little Flower growled. "But, I've never felt comfortable with her punishment. It's been long enough now that I'm sure she fully understands what she did to us, but someone has to take the first step if we're going to have peace between our people. I also thought we should offer residency to her family, if they still want anything to do with her."

Jer nodded. "I will check with the rest of the Seniors and make arrangements if they agree, which I believe they will. Your suggestion is well within the agreed upon parameters."

Little Flower nodded and then tried and failed to get up off the pillow, and then flopped back with a frustrated groan. "A little help here, Papa? I seem to have beached myself."

"Beached?" he asked, not familiar with the Hue-man word she signed.

"It means a fish washed up on the shore, flopping around trying to get back in the water. I'm thoroughly stuck."

Jer chuckled as the term was apt, and walked over, easily lifting his daughter up. He watched her waddle out, and shook his head in amazement at her. Then returned to his desk and fired off a message to the other Seniors, knowing it would take several hours to get a reply from everyone.

Marcus called almost immediately though. "You're serious, cub? She wants to reduce Tabor's punishment? I thought you said she was in a grumpy mood."

"Very much so, on both accounts. Be forewarned, she may take up Nazari's case at the Full Council meeting too."

"Ancient Gods, protect us," Marcus said, pinching the bridge of his nose, and hung up.

Jer chuckled at the blank screen for several minutes, before returning to his work.

# CHAPTER 14

# Little Flower: A New Beginning

The Senior Council approved her suggested change in punishment for Tabor. So a few days later, they took her father's new ship and flew over to the Agency. She hadn't been able to see much of anything the last time she'd been there, outside of the vague shapes of buildings in the storm, but now there was nothing. Nothing, but a single long building in the middle of a barren and torn up field outside of the old clinic, and yet her memories of the place threatened to overwhelm her.

She sat in the ship for some time staring out the window at that lonely building, her father waiting patiently beside her. Eventually, she carefully slid out of her seat with her father's help. Even though the seat was designed for her, her pregnancy was now advanced enough to make every movement more challenging. If her calculations were correct, she was now about eight Earth months pregnant. Grabbing the bag she'd brought with her, she followed her father down out of the ship, which he had to help her with as well. There were only a few steps but they were designed for the Sabers, and she was worried about falling. She'd never felt so unbalanced before. They walked over together at her slow, wobbly pace. The guards met them at the entrance of the building and followed them inside.

She'd expected to see the same long tan hallway that had been there before, but what she found instead was an even longer empty building, save for one tan cell near the middle. The floor of the massive room showed the clean outlines where the interior walls of the cells had been, stark against the faded rooms and hallways.

She stared at that cell for a long time before walking forward. Neither her father or the guards said anything, just waited for her. When she arrived at the cell, she took several deep breaths and nodded. The guard hit the switch on the cell, but she just stared at the former Senior Councilor, who appeared to be sleeping, curled up on a thin mattress in the corner, a small collection of puzzle boxes and toys neatly lined up beside her, and a half eaten tray of food.

Tabor woke and looked up as they entered, but then immediately looked away, refusing to meet her gaze. Little Flower stood there, staring at Tabor, lost in her own memories, and trying to control the rising panic she felt at being back here in this room. *Who knew a color could be so triggering,* she thought.

"I am truly sorry. I don't know how you remained sane," Tabor said eventually, which her father translated, after getting her attention.

"I didn't," she replied, simply.

Tabor tilted her head, accepting her point, but otherwise remained quiet, staring off into the distance, almost as if she was forgetting they were there. Her father said something to the guards, and they shook their heads.

"What is it?" she asked her father.

"She's having trouble speaking," her father replied. "I was worried about psychosis, but the guards state they've tested her, as they were concerned as well."

"After a while, you forget how," Little Flower said, and walked over to Tabor, handing her the bag. "The Agency has been dismantled, I'm here to move you to the compound."

Tabor blinked and refocused slowly on her, and opened the bag with a slight hint of curiosity. When she pulled out the carry harness and leash inside, she sighed, but nodded, putting it on without comment.

Little Flower took the end of the leash and led Tabor out of the room, past the guards, who both looked at her in astonishment. They didn't stop her, nor did her father. She hadn't told him what she'd planned. Whatever he was thinking, he kept it hidden behind his mask, and just followed out after.

Tabor blinked furiously in the bright sunlight, and looked around at the empty torn up field and the ship waiting for them. She gave Tabor several moments to recover before leading her onto the ship and motioning for her take a seat, giving her one of the window seats. Her father and the two guards followed, and once they were all strapped in, her father ordered the pilots to return home. Tabor stared out at the world around them, almost as if she couldn't believe she was seeing something other than those tan cells. Little Flower remembered that feeling vividly.

The first of the spring rains had finally arrived, and the desert had responded almost overnight. Once they were out of the torn up remains of the Agency, tiny colorful flowers dotted the landscape, and the first tender buds of other plants and grasses were now poking up through the sands. To Little Flower the overnight transformation seemed miraculous, but the native plants had little time to grow, so like her species, they grew quickly. Tabor seemed genuinely impressed with what they'd built as they approached the compound and landed neatly in the new shuttle bay, but still said nothing.

When they arrived, her father again helped her down out of the ship, and Tabor followed obediently after. She then paraded the former Senior Councilor slowly through the compound, with every resident, guest, and even members of the press lining the halls in silence, until they all ended up in the garden.

Tabor's partner and four young cubs were waiting for them by the pool under the shade of the tree. Tabor started to run forward at the sight of them, but Little Flower yanked hard on the leash, just as she came within feet of her cubs. She obviously wasn't big enough or strong enough to stop Tabor, but it was enough to remind the former Senior of what she had done to Little Flower, and that she was not free to see her family. Little Flower watched closely as anger, frustration, sadness, and then a gasp of understanding, regret, and acceptance flashed through Tabor's body. It was what she'd been hoping to see.

"Jennette Tabor," Little Flower signed, and Marsee, who was waiting with Tabor's partner, immediately began translating.

Tabor turned to face her, her face now a calm mask of acceptance.

"For the crime of forcing my species through more than eight standard months of total isolation, without the rights and care we should have been granted as a sentient being, you imposed upon yourself the same isolation, in the same cell I was once held in. You were given the same care I was given, the same amount of contact, and the same food, for the past month and a half. However, as you saw, the Agency is being dismantled, and to require someone to care for you in isolation themselves would be as much of a crime, so you have been brought here instead for the remainder of your term."

Jennette nodded her understanding, so Little Flower continued. "The Senior Council gave me permission to change, or shorten your sentencing, or allow visitation as I saw fit, and I am exercising that right. We, as a people, have agreed that no one, regardless of crime or illness, should ever be held in solitary isolation, for *any* length of time, as we were, and as you and your family are now residents of this community, that right now extends to you. As such, I am changing your punishment to community service, with the expectation that you will spend each day in service to this community, for the remainder of your sentence. Outside of that time, you are free to come and go as you please."

Jennette again nodded her understanding, although her ears flicked back in surprise that she was not just being moved to a new cell, but actually being allowed to reunite with her family.

"My understanding is that you are in need of a new career, and we have a brand new trauma ship in need of a competent pilot, if you're interested."

Tabor just stared at her and blinked for several moments before slowly nodding.

"Wonderful! Please take off your harness and leash." Little Flower grinned, and held out her hand for it.

Tabor did and handed it over, still not speaking, just staring at her in that same shocked and amazed expression.

"Mama, if you would be so kind as to destroy this vile thing," Little Flower signed and handed it over. Myra took the harness and tore it to shreds with a grin. When the harness was nothing more than tiny pieces, Little Flower walked over, carefully picked one of the lilies that smelled like chocolate, and held it up to Tabor. "Welcome to your new home, Jennette. May you find the same peace, love, and hope here that I have."

Tabor took the lily and sat down hard, staring at it, as if it were the most beautiful thing she'd ever been given. Eventually she looked up at Little Flower and tilted her head. "Are you really forgiving me?"

Little Flower paused and considered her words carefully. "When the asteroid hit, you saved my people, healed us, and welcomed us onto your world without a moment of hesitation, at great risk to your own people. Mistakes were made in our care that caused us a great deal of harm, and it will take my people time to recover from the trauma we experienced. But we are recovering, and I do not believe you intended to hurt us with the decisions you made, so yes, I at least, am forgiving you." She then gave the now completely overwhelmed and shaking former Senior Councilor a hug, before stepping back and motioning that she was now free to reunite with her family.

<div align="center">~~~~~</div>

That afternoon Little Flower and Marsee were in their room during the midafternoon rest period. As they often were, Marsee had her whiskers in a book, while Little Flower worked on the painting she planned to give to Ellie. Rubbing her back, she groaned and leaned back in the rocking chair Ellie had gifted her. Her back and sides had been bothering her all day, and it felt like the baby had a foot jammed between her ribs, making it difficult to take a deep breath. She really needed to pee as well, but the hole of muck was just too far away to bother.

"Marsee!" she called out. Her sister didn't respond, which meant that she must have her hearing aids in. It would take far more energy than she had to heave herself up out of her chair to get her sister's attention, so she just threw an eraser at her sister instead. Marsee jumped as it hit her squarely in the back of her head.

"What?!" Marsee asked, looking over at her with a glare, her ears back and tail lashing.

"I think it's finally done. Come see. Tell me what you think."

Marsee's ears flicked up and she tossed her book aside, jumped down, stretched, and padded over on all fours to peer over her shoulder. "Oh, it's amazing!"

"Do you think she'll like it?" Little Flower asked.

"I think she'll love it!" Marsee replied.

"I hope so. Will you help me put together a frame for it? It's too big for me to manage on my own right now."

"Sure, let me grab some supplies. I'll start working on it now," Marsee said, and bolted out of the room before Little Flower could ask for help getting to her padded throne of muck.

With a sigh, she sat there rocking and trying to find the strength and energy to heave herself out of the chair. Deciding she could wait for assistance, she went back to examining the painting to make sure there wasn't anything else she wanted to add to it, when a sharp pain wracked her stomach.

Little Flower groaned and breathed through it, frowning with worry. *It's too soon. It's probably just gas, or you've waited too long to pee.* Still, she called her mother, but she didn't pick up, which meant she was probably with a patient. Sending a message instead, she wondered how long it would take for Marsee to return, or if she should just start making her way over to the clinic on her own. *Pee first,* she decided, and finally heaved her way out of the chair and wobbled over to the hole of muck, exhausted and short of breath from the effort of that short distance, and the tiny foot that was still lodged between her ribs.

She had just made it back to her chair, planning to rest for a moment, before making her way to the clinic, when Marsee returned with her arms full of tools and supplies.

"Oh good, you're back," Little Flower signed and then paused as another wave of pain gripped her stomach. "Marsee, can you go find Mama for me, please."

"Sure. Why? To see the painting?" Marsee asked awkwardly, shifting the supplies to one arm so she could talk, as she started crossing the room to her work bench.

"No. I think it's time," she answered.

"Time for what?" Marsee asked, confused.

"I think the baby is coming. Help me up out of this chair and then go find Mama. I tried calling but she didn't answer. I'll follow you to the clinic."

Marsee's ears went straight back and her tail spiked out at Little Flower's words. All of the items she had been carrying slipped out of her grasp and fell to the floor in a clatter. Marsee ran over and carefully helped her out of the rocking chair before bolting from the room at a full run. Little Flower chuckled at her sister's reaction, and followed slowly behind, pausing briefly to look out at the vibrant landscape below, before carefully making her way down the ramp. She still couldn't believe how much it had transformed in just a few days. Massive herds of wild animals roamed in the distance, but closer by, small herds of animals grazed contentedly in their enclosed pastures below. She smiled at the horses and thought about her grandfather's old horse Buster, wondering what he'd think of this place. She missed him dearly. She hadn't made it over to the barns since they arrived, but she enjoyed watching the animals graze from her tower.

A railing and treads had been added to the ramp, for which she was very grateful, as the rains made the stone slippery, even with the static shield that deflected most of it, and she held on tightly as she made her careful way down. When she finally made it to the bottom, she found her parents' door wide open. Peering inside she saw the room was empty, so she closed the door and started wobbling her way down the hallway. She'd just spotted her grandfather running towards her as another contraction hit and dropped her to her knees with the pain.

The sharp pain in her side exploded, feeling like someone had stabbed her with a hot knife, and she cried out.

GrandFather made it to her side and she leaned into him, grabbing ahold of him for support until the pain subsided a little. "It's over, help me up," she said after the contraction passed, and after awkwardly struggling to her feet, they started slowly making their way down the hall again. She was gasping for breath, as every inhale caused her sides to hurt, and she had to stop often, as she was starting to feel dizzy.

They'd made it maybe a hundred feet when Marsee and both of her parents came barreling around the corner and down the hall at a full run on all fours. The few people in the hall scampered to get out of their way, and then turned to see what the emergency was. *Nothing to see here,* she thought. *Just a beached whale flopping her way down the hallway.*

Her parents skidded to a stop. "Marsee said the baby is coming?" her mother signed.

"I think so. I just had a contraction a few minutes ago. They're not very far apart."

"It's too soon! We need to get you to the clinic," her mother signed, and reached down to pick her up, but she pushed the paws away. Being carried hurt too much these days.

"I can walk," she signed, and started shuffling forward again. *Then again maybe not,* she thought a few moments later, as yet another contraction hit her stronger than before, causing her to scream. Eyes closed and crushing her grandfather's arm as he struggled to hold her up, she felt something wet gush down her legs. *Did my water just break?* She gritted her teeth through the pain, trying to avoid screaming again. She fought to stay on her feet as her knees threatened to buckle. It just took far too much effort to stand back up, and she didn't think she could a second time. When the worst of the pain passed, she opened her eyes and looked down. Instead of the water she was expecting, her legs were covered in blood. She looked up at her mother who had the same expression of terror on her face. It was the last thing Little Flower saw as the world spun, and darkness pulled her under.

# CHAPTER 15

# Myra: An Offering to the Ancient Gods

Myra scooped up her daughter and ran for all she was worth to the clinic, praying to the Ancient Gods to save her children once again. As she barreled through the open door to the clinic, she bellowed commands. The healers that had been preparing for Little Flower's birth jumped and ran to follow her orders. She carefully set her daughter down on the first operating table. Readouts sprang to life on the monitor above the bed.

She mentally swore in three different languages. Little Flower's pulse was erratic and her blood pressure was dropping fast. A second set of vitals showed the cub was showing signs of distress as well. She waved her hand and the screen changed to show a three-dimensional scan of her daughter. She zoomed in on her abdomen, and swore again. *How in the dark moons did that happen?* She swore a third time as she looked down at the bed. Blood was already soaking the table and dripping on the floor. Little Flower was losing far too much blood, and she was going to lose both of them if she didn't act quickly.

"Prep for surgery!" she bellowed, and ripped the dress off her daughter in one motion. "Why isn't that transfusion hooked up yet?"

"We're out of her blood type. The broken leg we had to operate on last night used the last of it, and he's the only one with a matching blood type," one of the other healers called back.

GrandFather pushed his way in through the crowd of healers all scrambling to get Little Flower ready for surgery, and yanked on Myra's fur, getting her attention. "What's wrong? How can I help?" he signed.

"The repair of her broken rib failed and it broke off. She's hemorrhaging and bleeding internally. We need to cut the baby out now and stop the bleeding, but we're out of her blood type. I need you to leave the surgery," Myra commanded, pushing him towards the door.

He didn't leave. "Use my blood," GrandFather signed, forcing his way in front of her again.

"I can't. Your blood type doesn't match. It would kill her," she said, and turned to yell another order.

He yanked on her fur hard, refusing to let her turn away. "I'm a universal donor. My blood type is good for everyone. Trust me. Use my blood. *Please!*" he signed.

She frantically considered the risk. *Was that even possible? If he was wrong...* Alarms started blaring and she turned to read them, and swore again. "Brice, hook GrandFather up to a direct transfusion, and get him started on fluids to help counteract the loss of blood. We're going to need a lot of his blood, and fast, if we're going to save her."

Brice picked up GrandFather and set him on the adjacent bed and began preparing for the transfusion. *Come on...Come on...* She willed her team to move faster in preparing Little Flower for surgery, watching the monitors as her daughter's vitals dropped lower and lower. *Don't you dare die on me, Little Flower. You need to fight. Fight like you've never fought before.* As soon as the transfusion was in place, Little Flower's vitals paused their downward spiral. The other healers moved out of the way so she could begin operating, and with a prayer to the Ancient Gods, Myra slammed her terror behind her mask, and began.

Carefully cutting into her daughter's belly, she cut through the various layers of skin, fat, and muscle, moved her daughter's bladder out of the way, and finally cut through the uterine wall exposing the amniotic sac. Her daughter's belly was full of the blood she was hemorrhaging. Brice suctioned it away. Thankfully, the scalpel tool cauterized the opening as she cut, preventing further blood loss. As she cut the amniotic sac, what remained of the fluid started gushing.

"Suction!" she ordered as she continued carefully cutting an opening, finally exposing the tiny cub inside. Claws sheathed, she reached in and removed one of the tiniest cubs she'd ever seen. Once the cub was out, another healer quickly clamped and cut the umbilical cord, and she handed the cub off to the team of healers waiting, and went back to saving her daughter's life. She couldn't worry about Little Flower's cub now. Before she could, another set of alarms went off and she looked over. GrandFather's monitors were showing he was in distress from loosing too much blood.

"Disconnect the transfusion!" she bellowed. Little Flower would never forgive her if her grandfather died trying to save her.

He tried to refuse, weakly pushing Brice's hand away and signing 'no'.

"Restrain him if you have to and disconnect that transfusion," she ordered, and returned her focus to Little Flower.

Transfusion disconnected, Little Flower's vitals started dropping again, dangerously low. She stopped breathing on her own, and the life support systems kicked in, breathing for her. Myra picked up her pace. She didn't have much time left. She began looking for the source of the bleeding and found the broken rib. She didn't have time to put the rib back in place and heal it, so she grabbed the evil thing with a pair of tongs and yanked it out.

"Suture!"

Trading tongs and the broken rib for the suture wand, she began repairing the surprising amount of damage it had caused, as Brice suctioned the pumping blood out of her way. She'd only just started when the absence of a noise blared louder than any of the alarms, and cut right through her soul. She looked up at the monitors for confirmation. Little Flower's heart had stopped beating.

"I told you not to die on me," she growled at her daughter. "Don't you dare disobey me! Fight!"

She went back to closing the rupture. She needed to stop the bleeding before they could try restarting her daughter's heart, otherwise she'd lose more blood the moment her heart started beating again, and she'd already lost far too much. The moment the wound was closed, she pulled away from the table.

"Clear!"

Brice applied the shock paddles, causing Little Flower to jump on the table. They waited.

...

Nothing.

"Again!"

Brice did as ordered, and they waited again.

...

Still nothing.

"Again!"

When the third try failed, Myra started to panic.

"Again!"

"Myra, it's been over five minutes," Brice said, looking at her with compassion.

"I said again!" she growled. When Brice didn't move, she ripped the paddles out of Brice's paws with a hiss and applied them herself.

*Please! I'll do anything!* she promised the Ancient Gods, begging them again to save her daughter.

Miraculously the gods accepted her offer and Little Flower's heart started beating again, weak but steady. *Thank you! Thank you! Thank you!* She closed her eyes in a brief prayer of thanks, and then tossed the paddles back to Brice with an angry snarl before going back to check for additional damage, remove the placenta, and begin the delicate process of repairing the incision she'd made to cut the cub out. It took over an hour to complete the repairs, but in all that time the beep of Little Flower's heart monitor never wavered. It was one of the most beautiful sounds she'd ever heard.

When the repairs were finally completed, Myra set the suture tool down, and examined the monitors and scans. Little Flower was weak but stable and the bleeding had all been stopped. She'd made it. Now the only question was, had her heart been stopped too long, and how badly had her brain been damaged from lack of oxygen. For her own species it had been far too long to not cause significant damage, but they had no idea how long the tiny Hue-mans could last, or how well they would or could recover from that damage. As fragile as the species was, in many ways they were far more resilient. The results of those scans were worrisome though, and she frowned. *I'll need Ammond's help,* she decided. While the monitors were the top of the line, they weren't designed to monitor brain activity in the same way his specialized equipment was, and he was far more experienced reading their brain scans than she was at this point. She turned her head to order Brice to go track down Ammond, and saw GrandFather watching her.

"Is she okay?" he signed, weakly.

"I don't know. She's alive. Only time will tell how badly she's been injured," she replied.

"The baby?" he asked.

She'd been so focused on Little Flower that she hadn't even checked. On a neonatal bed that had been set up next to Little Flower was the impossibly tiny cub. Several weeks premature, according to the information they'd gathered from GrandFather and the other Hue-man females, it would be far too soon for her own species to survive, but apparently still within the range of viability according to them. She carefully examined the monitors and turned back to GrandFather.

"She's tiny, but she appears to be stable," she signed with a relieved smile.

GrandFather closed his eyes and started crying. She knew how he felt, and wished she had time to cry too. Ammond arrived moments later with Brice. He took one look at the amount of blood on the operating table, frowned, slapped on his healer's mask, and got to work examining the existing scans. Frowning again, he left and returned a moment later with his modified brain scanner, adapted now to be able to fit the shape of the Hue-man's heads better, and took several more scans before unhooking everything.

"It will take time to go through these before I'm comfortable with any treatment," he said, looking up at her with compassion.

She sighed but nodded her understanding, not expecting anything less. Deeming Little Flower stable enough to move, she ordered her daughter and granddaughter to be cleaned and transferred to one of the beds in the trauma ward for monitoring. Ammond walked over and examined Little Flower's cub for a few moments, his mask softening as he peered at the impossibly tiny cub, before looking back at the cub's mother with a worried sigh, and left to examine his scans. She watched him leave, scared by the slip in his mask, and offered up another prayer to the Ancient Gods, who had shown her such favor only a few minutes before, asking for yet another miracle, and wondered what they would ultimately demand from her in return.

After cleaning the massive amounts of Little Flower's blood off her own fur, she left to inform those waiting out in the clinic. The room went silent as she entered. Marsee had been pacing, while Jer sat talking with Marcus and Ellie. *When did they arrive?* she wondered, but then took a deep breath and focused her thoughts.

"Little Flower has delivered a healthy baby girl," she said. The room interrupted into cheers, but she held her paw up for silence. "I'm not exactly sure how, but somehow one of her previously broken ribs broke again, this time causing her to hemorrhage massive amounts of blood. I was able to repair the injury, but not before she stopped breathing and her heart stopped. We were able to get it started again, but it took too long. There is a high probability that she will suffer from brain damage due to the amount of time her brain was without oxygen. Only time will tell how much and how badly. She is currently very weak, but stable."

"Can we see them?" Marsee asked. Her ears drooped to the sides in worry, and she held her tail clutched tightly in her paws, twisting it. Myra would have been doing the same if it hadn't been for all her training.

"She's being moved to the trauma ward now where visitors are limited to family and no more than two at a time. GrandFather is already there with her. Jer, if you would like to join him, I'll take you back. Marsee, we'll come find you later. The rest of you, there's little point in waiting here. It will be a few hours at least before we know more." She turned and led her partner back to the intensive care ward. As they passed the operating room, she noticed the other healers still cleaning the blood that had been tracked everywhere. *So much blood loss. How could such a tiny creature lose so much blood and survive without issues?* She sent out another silent plea and grabbed Jer's paw for support.

As they entered the trauma ward, they met Brice coming out of one of the rooms. Brice tilted her head in the direction of the room she'd just left, to indicate that was where Little Flower had been placed. They entered to find Little Flower still unconscious, the cub by her side in the neonatal cart. GrandFather reclined in a chair next to the cart, one of his fingers grasped tightly in one of the tiny cub's paws. A saline drip hung next to him, one for him and another for Little Flower.

Jer walked over and squat down to peer at the cub. "She's so tiny. I thought they would be bigger," Jer signed, and then moved over to sit on the other side of the bed taking one of Little Flower's paws in his.

"She's several weeks premature," Myra replied, which caused him to frown. Marsee had been a preemie as well, and had spent weeks in the trauma ward after she'd been born, and she had barely survived. "Everything appears to be functioning normally. She's healthy, just small."

Jer sighed with relief and turned his attention to his daughter, brushing a stray piece of her head fur aside. *She looks so small and weak in that bed,* Myra thought. With a sigh, she walked over and carefully picked up Little Flower's tiny cub and brought her over to her mother. Unsure of how the cub would nurse, but knowing she would need to nurse quickly if she were to survive, she gently placed her on her mother's chest, tucking the blanket that covered Little Flower around them both, to help keep the cub from falling. Myra's species nursed on their sides, but everything she'd seen so far from the other Hue-mans showed they nursed sitting up or reclined. Helping the cub find a teat, she sighed with relief when the cub latched on and began nursing. As the cub nursed, Myra watched the monitors, and ever so slowly Little Flower's vitals improved, not enough, but she'd take all she could get right now.

GrandFather had rolled over to watch, but shifted back in his chair and closed his eyes, looking pale and breathing hard. Worried, she flipped the monitors over to his readings and frowned. His blood pressure was still too low. She shifted over to him and touched him lightly on his shoulder to get his attention. "How are you feeling?" she asked him when he opened his eyes. He should be in a recovery room himself, but she understood why he was here instead. He'd refused to be put in his own room, and she probably would have done the same if she'd been in his place.

"Tired and light headed, but okay," he replied.

"Bring GrandFather some fruit juice," she instructed Brice, leaning out of the room to get the other healer's attention.

Brice quickly did as requested and returned with drinks for all of them.

"Drink," she ordered GrandFather, and grabbed a pillow, making him elevate his feet more. She left her drink untouched, too worried to drink.

When GrandFather was done, he set the empty glass down on the table beside him, and turned his head to watch his grandchildren again. They sat there a long time in silence, waiting, listening to the beep of the monitors, and watching Little Flower and her cub.

Eventually GrandFather shifted to look at her. "Be honest with me, Myra. Just how bad is she?"

She closed her eyes and took a deep shuddering breath. "She lost far too much blood, even with what you shared, and her heart stopped for too long. The scans show she's suffered some fairly systemic brain damage from the lack of oxygen. Ammond is trying to figure out a course of treatment. She's going to have a long road ahead of her and will need a lot of help...if she even wakes up," she signed, saying for the first time what her heart had been denying.

Jer stared at her for a long moment, and then swallowed hard before closing his own eyes offering up a prayer to the Ancient Gods as well. So much hung in the balance with her daughter's life. The cub needed her to survive, at least until one of the other pregnant women gave birth. Myra knew she would care for the cub and her daughter through whatever hardships her daughter faced, for the rest of her life if necessary. But if Little Flower died, she might not be given that chance. She didn't particularly care what happened to herself. Whatever the Council decided would be fair and just in her mind. All she cared about was the health of her children, and she was terrified for them both.

# CHAPTER 16

# Marsee: Blame

Marsee watched her parents walk back into the clinic, twisting her tail hard, not wanting to believe what her mother had said. Her sister had to be okay. She just had to be.

"Marsee, come on. Let's go get something to eat," Ellie said, putting a paw on her shoulder.

With a strangled sob, Marsee turned away and let them lead her out of the clinic towards the cafeteria, but they were only halfway back when she saw someone cleaning the floor where her sister had been. The scent in the hall was a mix of antiseptic and sister's blood, and with a strangled cry she took off at a run in the direction of her room.

"Marsee, stop!" her uncle called out, but she didn't stop, just kept running until she was in her room, only that was worse. The emptiness of the room screamed louder than any sound. Her eyes caught on the jumbled pile of materials and tools she'd gathered to make the frame for her sister's painting, and she gasped with horror.

*Oh Gods! It's all my fault!* she cried to herself. Grabbing a piece of the wood, she threw it as hard as she could at an exposed section of wall and it splintered into several satisfying pieces. Grabbing another piece she went to throw it, but something caught her wrist. Startled, she spun to find her uncle there. "It's all my fault!" she wailed and collapsed into her uncle's embrace.

"Hush, child. It's not your fault," her uncle whispered and held her tightly, grabbing her by the scruff.

"Yes it is," Marsee whimpered. Even the normally instinctive reaction to calm that grabbing her scruff should have had, did nothing to ease the pain in her heart.

"No, child, it's not. These things happen. Childbirth is dangerous," Marcus said. "And her pregnancy was always a risk."

"It is. You don't understand!" she yelled, trying to push away, wanting to throw or hit something, or just run into the wilds to escape her grief, but he wouldn't let go, and held tighter. "Let me go!" she growled, trying to push away.

"No," he said softly. "Not until you've calmed. Now tell me, why do you think it's your fault? Did something happen?"

She sagged against him, and he began purring to comfort her. "No. It's because I was the one that was watching her when she climbed the tree and broke her ribs that last time, and I should have never left her alone to go make that stupid frame. If I'd been here, she would have been at the clinic sooner, and she wouldn't be injured and fighting for her life now," Marsee explained through sobs and hiccups.

"None of that is your fault. If it's anyone's fault it's your mother's," her uncle replied. "She was the one who destroyed the harness and wanted you to help care for her. And it's not your fault that you weren't here when her labor started. She wasn't due for another couple of weeks."

"Mama! They're going to kill her aren't they?" she realized in horror, looking up at him. "If Little Flower dies, they're going to kill her too."

Her uncle sighed but nodded. "That's entirely possible. The Huemans are still very angry at us, and they rarely vote the way we expect them to. Your mother could appeal it, but I don't know if she'll have enough votes among the Senior Council."

She shook now with fear for both her sister and mother, and they sat there for a long time, Marcus holding her tightly as she cried out her fear and grief, until she finally calmed. He relaxed his grip slightly, but still continued to hug her and purr.

"That's better," he said. "You need to be strong for your sister and her cub. They'll need your help, now more than ever. You're going to need to be a mother for that cub. Your parents won't have time. Your mother will be busy trying to save your sister, and your father will be busy trying to get the Hue-mans on our side, if they're to vote in your mother's favor."

She wiped the tears from her eyes and nodded.

"That's my brave girl. Now, you know the drill," he said, lifting her chin with one paw, although he still had her wrapped tightly with his other arm and tail, hand near her scruff, and she sighed.

"I'm fine," she said, with a huff of annoyance, but turned her instinct on anyway.

"I know, but you ran at the smell of her blood. I need to be sure," he said softly.

"I wasn't reacting to the blood, not that way," she replied, but waited until he told her she could turn it off, wondering if he was going to swing at her like her father had that last time. He didn't though, just had her turn it off after a minute or so and nodded, finally letting go of her.

She sagged in misery, turned, and slowly walked over to pick up the broken pieces of wood, and tossed them in the recycler, before returning to pick up the rest of the mess on her floor. When she looked up, Marcus was looking at Little Flower's painting, with an expression of sadness on his own face, before hiding it behind his mask and turning back to her.

"Come on. Ellie's waiting for us in the garden with lunch," he said.

"I'm not hungry," she replied. "Go on without me."

He frowned, but nodded and left. She watched him leave for a moment, honestly surprised that he'd left without insisting. She turned and looked back at the painting, wondering if that would be the last thing her sister ever drew, and decided she would make a frame equally as fitting, and sat for a long time, just staring at the picture and trying to decide what she wanted to do, and then her attention caught on some of the other drawings her sister had done, and an idea sprang to life.

Grabbing the drawing tablet they now shared, Marsee pulled up the drawings her sister had completed for the cub's book, flipped through them, and started working on her design. It took her several hours before she was happy. Looking over the materials and tools she'd grabbed earlier, when she'd planned on a far simpler design, she decided they weren't nearly good enough. Returning to the guild hall, she dug through the supplies trying to decide what she wanted, until her eyes caught on a small supply of rainbow wood, and she grinned. It was incredibly expensive, one of the few natural exports from the Ice Planet, nearly extinct, like the creatures from Earth, and the hardest to work with. She was honestly surprised to see it here, but realized it must have been sent as a gift. If stained right, the grain would glow under the right lighting conditions, and these samples had burls that would make them even more interesting and difficult to work with. To her relief, there was just enough, if she was careful.

She winced at the price but bought it anyway, not caring that it took a huge chunk out of her credits, and then made her way over to the tool cabinet, grabbed several additional tools and checked those out as well, and returned to her room and started working. In an act of penance for not protecting her sister, for not being fast enough, she poured her heart and soul into her craft, and with every loving motion sent up a prayer to the Ancient Gods to save her family.

# CHAPTER 17

# Damon: The End of His Line

Damon watched as Marsee ran past him, followed by Councilor Surellis, and he frowned. He knew from the trail of blood that he'd been mopping up, that it couldn't have been good. Everyone was talking about it, although no one was helping him clean, which wasn't surprising. Very few people even acknowledged him, even after all the time they'd been there. Only a few of the guys would even speak to him, and most of those were only friends *because* of his tattoos, and the anger they felt at being denied access to many of the guilds, and not having any say in what happened to them. The guilds had denied their request to join, and so far, no one else had sponsored any of the other men. After the council meeting the other day, he now knew his people never would. The venom in their words had stung, but he didn't blame them.

*Did she die?* he wondered. *Marsee seemed pretty upset.*

He turned back to his mopping to find himself facing the Senior Guild Master. "Ma'am, did Little Flower..."

"She had a healthy girl, but suffered fairly severe consequences in the process. We don't know how bad yet," she signed, not really paying attention to him, her focus on the two that had disappeared down the hall. With a heavy sigh, she turned and walked away. To his surprise though, she returned a few minutes later carrying a mop of her own, and began helping him clean up.

She must have noticed his surprise, although he didn't say anything. "Just because I'm the Senior Guild Master, doesn't mean I won't do the work that needs to be done. How are you adjusting to things here?"

He shrugged. "Many things are far better here. My apartment is nicer than anywhere I've ever lived before, but with the way everything has been set up, it will be a long time before I'll be able to do what really I want to do."

"What's that?" she asked.

"I want to be a pilot in the Ship's Guild," he replied.

"Ahh," she replied, nodding her understanding. "There are plenty of things you can learn in the meantime. We have no age restrictions in the Guild."

He shrugged again. "I have carpentry skills and took a few of the guild classes, but they're not for me. My dream is to fly." In reality though, he'd been excited about learning some of those crafts, but the others had been far less than welcoming, and after being told several times to go find something else to do, and the dozens of nasty looks he'd received, he'd stopped attending. He was still attending all of the mandatory classes, and could read the basics of Saber now. He had also downloaded the training manuals for the shuttles and ships, and was slowly picking his way through them.

She nodded and kept working, and the long hallway was just about clean when Senior Councilor Surellis appeared again.

"I'll finish up and take care of that mop for you, ma'am," he said, holding out his hand for it.

"Thank you," she replied, handing it over and leaving with the Councilor.

"It won't work," a voice said from behind him, and he turned to see Paul walking towards him.

"What won't?" he asked.

"Trying to get on their good side. I saw your conversation. She didn't even consider speaking up for you to get into the Ship's Guild. You know as well as I do, they're not going to drop the requirements, and it'll be another twelve Earth years before you get to fly a ship."

"The cats might sponsor us," Damon replied, picking up the bucket of water to carry it back to the maintenance shed.

Paul snorted. "In your dreams. They won't sponsor us until one of the women does first, just like Aaron and the others have stated. And you know damn well they won't do that. They're going to make us wait the entire time."

He shrugged and walked off. There was little he could do about it anyway.

That evening he decided to eat his meal out in the garden rather than returning to his room as he usually did, but regretted it almost immediately, as the group he went to sit near, stood and left as soon as he sat down. Vera, an older black woman, did not, at least not right away, and he was surprised.

"Evening, Vera," he said, trying to be polite.

She looked up from her tablet, and he realized she'd just hadn't seen him yet.

"It was," she replied dryly, and started to get up and leave.

He sighed and looked away. "Look, I get why you're all wary of me. But I'm not that person anymore. I was young and stupid when I got those tattoos but I couldn't afford to get them removed. What do I need to do to prove it? I've never done anything to hurt you, or said anything, as far as I know. If I have, I'm sorry."

She snorted. "Damon, don't you get it. If our history has shown us anything, people like you don't change. They might hide it better, but deep down inside, you're still just as racist, even if you have removed your tattoos. I doubt you will ever prove yourself to any of us, and certainly not to any of the women. Most of us have been hurt by people like you and frankly, most of us wish you'd just leave. Why should someone like you have survived, when so many other good people died?"

"You don't think I wouldn't leave if I could?" he snapped. "But I can't. I can't learn the skills I want to learn because of the policies you've all put in place. I've even offered to give up my Council position if you made me an adult, just so I can leave. You get to fly all over the universe and learn anything you want, but I'm treated like nothing more than a..."

"A slave?" she interrupted.

"I was going to say child," he replied. "What was done to you and your people was wrong. I didn't know any better when I was a kid, but I know that now."

"Damon, you and the rest of the men are experiencing what every woman here has spent their entire life dealing with. I've lost count of the number of jobs and careers I was denied just because of the color of my skin or what was in my pants. When I was younger, I couldn't even own my own checking account or credit card, and even though I had a solid job, for a time I was homeless because the banks wouldn't issue me a mortgage, and no one would let me rent an apartment because of the color of my skin. My grandmother was born a slave. She didn't even know who her mother was. It's our turn Damon. Get used to it."

She stood and started to walk away but turned back to him. "I just hope that your antiquated and destructive ways die off with you and your line."

"What do you mean by that?" he asked.

She snorted again. "If you think any woman here is going to have your children, you're sadly mistaken. Whether nature or nurture, we're not taking that chance," she said, and left.

He stared at her long after she'd left. Like all of the men, he'd left donations of his sperm at the clinic, in the event that something happened to him. Myra had stated that the donations would be anonymous. Only the healers would know. In order to best save the species, they were artificially inseminating the women, so that there would be as much genetic diversity as possible. Only a few of the women had paired up to do it the old fashioned way, and only with those that were officially adults. There were far more men than women rescued, so all the men knew there was little chance for a partnership, but he'd hoped that maybe a small part of his daughter could live on again in some other child, but now it would seem that was no longer an option either.

No longer hungry, he left the garden, tossing his meal into one of the recyclers. He walked around the compound until it was time for the evening's council meeting, growing angrier every minute. *What right do they have to just end my line? I've not committed any crimes, not like Mitch did, at least not since before, and I did my time and made good on it. If our birth dates are based on the date of the Cataclysm, shouldn't our records be based on our actions since then too?*

Paul was waiting for him outside of the council chamber and took one look at him and shook his head. "About time you got angry. What are you going to do about it?"

"I don't know," he replied. "I might just leave."

"They'll never let you leave," Paul replied. "You're nothing but a cub to them."

Paul was right. Damon tried again to get the Council to change things so that he could leave, but as much as he could tell everyone wanted him out of there, they weren't willing to make that change.

Paul didn't even bother with an 'I told you so.'

# CHAPTER 18

# Jeran: Hope

A day had passed, and still Little Flower had not woken, although her vitals had improved. GrandFather currently dozed in his chair, while Jer walked around the room holding the tiny cub, who had started to fuss but had been uninterested in nursing. His bright copper fur was clenched tightly in her paws, and he was completely enamored with the tiny thing. He had stepped out several times, to deal with Council related business, and to allow Marsee to come visit and meet her niece, but Myra hadn't left the room, only stepping out when nature called, and to briefly talk with Ammond about his findings, which were not good. They had begun normal treatments but were seeing little in the way of improvements.

With a frustrated growl at the unchanging monitors, she stood and walked out of the room and started to pace in the hallway.

Brice must have seen her leave the room and come over, as he heard the other healer ask if there was any change.

He shifted so he could better listen in on the conversation.

"No, and it worries me that she hasn't woken yet," Myra said. "I'm considering another blood transfusion. Did you find any other donors or was GrandFather the only one with his blood type?"

"We found two others, but they're both young children," Brice replied.

"Moons! GrandFather's not recovered enough for another transfusion. What about Ezra?" Myra asked.

"We're trying now. He's not much better than GrandFather, so we're taking it slowly," Brice replied.

"Anything's better than nothing," Myra said, ordering Brice to bring the unit once it was collected.

He frowned at the conversation and turned around to walk in the other direction. When he made it to the other side of the room he turned, but froze, not sure he was seeing what he was seeing at first.

"Myra! Get in here!" Jer called out. Myra bolted into the room to find Little Flower's eyes open and looking at her. He leaned over and woke GrandFather. When he looked back, Myra had her eyes closed and he was sure she was offering a prayer up to the Ancient Gods. So was he. *Please let it be true!* he prayed. Myra opened her eyes again and Little Flower smiled weakly at her, and tried to raise her arms to speak, but they fell back down.

Myra raced to her daughter's side. "Don't try to talk. Save your strength. You're okay, and you have a beautiful healthy baby girl."

Jer came around the bed and handed the cub to Myra who held her up for Little Flower to see. Little Flower started crying, and she struggled to lift her arm up to touch her cub, which she managed for a few moments, before her strength gave out, and her arm fell back to the bed. Myra carefully laid the cub on Little Flower's chest, and then helped her bring her arms up to hold her.

Little Flower caressed the soft fur on her daughter's head for several minutes before looking up at Myra.

"Do you have a name picked out for her?" Myra asked.

Little Flower gave a slight nod and said something to her grandfather.

"She says her name is Hope," he signed.

He and Myra both gasped at the memory of the daughter they'd lost to save Marsee. "That's a beautiful name for her," Myra signed back.

Little Flower smiled weakly, looked back at her cub, let out a heavy sigh, and closed her eyes.

When her paw slid down and her next breath was slow in coming, his heart nearly stopped with fear.

Myra looked up at the monitors frantically, but sighed with relief, and his heart started beating again. He said nothing as Myra hooked up an oxygen feed and watched as the stats stabilized.

"She's sleeping," she said to them after a few minutes, and then after flipping through the other scans she carefully tucked the cub in, and sat back down in her chair.

"That's a good sign," Jer said with a grin on his face. "She woke up and was able to speak."

Myra nodded. "Yes, but she was very weak, and her vitals dipped for a bit. She's not out of the wilds yet."

Jer nodded. "I'll let Marsee know she woke up for a few minutes, and let her know of her niece's name." He left the room with far more enthusiasm in his step than he'd had for the past day.

He found Marsee in her room, whiskers down in one of her crafts, hearing aids in, and fully focused on what she was doing. She didn't notice him when he appeared in her open door. He leaned up against the sill remembering just how tiny Marsee had been when she had been born. *Now look at her.* He was so proud of his daughter, of everything she'd accomplished and overcome.

"Marsee," he called out, but she didn't look up. *Still, some things apparently never change.* He chuckled and walked in. When he tapped her on her shoulder, she jumped with a yelp.

"Papa! Did you have to do that?" she asked, ears back and tail lashing.

"Sorry, Kitten. I figured you'd want to know; your sister woke up for a few minutes," he said.

Marsee brightened and her tail spiraled with joy. "How is she?"

"Weak, but she was able to tell GrandFather the name she'd picked out for her cub, before falling back to sleep," he replied.

"Oh?" she asked. "What is it?"

"Hope," he replied.

Marsee gasped, and he realized that she must know about her sister. "You knew?"

Marsee nodded. "Mama told me after we found out about Little Flower being pregnant. Can I go see her now?"

Jer nodded, and she bolted out of the room, the tool she'd been holding clattered to the floor in her wake. He smiled as he watched her go, grateful to bring her some good news for a change, and bent down to pick up the tool. When he set it on her desk he looked closely at the project she was working on, and raised a brow in surprise. *What have we here?* He picked up the piece of wood she'd been carving. *This is beautiful,* he thought, tilting the wood to make it sparkle. The shifting light made it almost look like the creature she'd carved moved. Marsee rarely put this much effort into her crafts. They were solid and functional, but she rarely spent a lot of time embellishing them. *Ellie will need to see this when it's done,* he thought, looking at the image displayed on the tablet left behind. It was a fairly ambitious project she was attempting, and if the rest came out as good it would be a work of art. *She's changed so much since that day in the garden,* he thought with relief.

She'd put a significant amount of energy into translating the charters and other legal documents into sign, and then had even translated a few of the books the Hue-mans had recreated into the other languages, and was spending a lot of her time in the guild hall helping to translate and teach the Hue-mans the various crafts. He'd been learning the Hue-man's written language, but he was nowhere near as fluent as she was. The translation programs routinely messed up, leaving him scratching his head at the meaning most days, but Marsee seemed to have no problems.

He set the unfinished project back down on her desk, and walked outside to look at the view from the tower. He hadn't been up here in a while, and even he couldn't believe how much his home had changed in such a short amount of time. With a prayer of thanks to the Ancient Gods, that his daughter had woken up, he made his way down the ramp and back over to his office to continue working for a few hours before returning to the trauma ward.

"How is she doing?" he asked Myra when he returned.

"No change," Myra replied as Marsee handed Hope over to him and left. "She hasn't woken again."

Jer nodded and started walking slowly around the room, purring, as the tiny cub snuggled in close. The room was small though, so he left to walk out in the hall, whispering quietly to the cub that he doubted could even hear him.

Suddenly, both Ammond and Brice came running down the hall from opposite directions and bolted into his daughter's room. He hurried back and waited just outside of the room as the three of them rapidly spoke. He understood one word in three as they were examining her scans, but he knew enough to tell that Little Flower's heart was still beating, and she was still breathing at least.

Ammond left and returned a few minutes later carrying his specialized brain scanner and set it up, and they began another rapid fire discussion.

Jer swallowed hard as Myra turned away and Ammond placed a paw on her shoulder to comfort her.

"Myra? What's going on?" he asked.

Myra looked up at him, her face full of grief and heartbreak, and she left the room without answering.

"Myra?" he asked again, and then turned to Ammond for an explanation.

The ancient healer's mask was missing, and showed his own grief and worry. "I'm sorry Jer. Her brain activity has decreased substantially. She's in a coma, and I don't know how to fix her."

Darkness and silence surrounded her, and wrapped her in an agony of pain and confusion. She tried to move, to open her eyes, to scream, but her traitorous body refused to respond.

She drifted between dreams and this dark, silent, painful world, until she wasn't sure if she was awake or dreaming.

*It must be a dream,* she decided eventually, and wondered if she could control the dream.

She tried pushing away from her body and the pain. There was a stretching sensation followed by a silent pop that she felt more than heard, and suddenly she was floating above her body. A thin cord connected her, and held her in place like an anchor to a boat, and the agony of her body receded.

*Oh, this is so much better!* she thought, and relaxed.

Before long even the memory of the pain was forgotten.

# CHAPTER 19

# Myra: Coma

"It's been days. Why aren't any of our treatments working?" Myra growled, struggling to keep the anguish from her voice, as she poured through the dozens of scans they'd taken, trying to figure out what they were missing.

"I wish I had an answer for you, Myra," Brice replied. "We know so little about how their brains work or how capable they are of repairing damage as extensive as this."

Ammond changed the display back to the scan taken right before Little Flower had slipped into her coma, and pointed to several spots on one of the scans. "I'm pretty sure she was awake here, based on the increased activity in these areas."

"So what happened right afterwards? It's almost like she's been sedated," Myra asked. "We certainly haven't seen scans like that from any of the other bi-peds except for then."

Brice gave her a pointed look and Myra growled at her. "I know what you're thinking, don't." Brice pursed her lips, but said nothing.

The quiet beep of Little Flower's monitors filled the trauma unit, while they considered. Even though Myra had been a healer for over a hundred years, this was the first time someone in her immediate family had ever been this injured or sick. When her parents had died, it had been in a shuttle accident, and they'd died instantly. And while all of her cubs had their share of illnesses and broken bones, it had been nothing like this. Even the weeks Marsee had spent in the trauma ward hadn't been as bad, as every day she'd gotten a little better, and a little stronger. She'd known how to treat those injuries, but nothing they'd tried had worked on this tiny Hue-man she now called her daughter. She'd never felt so hopeless and out of ideas.

Plus, she was still reeling from that mornings session with the review board. Because of her prior conviction, Jer had been forced to request a review of Little Flower's case, to confirm that she hadn't made a mistake in her daughter's care that lead to this outcome. She was still waiting for their report, but they had identified several areas of additional study to fund, including figuring out why the repair on the rib hadn't held. Thankfully she wouldn't be charged for that as she'd reached out to the other Healers at the Agency when the rib hadn't healed the way she'd liked to begin with, and the review board had agreed prior to the trial that it hadn't needed to be surgically repaired. They still had no idea how it had broken, or caused so much damage in the process, but it did appear to be a fault with the bone knitter, as Ezra's leg had broken in the same place it had been broken when he'd been rescued from Earth.

Ammond looked over at Myra, snapping her out of her thoughts, and then refocused on the scans, zooming in and examining different areas of her daughter's injured brain. "You might be onto something, Myra. The worst of the damage to her brain is in the areas here and here, and that would be consistent from my research as the parts of their brain that controls waking and sleep, as well as fine motor control. It's possible she's stuck in a deep sleep state. It's also possible that even if she did wake, she might not be able to move."

"She was very weak, but she was able to move her arm and head when she woke that one time," Myra countered.

"If she's appearing to be sedated, maybe an anti-sedative would work," Brice suggested.

"It's worth a try," Ammond said with a shrug. "It certainly won't hurt her if it doesn't work."

Myra agreed and left the room to locate the required meds. A few minutes later she returned and injected it into her daughter's arm. They all watched the scans as Little Flower's vitals and brain activity reacted to the anti-sedative, giving them all a brief sense of hope, but that hope was fleeting, as within a few minutes she returned to the same nearly catatonic state as before.

Myra swore, but Ammond reached out a paw to comfort her. "We did get a reaction out of her. If nothing else, that tells us we might be onto something. Try upping the dose."

"We've never used a higher dose on them, Ammond. I don't know if that would be safe," Myra replied.

Ammond took the hypo from Myra and checked the meds she'd used and pulled up the information on that particular anti-sedative. "You should be able to use triple the normally recommended dose of this without any risk of harm. The initial trials used a dosage even higher on our cubs without any side-effects, but we should wait another hour until this dose is fully out of her system, just in case."

He handed the hypo back to Myra, and she set it down on the table next to her. Ammond flipped the scans back in time to review the changes they'd seen, zoomed, and rotated, frowned, zoomed back out, and tapped a claw absently on the railing of the bed.

"I know that look Ammond. What have you found?" Myra asked her mentor.

"This part of her brain flared with activity right before she started descending back into that catatonic state," he said, tapping a spot on the monitor.

"Isn't that where they process their sense of touch?" Brice asked.

"I believe so, but it has other purposes too," Ammond said absently, not particularly listening to either of them as his brain raced through the possibilities. He flipped to another scan showing chemical output. "That's what I thought," he muttered, tapping one of them. "This here is the same chemical they produce when they cry." Ammond carefully examined Little Flower's eyes ,and then gently ran a finger across one eye, feeling dampness, and then flicked back to the brain scan. "This part of the brain is used for processing touch, but unlike us, they also use it to process pain. There was a massive spike in activity here, but nowhere else. Add in the chemical change, and the fact that there's an increase in tear production, I'd say she's in pain, and quite a bit of it. I suppose it could be possible that her brain is trying to protect her from it."

Myra blanched. "That was a pretty invasive operation, and we didn't have time to administer the normal pain blocks, but it's been several days, so the worst of her incisions should be healed, and we've dosed her with several rounds of nanos since."

"That would only treat surface pain. She's missing half a rib, and there could be significant nerve endings in that bone, as well as any place those edges could be rubbing. Let's try injecting her with a nano solution around her incision points, and at the end of this rib, and I think we should administer a pain block even if she is unconscious. I'm sure you remember how uncomfortable it was for you after your emergency surgery to give birth to Marsee. Just because she's healed from her incisions, doesn't mean her body isn't still going through some fairly traumatic changes to adjust from no longer being pregnant. We only have a few pregnancies to compare to, but her hormone levels are still not back to what we believe is normal," Ammond said.

Myra nodded and left once more to retrieve the suggested supplies. Ten minutes later, the pain block was administered and Myra began carefully injecting the nanos.

"I really wish we could give Little Flower another transfusion. Her blood count is still far too low, and she's still spotting," Myra said while she worked.

"I checked on GrandFather this morning. He's improving, but I'm not sure he's recovered enough for another transfusion. His blood count was still far lower than normal too. We could try if we took it really slowly and pumped him full of fluids, but I'd feel better if we waited another day or two. I'm thinking we should put in a permanent feeding tube first. She's already losing weight," Brice suggested, as she handed Myra another syringe.

Myra nodded. "Hope is taking a lot out of her with her nursing. Did we hear back from the other mothers to see if they could donate or nurse?"

"Margaret has already stopped breast feeding and Janet was able to donate some but she doesn't have a lot to spare. The others haven't given birth yet. Maybe once they do we'll be able to have them start nursing Hope too," Brice replied.

"GrandFather said they had a formula made from the milk of one of their planet's other animals. Sadly that species didn't survive. I've got a few scientists working on trying to synthesize a replacement, but I'm worried that Hope won't get the nutrition she needs if she doesn't nurse. She's so small compared to the other two, and we've had such a hard time keeping weight on the Hue-mans as it is," Myra said, as she set the last syringe down. Brice brought everything back out to sterilize and they waited several minutes to allow the pain block time to fully take effect, before taking another scan.

"That chemical is going down. Looks like you were right," Myra said to her mentor.

"Can I get that in writing?" he teased, trying to lighten the mood a little.

"If you can get her to wake up again, I'll have one of the Hue-mans tattoo it on my forehead," Myra said, with a slight curl of amusement in her tail.

"Deal!" he chuckled. An hour later, they tried the anti-sedative again. Like the first time there was an increase in brain activity, but this time even though there was no spike in pain, Little Flower never woke, and after a while, returned to her prior state.

Myra growled the moment the monitors started showing a decrease in brain activity again, and left the room to pace in the hallway. Ammond and Brice followed her out eventually.

"Prep the surgery to put the feeding tube in," she told Brice, "and bring Rachael and Irene in and set them up in a recovery room for around the clock monitoring. If they have any complications when they go into labor, I don't want to lose any time getting them here."

Brice nodded and left to make the arrangements. Myra walked over to the nearest window and leaned her forehead up against the glass. Ammond followed her and wrapped an arm around her. "We'll figure it out, Myra," Ammond said, trying to comfort her.

"What do we even try next? All of the normal treatments have failed and even if we do wake her, there might not be anything left of *her* in there," Myra said, stating her fears.

"We start by trying to figure out why our treatments have failed, and treat her as best we can, and if not, we do our best to keep her alive long enough for Hope to survive on her own," he said gently. "And then we let her go."

Myra growled, but leaned into her mentor, hoping that day would never come.

Brice returned a few minutes later to let her know the surgery was prepped. Myra returned to her daughter's room and carefully carried her down to the surgery. They successfully implanted the feeding tube, and several of Little Flower's vitals increased and stabilized after her first feeding, but still, she did not wake.

# CHAPTER 20

# GrandFather: Apprentice

James walked into the newly built habitat known as 'The Barn' and took a deep breath as the smell of animals hit him. He found it oddly comforting and reminded him of home. The barn was a massive three story enclosed habitat designed to provide long term care and enrichment for the various species from Earth, although it resembled more of an indoor zoo than any barn he'd ever been in.

He'd been so busy helping Jer and the others with running the compound that he'd only been in here a few times since it had been built, and not since the last of the creatures had been transferred from the Agency. Between translating requests by his people, who were still learning to communicate with sign language, and managing the logistics of caring for everyone that lived here, he'd almost forgotten how much he enjoyed being in a barn.

The last few weeks though, as his granddaughter remained trapped in a coma, he'd felt useless and restless. He couldn't stand the hospital room any longer, and he needed to find a way to help her. He eventually decided to see if Nazari's offer of mentorship to the Healer's Guild was still on the table. He had decades of veterinary experience, but had been planning to retire from that trade and go into politics as a councilor, as he was getting too old to risk being kicked by an unruly horse, but now he hoped he could transfer some of that knowledge into helping his granddaughter. He'd tried helping Myra with what he knew about human anatomy, but the human brain wasn't his specialty, and none of the others rescued had been doctors or nurses either.

He'd asked several people to teach him, so far without luck. Myra was so busy trying to figure out how to save Little Flower, that she didn't have time to teach him the basics. Brice had taken over running the clinic in Myra's absence, so she was out, and Ammond had temporarily set aside his research on trying to figure out how to fix everyone's hearing loss, to focus on running hundreds of tests on how the human brain normally worked, to better help Myra, and the other brain specialists she'd wrangled into helping her. He'd shaved his head and spent days wearing an uncomfortable mesh hat and letting Ammond scan him performing every activity the ancient healer could think of, many of which were rather embarrassing.

Ammond was now busy scanning other volunteers for comparison, and didn't need him anymore. He tried helping with Little Flower's daily care but the ward was designed for the Saber's convenience in treating their patients, and not for someone as tiny as he was in comparison. The best he could do now was sit and watch his grandchildren while Myra and Ammond researched.

Nor was he willing to travel to the Healer's Guild in Council City and leave his granddaughter behind for the training offered there, which left Nazari, the only other master healer that still permanently lived at the compound. Most of the other healers had left to return home to their families, now that their care was no longer needed. Several of the journeymen who remained behind had offered to help tutor him and answer questions, but they weren't qualified or even allowed to take a protege yet, according to the rules of the Healer's Guild. Nazari had specialized and switched to Animal Healing after she'd earned her masters, so he was hopeful that she'd at least be willing to teach him the basics, if not mentor him outright, like she'd once offered.

His feelings for the healer were mixed though. She'd been his healer at the Agency, and while he understood why they'd been kept in isolation, there was still a lot of trauma there, which was another one of the reasons he hadn't taken her up on her offer before, and he wasn't sure if that offer was still on the table, as he'd voted against her bid for adoption.

He'd spoken to Little Flower about it before she'd gone into labor, argued about it more realistically. She'd wanted him to represent Nazari at the Full Council, to appeal the vote that had taken the child from her, but he honestly felt that the child would be better cared for by his own species in the long run, by most people anyway. He'd been surprised that Damon had volunteered, but, like everyone else, figured it was just a ploy to earn his adulthood, and there was no way he was giving him a child.

Looking around, and not seeing anyone, he decided to check the main floor first. Unlike the Trauma Center, the Barn was designed for both Human and Saber use, which was impressive considering that the adult female Sabers were twenty feet tall when they stood on their back legs, and practically the size of elephants when on all fours. The barn was broken up into multiple areas designed for the different kinds of creatures that had been rescued. The main entrance of the barn held stalls for the bigger creatures, but rather than the standard twelve by twelve foot stalls he was used to, each stall was at least ten times that size, designed to support multiple creatures, although smaller stalls were available for when a creature needed to be isolated for individual care. These all connected to much larger outdoor runs that spanned hundreds of acres of land that had been fenced in, for the parts of the day that were cool enough for the animals to go outside and run.

The Sabers must have landed at several farms during the rescue as most of the creatures were domesticated. Horses, llamas, sheep, goats, pigs, chickens, turkeys, dogs of various breeds, and mostly undomesticated barn cats, had been the predominant species rescued, although oddly no cows, which was making feeding Hope a challenge. There were a few female goats that had been rescued, but they were all currently pregnant and not actively nursing. There was also a smattering of deer, bears, a mountain lion mother with two cubs that had been born after the rescue, a couple of raccoons, half a dozen different species of birds, and one lone skunk. The biggest surprises were the three zebras, two female giraffes, and a porcupine.

There were also two very cranky geese. He'd stopped to look at them on the way over, and he wasn't sure if they were the same two that they'd been gifted by their neighbors, but he thought they might be. *They would be the ones to survive,* he thought bitterly. There were warnings on their pens and paddock in all six languages warning people not to approach. *I'd better tell Nazari to put a shield around that pen. A fence isn't going to be nearly good enough. I'm surprised they haven't figured out how to get out yet. We never could keep them in.*

The Water Sprites had rescued dolphins, three species of octopuses, three smaller species of whales, lobsters, a giant sea turtle, thankfully full of eggs, and a wide variety of fish and other creatures that had been rescued from a commercial fishing net, but these had all been moved to the Water World, where the oceans nearly matched the salinity of Earth's old oceans.

They'd found a few local replacements for needed protein sources, but no one really liked them much. So they were also hopeful that in another few months they'd be able to start gathering unfertilized eggs from the chickens, although there wouldn't be enough to feed everyone. The few fish that they had found both reasonably edible and containing the iron they needed had to be shipped all the way from the Water World, as most of the fish they'd rescued hadn't been repopulated enough to consider harvesting yet either.

For all their teeth and claws, the Saber's were vegetarian and were very uncomfortable with the idea of raising the other animals for food, although they understood that it was necessary for their species survival, since much of the foods they could eat didn't give them all the nutrients they needed. Everyone was on daily supplements and several groups of scientists were working on synthetic solutions to the problem, but the first few samples tested were horrid, and that was being kind.

They did have some domestic animals, like the chenzies, which they raised for their wool. The bodies of those animals when they died of old age were being donated for food for the carnivorous species rescued, rather than the current practice of placing their bodies out in the wild for local carnivores to use, but since those creatures lived for close to eighty local years, they were few and far between. They had tried grilled chenzie, but that had sadly proved to taste horrible. As of yet, there was still no equivalent to a steak or bacon cheeseburgers.

He was sad that so many species had been lost, but he was also pragmatic, in that if it weren't for their rescuers, they would have all been lost when the asteroid had hit, and if humanity had kept on with their complete disregard for the environment, the rest probably would have gone extinct in another few generations anyway. *I wonder how Little Flower was doing with that cub's book. Maybe Marsee and I can finish it for her so she'll have it when she wakes,* he thought.

He walked past several rows of stalls looking for Nazari without success. A bright purple 'wheelbarrow' sat outside of one of the stalls and shovel-fulls of horse manure were being tossed out of an open door. Unlike the wheelbarrows of home though, this miracle floated a foot or so off the ground, and could handle ten times the weight of a traditional one, and you didn't even have to push it. It would follow you around, and when it was full, you just had to push a button and it would empty itself in the compost and return. He turned and made his way down to the stall and found Henry Curtis, singing as he cleaned.

James leaned up against the wall, listening and watching appreciatively. Henry was a handsome and muscular man, with skin several shades darker than his own, and his deep voice stirred something in him that he thought he'd never feel again. He still grieved for his lost partner, and honestly had no idea if Henry or anyone else who had been rescued was gay or not. He'd been too afraid to even ask, and forming a relationship with someone hadn't mattered all that much, outside of the desire for company.

He'd been far too busy, but now with his granddaughter in a coma, he was finding he was lonely. The Chenziras that had taken her in and adopted her were good company, but he missed having someone of his own kind to talk to, someone that he could commiserate with about missing donuts and the like. Everyone he'd met had been nice enough, but no one had even remotely sparked an interest in him, and most of the men were still angry with him for going along with the age of adulthood. To his surprise though, the few men who had been granted their adulthood hadn't immediately turned around and sponsored any of the others yet either, like they'd all expected, but then the risks of making a mistake were even higher now.

Following the session, where his granddaughter had shown everyone what had happened to her, the Council had voted to make several changes around rape and sexual assault. Now any sexual assault that involved penetration was considered rape, regardless of whether or not the person could become pregnant. They had also raised the age of sexual consent to adulthood, added mandatory health classes as part of their primary education, and made all forms of birth control a protected right.

Now none of the women would engage in a physical relationship with any of the men until they earned their adulthood. This of course rankled with the men who hadn't been granted adulthood status. He honestly thought it was rather fitting, and it was proving to be more of an incentive than he'd thought. Behavior among the men had changed almost overnight, as they began courting in earnest.

Henry jumped in surprise when he saw him standing there, and then smiled sheepishly before nodding a greeting. "Morning GrandFather. How long have you been listening?"

His soft, southern accent was just as deep as his singing voice but Henry's greeting made him sigh. James's name sign was GrandFather, and most people had taken to calling him that even when spoken. He didn't mind since he was one of the oldest people rescued, not that he considered himself old, but he didn't particularly *want* Henry to think of him as a grandfather.

"James, please, and long enough to know I'd like to hear more. Haven't heard that song before. What's it called?"

Henry nodded to his request. "Guess you never made it on to TikTok. It was all the rage with the kids before. It's called 'The Wellerman'."

"Nah, I didn't have time for social media. Barely managed to keep up with my email most days, but you have a beautiful voice. You should sing some evening."

Most nights, if it wasn't raining, people would gather in the garden to socialize, sing, and play music. While just about everyone had suffered some form of hearing loss, Ammond had been working through the group and restoring what he could. About a fifth of the people rescued now had at least partial hearing restored, while the others were either waiting their turn, or like his granddaughter, experienced damage so severe that it was unlikely their hearing would ever be fully restored. It didn't matter much though, as everyone was now fluent in sign language to be able to communicate with the other species, since their vocal and auditory ranges didn't fully overlap. They could only hear the voices of the children, and the Sabers could only hear the deeper ranges of their voices. He expected they could probably hear Henry quite easily though. He'd never heard a deeper voice before.

Henry shrugged and looked away in embarrassment. "I don't really like singing in front of people, but thank you."

GrandFather nodded. "I totally understand. I was never one for karaoke myself. Then again, my voice is nowhere near as nice as yours. Oh who am I kidding, my voice is horrible. The one time I was drunk enough to try, I got kicked out, literally. Anyways, I was looking for Nazari, have you seen her?"

"Next aisle over, least she was about ten minutes ago," Henry replied. "Thanks!"

Henry nodded and tossed another rake full of manure into the wheelbarrow, a good fifteen feet away. James continued down the aisle and smiled as Henry started singing again, and made the decision to try and get to know him a little better. If nothing else, he could use some friends.

True to Henry's words, he found Nazari sitting next to a draft horse that was standing in cross ties in the middle of the aisle. The massive Belgian didn't even come up to Nazari's shoulders and the sight made him smile wistfully. The horse reminded him of Buster. He'd been a really good work horse and an even better trail horse, and he missed the old guy.

"Hello GrandFather! It's nice to see you again. What brings you to the Barn?" Nazari asked as he walked up beside her.

GrandFather gave the horse a gentle pat and then signed back. "I came to find you, actually."

"Oh, what can I do for you?" Nazari asked.

"I was hoping that offer of mentorship to the Healer's Guild was still on the table. I want to learn so I can help Little Flower, but everyone else is too busy to start training me, and I don't want to go to the Healer's Guild while Little Flower is still in a coma."

"I would gladly take you on as an protege, but on one condition," Nazari replied.

"What's that?" he asked, wondering if Nazari would ask him to advocate for her. He would, if she asked. As a Councilor he couldn't deny anyone's request for an advocate, and well, if it helped his granddaughter, he would do anything.

"That you teach me everything you know about the animals from your planet. Like this fellow here," she said, giving the horse a scratch on the withers.

The horse groaned with pleasure at the scratching, clearly not in the least bit uncomfortable with the giant predator sitting next to him, and James had to chuckle. The giant draft horse looked like a miniature pony next to the big cat.

"From what we can tell, it looks like part of his sex organs were purposely removed. Why would your species do that?" Nazari asked.

James snorted, not even remotely expecting that question. "That was a common practice. The stallions can be unruly and difficult to handle when the mares come into heat, and most breeders wanted to ensure that only their best would breed. It was big business and people made a lot of money that way, especially if the horse was used for racing and won regularly."

"I still don't fully understand your concept of money, but I could see how their bigger size could have been a challenge for you," Nazari said.

"It's a shame though that this big guy was gelded. I used to have a horse that looked an awful lot like him. He was the best horse I've ever known, and I've worked with a lot of them. We could have really used his genetic material."

"Oh that's not a problem. Once we had the scans from an intact male, we were able to regrow them. He's fully functional now and we've seen no signs of aggression from him."

"You can do that?" he asked, "That's incredible! Well aren't you a lucky guy? Bet all the ladies just love you!" he said, patting the big horse again.

"Well, as the only adult male horse, they do, although he seems to like you an awful lot too," Nazari said, as her tail curled. The horse had been sniffing him all over.

"If this was Buster, he'd take my..." he started to sign, but then the horse grabbed his hat and started waving it up and down just as Buster used to. "...hat", he finished. *Not possible...* he thought, and walked around to the other side of the horse to be sure. Sure enough on his back leg was a dark brown spot that looked just like a handprint. James put his hand on the spot and started crying as he leaned up against the side of his old friend, taking a deep breath of his familiar scent.

Nazari followed him around the horse and tapped him on the shoulder. "What's wrong, GrandFather?"

"I'm almost entirely sure this is my horse, Buster. Well technically he was my partner's horse. Ben raised him from a baby. Is there any way you could find out if it is? He would have been rescued close to where I was. I was out riding him when the shockwave hit and had only just left his side when I was knocked out by a Flyer. He had a badly broken leg that would have meant we would have had to put him down, but with your technology..."

"Well you were brought in together," Nazari said. "According to the reports I had. You never asked about him though, so I thought maybe not."

"Myra said that none of the males of his species survived," James replied.

"That was probably a translation issue. He wasn't fertile when we rescued him, so he wasn't listed as a male," Nazari explained, and then pulled her tablet off of her carry harness and started tapping away. A minute later, she handed him the tablet and he watched as two flyers swooped down, stunned him and Buster and carried them both off, Buster's very distinctive saddle still on him.

"Oh Buster! It is you! I can't believe it, but you made it too!" He gave the horse another big hug. "I just hope Little Flower wakes so I can tell her about you," GrandFather said to the big horse.

"So," Nazari said, her tail curled in happiness for him. "When do you want to start?"

"I don't have anything to do but pace in Little Flower's room, so now is as good a time as any."

"Perfect, tell me everything you know about this creature and then we'll compare that to what I've learned, and then I'll show you how to use the scanners. First though, what did you mean by 'you were riding him'?"

The look on Nazari's face as he explained was priceless.

# CHAPTER 21

# Marcus: War Room

Marcus placed his paw on the access panel to the Ancient Archives, one he had looked at hundreds of times over the years with the longing of an unrequited love. The door which until a few months ago had been off limits, now slid open to reveal a massive chamber filled with books that went all the way back to the founding. Stepping through he took a deep breath, and sighed with contentment, as the door slid closed behind him.

He'd spent most of the first two hundred years of his life dreaming about being in this room, an area of the archives that was reserved to only a select group of people. More than likely he could have asked former Senior Councilor Tabor for access, but he knew himself too well. He'd never have been able to pull himself away long enough to attend to his normal duties. Only his oath to his people kept him from spending every waking moment in this room now.

As it was, he *should* be preparing for the upcoming meeting of the Full Council, but he needed a break. With his unexpected promotion to Senior Councilor, his workload had quadrupled, and he had reached his limit. Not only was he dealing with the struggles of figuring out how to be a Senior Councilor, when the normal transition period had not happened, he was dealing with the needs of a district he wasn't familiar with, and trying to deal with the fallout from the Trial. *Paxton was right not to want this position,* he thought. *All my years as Acting Senior, and I still wasn't prepared.*

He knew the coming council meeting was going to be hard, if not downright brutal. The people were furious with both the Senior Council for their decisions at the Trial, and his council for their actions prior that had warranted it. Even though they'd not been found guilty, the people were still calling for his council to resign. He was shocked no one had actually been voted out yet, but it was close in a number of districts. The press had been hounding them hard as well, picking over every decision past and present, and the other planets were furious that he and Jer now had a third of the vote. It was especially bad on both the Water World and the Ice Planet, where protests had already started, but the unrest was spreading to Flyer and Digger as well, and it was all he could do to calm things down.

He'd even gone so far as to publicly state that he was intending to step down, after his term as Jeran's replacement was done, not that anyone believed him. The only reason he hadn't stepped down yet was because, while his ratings were the lowest they'd ever been for him, they were still higher than everyone else's, save for Paxton's, who repeatedly told him he didn't want the position. Marcus had made him his Acting Senior anyway, partly out of spite, but also because he'd come to respect Paxton over the past few months, even if he didn't always agree with him.

He was being very careful about what he brought forth for the Full Council Meeting, knowing that he would have a hard time getting anything through. Nazari had reached out to him to discuss the possibility of appealing the decision, and as much as he agreed with Jer that the vote had been cast in retaliation, public opinion was bad enough that he'd advised her not to submit her appeal until after the council meeting, as with how things were going now, he was quite sure it would not go well for her. He planned to discuss Nazari's case with the other Seniors, and see if they could come to a decision outside of the Full Council, if there was time. She was disappointed, but she understood, and to her credit, she was spending more time with the other cubs who remained in the nursery, and he hoped that if perhaps her appeal failed, they might allow her to adopt one of the other cubs. Interestingly none of the other Hue-mans had stepped up to adopt the other cubs yet either, although several had at least started spending time with them.

He was honestly surprised Jer still had full favor with his council, as was the press, according to the last broadcast he'd watched. In addition to being livid about Jer's promotion, they were angry about paying for the added reimbursement given to the Hue-mans, although no one denied that they deserved it. They just didn't think it was fair that they were the ones paying for the Council's crimes, and he supposed they were right. His council was fully aware that it was entirely likely that none of their budget items would pass, so as of his last meeting, they'd decided to only put forth critical infrastructure needs, to help offset the impact. He personally doubted that would be enough.

He let out a heavy sigh, and allowed the smell of the ancient books to soothe his stress, and willed himself to forget the challenges of the universe for a few minutes, as he wandered the stacks trying to figure out what to read. He had several pet research projects he was working on, but he was looking for something different tonight, but he wasn't sure what.

For the last several decades he'd taken his lack of access to this area as penance for not being brave enough to accept the senior councilor position before, for fear he'd be the one to have to put his younger brother and niece down, when they'd both struggled with their instincts.

The gods had answered his prayers and they'd both survived. It was fairly common for junior councilors to struggle with their instincts after their test, and Jer had been no exception. Thankfully his efforts had worked and Jer had regained control, but then his youngest daughter had been born an only cub too, and very early on showed signs of psychosis that had them all worried. They'd all tried working with her, to no avail, but amazingly she'd survived where no one else ever had, and they now had a possible cure, or at least a better treatment, if the reports coming in from the Guard were any indication. He still had nightmares of that night in the garden, and not just because Myra had attacked him when she'd thought he was going to execute her daughter.

Seeing his niece lost to her instinct, and knowing what he had to do, had very nearly broken him.

It had been months now and he still hadn't gotten over the unexpected events that had occurred at Little Flower's sentience trial, or the day after, and frankly neither had the rest of the Seniors. He'd been just as surprised as the rest of the Council when Little Flower had turned down the position of Senior Councilor, but had never expected she'd somehow manage to overturn Jeran's conviction, and get him sworn in instead. *Little Flower would have made an incredible Senior Councilor,* he thought. *We could really use someone who can adapt and think like her.*

He sighed with worry and sent up a prayer to the Ancient Gods for his newest niece. Shaking his head at how emaciated she'd looked the last time he visited, nothing like the vibrant young woman he had grown to respect, he refocused his thoughts on the room around him. There was little he could do to help his niece right now, and for the moment, he had a few free minutes to explore, and he shouldn't be wasting it on things he couldn't change.

Two hundred years of waiting to view the archives and he hadn't been disappointed. Every trip he allowed himself brought something new and exciting to read, and he wished he could read everything, even though he knew that was impossible. Unless there was something specific he needed to research, he usually just picked a random direction, and a different stack every time he went, letting fate, or the Ancient Gods perhaps, pick his path.

He pulled out his pair of the special gloves designed to protect the ancient documents from accidental damage by his claws, and wandered for nearly half an hour, waiting for something to catch his eye, heading further and further into the stacks, far past where he'd been before, when to his immense surprise, what caught his attention wasn't an ancient book or manuscript at all, but an access panel next to a nondescript door, in an out of the way and hidden corner of the archives. *Could be nothing more than a supply closet,* he thought, but walked over anyway. *But then a supply closet wouldn't be locked either.*

Marcus placed his palm on the reader and the door opened revealing the heavy scent of old books, and the stale air of a room not accessed in a very long time. A light flickered on showing him more stacks of books. Marcus started scanning the books and flicked his ears back in surprise as he realized just what he was seeing. He carefully pulled one out and brought it over to the workbench in the center of the room, designed to handle these old documents, yet clearly not touched for a long time. A thin layer of dust covered the table. He quickly cleaned it off and then with barely contained excitement flipped the cover to reveal the title page, and gasped. *This isn't just ancient! It's from before!*

He wasn't aware that anything existed from before. A few rare copies yes, but not the originals. The date on the book was in the old format, almost two hundred years before the Great Awakening, and before they came to their new world and started the new date system. This was from a time when years were identified by the reign of the current ruler. He carefully turned the page, marveling at the nearly perfect condition of the book, and began reading an ancient handwritten script.

*It is with a heart aching with grief unbounded that I record the passing of General Chenzira only a day after learning of a new world suitable for our species. Would that she could have made it to our new home, for she is the whole reason we survived what I pray will be the last of the plague wars. She fought the plague-ridden for fifty long years and was one of the few guards not to succumb to the plague herself. And so now I begin this journal in the hopes that her story at least should make it to that new world.*

*Chenzira was born on the third day of the fourth month in the third year of Edents Reign. Her father, a commander in the Guard, her mother a Medica, and she an only cub, there was great fear she would succumb to the plague, and for a time it appeared like she would, but the gods must have seen her worth because she was one of the lucky ones to survive. She rose quickly in the Guard and was promoted to Commander in the Port City of Presthsda at the incredibly young age of one and twenty, following the un-expected death of her father.*

*Only a month later the war would begin and her city destroyed in that first attack. Word reached her prior and she was able to evacuate her people before the attack began and drive off the invaders. Amazingly only one death occurred, a guard by the name of Renny Wintersday. Some state that Chenzira and Wintersday were considering partnership, but if that was the case, she never told me.*

*Following the attack, the Council of Elders promoted her to General for her success in protecting her people and driving off the attack. As with all attacks, many eventually succumbed to the plague, and before long our borders were under siege by the plague-ridden, sent to decimate us before the main forces. Time and again, Chenzira succeeded, and those highest in her ranks survived without succumbing. It would be impossible to remember the details of fifty years of war, but I witnessed many of those battles and recorded them for posterity in the hopes that we might one day be victorious. What is included is only a smattering of the many victories she won, but these are the ones most pivotal to our eventual success.*

Marcus read through the short journal fairly quickly and sat back stunned that he'd never even heard the name of their last General, and for her to have his brother's partner's family name was astounding. *I wonder if they're related,* he thought absently, wondering if psychosis was inherited, since this other Chenzira had struggled with her hunter's instinct before learning to control it, much like Marsee.

He carefully put the book away wondering what the General's first name was, since they never mentioned it. *Typical. People always leave out the important details figuring no one would ever forget them. Grace,* he wondered, remembering the name on Myra's deed. *No, the author said she died before they came here, her children, grandchildren perhaps? It would certainly explain why Myra's deed was so big.*

Marcus wandered and picked out another book and gasped when he realized this one was several thousand years older than the prior one had been. He'd never even seen a book this old, much less touched one. For that matter, he didn't even know their history went back that far. This one too described a war, and he realized quickly that it was the first of the plague wars, as the general who's journal he was now reading struggled to understand this new enemy, and what was happening to his own troops after engaging. It took him several hours to read that one, struggling with language that had shifted far more than he was used to. He yawned and considered heading home for the night but decided to check out one more.

*How odd,* he thought as he put the book away. He'd always been taught that their sentience had come from defeating psychosis, but this general described it like an actual plague that had destroyed their sentience. He took a picture of one of the descriptions and sent it off to the Senior Guild Healer in the hopes that maybe it would help.

He wandered the stacks until his eyes caught on another small book. *I should be able to finish reading that one fairly quickly,* he thought, and carefully slid it out. He walked back to the table, set it down, stretched, his back and tail popping with the motion, and sat down to read. Flipping open the cover he gasped.

*Of Belonging to*
*General Marsee Ezabet Chenzira*

He stared at the name for several long moments, overwhelmed with a feeling of importance, as if the similarity in names wasn't just a coincidence. He'd actually spent quite a bit of time researching Myra's deed, trying to figure out why the plot of land hadn't been bought up, mostly out of curiosity, and in all his time, he'd not found another Marsee Chenzira listed. Chenzira itself was a rare name among his people too. Blinking out of his surprise, he carefully turned the page and began reading.

*As with most in my position, I fully expect that my words here will one day be the study of future Generals, although I pray that the fragile peace we've so recently won, will last, and that my words will fade to the winds of time, before such need of my hard earned knowledge should ever arise. Yet my dreams are filled with the images of a future General Chenzira, who will one day need my guidance, for we are but a fragile and weak minded people, that lust for power and control at our very core, and no matter how much we wish it, someday, somewhere, someone will try again to wrest that hard won peace from us, whether it be us or the strange white giants you fight in my dreams.*

*Perhaps they are just the wild imagination of an old and starving General, but who knows what the Gods are capable of. Perhaps we will maintain our fragile peace only to lose it to some unknown species from a far distant world. Every cub for eternity past has looked to the stars and wondered what is out there. Perhaps now that we no longer fight amongst ourselves we will soon find out. I pray that our scientists are successful, for there is little left to this world, and it is all we can do to keep our cubs from starving to death from the destruction we've wrought on ourselves. I hope that by the time thee hast read this, we have found a safe haven amongst the stars, and that no cub ever again knows the pain of hunger, or the agony of war.*

*To thee, my dearest future Marsee, thee, who are but a cub fighting Leviathans that would swallow thee whole, who have known pain, suffering, and darkness, unlike any others of thy time, know that thee are stronger than all of them, for thee hast endured more than they could ever imagine, and survived. Thee hast taken their ridicule and abuse and absorbed every strike and attack and grown stronger, where others fell away, unable to stand what thee hast been forced to experience.*

*You are a General amongst a people who hast forgotten the horrors of war, who shy away at the very idea of killing to survive. But when diplomacy fails, you know that all that remains are thy teeth and claws and will to endure. I grieve with thee all that thee have lost, and will yet lose before thy battle is won, but take strength from that agony thou hast already survived, and hope from the knowledge that peace is possible, if thy honor and courage be great enough, for I have seen it with mine own eyes. Stay strong, young one. Love hard, fight to your last breath, and save thy people and thy cubs from those who wish them harm.*

*From the depths of time, I salute thee.*


He blinked hard and read it again, and then flipped the pages to find hand drawn tactical diagrams throughout the rest of the journal. He had enough training to understand some of the diagrams, and what he saw made him sick to think of the devastation forces of those sizes could cause.

*Ancient Gods Please let her name just be a coincidence,* he thought, and carefully put the journal away. But the letter unnerved him, and his dreams that night were filled with nightmares of long forgotten wars.

# CHAPTER 22

# Jeran: A Minor Problem

Jer leaned back in his office chair, and rubbed at his face with his paws, trying to focus. He'd thought being a councilor for his district and preparing for Little Flower's trial had been hard, but nothing had prepared him for the strain of the past two months, and he was exhausted.

He'd spent nearly five decades as a councilor, and decades more as a junior councilor and advocate, so he thought he knew what he was agreeing to. But he'd not counted on the fact that he had stepped into a well oiled machine of junior councilors and staffers, that managed the majority of the day to day slog of running a district, when he'd first been elected as councilor all those decades ago, and that none of that existed for his daughter's people.

Jer snorted. Nothing existed for his daughter's people. They were literally building a city in the middle of nowhere, and they'd all vastly underestimated what would be required when they'd designed the original plans for expanding the compound. Their original design had accounted for the expected population growth of the Hue-mans and the other land based species they'd rescued, but none of them had realized that every other sentient being on all five planets wanted to visit, and many even wanted to move here permanently.

He had a waiting list nearly ten years long for the guest habitats they'd built, and that was even after restricting it to the people who had a legitimate reason to be there. He even had requests to move here permanently by Ice Giants, and they were even less equipped to handle the heat than the Hue-mans were. Thankfully Ellie had taken on the mantle of coordinating and designing the expanded rebuild, but it still had to be reviewed and approved.

That they didn't have housing didn't stop people from coming either. The area around the village was surrounded by personal ships, shuttles, and ground crawlers, with people choosing to live in them while they stayed, just for the opportunity to visit, and that took a great deal of effort just to ensure that there was enough food to feed every-one. Jordan had claimed the kitchen as her domain, but how she was managing that was beyond him.

He was having a hard enough time just ensuring that shipments of food arrived on time, something that wasn't normally the responsibility of the Council, but with only one food source in New Hope, they couldn't justify charging people for food, and he'd never paid much attention to how much it cost to import foods for the other species.

They were expanding the greenhouses and hatcheries to support the other specie's dietary needs, but that took time, and it didn't ac-count for what they needed to produce the candies Jordan was making. Thankfully New Hope Confectioners was proving to be profitable, as Marsee had immediately realized it would. Surprisingly the dried fruits were popular with all of the species, even the Ice Giants, who were en-tirely carnivorous. Wincing at the total, he signed off on Jordan's latest requisition form without more than a quick glance at the contents, knowing if it was on her list, it was needed, and moved on to the next item on his list.

He'd been working closely with Marcus over the past few months, relying on borrowed staffers to manage the permitting process for the build, including running environmental and community impact stud-ies, while he and Marcus hashed out the plans on what physical land would actually belong to the Hue-mans going forward.

Never in their history had they been required to share a world with the entirety of a second sentient species. People voted with their species in whatever district they were registered, or legally transferred their species to the world on which they were inhabiting, as he'd done to qualify to become an elected official for Little Flower's people. He was currently flat out denying any and all other requests to transfer, until such time as the Hue-mans had full representation, unless a majority of the Local Council requested that change, and that had been backed by the rest of the Senior Council.

The transfer of the land to the Hue-mans had already received unanimous approval from Saber's Council. The plot of land was tiny and in a desolate part of the world that few wanted to live in. That the Hue-mans were not only happy here but thriving surprised everyone, especially considering how ill equipped they were as a species to survive in the heat without all the specialized clothing the Guild produced for them. Still, making the change required a unanimous vote by the Full Council, as it involved changing a protected right, and neither he or Marcus had any idea how the rest of the Full Council would vote.

The discussion was expected to take up a significant portion of the meeting, a meeting they were leaving for in the morning, and for which neither he or his people were even remotely prepared for, and he fully expected to work the entire trip to Flyer. Barely half of the Council had been filled yet. Grandfather and Little Flower had both warned them of this, fully expecting that few of the other women would sponsor the men for some time, but he'd not expected that it would be a unanimous decision. There hadn't been a single adulthood ceremony since that first day.

Additionally, nearly a quarter of the women had chosen to remain behind, as they were now pregnant, and everyone was on edge following the disastrous results of his daughter's pregnancy. A large contingency of healers would be traveling with them, in the event that there was a problem, since the other worlds did not have experience or training in how to treat Hue-man illnesses and injuries yet.

Further complicating things was the fact that very few of the Hue-mans had even expressed an interest in any of the work expected of a councilor, outside of showing up for the meetings, and GrandFather was spending more of his time with Nazari, leaving him to pick up the pieces, although he couldn't blame GrandFather for wanting to find a way to help Little Flower, or for her people wanting to learn a skill or craft that brought them joy. He'd spent the last month trying to prepare the others for what to expect, but half the time he couldn't even get everyone to show up for the planning meetings.

Every day seemed to bring a dozen completely new and unforeseen problems. Added to his responsibilities as a senior councilor, he was having to split shifts caring for his daughter and her newborn cub, although thankfully the Senior Council had understood, and had pushed the Full Council meeting off with the excuse that they were giving the Hue-mans more time to get settled and prepare.

His weren't the only people needing to prepare. The other council cities needed to be updated to provide adequate housing for his people, and the council chambers reconfigured for seating, and they needed time to allow the Council's translators the time they needed to become fluent in sign. They'd asked Marsee to translate again, but she had flat out refused after Hope was born, not wanting to leave her sister's side, and honestly, he was glad. Myra would need the help with everyone else gone.

This meeting should have been held on the Water World, but with the addition of a new species and planned renovations, which were more difficult to build underwater, they'd restructured the order and timing of the meetings from every three months, to every four, and lengthened the planned session slightly, to allow for the additional time needed for reviewing the needs of the additional species. Based on ease of construction, they were heading to Flyer first. As far as he could tell, it was the one decision they'd made that the rest of the Council was actually happy with, as it meant less time off world, which for some of the species was rather significant. His planet was fairly central to the others, but it was nearly eight days between the Water World and the Ice Planet, one way.

To help him, the Seniors had moved all of their preparatory meetings to Council City for the past week, rather than the expected tradition of having them on the hosting planet, which allowed him to attend remotely rather than having to spend days traveling to Flyer as he would normally have had to do.

He'd offered to host them here, but the Water Sprite habitats hadn't been built yet, or the tunnels hooked up, and with the spring rains, the grounds were a muddy quagmire, which made it difficult for Clear Seas to travel here and stay for any length of time, although he had visited one afternoon using the personal transport vehicles they used to maneuver on land. He'd come to meet Little Flower's daughter and bring the gift his family had sent. They'd spent hours afterwards talking about everything that had happened at the trial, and the struggles he was facing now, and they'd carefully repaired the friendship that had been damaged with the trial.

That had been the one good thing that had happened since his daughter had gone into her coma. Clear Seas had informed him that he would not add to his family's grief if Little Flower should die. That gave them a tie and quite likely Clear Seas the tie breaking vote, since the following Full Council meeting would be held on the Water World. If Little Flower lasted longer than that, then hopefully, he'd have earned the other Senior's friendship and compassion enough to save Myra's life.

On top of everything else, for the last half week, Marsee had seemed withdrawn and distracted, and that worried him greatly. That she'd survived psychosis was a miracle, but he'd not had the time he wanted to work with her, to make sure she was fully under control, and the last time she'd withdrawn this much it had been because she'd been struggling to control her instinct, and hadn't wanted anyone to know. Both he and Marcus had caught her with her instinct on, although she hadn't had any problems turning it off. Both situations had been reasonable, and they were giving her time to learn to recognize when it was on and learn to control it. In many ways, she was now reacting much like a young cub normally reacted as they learned to control their instincts, but he was still very worried. He needed to find time today to talk to her about it, but he'd just been informed of yet another completely unexpected and baffling problem, and he had no idea how to fix that either.

There was a knock on his door and he looked up to see GrandFather in the opening. "You wanted to see me?"

Jer smiled. "I did, GrandFather. Please come in and shut the door." GrandFather was the closest thing he had to an acting senior right now, and his go-to expert on Hue-man culture now that Little Flower was stuck in her coma.

GrandFather looked at him curiously but did as requested. Once his door was shut Jer put up his privacy shield, which made GrandFather frown.

"What is it this time?" GrandFather sighed.

Jer chuckled. "You know, you're starting to sound like Marcus."

GrandFather snorted in response. "Well, it could be worse, I could be sounding like my grand daughter."

"Ancient God's protect us," Jer replied with a curl of his tail. "Anyway, it's both baffling and concerning, and I'm not really sure what to make of it. I just received the final report from Healer Brice on the species repopulation programs, and one of her comments has me scratching my whiskers."

"Oh?" GrandFather asked as he hopped up into his usual chair. "Nazari hasn't mentioned any whisker scratching problems, so I'm guessing this has to do with my species"

"You would be correct. As you know, most of the adult women have chosen to be artificially impregnated rather than trying for a pregnancy the 'old fashioned way' as you called it. The vast majority of the men have also provided sperm donations to allow for this, and while the women don't know whose donation is being used, for the purpose of privacy as requested, Healer Brice indicates that every single woman over the past month has specifically requested that Damon Minor's donation not be used."

GrandFather snorted in amusement. "That doesn't surprise me in the least. Serves him right for that matter."

Jer flicked his ears back in astonishment at that statement. "I understand that he's been one of the most vocal about trying to persuade the others to change the age of adulthood for the men, but your reaction makes me think there is something else going on. Has he done something to harm someone that I am not aware of?"

"Outside of annoying just about every woman here, not that I know of. The problem isn't what he's done, at least not since the Cataclysm, but what he represents. Are you aware of the fact that he used to be covered in tattoos?" GrandFather asked.

"The skin drawings?" Jer asked for confirmation.

"Yes. He's since had most of them removed, or at least any that would be obvious, but word of them has made it through the Huemans. Tattoos aren't a problem, in of themselves, but what he had on his skin was, or so I'm told. I never saw them. Many represented groups or ideas that were considered dangerous. It's the main reason he's on the watch list, not for anything he's done, at least not that I'm aware of."

Jer's ears flicked back in surprise. GrandFather and Little Flower had added nearly a dozen people to the watch list over the past several months. He knew Damon was on the list, but he'd been under the assumption that it had more to do with continued efforts to change the age of adulthood, and association with Paul Markson and Danny Shuto, who were both on the list due to complaints of repeated pressuring to mate, when the female had already indicated 'no' multiple times, along with several others. Others had been added because of violent outbursts, although thankfully no one had been hurt. The men who had been harassing the women had been spoken to, and informed if they had another complaint that they would be charged formally with harassment with intent to rape. That had stopped those issues cold. They had expected people to push the boundaries of the law, both out of ignorance, and from years of not being held accountable for their actions. So as long as no one was actually hurt they were giving everyone one chance to adjust their behavior before punishment occurred.

The violent outbursts that had resulted in destruction of someone else's property had required reparations, although one person had been removed from the list when their violent outburst had been deemed to be caused by a medical issue and successfully treated. There was a great deal of discussion about whether or not the violence and intolerance experienced by the Hue-mans on their world was due to injury or contamination rather than nature following that incident, especially since so many of the Hue-mans had needed treatment from various toxins found in their system. It was also clear that many were still dealing with their past trauma and isolation sickness caused by their time in quarantine.

Jer flipped open his tablet and pulled up footage from the agency to show Damon's tattoos. "Which ones?" he asked.

GrandFather looked at the image and swallowed hard. "I had no idea it was this bad. These three here are the most concerning. In one way or another they represent hatred towards people with different beliefs and skin color, and I'm pretty sure these two represent gang symbols, although I could be wrong."

"Gangs?" Jer asked for clarification as he didn't recognize the Hue-man word.

"Those were groups that specialized in crime, usually involving the sale of illegal drugs, weapons, and extortion. This one is the worst of all. Do you remember the great war my daughter spoke about during the trial, the one where my district dropped massive bombs on three cities to end it? This was one of their symbols. Most of the rest of these were designed to instill fear and project an image of being tough. Jer, I'll be honest with you. I don't trust him at all, and if I'd met him on Earth, I would have run for my life. If anything ever happens to me or others with my skin color, he should be your primary suspect."

Jer frowned in worry. Little Flower had warned them about people like Damon practically within days of learning how to speak. "How concerned are you that he will actually try something now though? I've had no complaints about him, outside of the one comment that was made during Nazari's petition. I was under the assumption he was on the watch list because of his association with Paul and Danny."

GrandFather thought about it for a moment before answering. "Honestly? I'm terrified. Everyone is keeping watch on him, but even then he's constantly trying to rile people up about the vote. He's gained some followers there, but he's pushing everyone else away. If he's being shunned by the women that makes him more dangerous, and if he finds out that people are rejecting his donation too, it'll make him even more of a threat. We already have an imbalance and many of the men who want a partnership can't have one. I honestly don't know if any of the other men have a preference for partnering with other men like I do, but Damon would likely target anyone he found with that preference as well, based on several of these other tattoos." GrandFather pointed out several of the drawings and Jer marked and recorded them as hate symbols.

"I'll talk to Myra and some of the others who are remaining behind to keep watch while we're gone, and let the healers know not to let that information out. I'll also ask Brice to change the report so that it doesn't become official documentation. I can't legally do anything to Damon based on what he represented in your past if he hasn't done something to someone here since the rescue. But how do you propose we handle him going forward if the actions by the others are isolating him?"

"Honestly, I don't know. People like him often crave power and attention, but giving him that could give him the opportunity to harm others. I am surprised that he offered to adopt the child, but I and most of the people I've spoken to think that was just intended as a way to gain adulthood. After seeing these tattoos, I certainly wouldn't sponsor him or let him adopt. Maybe we could find a way to compromise with his demands around the vote, and find a way to allow the men to prove their worth rather than just having to wait, some sort of test or completion of education. Maybe anyone who reaches journeyman in their craft? Although from what I understand Damon hasn't stuck with any of the courses offered by any of the other guilds."

"My understanding is that he's working as a groundskeeper, rather than taking classes. I checked with his supervisor after I read Brice's report, and there were no complaints. He hasn't missed or been late for a shift yet, and takes on any additional work requested without complaint," Jer replied. "He's the only member of your species doing that work too."

GrandFather didn't comment for a while. "I honestly don't know what to make of that. The work he's doing, most people on Earth would have considered beneath them. I recognize that it's work that needs to be done, but everyone else is taking the opportunity to learn a new skill. He's not."

Jer leaned back in his chair and considered, and eventually nodded. "Damon has indicated more than once that he wants to be a pilot, and the fact that he can't is one of the reasons he's against the age restriction we have in place. The biggest complaint from all the men seems to be their inability to join many of the guilds because they're not recognized as adults yet. I will speak to the guilds again about allowing those who are interested in joining, even if they aren't legally an adult yet."

GrandFather nodded. "Maybe we could find him a mentor in the Ship's Guild, or at the very least teach him how to pilot a shuttle. The fact is, most of the males rescued would have been considered legal adults before. That should count for something, even if they aren't allowed to vote yet."

"Agreed. The problem is there's far too much risk involved to take someone in who isn't an adult because of the harm they could cause another. The guilds have all refused to change their charters or make exceptions in the past because of it."

"It wouldn't help Damon, but I could talk to Nazari about taking a few apprentices as animal healers. I know Henry has mentioned wanting to learn. There's less risk there. I'm not ready to sponsor anyone for adulthood, but there are people I trust enough to be an animal healer. Henry's certainly been putting in the hard work. Plus, most of the master level healers in residence are animal healers anyway, and have more bandwidth to take on an apprentice."

Jer nodded, and thought for a while longer trying to decide whether it was time to discuss 'The Test' or not, and pursed his lips as he considered.

"What is it?" GrandFather asked.

"It was your comment on testing them. How much did Little Flower talk to you about our hunting instincts?" he asked.

"Not much, outside of what happened that one day when we reviewed the Agency's footage and Marsee ran out of the room, why?" he asked.

"What I'm about to tell you is confidential information and I need you to take an official vow not to release this information to anyone."

GrandFather raised both eyebrows at that, but did as requested.

Jer proceeded to tell him about Marsee's illness, how close she'd been to killing his granddaughter, and how close they'd been to being forced to put Marsee down before she could hurt anyone else. GrandFather had been horrified on both accounts, and they spoke for some time about the disease itself. Jer then continued on and told GrandFather about the test the councilors took, and all of the various indications of psychosis in his people. He went into far greater detail than he had with his daughter and then spoke about what he'd since learned regarding the other species tests, information that was now available to him as a member of the Senior Council.

"I can see why you'd keep this secret," GrandFather said. "Not just to protect Marsee, but to protect your species as well, and why you'd be so cautious about who you put into power."

Jer nodded. "The stigma around the illness would have devastating consequences for Marsee if the general public found out about it, and I doubt that the other species would understand why we end up having to kill our young. Nor would they ever trust us again if they knew what could happen to any of us under the right circumstances. I just hope that what happened with Marsee is repeatable and that we never have to put down another cub again. It's the whole reason Marcus and I both turned down nominations for Senior Council in the past. It's hard enough to test my own junior advocate's control, but the idea of having to kill a child or someone I've known for decades…" Jer shook his head. "As just a councilor I had the option to delegate the test to the Senior Councilor, or bring in the Honor Guard if someone has already lost control, as it can take an entire contingent to control the situation, especially if it's a fully grown adult female. I've had to do so on more than one occasion, and frankly it's been the hardest part of my job, even knowing they were already gone. It's also one of the biggest reasons our Senior Councilor is almost always female."

"Is that why you hesitated to take the position when Little Flower nominated you?" GrandFather asked.

"No. Well only part of it. If it becomes necessary for me to execute someone as Senior Councilor and I find I can't actually perform the act, I can call in the Honor Guard. I hesitated because as Little Flower's Senior, it would have been my responsibility to oversee the execution of Myra, and the procedure to sterilize my children and grandchildren, if the Senior Council had chosen that as her punishment. I would have had to choose between my family and your people."

"Gods, Jer. I can't believe you agreed," GrandFather exclaimed.

Jer smiled wryly. "Realistically there was nothing I could have done to save her or my children, even if I did have visions of taking on the entire Senior Council and Honor Guard to try and free them. I still can't believe your granddaughter found a way out of that mess, but Myra made me promise back when we first found out about the rape to do everything I could to protect Little Flower and your people, even if it meant her death. That's why I ultimately accepted. By doing so, I was no longer committing treason to protect your people."

"Well it's pretty evident to me how much we need someone as dedicated as you to help us through this mess," GrandFather said. "Especially since most of my people have expressed little interest in leadership. I'd considered it, but with Little Flower…"

Jer nodded sadly. "I fully understand and respect your reasons for joining the Healer's Guild, although I wouldn't say no if you changed your mind. It's enough that you've agreed to step in as acting senior when there's need. Regardless it will be a long time before your species has enough people to even designate a senior advocate, much less require a full term as a junior councilor, but we should consider some form of test before that happens, and depending on what that test is, I could see using that as a method for designating adulthood in the men."

GrandFather considered for a long time before nodding.

"I'll think about what we might be able to use. That's not the kind of thing you decide on the spur of the moment," he said, and then chuckled.

Jer tilted his head in confusion. He didn't find anything funny about the comment.

GrandFather explained. "One of the science fiction stories we used to have before, had a similar concept called the Kobayashi Maru that was given to the equivalent of a ship master. It was a no win scenario. No matter what you did, people died. There was never a right answer. Little Flower was a huge fan of that show, and I'm sure it would tickle her to no end to try and design one."

"Let's hope she gets that chance," Jer said.

GrandFather nodded. "Agreed. Was there anything else?" he asked.

"No, but I can't guarantee I won't call you back in five minutes when something else comes back up. Are you sure you won't reconsider being my senior advocate?"

"Ha! No, I'd rather stick my hand up a chenzie's butt!" he joked in reply. "It's far less painful."

"Isn't that the truth," Jer muttered, and he turned off the privacy shield so GrandFather could leave.

He sent off a few messages regarding the report and issues surrounding Damon, and then decided it was time he talked with Marsee, praying she wasn't having a relapse.

# CHAPTER 23

# Marsee: Her Sister's Keeper

Marsee stared at the massive painting her sister had completed for the Senior Guild Master and sighed. *I should have waited until someone was around to stay with her, or carried her to the clinic instead of running off to find Mama. If I'd been even a little faster, she wouldn't be stuck in a coma now,* she thought for the millionth time.

It had taken her a full two months, but she was finally finished carving the most beautiful frame she'd ever made, or anything for that matter, and the painting was now ready to give to Ellie. It was what Little Flower had wanted, but she couldn't bear to part with it, not with her sister still in a coma, and not knowing if she would ever draw another thing again, even if she did wake up. Marsee lovingly ran a finger over the lily her sister used as her signature and sighed. *Little Flower should be the one to give it to her,* Marsee decided, and carefully hung the now framed painting on the wall above her sister's desk.

Once the painting was hung to Marsee's satisfaction, she backed up to look at it and frowned. *It needs more light,* she decided, and walked over to one of her own paintings, removed the lighting strips, and brought them over to the other wall. Lights in place, she stepped back again and smiled. *There, that looks better.* Painting hung, she snapped a picture to add to her journal, turned and leapt onto her hanging bed, and shifted around so she could lay down and look at it some more.

After kneading her pillows for a bit, she rested her head on her paws and sighed. It was hard to believe it had only been a few months since Little Flower arrived in her life. So much had happened that it was hard to keep track of it all. With another heavy sigh, she flipped open her tablet again and added the picture to her journal, and then scrolled back to reread a few of her favorite entries.

While no longer needed, she'd continued with the journal she'd started when Little Flower arrived in her life, and over the past two months had gone back in and filled it out. Now that she knew no one else would read it, she'd added everything she could remember about her sister, her time here, and everything her sister had told her about her world before. She didn't want to forget a single moment of her life with Little Flower, the good or the bad. If her sister never woke up again, she wanted to be able to tell her story, so that Hope would know her mother, and writing about her struggles with her instinct helped her to understand it, when there was no one she could talk to about what she was experiencing.

After a few minutes though, she flopped back down on her pillows with another sigh, and then pinned her ears back with a low growl at the sound of some distant machinery adding yet another building to the compound, or 'New Hope' as the Hue-mans had finally chosen. She didn't have a problem with the name, even though she hadn't been allowed to vote on it, but it still felt surreal to have her childhood home be a listed and named village on the census. With the way things were growing, she fully expected it would qualify for city status within a decade, if not sooner. *Probably a lot sooner*, she decided, since everyone on all five planets wanted to be here.

The once quiet halls and garden now housed thousands of sentient beings on any given day, and between the noise of people talking and the constant construction, Marsee was ready to pull her fur out. If it weren't for her hearing aids she'd never get any peace, but she couldn't keep them in all the time. When it was her turn to watch Hope, she needed to make sure she could hear the tiny cub, and it was uncomfortable to sleep with them in.

Her tower, which had once been the tallest structure for leagues, was now dwarfed by surrounding buildings, and only one door still had an unobstructed view into the valley, and the only reason for that was because the land in front of her tower had been reserved for animal pastures. Even with her doors closed, she could still hear people talking. Only in the middle of the night did she find any peace and quiet, but even then people would still be wandering the halls. The Hue-mans did not do well with the afternoon heat of her world, and were becoming far more nocturnal in their activity. Granted the days were nearly twice as long here as they'd been on their home world, so it wasn't surprising that their circadian rhythms were completely messed up.

To be fair, it wasn't all bad. She quite liked watching the Earth creatures grazing in their pastures in the early mornings and evenings, and the massive pool, greenhouse, and aviary were some of her new favorite destinations, even if they were full of people, most of the time people she didn't know. She couldn't really complain. Everyone, well mostly everyone was fantastic, and she was very popular with the Hue-man cubs. Marsee figured that was because she was one of the youngest, if not *the* youngest, Sabers currently in residence, outside of Tabor's young cubs, and far closer to their size than anyone else.

That thought made her curl her tail a bit. She'd snickered for hours after her little sister had chosen to name their species after the fiercest cat that had ever lived on their planet. When word had made its way around Marsee's planet and people learned what the word had repre-sented, it had become so popular that most people were now using that name instead. The drawing Little Flower had done was one of Marsee's favorites too, and she looked over at the wall of other paintings and drawings Little Flower had done.

She'd recently completed and translated the cub's book Little Flower had been working on, with GrandFather's help, and while she'd bound up several copies, she'd also printed out many of her favorite pages and framed them too. She hadn't shared it with Ellie yet, hoping that Little Flower would wake and get to see it first.

She lay there instinct on, as she examined those drawings, and envisioned the saber tooth tiger hunting the giant wooly mammoth of that world's past. There was something very primal about the saber, that made her instinct purr.

*That was a creature worth hunting with,* her instinct explained, *if it could take down something so much bigger than it was.*

She smiled before shutting her instinct down. *Yup, still in control,* she thought. She tested herself several times a day to be sure. Over the past few months, she'd developed a sort of truce with her instinct, and felt far more centered and in control than she'd ever been before, but it still felt strange to hear a voice in her head that wasn't hers.

It had changed from the insistent demands to hunt, to trying to help her deal with the changes and challenges in her life. In many ways her instinct was much like that ancient creature from Earth, a more primal version of herself. Oddly though, it was one that was more in tune with herself, than she was at times, and she found herself asking it for advice more often. It was the one person she could talk to about what was going on in her life.

She never stopped marveling at how beautiful the world was with her instinct on, and had drawn dozens of pictures through that lens, although she knew would probably never be able to share them with anyone, except for maybe her sister, if she ever got that chance. She didn't think her parents or uncle would understand. To them, her instinct was something to be avoided at all costs, but doing that hadn't ever worked for her, and she was in far more control now, now that she regularly used it, than she'd ever been before, and as far as she knew she hadn't had a lapse since the day Hope was born.

She really wished she could share what she was learning with someone, anyone, but there wasn't anyone she trusted enough to tell. Surrounded by thousands of people she barely knew, she felt terribly lonely. She was angry at herself for failing to protect her sister, and both scared and grieving. Both her parents were too busy, and she wasn't close enough to anyone else. Years of isolating herself to hide her growing illness meant she'd developed few real friendships. Little Flower had been the closest friend she'd ever had, and the only one she'd ever been able to talk to about anything and everything.

It wasn't just that she couldn't talk about her instinct with anyone, but she couldn't let anyone know how she was feeling about her sister or the changes in New Hope. Anytime she got even the slightest bit upset or angry, her father and uncle, if he was around, would check her control. She felt like crying all the time, but she was terrified if she let it out that they'd just kill her, and she'd never been good at hiding her emotions behind a mask like her parents or uncle did, and it chafed and hurt almost as badly as the hearing aids did.

As lonely as she was, she also missed her privacy, and the ability to go for a walk in the garden without tripping over someone. It had been weeks since she'd been able to find a quiet and safe place to draw, and she was sick of being stuck in the one room of her tower. Having her parents in the tower was proving to be a bigger challenge than she'd expected too. She might legally be an adult now, but her parents were still treating her like a cub, and she thought she might just lose it completely if either one of her parents asked where she was off to one more time. She even missed the flicker flyers that had been scared off by the sudden increase in population. She couldn't blame them for leaving, and wondered if they would ever return. She looked over at the small collection of gifts they'd given her sister in exchange for drawings of themselves, and sighed again.

After another loud screech from some distant piece of stupid machinery made her fur stand up on end, she popped in her hearing aids and turned off all sound, reveling in the silence for a few minutes. There was only one sound she wanted to hear, and that was the sound of her sister laughing. She flipped open her tablet again, and pulled up the video she'd taken that day of the flicker flyers, and watched it for probably the hundredth time and half sighed, half growled at what had been lost, because *she'd* been too slow to get help.

Frustrated, she tossed the tablet aside with a growl, pulled her hearing aids out, and tossed them back in their case, as they were already making her ears hurt. Reaching under her pillow where she kept the eraser that her sister had flung at her on her last day, she fiddled with it as she thought, absently flipping it from one claw to another, trying to figure out what she wanted to do with her life, and figure out a way to control the growing anxiety she felt before she exploded.

She felt both lost and trapped. She'd spent most of her life in school or the Guild learning what her instructors and masters wanted her to learn, but she was an adult now, and should really start thinking about mastering one of her crafts, but she couldn't pick just one. She loved them all and wanted to learn more, and she was contemplating switching Guilds again, maybe over to the Tech Guild or even to the Ship's Guild to learn how to fly one of the interplanetary ships.

She'd been working on translating and binding the Hue-man books with Little Flower prior, but it just wasn't the same without her sister to bounce questions off of. But when she wasn't helping to teach the Hue-mans, the rest of her time was used up watching and caring for Little Flower and Hope. So much so, that she'd had to stop her classes altogether. She loved spending time with Hope, and absolutely adored the cub, but being around her sister was exhausting and depressing. She loved her sister fiercely, but the ever present beeps of the trauma ward made her want to scream. So much of their care had fallen on her, as her uncle had indicated would happen. GrandFather tried to help but the ward wasn't designed for him to easily care for her, and between covering the night shift with her sister, and all of her other responsibilities, and the noise of the compound, she hadn't gotten a good night's sleep in weeks.

With a growl, she jumped down from her bed and paced in her room, trying to contain her grief and frustration, but the room wasn't big enough. In the past she'd run in the halls when her anxiety grew too overwhelming to handle, but the halls were crowded with people now. She grabbed a pillow and threw it with another quiet growl, but that didn't help. She grabbed another one, flicked on her instinct and shredded it into tiny pieces.

*I never liked that pillow anyway,* she thought. But it still wasn't enough.

*Of course it's not enough,* her instinct admonished. *We've allowed strangers to invade our territory.*

*They aren't invading. We invited them here. It was necessary to save Mama's life and our future cubs,* she reminded it.

*I'm not saying it wasn't, but we need to mark our own territory. Find someplace of our own where we can be alone, and roar out our dominance.*

"Where? Everywhere here is full of people, and I'm not leaving my sister or Hope," she spat back as she paced, too upset to care that she was talking to herself. She looked out her door at the acres of pastures and the Wilds far off in the distance.

*Yes. There!* her instinct agreed. *Find some place close enough we can run to when we need it, but far enough away to be our own.*

She didn't even stop to consider. Bolting for the ramp, she raced down and nearly collided with her father at the bottom.

"Easy there, Kitten. What's wrong?" her father asked.

"Everything," she growled and kept running. She bolted through the outside door with a bang, and ran with everything she had. She didn't want to talk. She couldn't talk, not to him, not to anyone. They just wouldn't understand the way her sister would have.

"Marsee stop!" her father called out, but she ran faster, needing to get away from him, from everyone, but mostly from herself, from her overwhelming guilt and grief. Her claws dug into the new grass brought on by the spring rains, and ripped out huge clumps of dirt as she ran. She gave herself over to her instinct, and let herself just feel. The stresses of her life vanished as she focused everything on running as fast as she could.

*Yes! This is exactly what we needed,* they thought, dug deeper, and ran even faster.

The next thing Marsee knew, she was flattened to the ground with teeth digging painfully into her scruff. She yelped in pain and struggled to spin around to fight whatever predator was attacking her, but then growled her frustration and anger, as she realized it was her father pinning her to the ground, but that only caused his teeth to dig deeper, making her yelp with pain.

"Stop it! Get off of me!" she yelled. He backed off immediately. She sat up glaring at him, and rubbed at her sore jaw that had been slammed into the ground. "Was that really necessary?" she hissed, tail lashing.

"Yes," he said matter of factly, as he grabbed her face hard, forcing her to look at him. He stared into her eyes, and she realized why he'd chased after her. He thought her psychosis was returning, and that she was running away to get away from everyone before she hurt them. She tried to pull away in frustration.

"Shut it off, now," he demanded, not letting go of her, and she felt the warning sting of his claws.

Marsee let out a frustrated sigh, half growl, and flicked off her instinct. "I'm *fine* Papa. I'm still me. I just needed to get away from all of *that*!" she said, waving in the general direction of the compound.

He took a deep sigh of relief and let go of her. "I'm sorry, Kitten. I had to be sure."

"Look, I get it. But you know, sometimes I'm just frustrated, angry, and scared, and need to run, to roar at the top of my lungs without waking the neighbors. I have it under control. See?" She flicked her hunting instinct on and back off again several times. "You don't need to pounce on me every time I'm running or don't answer you, and that really hurt!"

She rubbed at her scruff, and then checked her paw for blood. When she saw a drop of blood on her paw, she growled at him, held her paw up so he could see, and started walking away.

"Kitten wait..."

"Leave me alone, Papa. I don't want to talk right now," she growled, not looking back.

"Kitten, I know..."

She turned and roared back at him. "I SAID, LEAVE ME ALONE!" He flinched back in surprise. Marsee rarely raised her voice with her parents, but then she'd never needed to. With another angry growl, she turned back around again, and kept walking, ears pinned flat, and tail lashing furiously behind her. She made it up to the top of the small hill and looked back. He was still standing there watching her. She glared at him, turned back around, huffed with an annoyed flick of her tail, and took off running again.

Letting herself relax into her instinct, she tried to regain the calm she'd had for those few moments before he'd pounced, but her instinct was furious with him too. Far off in the distance there was a stream dotted by a few small scrub trees, and for lack of anywhere else to go, they made their way there, pushing themselves as hard as they could run. Panting, but still livid when she arrived, she let her instinct shred the bark on the larger of the trees and even spray it, until their anger and feelings of being trapped subsided, and she turned her instinct off again. It had felt so good to sink her claws into the tree, and let her anger and months of pent up frustration out. She flopped down next to the stream and took a drink from the cool water, and then rubbed the back of her aching scruff again. *How long is he going to keep testing me like this?* she wondered. *He's never pounced on me before, though. That hurt!*

**I do not believe he will ever trust us,** her instinct replied.

She sighed, realizing it was probably true. It had been months since she'd nearly lost herself to psychosis, but she'd been fully in control of her instinct since then. While there had been the two instances where it had turned on when she was stressed, she'd never lost control, or even thought about hunting anyone like before, Jordan's creations yes, but not anything living. She'd been practicing so much that she could turn it on and off with ease now. She didn't want to lose control and hurt someone either. A small crawly scurried in the brush beside her and she flicked on her instinct, just to prove to herself that she could control it. They watched the crawly walk towards the stream and calculated a dozen different ways they could pounce and kill it, before she flicked it off again, and sighed, flopping down to rest her head on her paws.

She sat there for nearly an hour, flicking small stones into the stream, before she heard a noise behind her. Flicking her ears back, she sniffed to see who it was, and growled a warning, both hurt and frustrated. He smelled of fear. "Leave me alone, Papa."

"Are you going to tell me what's bothering you, or are you just going to stay out here and growl at crawlies all day?" her father asked, not leaving her alone.

"Crawlies," she answered. "They don't ask annoying questions."

"Fair," he said, and sat down beside her, keeping her company but not talking for several minutes. "Talk to me, Kitten. What's wrong?"

"What isn't wrong, Papa!" she cried. "Little Flower's stuck in a coma. Mama hasn't been home in days, and you and GrandFather are both leaving tomorrow, which means I'm going to be stuck picking up the slack. I'm sick of cleaning up messes, and the infernal beep of Little Flower's monitors makes me want to tear my fur out. I hear it beep in my sleep now. There are people everywhere, and even in my room with the doors shut, I can still hear them, and apparently you don't even trust me enough to go out for a run," she spat. *And it's all my fault,* she thought to herself, and flicked another stone into the water.

"I'm sorry, Kitten. I'm sorry you've been caught up in all of our mistakes, and that you had to agree to give up your privacy and share your home. I know having to help care for your sister and Hope hasn't been easy on you, but I do trust you."

"No you don't. You smell of fear," she muttered. "You're never going to trust me."

He sighed and didn't say anything for a while, proving her right. "I'm just worried about you, Kitten. I'm sorry I hurt you. I didn't mean to. So what do you want to do? Do you want to move out, or maybe go live with your grandparents for a while? You could come with me tomorrow and stay there for a few weeks. You don't need to stay here and take care of Hope and Little Flower. The other healers will help."

"If I knew what I wanted to do I wouldn't be out here growling at crawlies," she hissed at him, and then flopped back down with another sigh. "Honestly, I just want things to go back to the way they were before, where it was just me and Little Flower the tower, when I could yell at the top of my lungs if I wanted to, without having to worry about you hearing or waking all of New Hope. I miss being able to go for walks in the garden and chasing the flicker flyers and throwing pillows at Little Flower every time she called me Chenzie Butt. I'm scared she's not going to get any better, and that I'm going to lose her forever, and Mama and Hope too when that happens. I'm surrounded by people everywhere and lonely at the same time. I don't have anyone to talk to at midnight or raid the kitchens with. I can't even sleep without her here. It's both too quiet without her snores and too loud with the sounds of the rest of the compound. There's just been too many changes, too quickly, and it's all just too much to handle sometimes."

"It has been a pretty crazy couple of months hasn't it," her Papa replied.

"That's the understatement of the millennia," Marsee muttered. "You need to stop hanging out with Uncle Marcus."

Her father chuckled, and then sighed. "I miss her too. I'd wake Little Flower right now, if I could. I don't know how to help her either, except try to help your mother as best I can. I know this has been really hard on you, and I don't know what we would have done without your help and support, but I'm not willing to trade Little Flower for your sanity. Tell me. What can I do to help?"

"Well you can stop biting me for one. I promise if I even have a hint of an issue, I'll come tell you, Mama, *and* Uncle Marcus about it right away. I won't hide it from you like I did before."

"Deal. What else?"

"Moons if I know!" Marsee said, throwing up her paws, and then with a growl, stood up to pace.

"Do you want to come with me for the Council meeting?" he asked again.

"Honestly, yes, but no. I can't leave Little Flower like this, and Mama needs the help. She can't watch Hope *and* find a way to fix Little Flower, and the other healers have their own patients to deal with. Besides, you know Mama, she won't sleep if Little Flower is left alone with the other healers." She sighed and continued to pace and then kicked a rock, flicking it into the stream with a splash. She grabbed another rock and flung that one in with an even bigger splash, and grabbed another one, and threw that one with a growl. Her instinct wanted to run, not stay here and talk, and it didn't like that her father was here in territory that they'd just marked.

"Little Flower is not your responsibility, Marsee. We're her parents. We took on that responsibility willingly, knowing that there might be complications with Hope's birth, but you're not. You need to live your life. Do what makes you happy. Focus on your crafts, learn a new one, travel and see the worlds," he said.

"Papa, you don't understand, I want to do all that *with* Little Flower, not by myself. How can I go off and enjoy myself while she's here wasting away to nothing with Mama right beside her? If Little Flower dies while we're both gone, who's going to care for Hope, or stop Mama from hurting herself? You know she holds herself responsible for Little Flower's condition, but it's not her fault."

Her father stood and walked over to her, and took the stone she was about to throw out of her paws, before making her turn to face him. "You're right, and it's not your fault either."

She glared up at him. "Of course it's my fault! I shouldn't have let her climb the tree. If I'd stopped her she wouldn't have broken that rib, and I shouldn't have left her alone when her labor started. I should have run faster, or for that matter called Mama and carried her to the clinic myself. If she'd gotten there even a few minutes sooner we might have saved her! But I didn't and we weren't fast enough!" she cried, and then bolted across the stream and started running again, trying to outrun her anguish.

"Marsee!" her father yelled. "Marsee, stop!"

She added speed and heard him splash across the stream after her. She tensed for the pounce, but didn't stop. When she didn't end up flattened to the ground again, she looked back and saw her father right behind her, and off to the side. She growled at him, not wanting to be around him.

He flicked his ears back, but then his expression changed, becoming fiercer and far more determined. It was an expression she'd never seen on him before. "Is that all you've got?" he sneered at her. "If you think you're going to be fast enough to save everyone, then you need to run faster than that. RUN!" he yelled, and then he swiped at her, claws outstretched.

She flattened her ears at him, shocked that he would threaten her, and bolted forward to escape the swipe, putting everything she had into the run. Her instinct flared, wanting to protect her, but she squashed it. "What are you doing, Papa? Leave us alone," she hissed at him.

His expression, if anything, hardened. "No. Keep running. No wonder you didn't make it to Mama in time. Look at how slow you are," he taunted, and she felt the hint of claws on her backside.

Marsee growled at him and kept running. She was tired from her long run before, and started to slow.

"Keep moving. I said RUN!" he yelled and swiped again. This one made contact, and it stung. She growled at her father, but he just pinned his ears and growled back. "FASTER!"

He kept after her, running and swiping until she'd had enough and turned on him, growling and swiped back. He leaped out of the way, easily avoiding her.

"Stop it!" she yelled at him.

"What happens next time if you don't push yourself to be faster? You're barely half grown. How under the three moons do you think you're going to be able to protect anyone. If you want to be a parent and take on a parent's responsibility before you've grown up, you'd better learn to run faster, be far stronger than you are now, because this isn't good enough."

He swiped at her making contact again, and it hurt. Both she and her instinct were livid at his continued attacks and taunts. She knew fighting back could be seen as losing control, but he'd attacked her first, and she didn't know what to do, or how to make him stop, and her instinct was demanding she act. It was all she could do to keep it turned off.

"Why won't you leave me alone?" she growled at him. "I just want space to think? Is that too much to ask?""

"No, you want to wallow in self pity. You're nothing but a tiny cub. If you can't protect yourself from me, how are you ever going to protect anyone else from harm?"

In the back of her brain, her instinct growled, reacting to her anger and pain. *He wants us to fight. Aren't we allowed to defend ourselves?*

*I don't know. I don't understand why he's doing this,* she replied. She just wanted some space to work things out, and his comments hurt worse than the swipe, giving voice to her deepest fears, that she'd never be a good mother.

*A parent doesn't hurt their cubs like he's doing now. We would never hurt our cub like this. Are you going to let him get away with this?* her instinct growled.

She agreed wholeheartedly. She would never treat Hope like this, and decided that if he wasn't going to let her have space, she'd make him. She dropped to crouch with a growl, ears back. "Leave us alone!" she growled at him. "If you don't back off, we will attack," she said, flicking her instinct on and preparing for his response.

"That's it. Get angry at me all you want, but you'd better keep running," he growled back, and snapped at her, nearly getting her in the nose.

She flinched back and took off running again before she even realized what she was doing.

"You're not nearly fast enough. I'm not even breathing hard and you're dragging your tail on the ground. Move! How are you going to save Little Flower or Hope if a crawly can run faster than you?"

Swipe.

*You want fast, I'll show you fast,* she thought, and let her instinct free. They roared their anger, as they bolted forward.

*Yes!* her instinct purred as they ran faster than they'd ever run before. *We are fast and fierce when we work together. Our prey will never escape, and we'll be strong enough to protect our cub.*

"That's all you've got? Pah, a bumble crawler could outrun you," he taunted.

Swipe.

"ENOUGH!" they growled and spun to face him again. Haunches down, they prepared to leap. If he thought he could keep doing this he was wrong. He faced them and they circled each other.

"What's the matter? Too slow to keep up with your Papa? Need a break, Little Kitten?" he sneered, and then swiped at them again.

They growled and leapt. He batted her out of the air mid leap and she landed hard on her side. With another growl she picked herself up and started circling him, her instinct trying to find a weak spot.

*There!* it told her.

She charged, ducking under his swipe, and leapt. He spun faster than she could watch, and she went flying again.

*How did he move so fast?* she wondered.

***You gave yourself away. Don't let your butt wiggle or your eyes show where you are going to attack. Find your target and explode,*** her instinct explained.

"Is that all you've got? A cub can move faster. I thought you were better than that," he sneered.

"Yeah well maybe I'm not. Maybe you should have taught me better," she hissed at him. "But how could you? You were never here, were you? Always off at the Council, caring more about everyone else than me, or Mama! You didn't think about what bringing the Hue-mans to Mama's clinic would mean for either of us, did you? You just offered up Mama to whatever plague the Hue-mans brought with them, and sent me a text message that you were going to be stuck at work, and left it up to me to find my own way home, as always," she roared, hurt by his words, and leapt again.

He ducked but not quite enough, and she made contact with her claws as she sailed over him. The smell of blood hit her nose.

***Yes! Much better,*** her instinct purred.

"I didn't even get to hug Mama goodbye before she was stuck in quarantine for months on end!" Marsee hissed, after landing and spinning to face him again.

"How would you even know if I was there or not? You always spent most of your days locked in that tower room of yours," he said, not even showing that he'd been scratched or even cared about what she'd said.

"Staying there was better than facing your disapproval every time the lights bothered me, or I couldn't sit still, or something triggered my instinct. Do you think I didn't notice how disappointed you were in me? Nothing I ever did was good enough for you!"

"Can you blame me?" he asked.

Furious, she gave her instinct more control. **"Yes. We can, and we do,"** they growled and leapt again. He frowned at her statement, but still managed to swat her out of the air barely trying, only this time they landed hard on a rock. They yipped with the sharp pain they felt in their shoulder, and lay there, gasping for breath, and watched him stalk forward, with an absolutely feral look in his eyes. His eyes dilated and his nose flared. *Was he losing control?*

He growled at her, and swiped again.

***He's going to hurt you. Move! Now!*** her instinct yelled, and pulled her out of the way of his swipe moments before it landed.

She scrambled to her feet and started running again, this time in fear, although her shoulder hurt badly, and she couldn't run nearly as fast as before.

Swipe.

They yelped as his claws dug deep and they pushed themselves further trying to get away from him. They were seeing their father as less and less a member of their family, and more as someone who wanted to hurt them.

***Fight back!*** her instinct insisted. ***We're injured and we can't outrun him. Stop running and fight back!***

"You really are a disappointment. We should have picked your sister Hope, instead of you," he said, and swiped at her again, this time clawing her hard in her already sore shoulder.

Marsee roared her pain and grief and gave herself completely over to her instinct. She'd had enough. It wrenched them around in a massive twisting leap, and grabbed his scruff with her teeth and dug her claws into his sides, pulling him to the ground, and pinning him there.

*That's it! Now we show him who's in charge!* her instinct purred with their victory, and showed her a dozen ways she could kill him.

"Marsee..." her father squeaked.

They growled at him to shut him up, and clamped tighter. He struggled to get loose, but they kept him pinned for several long moments, until he stopped fighting her.

As soon as he did, she let go of her bite to his scruff, but kept his head pinned down so he couldn't move, and pushed her thoroughly annoyed instinct back slightly, but not off. *I want to make him understand how he's hurting us, and make him stop, not kill him,* she told her instinct.

*Fine, but if he doesn't back off, then we kill him,* it said. *No one hurts us and gets away with it.*

Marsee agreed and turned her attention back to her father. He shifted to try and get up again, during her momentary lack of focus, but she growled in warning, and he stilled.

**"Maybe you should have picked our litter-mate instead. You never listened to us. You wouldn't believe us when we said the lights bothered us, not till Ammond proved us right. We almost killed Little Flower, and where were you? At a Council Meeting, where you** *always* **are. You say we're always in our room, but how would you know? You're never here. You care more about strangers than you do us. You've never seen us as anything but a disappointing monster. It wouldn't surprise us if you were just hoping that Uncle Marcus would kill us that night in the garden, so you wouldn't have to get your paws dirty. You knew we were having problems, yet you saw nothing wrong with bringing helpless, defenseless prey into our very home. Did you want us to lose control? What kind of parent are you? No father of mine would do what you just did."**

Her control slipped some as she gave voice to the pain she was feeling. They hurt, they were furious, and they wanted him to feel some of the pain and fear they had felt. He was twice their size, but they didn't care. They were in control now. They needed to destroy something and he was there. They roared their fury, at him, at the world, snapped once at him close enough to make him flinch and try to scramble up again. They could smell his fear and they purred with victory. They pinned him back down until he stilled, and then she flicked off her instinct, and turned and limped away on all fours, ears back and tail lashing in fury, and swatted at an unfortunate crawly in her path instead. If he was that disappointed in her, she would find someplace else to live. There was no way she was going to live in the same tower as him now.

*What are you doing?* her instinct asked. *We had him pinned!*

*And we can do it again,* she told it. *If we killed him, the Council and Guard wouldn't believe that he was attacking us, and would kill us instead, but if he ever tries to hurt us again, he won't get back up.* Her instinct purred with pleasure and settled back down, content with that answer. They were fierce and they knew it now.

"Thank the moons," her father whispered.

Ears back in astonishment she turned and looked back at him.

"If that didn't trigger you to lose control, nothing will. I'm sorry Marsee for what I said. I really am. I had to push you. I needed you so angry at me that you forgot to focus on your control."

She growled at him and limped away. *It was just another moons' forsaken test,* she thought. A hundred feet or so later she stopped. Her shoulder throbbed with every step now that her instinct was off, and she collapsed to the ground, panting hard, and began licking at her shoulder, trying to make it stop hurting, and wrinkled her nose at the taste of her blood.

He walked up and sat down beside her.

"When are you ever going to believe me?" she asked quietly, not turning to look at him.

"I do believe you. If it makes you feel any better, this is what Marcus did to me for months, and he was far worse," he said after a while.

"Not really. You just promised me you wouldn't do this anymore, and five minutes later you're at it again. When is it going to end?" she snapped at him.

"To be fair, I just agreed not to bite you anymore, and I didn't," he said, trying to lighten the mood.

She flicked her ears back, and growled at him. He immediately looked contrite, realizing his humor hadn't gone over well. "Don't you dare try to loop-hole your way out of this. You knew what I meant and you broke your promise to me. Your word as a Senior Councilor, implied or otherwise, is supposed to be sacrosanct. How am I supposed to ever trust you again?"

He didn't answer for several minutes. "I'm sorry, Marsee. I'm sorry I didn't believe you about your hearing. I'm sorry I didn't work with you more on your control, and I'm sorry I have to spend so much time away from you and the family, and that I wasn't here when you needed me the most."

"But you're not sorry about attacking me?" she hissed.

He sighed. "No. I did what I had to," he replied. "I'm sorry I had to, but I would do it again, if I felt you were losing control. It's my responsibility to protect the people of New Hope, even if that means killing my daughter. I wouldn't have been able to stop you on my own, as you've so clearly proven, and I wanted you far away from everyone else."

"So I'm never allowed to be angry or upset again?" she asked. "Do I have to live my life hidden behind a mask, so just so you won't kill me if I growl or want to go for a run?"

"Marsee, you had your instinct on, and you marked a tree. That's not just angry. By all rights I should have killed you," he replied.

"And I wouldn't have been so angry I needed to mark the tree if *you* hadn't pounced on me in the first place," she countered. "Would you rather I claw a tree or you?"

"I would rather you didn't claw anything," he replied.

"And you've never gotten so angry that you didn't hit or claw something? Not once?" she spat at him. He didn't answer, which told her everything. "That's what I thought."

He was silent again for a while as she continued to lick her wounds, knowing they would need to stop bleeding or her mother would sniff them out, if not some predator. She just hoped they didn't need suturing, as she didn't want to explain what happened to a healer.

"What happened to Little Flower is not your fault Marsee, if it's anyone's fault, it's mine. You're right. I am the one that brought them to your mother's clinic, without asking her or you about it first, and that was wrong of me. Maybe another location and another senior healer would have meant Little Flower wouldn't have ended up in a coma, but then you would never have met her, and without her here, I would have lost you, and we wouldn't have Hope either. It wasn't your fault that Little Flower climbed the tree and broke a rib. If it's anyone's fault, it's mine. I chose not to stand up to your mother, even though I knew she was breaking a direct order of the Senior Council by destroying the leash. By all rights, I should have reported her, but I didn't, just like I didn't report you, even though I knew I was losing you to psychosis. When you went non-verbal on me in my office, I should have ended it there, but I couldn't. That night when you walked into my office, I was typing up my resignation letter to the Council. I knew what was coming, and I couldn't bear to be a part of that. I texted Marcus, not because I wanted him to do it, but because I knew I couldn't, wouldn't be able to. I was sure I was walking with you to your execution, and when you lost control I should have killed you before you could escape and harm anyone else, but I just couldn't. I had to give you the same chance that Marcus gave me. I wasn't disappointed in you, Marsee. I have *never* been disappointed in you. I was disappointed in myself, for not being able to help you, for not knowing *how* to help you. Every time I saw you struggle, I was right back to that day with Marcus when I lost control and almost killed someone I cared about. I should have spent more time with you, like Marcus did with me, but I was afraid, afraid I'd push you over the edge and then have no choice but to kill you. It was easier to pretend you weren't struggling, that you were doing better, that you had it under control, and I'm so very, very sorry." His voice broke with emotion, far more emotion than she'd ever heard from him before.

"How did you stop it, when you lost control?" Marsee finally asked.

"I didn't," he said softly.

Marsee turned her head and looked up at her father.

"Marcus did. That first time. Marcus managed to snap me out of it with pain and a bite to the scruff. That sometimes works. I got lucky. Something about that motion triggers the same reflex to stop as when we're cubs. After that, Marcus and I spent months out in the Wilds where he pushed me daily to make sure I didn't lose control again, and that meant stopping mid hunt after fasting for days, and far worse than what I did here today to you. Marcus didn't let me return home until my instinct saw him as dominant, and I don't even want to describe what he had to do to make that happen. I could never do that to you. Your mother almost left me because I was gone for so long, and I couldn't tell her why. I tried to snap you out of it that night in the garden, but it didn't work with you. If anything it made things worse and I almost lost my grip on you. I don't know why. Maybe it was because I wasn't around enough that your instinct didn't recognize me the way it did with Little Flower, the way mine did with Marcus. Maybe it was because you were further along than I was. I never struggled with it the way you did as a cub, and I only ever had that one slip where I lost control of who I was. Maybe that's why I didn't know how to help you. Obviously what I tried didn't help, and I'm sorry."

Marsee sighed and sat up, wincing with pain. She carefully tried moving her sore shoulder, and hissed. "It's getting late. We'd better get going or I'll be late for my shift to watch Hope," she said, and carefully stood up and started limping back. She really didn't want to talk about this, or even be around him right now, but she knew he would just follow her back.

"Marsee..."

She stopped but didn't turn around to look back at him.

"I've always been proud of you, and I always will be. You amaze me every day with how talented, caring, smart, and tenacious you are, and I'm so very sorry if I've ever given you the impression that I wasn't."

She sighed, nodded once, and kept limping her way back to the compound.

He walked up beside her and they walked in silence for a while. "Are you hurt?" he asked eventually.

"Yes, but I'll live," she said, and kept walking.

"That's good. I might not," he replied. She looked over. "You got me good. I underestimated you," he said with a wink.

"Yeah, well, you might want to stop doing that," she said with a growl. "Because you won't walk away if you ever try this little stunt again, and it won't be my hunting instinct in charge either. This ends today. No more tests. Ever." She didn't care that she was threatening a Senior Councilor. She would not allow anyone to treat her as he'd treated her today, test or otherwise.

He nodded, and they continued walking back to the compound in silence for some time.

"Do you want me to call my ship?" he asked, when she shifted to walking on two feet. It was much slower, but it hurt too much to walk on four.

"No," she replied. She didn't want his pilots to see her injured, and she was just peeved enough to make him want to feel uncomfortable watching her limp back, even if it hurt.

"You should have a healer check out that shoulder," he replied after a while.

She stopped and stared at him. "You're seriously recommending I walk up to Mama with these injuries? How am I supposed to explain dozens of claw marks and bite marks to my scruff?"

He sighed. "I suppose you could say you went for a run and a wild animal attacked you."

She snorted and kept walking. "I wouldn't have allowed a wild animal to do this to me. You're lucky you're alive."

"I know," he replied, and they walked the rest of the way back to the tower in silence. He raided his ship's first aid supply, while she showered, and brought her a small tube of nano-cream and helped to treat the worst of her injuries, but she just glared at him when the tube was empty long before all of her wounds were treated, and left him standing there holding the empty tube. Not surprisingly, she arrived late for her shift to watch and care for her sister and niece. When she finally arrived in the ward, her mother was outside of the room pacing as she carried Hope.

"Sorry I'm late. Papa and I were talking and I lost track of time. Is everything okay?" she asked.

Her mother sighed and twitched her whiskers. "Yes. No. There's no change. I'm just restless and frustrated and sick of that room, and Hope wouldn't go to sleep. This is no place to raise a cub."

Marsee nodded. "I don't blame you. I'm starting to loathe this place too. Does Little Flower really need to be here, or could we bring them home?" Marsee placed her tablet and the craft supplies that she'd brought with her on the small desk that had been added to the room after the first week.

Her mother stopped pacing and looked at her, considering. "I suppose we could convert the family room into a ward to treat her, but there's a lot of equipment she needs or might need if something goes wrong. It would take too long to get her to the ward, and with all of that equipment, it would feel just like here anyway."

"I could build something to hide it all, and we'd be able to add plants and flowers and make it more comfortable for us to care for her. Plus nothing in this room is designed for GrandFather. You know how much he wants to help. Little Flower loved my hanging bed and Hope loves motion. I could build a bed like mine that GrandFather could raise and lower so he could help more."

"Hope is starting to move around more. She lifted her head the other day on her own. I'm worried she might roll off of a bed if we aren't watching her," her mother said, as she considered Marsee's suggestions. "Could you make the bed with sides that could be raised and lowered, like her bed here?"

"I don't see why not," Marsee replied.

Her mother nodded. "Then let's do it. I'll put in the order for new equipment. I don't want to take anything from here. I'll send you a list of what I've ordered so you can figure out a way to hide it. Let me know what you need and I'll clear it with Ellie if we don't already have it in the guild hall."

"Okay, I'll start on some designs tonight. Why don't you go home and spend some time with Papa before he has to head out for that Council Meeting tomorrow," she said, wanting her mother gone before she started asking what she'd been talking about with her father.

"What would I do without you, Marsee?" her mother said, and gave her a one armed hug before carefully handing Hope to her, trying not to wake the tiny cub.

Marsee tried hard not to wince as her mother squeezed her throbbing shoulder. She watched her mother as she made her way out of the ward, and then sighed before turning and walking into Little Flower's room. She carefully placed Hope down in her crib and then went over to her sister, patting her head. "I wish you'd hurry up and either wake up or pass on, little sister. This waiting is killing Mama. I miss you so much, but I can't stand seeing you like this," She knew that her sister couldn't understand, and likely couldn't even hear her, but she needed to say it.

With a sigh, she emptied the waste bags, cleaned and fed her sister, and then began the exercises her mother insisted they do with her. She wasn't sure what the point of it was since Little Flower just seemed to get smaller and weaker every day, but it was something to do, and it helped pass the hours. When the exercises were done, she picked up her tablet and started sketching the new bed.

When she was done with that, she checked on her sister and Hope again. They continued to sleep, so she switched to working on translating one of the books that the Hue-man's had written. It was slow going but her ability to read their written language was improving. This was the fourth book she'd worked on since they'd arrived at the compound, not including her sister's book. Dozens more had been written by the Hue-mans trying to preserve their history before it was forgotten, and they were all awaiting her translation. This was the first one she'd worked on entirely by herself, and she really missed collaborating with her sister on it. It just wasn't the same, and she found it hard to focus on.

Still, she worked on it for several hours until Hope woke and started crying. "Hey there, what's the matter?" she asked, before sniffing out the answer. Sure enough, Hope had made a mess. Wrinkling her nose, she carried Hope over to the sink to wash her down and dry her off. The Hue-man mothers had some sort of baby poop sack that they used, but her parents' hands were too big to easily manage the tiny articles of clothing. After the third time trying, they'd given up and decided it was easier to just wash her down and clean the bedding when she messed, like they did with their own cubs.

Once Hope was thoroughly clean, she brought her over and set her down on Little Flower's chest so she could nurse, tucking the cloth strap around her so Hope wouldn't fall, and went over to change the bedding in Hope's crib. Careful not to touch any of the stinky, goopy mess, she quickly deposited it into the cleaning unit that had been installed in the room shortly after Hope had been born. That taken care of, she pulled out a fresh set of bedding and quickly made up the crib.

She checked on Little Flower to see if she needed cleaning again too, and emptied the containers into the waste hole, recording how much was there. Why her mother needed to know that, she had no idea either, but she did as she was asked. When Hope finished nursing, she burped the tiny cub, cleaned that mess, and then carried her around and purred until Hope fell asleep again. Gently setting her down next to her mother, she yawned and left to use the waste room herself.

On the way back, she grabbed a snack from the refrigeration unit in the ward and decided to have the healer on duty look at her shoulder, which was really starting to bother her. The nano cream her father had given her had long since worn off.

The Healer frowned at her scanner and looked hard at her. "How did you hurt yourself so badly?" Marsee refused to answer. The Healer glared at her but then sighed. "You have a hairline fracture in your shoulder, bruises everywhere, and what look like multiple claw and bite marks. Did someone attack you?"

"No, and I'd prefer that my mother not be informed of this either. She has enough to worry about with Little Flower," she lied, but refused to give any further information. The healer frowned at her, but nodded. Marsee was an adult now, and if she didn't want to divulge information, she didn't have to. A few minutes later her fracture had been repaired and two of the deeper cuts cleaned out and sutured. She was then handed a large jar of the nano cream and sent on her way.

When she returned to her sister's room, Hope had messed all over Little Flower. "You just went! Where do you keep it all? You're nothing but a little poop machine," Marsee muttered, as she set the jar down and went through the effort of cleaning both of them up and changing Little Flower's bed. This time she put Hope back in her crib, as she decided she wanted to curl up with her sister instead.

After applying a liberal dose of the pain cream to her shoulder and the rest of her other cuts and bruises from her little 'talk' with her father, she carefully picked up her sister and curled up with her on the massive chair next to the bed. Little Flower had a monitor embedded in her skin and the room's display programmed to focus only on her, so she was able to move her sister without having to worry that she'd set off an alarm. "Please wake up, little sister," she whispered and started purring. With her sister now safe in her arms where she belonged, Marsee fell instantly asleep.

She was still curled up like that when her father woke her early the next morning to say goodbye before he had to leave for his council meeting.

"Hey, Kitten," her father said, giving her a gentle shake, "Time to wake up."

"Oh. I guess I was more exhausted than I thought. I didn't mean to fall asleep," she said with a massive yawn. He gently lifted Little Flower out of her arms and transferred her back to the bed while she uncurled from her position in the oversized chair and cautiously stretched.

"I won't tell your mother, and you did run halfway across the wilds yesterday," he chuckled. "How's your shoulder?" he asked.

She frowned at the reminder. "It still hurts, but it's better. I had the healer check it out last night. There was a fracture and several of the cuts you gave me had to be sutured," she said after testing it out. She was still furious at him, even if she understood why he'd done it.

He frowned. "I really am sorry about that."

She just glared at him, and then sniffed. "Ugh, Hope messed again. Where does she keep it all? I swear their bellies must exist in another dimension," she grumbled to her father.

She tried to pick up Hope carefully, so as to not wake her, but Hope had other ideas, and started crying loudly. The high pitched noise made her pin her ears back.

"It's alright, Hope. I'll have you cleaned up in a minute. Then you can go have your breakfast and mess all over again, but then it'll be Mama's turn to clean you up."

Her father laughed, but helped her by cleaning up the crib while she washed and cleaned up Hope, and then applied some of the nano cream, noticing that Hope was looking a little sore from having slept in her mess. "Sorry about that, Hope," she said. Hope stopped crying almost immediately. "I bet that hurt huh? Poor little cub. I'm a terrible Mama, I know. Everyone says so." She was unable to keep the hurt out of her voice, and she felt horrible that she'd fallen asleep on her watch, and that Hope had suffered for it.

"I didn't mean what I said, and I'm sorry. You're doing just fine," her father said, "especially considering that you shouldn't even be doing this for another twenty or thirty years. I really appreciate your help though. I doubt I'd ever get your mother to come home to sleep if you weren't here."

Marsee just frowned. "Papa, How long is Mama going to do this? Little Flower isn't getting any better. It doesn't seem right to just let her waste away like this," she asked after setting Hope down to nurse again.

"I don't know, Kitten. I really don't," he finally answered, walking over to give her a hug. "She won't talk about it with me. Every time I've tried, she's practically bitten my ears off. I'm guessing until Hope is old enough to wean."

"Papa, if something like this ever happens to me, let me go. This is no kind of life," she said.

He hugged her tighter. She yelped as sharp pain throbbed in her shoulder, and he backed off immediately.

"Sorry, Kitten. I hope I never have to make that decision, but I promise you, I won't let that happen, even if it means I have to fight your mother," he said.

"Dark moons! She'll tear you to pieces! Look what she did to Uncle Marcus. Looks like we're both doomed," she chuckled, although part of her was highly amused at the idea of her mother giving her father a piece of what he'd done to her the day before.

"You're probably right. Best thing for both of us is for you to keep that furry little brain of yours safe, then."

"Sounds like a plan," she said. "Will you bring me something back from Flyer?"

"Don't I always?" he asked.

They talked further about the day before, and he asked her again if she wanted to come with him, but she declined. She was still furious with him for everything he'd said, even if it had only been intended to push her control, and frankly she had no desire to be stuck on a ship with him for two days, not in the mood she was in. He gave her another far more careful hug, and left to catch his ship.

She watched him leave and sighed with mixed feelings. She was used to him leaving and being gone for days or weeks at a time. He'd been a councilor for longer than she'd been alive, but the needs of being a Senior Councilor required far more of his time than she was used to, even with everyone he represented living under the same roof. She usually hated to see him leave, but today she was both glad he would be leaving, and worried what her mother would do with him gone for a full week. As she leaned up against the doorway, her nose picked up the smell of mess again.

"Not again!" she groaned, and with a tortured sigh, pushed herself off of the door sill and went back into the room to clean her niece and wait for her mother. When her mother arrived, looking far more rested than she'd been in weeks, Marsee was relieved. *At least someone in this family managed to have a decent night's sleep,* she thought, bitterly.

"How did everything go last night?" her mother asked.

"Fine. Hope sure makes an awfully big mess though," she said through a yawn.

"So did you when you were little. Even more, since you were more than twice her size" her mother teased.

"I'm pretty sure that's impossible after how many times I've had to clean her and Little Flower. She nursed about an hour ago, so you should have a couple of hours of quiet before she wakes. I'm going to bed," she yawned again, and grabbed the jar of pain cream and the other items she'd brought with her.

"What's with the nanos?" her mother asked with a frown.

"It's nothing, I just banged my shoulder into something yesterday. I had Healer Samin take a look at it last night. She said it's just bruised. Night," she said with a fake yawn. She didn't want to go into *how* she'd hurt her shoulder with her mother, and she hoped her mother wouldn't bother digging into the medical report if she thought it was just a bruise.

"Reading while walking again?" her mother asked, tail curled.

Marsee just rolled her eyes.

"Sleep tight, Marsee, and thank you. You've been an amazing help, and I'm sorry I've had to ask it of you," her mother said, giving her a kiss on her forehead.

"It's okay. Little Flower would do the same for me," she said, and yawned again, this time for real.

"Go on, off to bed with you! If you keep yawning like that I'm not going to make it ten minutes into my shift," her mother said, with a little push in the direction of the door. Marsee bolted before her mother could change her mind.

She lost all sense of time and self as drifted in the darkness tethered above her body. Only the occasional tug by a weight on her chest reminded her that it was even there. She knew there was something important about that weight, but it never remained long enough for her to figure out what it was, and she'd soon forget about it and drift off back into nothingness the moment it was gone.

One day, motion twanged along her tether, but then a feeling of warmth and love surrounded her. Sighing with happiness, she burrowed into that warmth, feeling like a piece of her that had been missing had returned. It took her time to realize that the source of that warmth and love was surrounding her body, and she started to drift closer to it again to figure out what it was, curious for the first time in as long as she could remember, but like the other feeling it too eventually vanished.

She cried out into the ether and mourned its loss, not knowing what it was, but desperately wanting it back. She tried to follow it, but it was like trying to follow the memory of a dream, and it too eventually vanished, until one day she felt another twang, and found herself being pulled by her tether. It didn't last long though but the still darkness around her was now a gently rocking sea. At first the motion was unsettling after so long in stillness, but she soon grew to welcome it, as there was little else in this dark endless expanse.

The feeling of love and warmth returned along with that gentle rocking motion, but it was different somehow. It didn't fit her the same way the other feeling had, and while it was nice, she eventually drifted off again. Each time the feeling of warmth and love returned, she woke a little, realized it wasn't what she was looking for, and drifted off again in search. Eventually she stopped checking and just allowed herself to drift on the sea, her tether stretching as she drifted further and further from her body, hoping perhaps one day she might find what she was missing again, and eventually she forgot that there had ever been anything but the sea, or what she was looking for, or that she was even looking.

# CHAPTER 24

# Kendra: Flag

Kendra sat in her office digging through her backlog. She honestly looked forward to the weeks the Council was off planet, as it was usually far quieter, and she could get caught up on her work. At the very least, she wasn't buried in as many meetings, and she could usually get in a couple of extra training sessions, which is what she planned for the coming week. She normally sent her second, Quinn Bluestone, to the Full Council meetings, but this time she'd sent her nephew Avery, as he needed the practice. She fully expected that the Hue-mans wouldn't form a guard once they reached town size, and was planning to transfer Avery and his squad to New Hope.

Yawning, as she'd woken up far too early to check over the council's transport ships before they left, a task she never left for anyone else, she pulled up the next ticket in her queue, and swore in three languages.

*It would have to show up now while they're both off planet,* Kendra thought bitterly, as she read through the flag on Marsee's medical record. She had seen enough of these scans in her life to know Marsee had been fighting. *The question is, with who, or what, and why.*

"Quinn, my office," she ordered, hitting the comms.

"Yes, ma'am," he replied, and a few moments later appeared. She motioned for him to shut the door, and then activated her privacy screen before putting the flag up on the monitor. "Your thoughts?"

He frowned as he examined the scans and the Healer's notes. "She only wanted it hidden from her mother, which likely means her father already knows. Based on the size of these bites and cuts, my guess is they came from him."

"Agreed. So did he attack her as the healer believes, or was he stopping her?" she asked.

"Your guess is as good as mine, but I'm leaning towards stopping her," Quinn replied. "Shall I bring her in for observation or question her?"

"No," Kendra ordered.

"No?" Quinn replied, surprised. "Test, psychosis, or abuse, we're duty bound to act."

"I have my orders. We do not bring her in until she comes to us on her own, or transitions," Kendra replied.

"By who's orders?" Quinn asked, stopping her with a frown. "No one has the authorization to give you orders like that. Not even the Senior Council."

Kendra frowned at her second, the only one she'd ever allow to talk back to her like that, and considered. *I suppose it's time he knows.* "The General's orders," she finally answered.

He looked at her in surprise for several moments and then snorted with laughter. "You had me there for a second," he replied, tail curling, and then stopped, and stared at her. "Wait, you're serious? *The General?*"

She replied with a single nod and stood, retrieved the hidden key, opened the secret compartment in her desk, and with a heavy sigh handed him the ancient document. He took it with curiosity that shifted to shock as he read.

"You're serious. Marsee's the General?" he asked. "The prophecy's real? That wasn't just some ghost story to make new guards cautious?"

"I honestly don't know, but I'm operating under the assumption she is. I saw nothing concerning at the Trial, but it's been a while since we've had a guard in New Hope. The Hue-mans are stupid and short-sighted, but I understand why they don't want us around. You tell no one about this except your second, after I'm long dead and gone. Is that understood?"

"Yes, ma'am," he replied, and handed the document back. She carefully locked it back up, after reading it again for the hundredth time, and hid the key. She stared at her bookcase for a moment before turning back around.

"But you're right. We are duty bound to act. Come on. I want your opinion on her too. If she is losing control or close to transitioning, I don't want that to happen when there's no one around to protect the citizens of New Hope, and if she's being abused, we should gather evidence to bring to Surellis when he returns."

An hour later they were landing in New Hope. "She's likely at the clinic with her sister, her home, or the Guild," Kendra said to Quinn, and ordered the squad of guards she'd brought with her to wait on the ship. She didn't want to give the people of New Hope concern if they saw them, unless there was a good enough reason to bring them out. She and Quinn should be able to handle an in-betweener long enough to call in the rest of the guards if it came to that.

It was still early, so she decided to take the new underground utility tunnels to the watch station just outside of the tower, hoping to catch Marsee as she left for the morning, while she sent Quinn to the clinic to check there, so it was with a bit of a surprise that she found Marsee making her way back to her tower instead. She called Quinn to let him know she'd found her, and a few minutes later, he joined her in the tight space.

"She just arrived home," she told him quietly. "She looks exhausted, but I didn't see any issues, outside of being angry and pinning her ears back at her parent's door. I expect she'll probably sleep for a few hours at..."

She stopped talking as Marsee left her room and started trudging down the ramp again, with what looked like art supplies in hand. *On the way to the Guild?* she wondered. At the bottom of the ramp though, Marsee hesitated, first looking outside and then towards the inner compound. She seemed to make up her mind and entered the courtyard and made her way into the garden.

Kendra frowned as she'd have to leave the tunnels to follow. Making up her mind, she sent Quinn to the other side, in the event she was just cutting through on her way to the guild hall, and waited for the halls to clear before following after. People might recognize her, but most wouldn't care, or see anything odd about her being here, as it was her right.

She followed Marsee's trail into the garden. While she'd seen it before, she still marveled at the space Myra had created here. The overwhelming scents of the flowers made it difficult to track, but she wasn't the Senior Honor Guard for no reason. Still, it took her a while to find Marsee without giving away that she was in the garden, and when she did, it was to find the child curled up in an out of the way clearing, drawing.

It took her a good half hour to work her way around so she could get a clear look at Marsee without her knowing she was there, but frowned again in confusion at what she saw.

*She's drawing with her instinct on?* Kendra thought, sure she was mistaken. There was no sign of jaggedness around the child, but her eyes were dilated, and she was actively sniffing her surroundings. Kendra's ears flicked back as Quinn joined her. Eventually, Marsee closed her sketchbook, turned off her instinct, yawned, laid down, and moments later was sound asleep and snoring lightly.

Quinn said nothing, but she could sniff his astonishment too. She considered approaching, but decided to wait. That moment between sleep and awake was one of the times when a person's instinct could take control. An hour or so later, Marsee's alarm went off. She startled, hit the tablet with some force and went back to sleep. The tip of Kendra's tail curled and she could sniff Quinn's amusement, but she'd hadn't seen a waiver, which was a good thing. A few minutes later the alarm went off again and she groaned awake, rubbed at her eyes, and trudged her way back up to the tower, where she dropped off the sketchbook and left again. They waited until they were sure she was gone, and made their way up into Marsee's room. It didn't take her long to find the hidden sketchbook, and started flipping through it, frowning at what she saw.

"These are beautiful," Quinn said. "But it's pretty clear she's using her instinct to draw them. I didn't even know you could do that."

"She had her instinct on for more than an hour, without issue. Not even the slightest twang, not until she got back here. Whatever happened, happened at the bottom of the ramp or outside, since she looked towards the door again," Kendra said, and placed the sketchbook back where she'd found it, and continued examining the room. "She was angry there twice." She checked Marsee's desk looking for a journal, but found nothing. And after a thorough search found nothing concerning in the room, they left. At the bottom of the ramp, she sniffed hard, examining the hundreds of scents, and filtered it down to just Marsee's and the Senior Councilors.

She followed their trail to the door and outside, with Quinn following behind.

"He stopped her here," Quinn stated, examining a patch of the ground. "I'm smelling blood."

"Same," Kendra replied, as she examined it too, and continued examining the trail, thankful it hadn't rained the night before. "She walked off though, and he didn't follow for a while."

They continued on, and she honestly wished she hadn't, when they came to the clearly marked scrub tree. Her nose scrunched with the bitter scent of spray, and Quinn sighed, with a hint of grief. "This is not good, not if she's marking her territory."

Kendra didn't say anything as she leapt over the small stream and continued following the trail. An hour later, they made it to where the trail ended. She rubbed her ears as she examined the trail left behind, trying to make sense of what she was seeing. "There's blood. We know she was injured, but I can't tell who pinned who. It almost looks like she pinned him."

Quinn snorted. "Unlikely. He'd be dead if that were the case, but we need to bring her in."

"No," she said. "I'm not doing anything while both Senior Councilors are off planet. If he attacked her without just cause..."

"She sprayed. He had just cause," Quinn interrupted. "This shows every sign of being a test. He chased her off and attacked."

"Perhaps, but she didn't spray until after he pinned her the first time," Kendra countered. "I've been known to claw a few things myself in the day, when I've been angry enough, and if it was self defense, it would take time for anyone to calm down, even in the best of situations. Besides, when's the last time you've seen anyone as calm as her after something like this happened, test or otherwise. If she was a risk, she'd have been struggling hard in the garden, not calmly sitting there drawing with her instinct on. We need more information. We need to know what really happened and how often she's using her instinct, and if she's hunting. After what she's been through, I wouldn't be surprised if she's been practicing secretly on her own. If she's just practicing her control in what she feels is a safe manner, that's not a problem, yet. If she's hunting, that's a different story. I'm leaving you and a couple of guards here to watch her for the week. When the Senior Councilors get back, we'll deal with it then."

As her second, Quinn was high enough in rank that he rarely had watch duty, but Marsee was an anomaly, and she wouldn't be able to hide many guards in New Hope. Without a guard hall, she'd have to house him in the suite she had available for her use, and if there was a problem, Quinn was her best fighter, and that would be needed to contain the situation until help could arrive.

"You're seriously going to let someone who's sprayed walk free?" Quinn asked in surprise. "She should be tested."

"By all accounts, she *has* been tested. Enough to draw blood. We watch and wait," she ordered.

"Yes, ma'am," Quinn replied, although he didn't look or sound convinced.

She sighed. "I understand this goes against protocol, but everything about her is new, and we need to understand it better, before we deal with it. If drawing with your instinct helps people regain control, I'll raid the Guild with every last credit in my budget, if it saves even a single child. Until we know more, I'm considering this a case of abuse, not a loss of control, and treating it as such. New Hope is practically empty right now, or empty as it ever gets. Watch and report back, but do *not* approach, or arrest, unless she's actively out of control."

"Yes, ma'am," he replied and followed her back to her ship. He picked the guards he wanted with him, and she flew off, back to Council City, praying she wasn't making a mistake.

As she returned, she dug into Marsee's medical record and account, looking for other signs or evidence of abuse, as was both her right and responsibility as a Senior Honor Guard. Marsee's medical records were surprisingly clean, but then with her mother a master healer, there would be little need to seek out treatment. *Or it could have been hidden.* She was about halfway back to Council City, when she found Marsee's journal, and began reading.

When the ship landed, she ordered the rest of the guards off the ship, and continued reading, knowing if she returned to her office, she'd be interrupted and buried in other work. The insight into Marsee's experiences, both with her instinct and the Hue-man's culture and behavior were incredibly informative, and far more detailed than Marsee had shared with the Seniors. The final entries didn't explain in detail what had happened, but there was enough there to be concerning on multiple fronts. She saved a copy of the journal to the ticket for evidence, and then stared out her window into the shuttle bay as she considered what she'd read, then with a heavy sigh, returned to her office and the mountain of other work that awaited her.

# CHAPTER 25

# Marsee: Council City

The next week was pure madness as her mother filled her father's absence by renovating the family room. The medical supplies her mother ordered arrived in two days, and Marsee spent the rest of the week crafting the hanging bed, and designing the various furniture pieces to store the equipment, including adding a hidden compartment under the bed to hide Little Flower's mess until it could be emptied, and legs that could be lowered and set to different heights so that the swinging bed could be converted into a stable platform when needed. The bed was much smaller than hers and rectangular rather than circular to make it easier for everyone to care for her, but she still made it just big enough that the three of them could fit, after realizing just how much better she'd slept with Little Flower in her arms.

When the frame was done, she tested it out by carefully crawling onto it, bouncing hard several times, and then rocking it so hard it almost touched the sides of the room. When it didn't so much as creak, she deemed it safe for Little Flower and the cub. Rather than just pulling on a rope, she added a crank handle and several additional pulleys to reduce the effort to raise and lower the bed. Then she had Ben see if he could raise and lower it with her in it. He could without issue, which meant GrandFather would have no problem with Little Flower, when he returned from the Council meeting.

Once the special hydrophobic fabric had arrived, she fashioned a soft pillow to fit the bed that would be easy to clean, but then covered the whole thing with soft absorbent fabric that was easy to wash, and far softer than the bed coverings in the Trauma Center. She brought the soft chenzie fur blanket, Little Flower's stuffy that she'd been given at the Agency, and the beautiful rocking chair that the Guild Master had made, down from her room for GrandFather and Hope's use. Her mother replaced the monitor that had been in the family room with the latest in medical grade tech, and set up the needed equipment on temporary furniture until Marsee finished crafting the cabinets that would hide everything.

The day before her father and the others were due to return home, everything was finished, and they moved Little Flower and Hope. Her mother carried her sister while she carried Hope. There were only a few people in the halls when they moved them, and most watched with respectful silence or a nod in sympathy. All but one, Damon. He didn't say anything but something about his mannerisms bothered her. She still misread their facial expressions at times, but for a moment, he seemed positively gleeful that her sister was still in a coma, and then he frowned at Hope. She glared back at him and he turned and walked away. She made a mental note to talk to her father about him when he returned, and hugged Hope tighter. Her instinct's hackles were raised, but she reminded herself there was little he could do to hurt Hope, protected as she was by both her and her mother.

Once her sister and niece were settled, and Hope had happily claimed the stuffy as her own, Marsee flopped on the couch in the room and immediately fell asleep. She was exhausted, but she didn't get the chance to sleep for very long. Ellie surprised them all by showing up an hour later with a gift of a matching rocking chair that was big enough for her mother to use, along with multiple warnings to watch their tails.

She'd apparently sent Nardal to the Council in her place and had taken an actual vacation, and spent part of it crafting the chair. Marsee wondered what it meant that the Senior Guild Master had to take time off from her work at the Guild to find time to craft. Hope absolutely loved the rocking chair, and they found that even Little Flower's vitals seemed to strengthen when they rocked her. Marsee carefully tried it out and found she loved it too. It worked on her much the same way her swinging bed did, to calm her anxiety, and she decided she'd set credit aside to requisition one for her room, knowing it would probably take months to earn enough to pay for Ellie's craftsmanship.

She thought about trying to craft one herself, but knew she just didn't have the time or skill to even come close to what Ellie had made for them. While she rocked Hope, Ellie wandered the room checking out the various pieces of furniture that Marsee had made. "This is all beautiful work, Marsee, functional and elegant at the same time. I'm impressed at the design choices you made to make it easy to use by both your mother and GrandFather, as well."

"Thank you," Marsee said, nearly ecstatic with the praise.

She was embarrassed and nearly catatonic as *the* Senior Guild Master started to closely examine her work, after her mother pointed out all of the pieces she'd made. It had been bad when she'd checked out her tools and workbenches, but those had all been fairly utilitarian and designed to take the abuse of further crafting, and while Ellie had run off with several of her paintings they hadn't been given more than a cursory examination, and she knew artwork was subjective. What one person could love another person might hate.

But Ellie was a skilled crafter, and one of the best too. She'd put far more effort into these items than normal, since they were for her sister and would be seen by visitors, but also as an excuse to avoid her mother, and as a way to calm down, as crafting always helped. Even still, Marsee could see so many flaws, a smudge in the stain there, a seam that didn't quite line up on another piece, and if she could see them, they must be glaringly obvious to the Guild Master.

"It's nothing like the quality of this rocking chair, but I'm pretty happy with how it all came out," Marsee said, as Ellie examined how one of the equipment cabinets worked.

"As you should be. I've been making furniture for well over a hundred years, but I'm not sure I would have come up with some of the ingenious ideas you did for all of this equipment, especially in such a short time. You did good, Marsee."

Marsee just beamed with the praise.

*I like her,* her instinct purred. *She smells of power and strength, and she recognizes our worth, unlike some people. She can stay.*

Marsee blinked in surprise. The only time her instinct had spoken about someone like that was with her sister, and it rarely spoke now, when not called forward. *What does that mean?* she wondered.

*It means you should listen and learn from her. She will make us powerful and strong, and then no one will dare push us around or threaten our cub,* it replied.

~~~~~

Later that evening, Marsee sat out on the balcony overlooking the paddocks and watched the suns set. Her father and the others would be home tomorrow afternoon, and she wasn't looking forward to talking with him about their last conversation, or dealing with the fallout.

"Mind if I join you?"

Marsee looked over to see the Guild Master walking up the ramp and flicked her ears back in surprise. Her instinct purred with pleasure, but Marsee was out of sorts. "I'm not much company right now," she warned, turning her head back to look out at the view.

"I figured as much. Your mother said you were struggling with all the changes, and I figured you could use a friend. If you need someone to talk to, I'm here."

"Thanks," Marsee said, surprised that Ellie considered them friends, but didn't respond otherwise. Ellie didn't say anything either or push her to open up, just sat there with her in companionable silence as they watched the suns set and the animals graze below.

"I'm thinking about switching guilds again," Marsee said eventually.

"Oh? To what?" Ellie asked.

"Not sure. Maybe the Tech or Ship's Guild. I avoided most of the Tech disciplines because they made my ears twitch, but now I have those hearing aids, and well, I've always wanted to learn how to fly."

"What about the translations you're working on?" Ellie asked.
~~~~~

"They're fun and interesting, but it's not the same without Little Flower," Marsee explained.

"Ah."

"You're not upset?" Marsee asked.

"Why would I be?" Ellie replied.

"I don't know. Because I should be focusing on one or two sub specialties by now, not changing guilds again, maybe?"

"So why don't you?" Ellie asked.

Marsee thought for a while. "Because I can't decide on any one. I like them all, but at the same time, I can't see myself focusing on just one thing. Every time I've tried, I end up wanting nothing to do with it. I like to bounce around, work on one thing for a while, and then try something new, and learn whatever skill I need to complete whatever project I have in mind."

"Is that why you want to switch guilds? To try something new, or do you have a project in mind?" Ellie asked.

Marsee opened her mouth to answer and then closed it when she realized she didn't have an answer.

"Or are you just trying to run away from all of this?" Ellie asked, waving her paw at the compound.

"I...I don't know," Marsee finally admitted. "Maybe a little of both."

"That's fair. Do you mind if I give you some advice?" Ellie asked.

"Not at all," Marsee replied.

"I think you should learn anything and everything that interests you. To the moons and back with becoming a master in any one discipline. If there's something you want to learn or a class you want to take at the Guild, do so. You let me know and I'll make sure you have a spot, no questions asked. As for learning to fly, you don't need to join the Ship's Guild to do that. Personally, I don't think you would do well over there. It's too...regimented for someone with your level of creativity. But one of the benefits of being the Senior Guild Master is that I have my very own ship and several very competent pilots on my staff to cart my furry butt from planet to planet, and right now they're bored silly, since the only place I've gone in the past few months is here, and I don't really need them for that."

"Really? You'd do that for me?" Marsee asked. She hadn't even thought about asking her father to learn on his ship, knowing that he might have to leave at a moment's notice.

"Of course! What's the point of having all this rank and privilege if I can't share it with my best friend's daughter? But I also think you should take some time away from here, even if it's just for a few days. Your father and GrandFather will be back tomorrow and there are plenty of healers around to help watch and care for Little Flower and Hope. Why don't you fly back with me in the morning and spend a week or three at my place. You can audit a few classes, see what interests you, take some lessons with Petra, wander the city, or even just take a nap, if that's what you need. Stay as long or as little as you'd like. What do you say?"

"Honestly, that sounds perfect. Thank you!" Marsee said, giving the Senior Guild Master a hug.

"You're welcome, child. Now, I think it's time for me to go yell at a few guild masters before bed. I always sleep so much better afterwards. I'll meet you in the shuttle bay at seven?" she asked.

"I'll be there!" Marsee said with a grin. "Have a good night, and thank you!"

~~~~~

The next morning, Marsee's alarm went off far earlier than normal. She groaned and nearly hit the snooze before she remembered why she'd set her alarm. "Ellie!" Bolting awake she quickly made use of the waste room and grabbed her toothbrush, shoving it into the bag she'd packed the night before with the other items she was taking with her, which included her drawing tablet, several of her sister's pictures, half a dozen of her favorite books, including Little Flower's cub's book, a small collection of her favorite art supplies, her sister's eraser, and her grooming supplies. She threw on her carry harness, clipped on her tablet and hearing aids, and looked around the room, trying to decide if there was anything else she wanted to take with her. Frowning, she
~~~~~

flipped open her desk and stared at the sketchbook. Deciding she didn't dare leave it behind, she stuffed it in her bag too, and looked around the room again.

*If Ellie doesn't have it, I can always pick it up in Council City, and if I decide to move there permanently, then I can always have everything shipped over later.*

She'd told her mother she was too tired to take the night shift the night before. But in reality, she wanted to have time to pack and to be able to sneak out before the normal shift change. She had absolutely no desire to deal with the discussion she'd face if her mother knew she was leaving, as she'd want to know why, and she had absolutely no desire to be around when her father returned. After a final look around the room she quietly made her way down the ramp and peered in her sister's room.

Her mother was curled up sound asleep on the spare bed, while Little Flower and Hope slept on their hanging bed. She hated the idea of leaving them, but she had to get away before her father returned. Her instinct was still far too angry with her father, as was she, if she were being honest with herself, and she needed both time and space to calm down. She didn't feel like she was at risk of losing control, but she saw no point in tempting the gods. She'd been far too busy to fully process what had happened the week before, and much of what he'd said now dug and clawed at her fragile self esteem, much like her instinct had.

***We need to find our own territory. Our father does not respect our boundaries. Ellie will make us strong and powerful so we can protect our cub better. She can see our worth,*** her instinct stated, although Marsee could tell it was not particularly convinced that her plan would accomplish their goals.

Marsee nodded to herself. She had been up late 'discussing' the trip to Council City with her instinct, the only 'person' she could talk to. The idea of leaving their cub behind with her father had bothered her instinct greatly, but she couldn't care for Hope in Council City. Legally Hope wasn't hers, even if she'd been the one responsible for most of Hope's care over the past few months, and Hope needed her mother's milk to survive. Neither of them expected her sister to recover, but when that horrible day arrived, she wanted to adopt Hope. She'd been thinking about it for a while, but her father's actions had cemented it.

She fully expected that the Hue-man Council would call for her mother's execution when Little Flower died, and normally that would mean Hope's care would go to her father, but after what had just happened, there was no way she was letting her father have Hope. She'd rather Hope went to one of the Hue-mans first, if she couldn't have her. Her father was too busy with the Council to care for Hope properly, but she could easily manage it, and had been managing it.

The Hue-mans had denied Nazari on the grounds that she didn't understand Hue-man culture and couldn't even speak their language, so she had been working hard to learn as much as she could about the Hue-mans, and was the only one that could even speak Hue-man at this point. What she'd also learned was that her ability to provide for Hope was a paramount consideration for them. She had more than enough credit to care for herself and Hope, but she hoped that maybe just maybe, she might impress one of the masters in Council City enough to offer to be her mentor, as that would significantly help her case, as it came with a major increase in her guild rate, and would provide her with enough credit to higher someone watch Hope when she couldn't.

She sighed, wishing she could hug her sister and cub one last time before she left, but doing so might wake her mother. *Goodbye little sister. I promise I'll take good care of Hope for you.* With another pained sigh, she turned away from the window and padded quietly down the rest of the ramp and through the courtyard and garden on her way over to the shuttle bay, where Ellie's ship was parked.

She was a full hour early when she arrived, but the door to Ellie's ship was open, and Ellie was already inside waiting for her.

Ellie grinned at her as she stepped in. "Good morning, Marsee. You're early. Ready to go?"

"All set!" Marsee grinned back.

"Good. Did you have breakfast?" Ellie asked.

"No. I was too..." Marsee struggled to figure out what term really fit, *nervous, excited, terrified.* "Worried I'd be late," she finally decided.

Ellie grinned. "No worries, I just sat down to eat too. Grab something from the kitchen before we take off, if you want."

Marsee tossed her stuff in an empty seat, and quickly grabbed the first thing that looked good. She sat in the seat Ellie indicated, directly across from her, and clipped into her safety harness before eating. Once she was situated, Ellie informed Petra they were ready to leave and the outer door slid shut. Moments later they took off.

"So, do you know what classes you want to audit?" Ellie asked.

"Not really. I'm not even sure what's available in Council City. I've taken all my classes in Sand Dune or remotely," Marsee replied. "What do you suggest?"

Ellie flicked an ear back to consider, and then unclipped her tablet. A few moments later Marsee's tablet chimed with the sound she used for Ellie. It was from one of Marsee's favorite fantasy entertainment programs. She'd chosen it after her sister had explained the name she called Ellie, as it was the closest thing that matched 'fairy godmother' in their culture. The program was fairly popular too.

Ellie's whiskers twitched in amusement, letting Marsee know she recognized it, but she didn't comment on it. "I've sent you the current course offering. We've just started a new semester so you should be able to hop into any of the classes that interest you without too much difficulty. There are several master level language courses that I think might challenge you. I highly recommend Native Flyer with Master Yellow Tail. He's a riot. I try to hop into his classes as often as I can just because he's so funny. He'll love someone new to pick on, especially someone with your abilities that would get the absolutely horrible puns he likes to use. As for your interest in the tech guild, I suggest any of the classes Master Tech Lowell is teaching. With your skill with languages, I recommend taking at least one programming course, but if you're looking for something more hands-on, there's a robotics course being offered, which is always very popular. I spoke to Petra as well, and she said she'd be glad to teach you to fly. We'll schedule that in around whatever other classes you're interested in."

"Thanks!" Marsee said, and dug through the course listing, flagging several that she was interested in, as she absently ate her breakfast, and then discussed several of the classes with Ellie to get her take on them. By the time they were approaching Council City, Marsee had her classes picked out and Ellie used her authority to sign her up for them, most of which she shouldn't even qualify for yet.

While Ellie did that, Marsee decided it was finally time to let her parents know what she'd done and fired off a message, trying hard to keep the snark out of her tone, although she was pretty sure she failed. She did wonder what her parents would think when they read it.

Ellie had the pilots land at the Guild, and then gave her a quick tour to make sure she knew where her classrooms were, and then left her outside of her first class, wishing her luck. Marsee was surprised to be taking classes on her first day, having figured Ellie would drop her off at her home instead, but shrugged. *No time like the present,* she supposed. Squaring her shoulders, she hit the switch on the door and walked in. She was the first person to arrive, so she found a spot in the back, hoping she wasn't taking someone's preferred seat, and plunked her bag down to wait for the others to arrive. She was fairly early, so she pulled out her tablet to distract herself. She was whiskers down in a book when the next person arrived without her notice.

"Well, it's about time you showed up," a musical voice said in Flyer.

Marsee looked up to see a golden Flyer standing in the doorway looking at her with a rather cross expression. The room was still empty, so she knew he was speaking to her, but she didn't even begin to know what to say in response.

His eyes twinkled with amusement at her loss of words. "Normally, people take my classes because they want to become a translator for the Council, not after. You've been doing a passable job from what I've been able to determine. Still there are quite a few words you've mis-translated into the other languages. Most are common mistakes, so I'm not surprised. I'm assuming your father and uncle taught you the other languages as a cub?"

Marsee shook her head. She hadn't been aware of any mistakes, although she did know others were adding to the guide on a regular basis. Mostly guild specific terms however. She'd added a flag to notify her on additions, but realized she should have flagged for edits too. *How many mistakes did I make?* she wondered.

"No, sir. I took the basics in primary school, but I didn't start focusing on language studies until I switched to the Writer's Guild, about a month or so after the Cataclysm. I was in the Crafter's and Artist's Guilds before that. I was rated as fluent in all but Water Sprite by the time Little Flower arrived at our home. I spent the month learning Water Sprite from Rainbow Scales for the trial."

The Flyer flicked his wings back in their equivalent of surprise. "You're serious? That's it?"

She shrugged. "I'm much better at reading and understanding people than speaking the other languages. I have a hard time making many of the sounds. Until a few months ago, I didn't have a lot of people from the other species to practice with. Granted most people speak sign language in New Hope. They're all easy compared to the Hue-man's language. Their language is a real tongue twister and it's a mess. Every word seems to have multiple meanings and pronunciations, and half the time I think they're just making up words to mess with me."

"You speak Hue-man too?" he asked, with another surprised shake of his wings. "I thought they were deaf."

"I do, sir, and not all of them are. They've been making progress in restoring their hearing."

"How do you even hear them though?"

Marsee shrugged. "Apparently my hearing is better than normal. I can hear things like the flicker flyers or the lights buzzing too. It's kind of annoying at times. Plus, some of the Hue-mans have voices that are within our normal range of hearing too, and they've learned to lower their voices when speaking with me, which helps."

He looked up at the lights in the room. "You can hear the lights?"

"Yes, sir."

"Huh," he grunted, and flicked his wings again before settling down in the front of the class to wait for the others, who began arriving shortly after. Just about everyone recognized her, which was rather embarrassing, but she did her best to ignore it and answer their questions.

"Settle down class. I know it's exciting to have someone new join us, and I'm sure you have a million questions for Marsee about New Hope, but that can wait until later. However, on behalf of our resident translator, who graciously honored us with her presence today, I thought we'd spend today's class going over a few mistakes I've found in her language guide. Starting first with the word 'visit'..."

By the end of the class, Marsee was slumped low in her seat, and it was all she could do to not bury her head under her tail. Master Yellow Tail spent nearly half an hour on the various connotations of 'visit' before moving on to another word, and then left them with homework to read the chapter on the forty three words for 'mother', for the next day, with a warning that there would be a quiz. On the plus side, Ellie had been right, he was rather funny, or would have been if it hadn't been directed at her the entire class. She escaped the class as quickly as she could.

"Don't let him get to you. He only does that to the people he's impressed with," one of her classmates said. "Although I'm not sure he's dedicated an entire class to one student before. That might be a new record."

"Thanks, I think," Marsee groaned, with a roll of her eyes.

Her next class was with Master Tech Cynthia Lowell. Thankfully there were no expectations there, as it was an introductory programming class, and while she was behind the others, Lowell was such a fantastic teacher that she had no problems following the planned material for the class.

Hours later, she made her way back to Ellie's office, only managing to get turned around twice in the massive twisting complex, to find that Ellie was in the middle of a meeting. Ellie saw her and sent her a message that it was going to be a while, so she should go find Petra for a lesson.

So Marsee backtracked to the Guild's shuttle bay and was surprised to find that she had access to the ship when she arrived. She dropped her bag off on a seat again, and made her way forward to the pilots section of the ship, where she found Petra curled up reading a book.

"Good choice," Marsee said as she walked in. "I've read that one half a dozen times."

Petra looked up. "Hey Marsee! I wasn't expecting anyone for a while. Are we heading out? Ellie usually lets me know ahead of time."

"No. Ellie says she's stuck in a meeting and that I should come see you for a flying lesson, but I don't want to interrupt you if you're in a good spot in your book."

Petra snorted and tossed her book aside. "I will never turn down an excuse to go flying. Besides, I'm going to be spending the next hundred years doing nothing but reading and popping out eggs."

Marsee flicked an ear back at the frustration in Petra's voice and body language. "I thought you were looking forward to being a Nest Mother."

Petra sighed. "I don't really have any choice there, so I'm doing my best to at least *pretend* I'm happy about it, the joys of being a female Flyer and all."

"My sister wondered about that when we were discussing the various life cycles of the species. I thought you could control how often you had a mating flight," Marsee said.

"I can, but it's required that I have at least four clutches a year," Petra replied.

"Required?!" Marsee exclaimed. "Can they do that?"

"Unfortunately, yes. It's not widely known, but our birth-rate has been steadily decreasing over the past few millennia. Not enough to be noticeable from year to year, but enough that there's typically only one Nest Mother per city now. If it weren't for Ellie, I wouldn't have even been allowed to leave Flyer," Petra said with a sigh. "I have several cities courting me right now, but ultimately it will be up to the Council to decide, based on where the greatest need is."

"You don't even get to choose where you live?" Marsee asked, horrified.

"They usually pick the person's preference, if they can, but my *mother* can be very persuasive," Petra replied. "I personally want to be as far away from her and the Council as I can get."

"I know that feeling," Marsee muttered. "I've about had it up to my whiskers with my father and the Council. I can't even go out for a run without causing a scene. That's half the reason I'm here."

Petra snorted. "Well, thankfully, flying is much easier than being the daughter of a diplomat. The controls don't care if you remember everyone's name or the proper way to greet everyone in their language."

Marsee's tail curled. "Did you ever hear about how my uncle first met your mother?"

Petra laughed. "Of course! It's one of my mother's favorite stories. I've helped her on a number of occasions locate new fish shaped things to decorate Marcus's office with. I am running out of ideas though."

"Well there's all the new fish species from Earth," Marsee suggested.

Petra grinned. "That's not a bad idea. I'll keep that in mind the next time I'm in New Hope or on the Water World. Now, how much experience do you have flying?"

"My father took me out a few times in his old shuttle, just enough that I could manage in an emergency," Marsee explained.

"Well, that's better than nothing," Petra replied, and began explaining all of the controls on the ship, of which there were far more than her father's shuttle, although the flight panel was much the same. When she was done, Petra made her repeat everything to see what she recalled. "Not bad!" Petra said after she was done and corrected the one she'd missed. "Alright, tell me what you would do to exit the shuttle bay."

Marsee gave it her best shot, which Petra corrected slightly, and then to her surprise, had her take off. Swallowing hard, Marsee opened the shuttle bay door, and carefully exited. She managed not to hit the walls or any of the nearby ships and shuttles. They practiced landing and taking off several times and then Petra helped her log a flight path, which marked her as the pilot, and notified everyone in the immediate vicinity that she was a student pilot, and that they'd better watch out, especially those out for a walk. Marsee's tail curled at Petra's teasing as she pretended to duck and cover. They managed to take several slow laps around the city before Ellie called to let them know she would be done in fifteen. Petra helped her to land the ship, this time not using the shuttle bay's auto pilot. Thankfully she managed not to land on Ellie, who was waiting for them by the entrance.

"Thank you, Petra," Marsee said. "That was fun!"

"Of course. Any time you're free, come back for another lesson. Ellie said you're planning on staying for a few weeks?"

"That's the current plan. I haven't decided if I'm going to move to Council City or return to New Hope. I'm kind of mad at my father right now," Marsee admitted.

"Well, we should have enough time to get you your shuttle pilot's license at least while you're here, if you can manage an hour or two each day," Petra said.

"That would be fantastic!" Marsee replied, and started to stand when Ellie called forward.

"Alright Marsee, take me home," Ellie ordered.

Marsee nearly froze with panic, and Petra chuckled, but motioned for Marsee to take her seat again. Tail curled tightly around her, and fully poofed, she took off. Thankfully they made it safely to Ellie's home, which wasn't all that far away, and she managed not to land on Ellie's house in the process.

"Well done, Marsee!" Ellie said when she made her way back to the common area. "You didn't even scuff the paint. I'm impressed."

"Thanks," Marsee replied, rolling her eyes. "It's good to know someone's impressed with me. I'm not sure I can show my face in Master Yellow Tail's class again."

Ellie burst out laughing. "I heard about that from about six different people today. Trust me, he's impressed. He only does that to people he likes."

"I hate to see what he does to people he doesn't like," Marsee muttered.

"Oh that's easy. How do you think Marcus ended up calling Wind Rider a smelly fish?" Ellie's tail was curled tightly in humor.

"Seriously?" Marsee asked.

"There is nothing the Flyers enjoy more than a good practical joke, trust me. I've completely lost count of the number of times I've been pranked by their guild masters over the years. None of the other species dare, but they seem to think it's a right of passage or something, once promoted. One time my entire office was filled with packing foam."

Marsee snorted. "I would have loved to have seen that."

Ellie laughed. "Well, I'm pretty sure I have a picture of that somewhere. Come on, let me show you to your room, and then I thought we'd pick something up at one of the vendors in the park for supper."

"That sounds perfect," Marsee replied with a grin and grabbed her bag as she followed Ellie out of the ship.

Ellie led her inside, showed her upstairs to her room, and left again giving her a few minutes to unpack. Marsee pulled out her books, placing them on an empty shelf, but stopped and stared at Little Flower's cub's book and started crying with homesickness, grief, and worry for her sister and Hope. Ellie came looking for her after a while, and found her curled upon the bed, wrapped tightly around the book, still crying.

Ellie walked over and sat on the bed next to her, as she sat up and wiped the tears off her face. "What's wrong, Marsee?"

Marsee couldn't speak, just handed the book over. She didn't know how to safely express everything she was feeling.

Ellie took the book and realized immediately what it was. "You finished it?"

Marsee nodded, swallowed hard, and forced the words out. "I was hoping she'd wake up and see it before it was published, but..." Tears started streaming down her face again. Ellie set the book down, leaned over and wrapped her in a hug, purring as she cried out her fear and grief. "Oh Ellie, I miss her so much!" she wailed.

"I know, child. I do too," Ellie said softly, and continued to hold and rock her until she was finally able to stop crying. "Better?"

Marsee nodded and wiped the tears off her face. "I'm sorry," Marsee said.

"For what, child?"

"For keeping you waiting," Marsee said. "And crying all over you."

Ellie snorted. "That's what friends are for, and what you clearly needed. I have strong arms and they're here anytime you need a hug or a shoulder to cry on. Grief is like that. It hits you out of nowhere and knocks you to your knees, and there is nothing you can do but ride it out. With what you've been through, I would be more concerned if there hadn't been an ugly crying session. Do you want to talk about it?"

Marsee shook her head. "I don't have the words."

Ellie nodded her understanding and picked up the book again. "So, what do you want to do about this? Do you still want to wait until she wakes up?"

Marsee sighed and shook her head. "No. This is her legacy and dream. It's what she always wanted to do with her life, and I want everyone to see it, to remember her for her artwork, for achieving that dream, and not for the trauma she endured. I only brought the one copy, but I have it translated into the other languages and ready to print."

Ellie looked at her with pride, compassion, and understanding. "Send me the files, and I'll make sure it's the most popular cub's book ever written. Not that I'll have to do much there. I'm sure it will fly off the shelves."

Marsee nodded, stood and walked over to her tablet, but looked up with a frown after sending the files over. "I don't want any credit for translating it. I want everything to go to her."

Ellie nodded. "That is your choice," she replied. "Now, why don't you go take a shower, and I'll take care of getting this published while you do, but rather than going to the market afterwards, I think we should go celebrate Little Flower's success at Sweet Reeds, which just so happens to be my favorite restaurant."

Marsee grinned and left to do as ordered.

~~~~~

Ellie watched Marsee leave, her expression turning to one of worry and grief once Marsee was safely out of sight. She was worried about Marsee, and had a feeling far more was going on than just her grief for Little Flower and fear of the consequences when she died, although that was more than enough to turn anyone into a blubbering mess. With a sigh, she picked up the book left behind and rubbed her thumb over Little Flower's signature on the cover and flipped through a few pages before closing it. As always, Little Flower's drawings were incredible, but Marsee had done a fantastic job arranging the book to best highlight her sister's work without the information detracting from the drawings.

She set it down, and forwarded the documents Marsee had shared to her team to have the book published immediately, and start printing copies, knowing there would be an instant demand. By the time Marsee had returned, looking far calmer, Ellie had her emotions back under control.

"Ready?" Ellie asked. "I don't know about you, but I'm starving."

Marsee looked up at her and grinned. "As long as it's not a smelly fish."

Laughing, Ellie walked over and wrapped her tail around Marsee and they made their way out as she told Marsee about several of the other practical jokes that had been played on her over the years. By the time they made it over to Sweet Reeds, Marsee's tears of grief had turned to tears of laughter, and Ellie's tail was starting to ache from how tightly it was curled, but her worry for Marsee still remained.
~~~~~

# CHAPTER 26

# Jeran: Fallout

While Jer had taken the public transport ship with the rest of his council to Flyer, rather than using his own ship, he decided to fly back with Marcus. He needed the privacy to relax for a few moments, and they needed to discuss the fallout from the Full Council meeting, as they had left right after the last session, so he could get home as quickly as possible. Once they were safely in jump, Jer unclipped from his seat and made his way over to the kitchenette and grinned when he saw what was stocked.

"I'm having a fuzzle knocker. Do you want one?" he asked Marcus.

"Please," his mentor replied. "That last session was brutal."

"Oh good. It wasn't just me," Jer replied. "Remind me again why I agreed to this?"

"Because your daughter is apparently far more intelligent than either of us," Marcus replied.

"Was," Jer said, taking a large swallow of his drink, but the burn of the alcohol did nothing to counteract the grief and worry he felt. "It's been two months Marcus. You and I both know she's never waking up." He refilled his glass before filling Marcus's and carrying it over.

"Myra's stubborn. She'll figure something out," Marcus replied.

Jer sighed, and sat back down with a wince. Unable to see a healer, the cuts and bruises Marsee had given him still hurt. "Honestly, I just wish it was over, one way or the other. This waiting is tearing my family apart. Myra hardly speaks to me and Marsee..." He sighed again, letting his worry surface. "She's taken the brunt of caring for Hope, and she's running herself into the ground."

Marcus looked sharply at him. "Did something happen? You've been moving like Ammond for the past week."

He didn't answer right away. He wasn't sure how to explain, and he didn't want to give Marcus reason to worry. "Not really," he said eventually, with a heavy sigh. "Marsee was feeling a bit overwhelmed with everything going on and went for a run. I followed after to make sure she was okay and she ran far further than I expected. We had a bit of an argument. She wasn't too happy about me following her and not trusting her to go for a run. She was still really mad at me when I left and I'm honestly not looking forward to going home and back to all of that." Jer waved his paw to encompass everything that was wrong in the universe. "It's honestly been nice to just focus on one thing this week, even if it was grueling."

Marcus nodded. "I can understand her frustration. Thankfully she and Myra should be off the watch soon. I do have some good news about that though. Kendra said they appear to be having success with using sign language. It's far too soon to tell, but she's hopeful, and all of the guards now have the basics of sign language down. I haven't been called in to test anyone yet, which in of itself is surprising. There's usually a couple of dozen each year according to her, so we should have had a few by now, statistically speaking anyway, but apparently everyone the guard has brought in has been doing well. There's only been one cub that was already gone when the guards arrived. We're hoping that we can eventually break through like we did with Marsee, but Kendra thinks she was already too far gone when they arrived. Still, it's better than it was."

"That is good news," Jer replied. "Ten thousand years too late, but I'll take any improvement."

Marcus nodded and took a sip of his drink and wrinkled his nose. "I don't know how you drink this stuff, Jer."

"You get used to it after a while," he replied. "So was it just me, or were the other councilors..." he paused trying to find the right word.

"Downright obnoxious?" Marcus asked. "Vindictive? Rude? Yeah. The vast majority of everything I brought forward was turned down or torn to shreds. I'm honestly surprised they approved the change to the Charter to allow your people land of their own."

Jer snorted. "The only reason they did that was because it took resources and land away from Saber. They seemed positively gleeful about that."

"You're probably not wrong there. We did redirect a vast amount of resources to New Hope after the Trial, which put a lot of projects on hold. It's not surprising that they'd make my council pay for that," Marcus replied. "Or for needing the Trial in the first place. Frankly we deserved it, even if we weren't convicted."

"Well, hopefully the next one will be better," Jer said.

"If we make it that far. Have you looked at our ratings recently? We're all scraping the bottom. A few more votes of no confidence and I'm going to be out a council anyway. My ratings haven't been this low since my first term."

Jer snorted. "I have looked, but I doubt you'll be kicked out any time soon. They may be low for you, but they're still far better than what I was averaging before the Trial."

"You're doing well now though," Marcus replied, taking another tentative sip of his drink, wincing again.

"As if. The only reason my ratings are good is because no one wants my job. It'd be a different story if the rest could vote. They're all still mad at us, and getting everyone ready for the meeting was like herding an entire school yard of cubs most days," Jer replied.

"That is rather surprising after everything Little Flower and Grand-Father told us," Marcus said.

"Perhaps. The majority of the females are spending most of their time in classes, exploring the different guilds, so I can't blame them for wanting to explore what's available, or do something they're more interested in. I imagine many of the males would if they were allowed.

They're still very angry at not having a vote, even after what Little Flower did to try and get them to understand why they're not being sponsored, which would fit with what Little Flower told us. Plus, I've seen several comments when people thought I wasn't around that clearly showed the biases we were told about."

Marcus frowned at him. "Is there reason for concern?"

Jer thought for a bit and shrugged. "I don't know. We've had a few issues, but those calmed significantly after the first few warnings were given. GrandFather's still worried about several people though. I've been trying to get the guilds to relax their admissions programs to let some of the males join before they've officially earned their adulthood. That seems to be the biggest complaint. They've said no in the past, but I'm hoping that maybe we can find a way to work around it, possibly see if we can get someone to volunteer to mentor them."

"I doubt anyone would, unless they knew them directly," Marcus replied. "That would be fairly risky, just as much as being their guardian would be."

"I know," Jer nodded. "And no one will offer guardianship, outside of offering for the cubs, not that the Council would allow it. I still feel horrible about Nazari."

"I'm glad I advised her to wait to submit her appeal. With the council we just had, they'd have probably thrown her in a cell, revoked her healer's license, and taken her adult children away from her too."

Jer snorted. "You're probably not wrong there. I've talked to a few people about mentoring or offering guardianship to the others. No one will offer until the Hue-mans start doing so. I was going to talk with Myra about it, since she offered in the past, but then Little Flower happened, and I'm not going to add that stress to her, especially not now. I honestly wouldn't put it past some of them to commit a crime just to make her pay for it."

"Do you really think they would?" Marcus asked.

He shrugged. "I have no idea. I can't understand them half the time. About the only thing I've figured out is that the odds are they'll vote completely differently than I would. I leave scratching my whiskers after just about every meeting."

"How so?" Marcus asked. "Are they making bad decisions? I didn't see anything wrong with how they voted this past week."

Jer snorted again. "That's just because they're the only council that voted in your favor."

Marcus chuckled. "Fair point."

"No. There are only a few votes I haven't agreed with, like the lack of a guard or Nazari. It's just that they're just not what I would expect. They're...creative. I'll go into a meeting with several ideas on what we can do on some given topic, and inevitably they'll come up with something completely different. Take the expansion project. The initial plans we designed had us adding more covered walkways and trying to figure out how to shield everything, and they suggested underground walkways next to the Water Sprite tunnels instead. Not only can it be used in all weather, but it won't require heating or cooling to keep at a safe temperature for them, or shields, just fans to keep the air flowing, and we'll be able to shield individual buildings instead of the entire compound. Ellie's redesigning everything using Digger and Ice Giant plans, including moving most of the buildings underground, leaving only the top floor above ground. Once suggested, it was obvious, but not something I was even remotely thinking about. I'm familiar with the habitats we have on the other worlds, but I never even once thought about using them in New Hope."

"Well if your daughter is an example, they're very inventive as a species," Marcus replied, sniffed at his drink, and set it down instead.

Jer took another large swallow of his, finishing his glass in a single gulp. He enjoyed the momentary distraction of the burn, and finally felt himself relax a little. "Moon's Marcus. I'm exhausted. I don't think I can keep doing this, not and care for Little Flower and Hope."

"Well, most people in your situation would go on leave," Marcus replied.

"I can't. There isn't anyone to hand it off to. The only one I'd trust enough is GrandFather, and he flat out refused, and my family is paying the price. I know I gave my oath, but I had no idea it would be this difficult," Jer admitted.

"You and me, both," Marcus replied.

Jer raised a brow at his brother. It was rare that Marcus admitted that anything was difficult.

"I didn't exactly have a normal transition either, and between you and me, Tabor left a bit of a mess," Marcus explained.

"Are you referring to the fallout from the Trial?" Jer asked. "Or something else?"

"Both," Marcus replied. "Samantha has been a gift from the gods there. The queue was a disaster. I'm honestly surprised Tabor wasn't voted out decades ago. There were tickets in there that were several years old."

Jer snorted. "Well, you and I both know, she wasn't elected Senior because of her organizational skills."

Marcus's tail curled in humor. "Too true. Well, now that the meeting is over, you should be able to take a few days off at least," Marcus replied. "I personally intend to go lick my wounds deep in the archives where no one can find me. Is there anything I can do to help?"

"Can I steal Samantha back from you?" Jer asked with a grin.

Marcus laughed. "Anything but that. She's mine now."

Jer rolled his eyes and shook his head. "You always were greedy. After all these years, you'd think you'd learn how to share."

"That's not true at all. I did just let you have several hundred leagues of my land," Marcus replied. "And I didn't even charge you a credit for it."

"That's just because Myra gave it to you in the first place, and no one else wants it," Jer snorted, and then reached over and grabbed Marcus's abandoned drink, downed it, and stood up. "I'm going to bed. If there's an emergency, please don't wake me."

"Good night, little brother," Marcus replied. "Don't let the crawlies bite."

Jer made his way back to his room, feeling slightly tipsy from the extra drink. He rarely had more than one, and with a heavy sigh, crawled gratefully into bed, but as exhausted as he was, sleep was a long time coming.

The next morning he overslept and Marcus woke him by pounding on his door.

"What did I say about waking me up?" Jer grumbled, wincing at the pain the noise caused in his head.

"We're exiting jump in a few minutes. If you'd rather end up splattered on the other side of the universe, by all means go back to bed," Marcus replied.

Jer snorted and crawled out of bed. Whether he was in his jump seat or sleeping, it wouldn't make a lick of difference if there was a problem coming out of jump. He'd be splattered either way. Still, he crawled off his bed and made his way out to his seat, flopping down with a groan, after grabbing some pain meds from the first aid kit. He'd drunk too much the night before, and had a throbbing headache now.

Moments later the universe imploded and they were back in normal space. He pulled out his tablet as the ship connected with the planet's network and messages started flowing in. There was one from Marsee, so he opened it and frowned as he read it.

"What's wrong now, cub?" Marcus asked, after Jer let a sigh slip out.

"Marsee's gone and flown off with Ellie, and said she's not sure when she's coming back, if ever," Jer replied with another heavy sigh, and tossed his tablet down, furious with himself, even if it had been his responsibility and duty to test her.

"Just what kind of argument did you have?" Marcus asked, but Jer didn't answer, and just shook his head.

"Jeran Frederick Chenzira, answer me. What really happened?" Marcus demanded.

He sighed. "When she ran off, her instinct was on, so I chased her until we were out of sight of the compound...and tested her."

"*Tested* tested?" his brother asked for clarification.

Jer shrugged. "As much as you ever did with me anyway. Not the full council test though. I...couldn't bring myself to do that."

"And she passed?!" Marcus exclaimed.

"She's alive isn't she?" Jer replied.

"Astounding!" Marcus whispered.

"That she is," Jer agreed. "And I may have lost her with that act."

"I'm sure she'll forgive you once she's had a chance to calm down," Marcus replied. "You did."

Jer snorted. "I knew what you were trying to do at the time. She didn't, and I hurt her, enough that she needed medical treatment."

Marcus frowned at that comment. "What did she tell the healer?"

"I don't know," he replied. "I haven't heard from Kendra yet though, so either her record wasn't flagged, or there will be a squad of guards to arrest me for abuse when we land." He looked out the window as they entered the planet's atmosphere and said nothing else until they landed in New Hope. "Marcus, keep watch of her please," Jer asked.

"Of course, little brother," Marcus replied. Jer grabbed his bag and left, surprised not to see guards waiting for him. He heard the sounds of Marcus's ship take off as he crossed the courtyard. After dropping his bag off in his room he climbed up the ramp to the second floor, where he assumed Myra was. She was curled up sound asleep on the couch next to the window. Little Flower rocked gently in the new hanging bed that Marsee had crafted for her, as Hope waved her tiny paws in the air, and looked to be crying.

Jer sighed and walked over to the cub. "Shhh, it's okay, little kitten. I'm here now," he whispered, and began purring as quietly as he could, trying not to wake Myra, and started walking around with her. Hope settled down immediately and snuggled into his fur. "What's the matter? Are you hungry, little one?" he asked, as a few moments later she started crying again. He couldn't hear her, but her face scrunched up and turned red, so he walked over and laid her down on her mother so she could nurse. That seemed to be just what she wanted, as she stopped crying instantly and started nursing. He wrapped the blanket around her and began rocking the bed slowly.

"Jer, you're home early. When did you get in?" Myra asked sleepily.

He looked over at her. "Just now and I'm sorry, I didn't mean to wake you."

"I'm glad you did. I didn't mean to fall asleep. Marsee was exhausted so I gave her the night off," Myra said.

Jer raised a brow. "I take it you haven't seen her message then?" he asked.

"No, what message?" Myra asked, looking concerned.

"She left this morning with Ellie," Jer replied.

"She what?!" Myra exclaimed, and then let out a weary sigh. "I'm not surprised. I've asked far too much of her these past few months. She deserves some time to be her own person and not trapped dealing with the consequences of my crimes." Myra stood and stretched before caring for Little Flower. Moments later he heard the sounds of the transport ship landing with the rest of his council.

"Looks like the rest are back. I hope GrandFather will help," Jer replied. "I'm not sure what we're going to do without Marsee's help."

Myra shrugged. "I'll manage."

"You're exhausted too. Why don't you go get some sleep. I can watch her for a while," he said.

She shook her head though. "Thanks, I have work to do, but you're welcome to stay."

"Myra, how long are we going to do this?" he asked.

"For the rest of her life," Myra snapped at him. "I am not giving up on her. I will find a way to fix this if it's the last thing I do. I'll understand if this is too much for you. You can leave too. I won't hold it against you."

He pursed his lips but said nothing for several long moments. "Myra, I'm just worried about you. You're not taking care of yourself. You're losing weight and if you've been up all night, you need to rest."

"I'm fine, Jer. She's stuck in that coma because of me," Myra growled at him. "She's my responsibility. I promised to care for her and her cub, and I will, even if it kills me."

"If you're dead, who will find a way to fix her then? Go to bed Myra. A few hours won't make any difference."

"Enough, Jer. I have work to do," Myra said, and pushed him out of the way.

"No," he replied, stopping her. "It doesn't take a healer to see just how tired you are. Go to bed. That's an order from your Senior Councilor. If you don't, I'll have you removed from her care entirely."

She snorted at him. "You wouldn't," she replied.

"Try me," he said, slamming his mask firmly in place. "Go. To. Bed."

Myra huffed at him, glared when he refused to back down, and turned and left, tail lashing behind her. He heard the sound of her door slamming shut moments later, and he sighed, wondering if he'd just ruined things with her too.

When GrandFather appeared a half an hour later, and said he would gladly watch Little Flower and Hope, Jer left to try and patch things up with Myra, but found the ancient door locked. He peered in the window and found her curled up sound asleep. *If she's already fallen asleep, as angry as she was, she must have been far more exhausted than I thought.* He sighed and pulled out his tablet to make sure she hadn't kicked him out entirely, but seeing little evidence of that, he decided to just let her sleep. He'd been on Myra's bad side a time or two, and knew he would have a much easier time talking with her after she got some rest. She always got grumpy when she was tired.

Instead, he decided to see if he could make some progress on his little problem with Damon and the others, and made his way over to talk with Brice, and eventually found her in her office.

"Councilor, what can I do for you?" Brice asked, surprised to see him, and motioned for him to have a seat.

"I have a bit of a problem, I'm hoping you might be able to help me with," he said, and took the proffered seat. She tilted her head indicating he should continue. "I'm sure you're aware of the issues we're having with many of the Hue-man males, as they can't join many of the guilds without being an adult or having a sponsor, and I was wondering if there was any way your healers would be willing to start sponsoring, or even mentoring those who were interested."

Brice sighed. "I'm sorry, Councilor, but I seriously doubt it. We're all far too busy, and most of the healers here are only master level one, so they don't qualify to take a protege. I can ask the others, but I doubt they will. I know I don't have time. It's all I can do to keep this place running, with Myra being out. Myra and Ammond are the only two without apprentices, as far as I know, and neither of them have time. Everyone else that qualifies has already taken a protege or three among the Hue-man females. I have a waiting list of healers that want to transfer here, but I'm full up with as many healers as I'm allowed. If you can get the Healer's Guild to authorize more, that might help. Frankly we're seeing enough volume to qualify as a Level Two Trauma Center now. That was something I wanted to talk to you about. I think we need to expand, and likely plan for us to become a Level Three before the year is out. We're seeing far more visitors to New Hope than we're rated for, and that goes up every day."

Jer nodded. That was at least something he could look into. "I'll see what I can do there. Thanks," he said. "Do you know if Tabor is working today?"

"She hasn't missed a day," Brice replied. "She's usually flying Trauma Ship One."

He nodded again, and left, making his way back to the trauma bay, and exited to find the three ships they now had, parked outside. He made his way over to Trauma Ship One, hit the switch to the door and entered. Unlike his personal ship, the cockpit was not hidden behind doors to keep it from the main passenger area, as the healers needed to be able to talk to the pilot.

Tabor turned when he entered and Jer motioned the healers off the ship so he could speak with Tabor privately. Tabor called Command and signed off, so she could give her full attention to him.

"Councilor," she nodded, taking her headset off. "Are you here to check on me?" she asked.

"No, I doubt I have to worry about you. I'm here to ask a favor of you," he replied.

She raised a brow at that. "How can I help?" she asked.

He grinned. "I have a bit of a problem, which you may or may not be aware of. Several of the Hue-man males are rather annoyed that they can't join the Ship's Guild until they earn their adulthood, or get a sponsor or mentor. I was wondering if you would be willing to do so or even teach some classes."

"I would, but I can't," Tabor replied, without hesitation. "Now that I've gone and convicted myself, I'm no longer qualified to sponsor or mentor anyone. The only people I would be able to teach to fly would be my own family. Guild charter. Oscar's the only one who could reverse that, and I seriously doubt he would even consider that until I'm done with my community service. Although I suppose you could ask. He's been known to surprise me a time or two."

"Would you be interested in adopting a few Hue-mans then?" Jer asked with a grin.

Tabor chuckled. "Do you really think a convicted criminal is the right person for that?"

"If I qualified, so do you," Jer replied.

Tabor grinned. "I will talk with my partner, but frankly most everyone is waiting for at least one of the Hue-mans to offer guardianship first. At least that's the scuttle I've heard."

Jer sighed. "I know. I appreciate you considering it though. Thank you."

Tabor nodded and he left, frowning as he tried to figure out what to do next. He tried the rest of the pilots, including his own, but they declined for various reasons, all more than reasonable. Giving up, he made his way back to his office to work, and put in several more requests to the various guilds. He was digging through his messages when there was a knock on his door, and he looked up to see Damon in his doorway.

*I wonder what he wants,* Jer thought, motioning him. "Come on in, Damon. What can I do for you?"

"Sir, I'd like permission to move somewhere else," Damon opened with. "I don't really care where, just not here."

Jer sighed. "I'm sorry. I wish I could give it to you. I can't for the same reason I haven't been successful in getting the guilds to relax their permissions. Living on your own requires you to be an adult."

"I know that. You could make me an adult. You and I both know I was one before. I even had a family and a daughter," Damon replied.

"I've done everything asked of me, and taken all of the jobs no one else wants to do, to try and prove I deserve it."

"I believe you, but I have no way of proving that you were an adult before, and the rest of the Council voted unanimously to keep things as they are. I can't change that, but I am still trying to get someone to sponsor or mentor you."

Damon frowned. "You know damn well no one will, not until one of the women do, and they have no intention of doing so, not until our time is up. Sir, I'll be honest with you. I don't fit in here, and I'm tired of the looks and comments. I just want to go somewhere I can start fresh. I don't even care about being able to vote or being on the Council. I'll give that up if that will help get me out of here."

"Have you told the others that?" Jer asked.

"Of course I have. If you remember, I bought it before the Council almost two months ago. They don't care. They think it's poetic justice that we have to wait," Damon replied. "And I don't blame them. Like I said, I just want to leave and do my own thing, where at least I'd be welcome."

"What would you do, since you can't get into the Ship's Guild right now?" Jer asked.

"What I'm doing now, if I have to. Maybe take some classes at the Guild. I was a builder before," Damon replied. "Or the equivalent anyway."

"There are plenty of classes being offered here," Jer stated.

"Would you want to take classes with people who want nothing to do with you?" Damon asked.

Jer sighed, Damon had a point. "I will check with the Senior Guild Master and see if she can get someone in Council City to sponsor you. I can't give you a place of your own, but if someone is willing to let you stay with them, I'll approve it. It would help if you did take some of the classes at the Guild, then I'd at least be able to show you were actually interested."

Damon nodded, "That's fair. Thank you," he said, and slid out of the seat he'd taken, and left.

Jer sat watching the empty doorway thinking about what Damon had said, and fired off another message to Ellie about finding someone willing to house Damon, and another to the Senior Council, based on GrandFather's suggestion about changing the other guilds so that people who weren't adults could join, and use earning their journeyman rank as proof of adulthood. He couldn't get rid of the existing rules on his own, but they could enhance them if he had support from the other Seniors. If nothing else, they could put it on the docket for the next Full Council meeting to discuss.

He was just about to head back to the Tower when his tablet rang with an incoming call from the Senior Honor Guard. Taking a deep breath he answered the call, praying that this was in response to his message, and not Marsee's unexpected arrival in Council City.

"Kendra," he nodded in greeting. "What can I do for you?" His heart sank with a heavy thud when she didn't answer right away. "What is it?" he asked, not really wanting to know.

"Councilor, what's going on with your daughter? I just received notice of her transfer to Council City, by your brother, not you, and there's a flag on her medical record that shows injuries consistent with fighting." Kendra glared at him, putting the full weight of her authority behind that look.

He sighed. "She's not at risk. She left unexpectedly while we were in jump. We just found out about it. She'll be staying with the Senior Guild Master."

"That wasn't the question I asked," Kendra glared. "Has she been fighting?"

He pursed his lips but nodded. "I tested her Kendra, enough to break her shoulder. She passed."

Kendra flicked an ear back dismissively, and then glared at him. "No one passes."

"She did. She had me pinned to the ground with my neck in her mouth, and just walked away."

"You're serious?" she asked.

"Very much so. She's furious with me, but fully in control. Marcus is aware of what happened, and has said he'll keep watch of her."

He spent the next half hour reviewing what he'd done, and what he'd seen, knowing that the lives of other children depended on it, even if it meant Kendra might find his own child to be too much of a risk to live.

"I don't like that she was talking in plural, or marking territory," Kendra said eventually.

"Neither did I, which is why I tested her in the first place," he replied, "but outside of that, she remained in full control, even after biting me hard enough to draw blood. She got me good several times, and I'm still sore. You and I both know that if it were anyone else, I would have died at the first sniff of blood, much less taste."

Kendra leaned back and sighed. "Did you notice any other odd behavior from her, then or afterwards?"

"No, she was back to normal afterwards, furious, but normal. We talked for a while and it took a good hour to walk back. She spent the night caring for her sister, but I checked on her in the morning before I left for Flyer, and she seemed calmer, if just as angry with me."

Kendra nodded. "Very well. We'll continue to watch her. I advise you to keep your distance for a few weeks, and try to be as unthreatening as possible. Don't approach her unless she approaches or contacts you first. Treat her no differently than if you'd pulled a cub from an abusive situation. She's likely to be jittery and scare easily."

Jer pursed his lips at the phrasing, but nodded. "Do you intend to bring her into the guard then?" That was the normal protocol in a situation like this.

"No. If she's already feeling like she's not in control of her surroundings, bringing her into the Guard will just make things worse. She's with someone she trusts, and Ellie is more than capable of recognizing the signs and...dealing with a problem if it comes to that, and has done so in the past, which is good enough for me," Kendra replied.

Jer raised a brow at Kendra's phrasing. "Are you indicating that Ellie has..."

"Yes," Kendra replied. "On three occasions that I'm aware of, and contained at least half a dozen others until we could arrive. Now, as for your most recent request, I am not relaxing membership requirements into the Guard, but we do have training programs for cubs that are brought in, and for training our own cubs. It's something we can consider once we've built a guard hall. If one of the guards chooses to mentor someone, I won't stop them."

He blinked at the sudden change of topic. "That's fair. I was planning on talking to you about that anyway. I fully expect by the next Full Council, we'll qualify as a town, as we should have the next round of apartment buildings completed by then, if not shortly after. I'm quite sure that my people won't form a guard of their own, and now that we're considered our own planet, I'm going to need to officially borrow guards."

"I expected as much, and already have guards signed up, ready to transfer when you approve it. They're aware that they won't be able to officially transfer to your species until you open things back up, but they're willing to offer their oath anyway, if you want," Kendra replied. "And in an emergency, you can always call on more. As far as I'm concerned, legally you might be on another planet, but I still consider New Hope my responsibility."

Jer raised a brow in surprise, but nodded his thanks. "That works. I'll let Ellie know to schedule that build out. Expect her to be in contact with you to discuss the changes we're making to all of the buildings. Be aware though, my people are still quite angry at us, although they're getting better, so your guards should be prepared to be invisible, as much as possible."

"Understood and understandable." With that Kendra nodded, and hung up.

Jer leaned back in his chair with a sigh. *Well I suppose that went better than it could have,* he thought, but still put up a prayer to the Ancient Gods to protect Marsee, and hoped he hadn't made things far worse for her. Her survival was now entirely in Kendra and her brother's paws, and there was little he could do now to protect her.

# CHAPTER 27

# Kendra: Watch

Kendra disconnected from the call with Councilor Chenzira and stared at her blank monitor for a moment, before turning to face Quinn who was sitting in the corner, out of sight of the camera.

"Thoughts?" she asked him.

"Marsee's exhausted, jagged, but still in control," he replied. "I think the break will do her good. She spent most of the week crafting and caring for her sister and cub in the trauma center. I didn't witness any further uses of her instinct, but she grew increasingly more anxious as it came closer to her father's return. Last night she spent several hours sitting on her balcony, anxious and jagged, until the Senior Guild Master offered to let her come stay with her. She told her mother she was too tired to watch her sister, but then was up late packing and pacing in her room, and muttering. I couldn't catch everything, but she seemed fairly conflicted about leaving. She didn't go in to say goodbye either when she left this morning, and she twanged pretty hard. The worst I've seen all week."

"I would expect anyone to be jagged after what Jeran just admitted to. With anyone else and in any other situation, it would be considered abuse," Kendra replied. "And she's fairly attached to the cub. Have you read her journal?"

"I have, and I agree. If her instinct is seeing Hope as her own cub, leaving her behind with someone who had just hurt her, would have been a fairly difficult decision. I'm surprised she was even able to leave."

"As am I, in both situations. Jeran's lucky to be alive. Testing her without backup was a foolish thing to do, but if she had been losing control, we wouldn't have been able to get there before someone was hurt or killed. If she's in control enough to walk away after that, then she's probably safe, but we're still keeping a full watch on her while she's here. Your thoughts on Myra?"

"Exhausted, frustrated, and scared, but in control," he replied.

"Normal for what she's going through and facing. If there's going to be a problem it'll probably happen if or when Little Flower dies," Kendra said. "She knows she's facing a possible death sentence, and I expect her instinct will fight to stay alive, although I expect she will remain in control until the Council gives their verdict, seeing as she managed to do so before. What of the Hue-mans?"

"I'd say at least half of the males are still angry, as Chenzira said. Several, I'd put a watch on. One in particular made me uncomfortable with his reaction as they moved Little Flower and the cub to the tower. Marsee picked up on it too. I put my guards on him for a bit, but we didn't find anything. He's fairly isolated, which is concerning, but other than that, it's hard to say. The females I saw all seemed fairly moody and worried, but then they're pretty late in their pregnancies, so that's not surprising either. Overall though, honestly better than I expected."

Kendra nodded and dismissed him. She sat and thought for a bit, before returning to her work.

That evening she joined Quinn in observation as Marsee and the Senior Guild Master wandered the vendors in the park after their evening meal. To her surprise, Quinn had decided to continue watching Marsee, rather than assigning it to one of the other squads as he normally did.

"Are you sure she hasn't transitioned?" she asked after a while. Marsee was twitching at noises like a new Guard.

"I saw no signs of it," Quinn replied. "She just seems overly sensitive to sound."

That wasn't unusual for people brought into the guard so she dismissed it. "I see what you mean about being jagged," she said eventually.

"She's actually far better than she's been," Quinn replied. "She's at least excited and enthusiastic, which is a far better state than she's been in all week." Kendra raised a brow but nodded and left.

~~~~~

Over the next several weeks, she randomly joined in on the night watch, when it became apparent that Marsee and Ellie spent most evenings checking out the city, and slowly began to relax as Marsee's jaggedness decreased, and she stopped jumping at everything.

She was working late one evening when a message came in from one of her guards on Marsee's watch, informing her that Senior Councilor Chenzira was at the Senior Guild Master's home. *What is he doing?* she growled.

She tapped her claws on her desk for a moment, considering. *Is she ready enough to be around him?* she wondered, but shook her head. *She's better, but still a risk.*

As Marsee hadn't blocked or reported him for abuse, she had no legal recourse to stop him from approaching his daughter, but deciding the safety of her people was more important, she placed a call to Quinn. "Where is she?" she asked.

"She just arrived at Sweet Reeds with the Guild Master and Petra, why?"

"Her father just appeared at the Guild Master's home," she replied.

Quinn sighed. "She's not ready. Didn't you order him to stay away?"

"I did," she growled. "Call the rest of your squad in, but keep them hidden. I'll follow Chenzira."

Ten minutes later she was outside of the Senior Guild Master's home. Chenzira was sitting on the stoop waiting, and he looked exhausted. She observed for a few moments, before slinking out of the shadows where she was hiding, and approached.

"I thought I told you to stay away," she said, at nearly a growl. "She's not ready, and you could be putting her life and others at risk by being here."
~~~~~

He jumped and spun, not having heard her approach, but then let out a heavy sigh, looking far more dejected than any Senior Councilor she'd ever seen. "I know, but I need her help, or rather, Myra does. Little Flower isn't doing well, and Myra won't accept help caring for Little Flower or Hope from anyone else, stating it's her responsibility and punishment, and I need to fly to Digger for the week. I'm hoping she'll allow Marsee to help."

Kendra pursed her lips and considered. *If he's not there, it might be okay.* "I want guards in New Hope, and on your ship, in case there's a problem," she replied.

He nodded without hesitation. "I figured as much, and rooms are already available."

Kendra glared at him. "If she says no, you leave. If she tells you to leave, you leave. If I see a problem and tell you to leave, you leave. Understood?"

He nodded again.

"Your oath, Councilor," she demanded.

He raised a brow at her insistence, and she sniffed his surprise, but he gave his oath anyway.

She sighed and nodded. "Remain as small and unthreatening as possible, and keep your distance unless she makes the first move." With that she turned and disappeared into the shadows again to wait.

# CHAPTER 28

# Marsee: Favor

The next several weeks passed quickly as Marsee dove into her classes, and found every minute she could to go flying with Petra, and occasionally Ellie's other pilots, Leaf and Willow. When it was just her and Petra, they talked for hours about everything, the challenges of being the daughter of a counselor, and their hopes and dreams. She was even able to confide in Petra about how difficult it was watching her sister waste away, and deal with the changes to her home, and even her desire to be Hope's mother when her sister eventually passed away, while Petra confided about how conflicted she was about having to give up her eggs, even though she knew she couldn't raise them all.

Most nights, she and Ellie explored the city together, and Marcus even joined them a few times. He said nothing about her father's test, and didn't even bother to make her turn her instinct on or off, which she'd expected. Instead, he focused on everything she was learning, and seemed genuinely interested and happy for her.

The lengthy walks were usually enough to tire her out, and did nearly as well as running or swinging in her bed did to control her anxiety, but one night, she was feeling particularly twitchy again. It had rained the two past nights, so they hadn't gone out, and Ellie's meetings had run late, so they had decided to eat in and read instead of explore.

"What's bothering you?" Ellie asked after Marsee changed position on the couch for the fourteenth time. "You're wiggling like a cub tonight."

She shrugged. "I don't know," Marsee said eventually. "Sometimes I just get like this. When it gets bad I usually swing in my hanging bed or go for a run. That usually helps."

"Well you have been cooped up in classes all day, and for that matter, I've been stuck in far too many meetings. A run in the woods would do us both good. Come on, I show you my favorite trail."

Marsee just stared at her in shock.

"What?" Ellie asked, as she set her book aside.

"You're okay with me running?" Marsee finally managed to ask.

"Why wouldn't I be?" Ellie asked instead. "Exercise is important, especially when you're stuck inside all day."

Marsee just shrugged again, unsure how to explain without giving away what had happened.

Ellie glared at her. "What's going on, Marsee?"

"Nothing, I'm just surprised that you're not upset or questioning my control," she replied. "Every time I've gotten even the slightest bit twitchy since that day, my uncle or father have been all over me."

"Ah," Ellie replied. "Yes, I can see how they would be worried, but isn't it better to find ways to relieve your stress and calm down, rather than letting it bottle up inside? I know you run when you're anxious or stressed. It's a good outlet, and one I use regularly. If I didn't, the guards would be dragging me in for clawing the fur off of some poor unruly Guild Master on a daily basis."

Marsee just blinked at Ellie and felt some of her own stress fade, realizing Ellie understood her, and wasn't judging her for needing to move. "Really? You like to run too?"

"Well, I don't know if I would go so far as to say I like it, but I'm stuck in meetings all the time. If I didn't do something, I'd be so fat and out of shape that I wouldn't be able to catch my own tail. Come on," Ellie replied.

Marsee chuckled at that mental image and followed after. A few minutes later they arrived at the entrance to a  wooded trail.

"The North Woods is mostly a nature preserve, but there are guarded and lit up trails all throughout.  Feel free to go out for a run any time you want or need.  If you get lost, just look for the green trail. That'll get you back to this entrance. Now, try to keep up if you can," Ellie replied and bolted forward.

Marsee kept her instinct off, but ran as fast as she could. Ellie was twice her size and her longer stride easily covered distances that Marsee had to push to keep up with. They passed several others out for a walk or jog of their own, but Marsee mostly ignored them as the trail was challenging and required her entire focus. The only time she got worried was when she passed a pair of guards trotting in the other direction, but they just nodded at her and Ellie. After that, she stopped worrying, and just let herself enjoy the run. It was exactly what she needed.

When Ellie finally came to a stop, Marsee was panting hard, although Ellie didn't seem winded at all. She found herself on the top of a hill overlooking the city.  Several others were sitting or lounging about in small groups, enjoying the view.

"This is why I like this trail so much," Ellie said, after finding a spot to sit. "It's not quite as nice as your tower, but it is one of the best views of the city."

Marsee flopped down beside her, too tired to even talk for several minutes.

Ellie looked over at her and grinned. "You did pretty good keeping up with me. I'm impressed. Feeling better?"

Marsee just nodded.

Once Marsee could speak again, they spent a good hour chatting about her classes and watching the suns set over the city before making their way back at a much slower walk as they continued their conversation. The trail was now lit up, and to her happiness, she even saw a few flicker flyers fluttering about. There were more guards around too, now that it was dark, but they mostly just nodded to Ellie or ignored them completely, and by the time they made it back to Ellie's house, she was so tired, she barely had the strength to climb the stairs to her room.

She grinned as she curled up on her bed to read for a bit, feeling happier than she'd been in a long time, and she was seriously considering moving to Council City permanently. She'd always loathed the city before because of the people, but it was far more manageable with her hearing aids now, and it honestly felt less crowded than New Hope did at times, even though there was close to half a million people living in Council City. She managed to get two whole pages into her book before falling fast asleep.

~~~~~

Three weeks after her arrival in Council City, she passed her shuttle pilot's test. So that night they went out to celebrate at Sweet Reeds again, and brought Petra along to thank her for all of her help. It was a beautiful night, so they decided to walk. They were laughing hard on the way back afterwards, as Ellie told another story about all the pranks that had been played on her over the years, but her laughter stopped instantly as they approached Ellie's house, and she found her father sitting out on the stoop.

"Hey, Kitten," he said, looking up at her. "You're looking good."

"Papa," she replied drily, and crossed her arms to keep her claws from coming out. "What are you doing here?"

"I came to talk to you," he replied. "And to ask a favor of you."

Marsee raised a brow.

"I have to go to Digger and will probably be gone for a while. I was hoping you might return home and help your mother while I'm gone," he explained.

She frowned at the idea. A big part of her missed Hope dearly, but another part of her didn't want to return and witness her sister fade away. "I don't know. It's too hard watching Little Flower waste away, and I've been thinking about moving here permanently. I'm really enjoying the classes I'm taking. Plus, I just earned my shuttle license today, and I want to earn my pilot's license too."
~~~~~

"Congratulations," her father said. "And if you want to move here, that's fine. I don't expect you to give up your goals or your future, but your mother can't care for your sister and Hope alone, and I don't know what else to do. She won't even leave your sister's room anymore, unless it's to consult with Ammond, and she's refused to allow anyone else to help her, even GrandFather. Please? Just for a week?"

Marsee sighed, but nodded.

"Thank you!" he said, brightening.

"I'm doing this for Mama and Hope, not you," she said, glaring at him, unable to keep the shiver out of her tail.

He nodded, and she left him on the stoop as she stormed her way to her room and angrily began packing.

Ellie appeared moments later. "Marsee, what happened between you and your father?"

"Nothing," Marsee replied, stepping around her. Ellie stopped her, and frowned at her. Marsee sighed. "We had a fight. That's all."

"I doubt it was just a fight after that last comment to your father," Ellie said, crossing her arms and scowling. "Are you sure you're okay?"

"I'll be fine," Marsee replied, and decided to try to distract Ellie. "I miss Hope, but it was nice to forget my sister's illness for even a few weeks. Thank you for letting me stay, and for being such a wonderful host. I had an amazing time."

"You've been a wonderful guest. I've missed having people here. It's been far too long. You're welcome back any time, and I mean that. If you want to move in or need a place to stay, my home is always available to you, even if I'm not here," Ellie replied.

Marsee looked up at Ellie in surprise. "Seriously?"

Ellie snorted. "I don't make offers lightly and well, there's more than enough room. I often stay at the Guild because it's too quiet here, but I want to know what's going on between you and your father, before I feel comfortable with you leaving here with him."

Marsee sighed and sat down on the bed trying to figure out what she could tell Ellie. "I was feeling overwhelmed by everything going on, and took off for a run, to try and calm down before my father left for the last Full Council meeting. Papa saw me and thought I was losing control again, but I just needed some space to think. He pounced on me to make me stop."

Ellie looked hard at her. "I can see why you'd be upset about that, but that's not nearly enough to explain what I saw today. What *really* happened?"

"Nothing," Marsee said, and looked away.

Ellie snorted. "You're a *horrible* liar. Tell me. What did he do or say to you that made you so angry?" She didn't answer, and after a moment Ellie sat down directly in front of her. "Marsee, I can't help or protect you if I don't know what's going on."

"You can't protect me anyway," Marsee said quietly, and then stood and walked away from Ellie to look out the open window. "No one can. Do you know what it's like just waiting for the people around you to decide you're a monster that can't be trusted anymore, and should be killed? If I even show any anger or frustration, I'm liable to be put down without even so much as second thought. I can't talk about what I'm experiencing with anyone or they're likely to think I'm losing control, not just stressed and overwhelmed by all the changes in my life. I can't even go for a run without being pounced on by my own father. I can't even begin to say what it meant to be able to running with you the other day, for you not to smell of fear around me when I even mention my instinct."

"You are *not* a monster," Ellie said, and wrapped her tail around her. "You're dealing with an illness no one understands, and you're so much better than you were even a few months ago. Now if something is happening, I want to know so I can help you work through it *before* it becomes a problem. You can trust me and tell me anything. Whatever it is, we'll work through it. I give you my oath not to tell anyone. Please tell me what really happened."

Marsee looked over at Ellie, shocked by her offer. "Why would you do that?"

"Well for one, I'd rather find ways to save people like you, than have to send them off to the guard for testing, and for another, everyone needs someone they can talk to," Ellie replied.

Marsee stared at Ellie for a few moments, trying to decide if she could trust her, and eventually decided to take the chance. She really needed to talk to someone, or it was just going to eat her up inside, and Ellie was probably the only one with enough rank to take on the Council to save her. She turned back to her bag, pulling out her sketchbook and handed it over to Ellie. Ellie flipped it open with curiosity, and Marsee watched Ellie's expressions go from amazement to concern.

"I've been practicing. I know I'm not supposed to use it, but I feel so much calmer when I'm drawing like this. Like I'm wholly me. I can't even explain how beautiful the world is when I have my instinct on. There are colors I can't even name or reproduce, and it's like I've never even seen or sniffed a flower before. Every one of them smells better than fried star fruit, and I can give as little or as much control to my instinct now as I want. That day, I was feeling trapped and anxious, and the sounds of New Hope were overwhelming. I used to run around the loop when it got bad like that, but I can't do that anymore. It's far too crowded. So we took off for the Wilds to find someplace to claim as our own, where we could go when we needed to get away from everything. Unfortunately Papa saw me with my instinct on. I was so mad at him after pouncing on me that I pretty much destroyed a scrub tree afterwards, and even allowed my instinct to spray it to try and get it to calm down. I figured it was better to let it have a safe target like a tree than clawing up my father like it really wanted to."

Marsee looked up expecting to see the same look of disgust she'd seen on her father, but Ellie just nodded. "That makes sense, and I've been known to claw a few things in my day."

"Anyway, we talked for a while and I told him some of what was bothering me, but I got overwhelmed with everything again and ran off, only this time he didn't stop me. He forced me to run into the wilds, swiping at me and saying some pretty awful things, many of which hit on some of my deepest insecurities. Eventually I had enough and we fought. I'll be honest, for a moment, I thought he was going to kill me, but I managed to pin him instead, and after giving him a piece of my mind, and letting him know just who was in control, I walked away. He apologized for what he said and explained afterwards that he was just testing my control, but it still hurt, as did the broken shoulder, and multiple cuts and bruises," she added with a mutter.

The look of shock on Ellie's face would have been comical if Marsee was in any mood to laugh. "That's abuse, Marsee. I don't care what his reasons were. You need to tell your uncle," Ellie replied, when she finally recovered.

Marsee shook her head. "He was doing what he needed to do, to keep everyone else safe. If I had been losing control, he wouldn't have been able to stop me, and at least I would have been away from New Hope, and maybe I was out of control a bit. I don't know. I don't know what counts as losing control. He says he should have killed me for marking up the tree. How am I supposed to know what will get me killed if no one will tell me? I can't run, I can't get mad or upset. I don't have the privacy to just roar my grief and frustration at the world. I can't even go to the cafeteria for a snack without being asked where I'm going, and I know now, no one is ever going to trust me even after the watch is over, informal or otherwise. Ellie, it's been like this my whole life. I moved to the tower to get away from the looks of disappointment every time I couldn't sit still, only now it's worse. Instead of disappointment, I see fear. Sometimes I think Marcus should have killed me that night. It would have been easier for everyone, then they wouldn't have to live with a monster."

"I trust you," Ellie said softly, and hugged her. "And you're *not* a monster. If you could walk away from your father after all of that, you're fully in control. The only monster I see here is your father for putting you through that. No matter what the reason, he shouldn't have done that to you. Please, you should talk to Marcus about it."

Marsee shook her head. "No. As mad as I am at him, he nearly lost his own life, to keep everyone else safe. Please don't say anything to Marcus or Mama. Papa promised it wouldn't happen again, but if it does, well, let's just say it won't be my *instinct* he'll need to worry about."

Ellie snorted, and then looked at her with a serious expression. "I promised I wouldn't, and I keep my promises. Now, has he ever hurt you before?"

Marsee shook her head. "No. Not like that anyway."

"But he has hurt you another way?" Ellie pressed.

"He's never physically hurt me before, but..." Marsee shrugged, not sure how to explain. "The needs of the Council always came first, and I always felt like a disappointment before because of my issues. He said he was disappointed in himself for not being able to help me, but I don't know if I believe him or not."

Ellie pursed her lips but eventually nodded. "If something does happen, do your best to stay calm, don't fight the guard, and demand a Full Council trial and an advocate. I promise I'll do everything I can to help."

Marsee nodded and resumed packing.

Ellie handed her the sketchbook back. "These are stunning by the way, and I'd love to see more."

She looked up into Ellie's eyes, trying to tell if the Senior Guild Master was being serious and decided she was. "Thank you."

Ellie smiled at her. "I look forward to the day when I can safely share these with the world, but until then, thank you for trusting me enough to show them to me."

When she had everything in her room packed up, she made her way to the waste room and grabbed her toothbrush. Then, squaring her shoulders, she made her way back down to the family room where her father now waited. She hugged Ellie goodbye and turned and walked out, thoroughly enjoying the glowering look Ellie was directing at her father, and watching him wilt under her gaze.

As they walked back in silence to the council building where her father had parked his ship, she noticed that clouds had started to roll in. It fit her mood perfectly.

Her father said nothing until they were in the air and on their way back. "I am sorry I hurt you."

Marsee glared at him. "Papa I get what you were trying to do, but you just made things worse, not better. My instinct is still very angry with you, and doesn't trust you now. If you value my life at all, don't ever raise a paw to me again, for any reason, as I don't know if I will be able to control it if you do."

Her father frowned at those words. "Are you having issues?"

"No, I am in full control, but I don't think it will fully calm until I do, and I don't know how it will react if you were to hurt us again. That's half the reason I left with Ellie. I was worried that if you even scared me by accident, like you often do when I'm crafting or reading, that I might react before I could stop myself. I know you didn't mean what you said to me, but your words still hurt, far more than your claws did, and that's going to take time to get over."

"I'm sorry," he said with a heavy sigh. "What can I do to make it easier?"

"Well for one, give me space and respect our boundaries and territory. I'm having a hard time with everyone in our home, and I need space to call my own. That was half the reason I ran off that day. I needed a place where I could go and just be me, and my instinct is furious that you didn't respect our boundaries. Treat me like the adult I am. If I go for a run, just let me. Don't ask where I'm going every time I leave the tower. Don't try to make me talk to you, or if I do talk to you about something, listen to me. Don't just try to fix it, be my father, not my Senior Councilor. Sometimes I just need to vent or let off a little steam."

Her father nodded. "Those are all reasonable requests. Would you like me to set you up with your own apartment?"

"I'll think about it. Ellie's offered to let me move in with her," Marsee replied.

Her father's ears flicked back in surprise, but he nodded. "That's quite the opportunity. You should take it."

"We'll see," Marsee said.

"I would expect you to be jumping for joy over that opportunity. Why are you hesitating?" he asked.

"It depends on what happens with Little Flower," she replied. "If the Council calls for Mama's execution, I intend to fight for custody of Hope."

"You?!" her father asked in surprise.

"Yes, me," she growled. "I've taken care of her more than the rest of you all combined, and I'll be sent to the dark side of the moons before I let *you* have her. You don't have the time to raise a cub on your own and be a senior councilor. You barely had enough time for me and you were only a councilor then."

Her father flinched at the venom in her voice, but was silent for several minutes before nodding. "You're right. I can't do both. The past few weeks have been grueling without your help. I won't fight you. If that day comes and you want her, I'll gladly sign over custody so it doesn't have to go before the Council, as I doubt they would vote in your favor. Your sister put you down as her preference after your mother and I, so I have the legal authority to make that decision. She wants Hope raised by one of us. I promise to help you any way I can, if you'll let me. You won't have to do it on your own. The only caveat is that I'll have to wait until a full six months have passed since the date Marcus put you on the watch list. Legally I can't give you full custody because of that, even if he did rescind it."

She sat there in shock, for several moments, before she found the ability to speak. Even her instinct was stunned. "Seriously? You won't fight me for custody?"

"I keep my promises, even if it doesn't seem that way sometimes," he replied. "I think you'll make a wonderful mother. No, correction, you *are* a wonderful mother. I'll talk with your mother about placing you as one of Hope's guardians when I return, assuming she's in a better mood. That I can do. In her current mood however, your mother is more likely to throw me off the tower if I even suggested it."

Marsee nodded and her tail curled slightly at that mental image. "Well if you do, make sure you warn me first so I can get it on video. That way I can watch it over and over again."

Her father snorted. "I'm honestly just thankful there wasn't video of you pinning me. I told your uncle what happened and he's been teasing me non-stop since."

Marsee's tail curled further. "He didn't mention anything about it when I last saw him. I wonder if I could get him to trade access to his archives for a repeat performance."

Her father groaned. "Knowing Marcus, I'm guessing you'd be able to trade access to the Ancient Archives for that."

Marsee grinned wickedly at the idea, although she seriously doubted her uncle would go for it. He was far too honorable for that. Still, it might be worth a try. Her father just rolled his eyes.

"So why are you going to Digger?" Marsee asked, changing the subject.

Her father sighed. "How much have you been watching the news lately?"

"Honestly not much. I've been too busy," she replied.

She waited while her father considered his words. "Let's just say, there's a great deal of unhappiness at what happened during the trial. There's a growing call for Saber's Council to step down, and the Senior Council too. Marcus wasn't able to get any of his budget items passed at the last meeting, which isn't surprising, even though most were critical items. The people are angry that they're having to pay for the Council's mistakes, even though what we ended up giving to New Hope was less than what we expected the sanctions would be going into the trial. Digger is showing the least amount of unrest at the moment, so we're going there to discuss whether or not we need to call for re-elections, and figure out how to pay for a few critical items that are needed here."

Marsee raised a brow. "I saw a little bit of that, but I didn't realize it was that bad. What do you intend to do?"

"I honestly don't know. My personal preference is to leave it up to the people and wait for them to call for re-elections. What do you think we should do?"

"Me?!" Marsee asked.

"Well, many of your arguments and concerns with the Senior Council are the same as the others, even if they don't know everything else that happened during deliberation. What would it take to restore your faith in the Council?" her father asked.

Marsee sat back in her seat and looked out the window as she considered his question. It was honestly the first time he'd ever asked her about her opinion on anything that really mattered, outside of her observations with Little Flower early on, and it was a long time before she spoke. Her father waited patiently. "Even if you all stepped down, I don't think it would help, not in the long run. The problem isn't with any one councilor or senior councilor, but with the decisions that were made and your actions since."

"How so?" he asked.

"The Senior Council chose to go with precedent rather than what the people and the rest of the Council thought was right. You and Mama took responsibility to save everyone else, which they respect, but what the people saw was the Council saving themselves at your expense, and punishing innocent people in the process too, not just me and my siblings and nephlings, but all of the people that are having to put time towards New Hope. Even if it is only an hour or two per person, we're still paying for the Council's mistakes, while the Council, outside of Tabor, suffered nothing. Most haven't even visited or made an attempt to get to know the people of New Hope, and it's been months now. As far as I know, only Clear Seas has visited out of the original Senior Council, and they were all here on the planet for a week before the last Council Meeting. Even for Remembrance Day, only Marcus came."

Her father nodded the point. "Most are just waiting until we have a place for them, and as for Remembrance Day, the Local Council decided they wanted to keep the ceremony small. The Hue-mans needed time to grieve."

"That may be, but the other Seniors could have attended, and the rest of Saber's Council could visit at any time and sleep in their shuttles just like everyone else has been doing," Marsee replied. "But they're not, and that makes people think they're ashamed of their actions. At least that's what I've heard. Even the Hue-mans are wondering why they haven't visited."

"Those are all very good points," her father said. "However, you still didn't say what you would do to fix it."

"Isn't that *your* job?" she asked him, rolling her eyes.

He chuckled. "It is, but I'm still curious."

"Well, for one, a public apology would be nice, but I'd personally prefer that *that* particular precedent never be used again. Victim's choice yes, punishing those not involved, never again. That was wrong and shouldn't have even been considered. No one should ever be punished for someone else's crime. And well, if you want people to trust you and your people, then they need to see what you've done for the people of New Hope, and how their investment is paying off. Show them what you've built and what the Hue-mans have accomplished in their short time here. Maybe celebrate one of the Hue-man holidays and invite everyone. The Council can sleep on their transport ships and eat in the cafeteria like everyone else, and maybe even do something like help set up, or some other form of community service like Tabor's doing."

"Those are excellent ideas. When did you get so smart?" he asked.

"When you were off at a Council meeting," she replied with a glare.

Her father sighed. "Fair point, well made, and I thoroughly deserved that."

Their conversation ended as the pilot announced their approach to New Hope. Marsee turned her attention to watch the approach. "I can't believe how much the compound has changed in just a few months," she said.

"You're telling me. I can barely keep up with Ellie and Gregory these days. I'll need to leave as soon as I drop you off. Thank you so much for coming back."

Marsee nodded, but didn't look away from the window until they landed. Once the ship was down, she unclipped from her harness, grabbed her bag, and started walking towards the door.

"Marsee," her father said. She turned around to face him. "I am truly sorry that I hurt you. I saw no other choice. I thought you were losing control again. I hope someday you can forgive me."

She sighed. "Papa, I understand why you did it. I'm just...angry and disappointed in you. You're better than that. What hurt the worst, is that you didn't trust me to tell you if I had a problem, that you didn't listen to me, to what I said I needed, *again*. My whole life, I've been forced to fit into a mold, into a world that doesn't fit me, reprimanded because I couldn't sit still, when all I really needed was to run, and forced to attend functions where I felt overwhelmed by the sounds I could hear, that you didn't even believe I could hear. I lost control because I tried to deny a part of me. I didn't gain control until I allowed myself to be whole. That which you see as broken, I see as beautiful. I can hear Hope laugh, when you can't. I can see colors that I didn't even know existed until a few months ago, and I am capable of defending myself from someone twice my size. This is who I am now, and you need to find a way to accept that. If that presents a danger or a risk, then you'd better kill me now, because I have no intentions of becoming that other Marsee ever again. For the last few weeks I was allowed to be myself, to do the things that interested me without judgment, without someone looking over my shoulder and making sure I behaved exactly the right way. Don't assume the worst in me. Treat me like a normal person. I know it's your responsibility to make sure I don't hurt anybody, but all you've done was hurt me and make it harder for me to control. You chose to see me as a danger and attack me, and not as your grieving and overwhelmed child, who just needed a hug and a shoulder to lean on. What am I to you, Papa? Your little kitten, or a monster?"

With that, Marsee turned and stormed off the ship without waiting for him to respond, and slammed the door shut behind her. She half expected him to follow out after her, but to her surprise, he didn't. Shortly after she exited the shuttle bay, she heard the ship take off. She took a few minutes to wander through the garden until she felt calm again, and then made her way up to her sister's room.

When she arrived though, she was horrified by what she saw. Her sister looked far worse than she'd been when she'd left, and her mother had lost a lot of weight and looked exhausted. She swallowed hard and plastered a calm expression on her face before walking in.

"Hey, Mama," she said quietly, so as to not wake Hope, who was currently sleeping in her mother's arms.

"Marsee! What are you doing here?" her mother asked, looking up from the tablet in her other paw.

"Papa brought me home, saying you needed help while he was gone," she explained. "You look exhausted. Why don't you go get some sleep?"

Her mother must have been as exhausted as she looked because she didn't argue, and instead handed Hope over to her and left without further word. Hope woke briefly in the exchange, but quickly snuggled back down. Marsee purred and walked around the room with her until she fell asleep again, and then gently laid her on the bed next to Little Flower.

"Oh, Little Flower," Marsee said softly, rubbing a paw against the side of her sister's face. Her sister looked emaciated, tiny, and frail, and far worse than she'd ever seen her, and there was no doubt in her mind that her sister was dying.

It was only a matter of time.

# CHAPTER 29

# Jeran: Tests

Jer watched out the window as his ship approached New Hope. Two full weeks had passed since he'd brought Marsee back from Council City, as they'd struggled to solve one problem after another that kept popping up. They hadn't ended their conference until Clear Seas had been forced to return home to deal with protests that were showing signs of becoming violent. They'd made some progress, but not nearly enough. It was dark, raining hard, and turbulent as they landed, which matched his mood and thoughts perfectly.

There'd been nothing in the way of communication from either Marsee or her mother the entire time, so he had no idea what he was flying into either. Kendra had been silent as well, which he hoped was a good sign. He hated having the guards watching Marsee, but he had absolutely no right to say no, and if he had pushed Marsee over the edge, his people needed their protection.

*What am I to you, Papa? Your little kitten, or a monster?*

The pilot struggled to land the ship in the storm and he felt sick to his stomach, but it had little to do with the bucking motion. Marsee's words had haunted him the entire trip, as had Quinn's.

Quinn had ordered the squad of guards that had been hidden on his ship and listening in, off the ship, and then shut the door and turned back to him with a look that had surprised him, a mix of fierce protectiveness, and a hint of disgust directed entirely at him. "Councilor, if I can see the fear you have towards her, so can she, and you can't hide that behind a mask. No matter how hard you try, children always know. I've seen it far too often in my career, with parents who bring their children into the Guard, my own parents included. It's been over a hundred years, yet I can still remember the look my parents gave me the day they abandoned me to the Guard. It took me years to work through the trauma of that day, and I won't let you do that to her. If you want her to survive, you need to love her unconditionally, and without a trace of fear. If you can't do that, she's right, you might as well kill her now, because that would be far kinder than what you're doing to her. If you keep going down this path, you might not lose her to psychosis, but you will lose her, and she deserves far better than that."

It took him several minutes to find the courage to leave his ship after it landed. Even still, he didn't return home right away. He wandered the garden for nearly an hour, not caring that his fur was thoroughly soaked, as he tried to calm his thoughts. Eventually he made his way back to the tower. Not surprisingly, his room was empty. He made quick use of the sonic shower to dry his fur and made his way up the ramp to Little Flower's room, where he'd seen a light on. He'd expected to see Myra there, but Marsee was there watching her sister, sprawled out on the floor playing with Hope.

"Hey, Kitten," he said quietly, not wanting to scare her. "Where's your mother?"

She looked up and gave him a half smile. "Trauma Center, talking with Ammond and others. She thinks she's found something. I don't understand any of it, but it sounds like there's some sort of barrier preventing the nanos from making it into her brain."

"That's exciting news," he replied.

Marsee shrugged. "If they can find a way around it. I'm not holding my breath. What's more exciting is that Hope took her first steps this morning."

"Already?!" he asked. His cubs hadn't learned to stand on two feet until they were almost three years old.

Rather than answering, Marsee picked up Hope. "Alright Hope, show your Grampa what you can do," she said, and held on with just a single claw to each of her tiny paws and helped the cub to walk a few steps."

"Well, look who's a big girl now," Jer said, as he scooped Hope up and tickled her. Hope squealed with laughter that was just barely within his range of hearing. He flicked an ear back in surprise. "I think I heard her!"

"Yeah, I'm not sure if her voice is lowering as she's getting older, or if she's doing it on purpose," Marsee said, and climbed up off the floor. She turned away from him and checked on Little Flower. "It's easier for me to hear her too, and she apparently can hear us, according to Ammond. She's been growling lately and responding to her name. So how did your meeting go? You were gone longer than I expected."

"Grueling, but we made some progress. The Seniors really liked your ideas about celebrating one of the Hue-man holidays and showing how the credit invested in New Hope is benefiting others. We're tentatively planning to hold a holiday celebration here in a month or so, and a Full Council meeting to sign off on a few of the critical budget items at the same time. I just need to convince my Council to go along with it, and figure out what holiday they're going to celebrate. Any ideas there?"

She stopped what she was doing to consider. "The older cubs have told me about several of their favorite holidays, many of which would work, but Little Flower's favorite was Hallowed Eve." Marsee looked down at her sister with a sigh. "She spoke about it several times. It was always scheduled at the end of their growing season, which we're approaching now, so it would fit. She said they used to go door to door saying 'trick or treat' and if you didn't give the cub candy, you'd get some sort of trick or prank in retaliation. The Flyers would love that."

He chuckled at the thought of the chaos they would create, "I'm not sure we should tell the Flyers about that, but what's candy?" he asked, not familiar with the Hue-man word she used.

"Sweet foods, like dried star fruit," she replied and used the sign he was familiar with.

He nodded. "She mentioned that to me as well. I'll talk to Jordan about it and see what other creations she can come up with."

"Did you talk about my other suggestions?" she asked, without making eye contact. "About the precedent?"

"We did, but no decision was made there. The Seniors are split. They all fully acknowledge your right to be angry with them, but they're worried that a reduction in the possible consequences could mean that someone else gets hurt. We plan to have that as an agenda item for the Full Council meeting on the Water World."

She nodded once in acknowledgement and squared her shoulders. "I suppose that's fair. At least you're considering it."

He sighed with relief at her understanding. He'd been worried about how she'd take their decision. "So, now that I'm back, do you want to borrow my ship to head back to Council City?"

To his surprise, she shook her head. "No, I'm staying." She reached over and stroked her sister's head. "I don't think she's going to make it much longer, and as painful as it is to see her waste away, I want to be here when that happens. I'm not moving out either, at least not until after. I want to be close to her and Hope."

He walked over to the other side of the hanging bed and looked down at his adopted daughter with his own sadness and grief. Marsee looked up at him with grief in her eyes, before turning away from him and walking over to the window. She stared out the window at the storm, absently wringing her tail. He sighed, not knowing how to help either of them.

"Marsee," he started and stopped, trying to find the right words. She didn't turn to face him. "Marsee, no matter what happens, you will always be my little kitten."

She sighed and finally turned back around to face him, her expression at first full of her fear and grief, but then it hardened as she glared at him. "But there's still a monster inside of me, isn't there?"

"No more than the monster inside of me," he replied. "I don't trust myself half the time. Is it not surprising that I have a hard time trusting you?"

She growled at him and stormed out. He sighed, instantly realizing he'd said the wrong thing, again, not that he had a clue what the right thing was anymore. He brought Hope back over to her toys and sat down on the floor with her, considering all the ways he'd messed up over the past year, but a moment later, to his surprise, Marsee returned carrying a sketchbook.

"You might see a monster, but I don't. Not anymore. I trust my instinct far more than I trust you right now. It's a part of me and it loves me unconditionally. It wants to protect me and those I care about. It wanted to kill you for hurting us, but it listened to me and respected my goals and desires, and didn't fight me to give up control, not like it did before. I gave myself up entirely to my instinct to try and stop you, because I thought you were trying to kill me, yet even though it wanted to kill you, I didn't, and it respected that. It's why I was able to shut it off and walk away. I just wanted you to stop hurting me, not kill you. My instinct is me. You can't separate one from the other, and we are far more balanced and in harmony than we've ever been before. I'm not even sure I could explain the difference, and I don't know how to prove that to you either. I don't know how to earn your trust or stop you from looking at me with fear. Even after what you did to me, you still look at me in fear and don't trust me. What do I have to do to earn your trust Papa? What more *can* I do? I don't even know what will get me killed, what imaginary line I need to cross that will be one step too far. Everything you or Marcus or Mama ever tried with me failed to work, and everything you say I should be doing only makes things worse. I haven't hurt anyone, haven't even had the urge to hurt anyone since that day in the garden, because I stopped fighting myself and started to listen to my body and my instinct, to learn what I needed to do to maintain control, to practice and find that balance, to release pressure, before I exploded and hurt someone. Yes, I had my instinct on the other day, but I wasn't out of control. It was intentional. I was actively working to maintain control the only way I know how, the only way that works for me, by giving my instinct a way to calm down, by respecting its own needs and desires too. We were both feeling trapped and like our territory had been invaded. You said I should have been killed for marking that tree, but I compromised and allowed it that little bit of control so it wouldn't demand more, and it worked, until you invaded our territory again. Running helps keep me calm. Movement of any kind helps keep me calm. I don't know why but it always has. It's why I built my hanging bed. Yet I wasn't allowed to do that as a cub. If I wiggled too much or ran you'd frown at me, and the more I tried not to, the worse it would get until I exploded and pounced on something. I'm not doing that anymore. I'm going to keep doing what keeps me calm and in balance, and you need to stop seeing that as a loss of control, but as me actively maintaining my control."

She stared at him for several moments waiting for him to respond, but he didn't know what to say, terrified for her. If she was needing to give up control to her instinct at all, that was bad, really bad.

She sighed and glared at him. "Tell me Papa. Would a monster be capable of doing this?" She practically threw the sketch book at him, and left again, storming back up to her room.

He stared out the open door for a moment and then looked down at the sketchbook, carefully opened it, and gasped at what he saw, absolutely stunning works of art that could never be displayed, and an undeniable admission of guilt that could very likely mean her death. After he finished flipping through the book, he closed it with a conflicted sigh, and then picked up Hope and walked up to Marsee's room.

She was curled up in a ball, hearing aids in, and swinging hard on the bed. He walked over and stopped the bed. She looked up at him with a mix of fear and defiance that nearly broke his heart. "Take your hearing aids out," he signed. He wanted to be sure she could hear him and signing while holding onto a wiggly cub was difficult.

She sighed, but did as ordered.

"How long have you been using your instinct to draw?" he asked.

"The first time was the day you caught me sneaking into the garden," she replied. "I made sure I was safe around the Hue-mans first. Papa, the world is so vibrant and beautiful when my instinct is on, and unlike before, I feel calm and relaxed, especially in the garden. Like I said, I didn't start gaining control of myself until I accepted that this was part of who I am. It was a safe way for me to practice. I promise I've never even remotely had the urge to hunt anyone."

"You shouldn't be using your instinct at all," he replied. "It's not safe. Every time you use it, is another chance for it to take control."

She snorted at him. "Papa, how many times do I have to tell you. I spent my entire life trying not to use my instinct, and failing miserably. By practicing, I'm now able to give up as little or as much control as I want, and still remain me, something I couldn't do before. Maybe your way doesn't work for people like me. What matters more, that I don't use my instinct, or that I find ways to remain balanced and in control?"

He sighed, but considered her comments. She *had* remained in full control and walked away. He was alive because of it, but the law was clear, and unlike the rape trial, he had ten thousand years of precedent backing it. He should report it, and bring her in for a full test before Kendra, but that was usually done after there was an incident, not a voluntary admission of use in which no one was hurt, and if she was going to continue being honest and forthcoming with him, he couldn't just turn around and immediately punish her for it. *I need to talk with Marcus,* he decided, and handed Hope back over to her to watch. She hugged Hope tightly to her.

"Don't do it again," he ordered, and left to make his way to his office. When he arrived though, he locked his door and just sat and stared at the beautiful drawings in the sketchbook. He'd honestly never seen artwork that was more captivating before. It put everything Little Flower had ever done to shame, but it was so very different from his own experiences with his instinct. He'd never once used it in a situation that wasn't life threatening, and he'd never found beauty or balance with it either. His was a monster that needed to be controlled and dominated, just like Marcus did with him, yet there was a part of him that yearned to be free, to be whole and balanced, and see the world with the beauty the way Marsee did.

With a heavy sigh, he flicked on his busy light and privacy screen and called Marcus.

Marcus just sighed when he saw Jer's expression. Jer said nothing, just flipped his camera around and showed Marcus the drawings.

Marcus realized what they represented immediately and grabbed the back of his scruff. "Oh, Jer, no," he whispered, his voice rough with grief and denial.

"She volunteered this information without being asked, and said drawing with her instinct helps to keep her calm," Jer replied.

Before Marcus could comment, Jer jumped in surprise as his office door swung open, and Kendra stormed in, without so much as a knock first. Kendra was one of the few people authorized to enter his office when locked, and it automatically shut off the privacy screen too.

He closed the book quickly. "Kendra, what's wrong?" he asked, figuring there was an emergency if she ignored his busy light, and nodded towards the monitor to let her know he was on a call with Marcus.

"I came to talk to you about the sketchbook, before you did something stupid," she replied, as she sat down across from him and reactivated his privacy screen.

He snorted at that comment, but then sighed, not even sure what to say to save Marsee, and just slid the book over. To his surprise though, Kendra didn't open it.

"I've seen it," she replied. "And I've watched her use her instinct as she drew, twice now."

His heart sank. "So you intend to test her?"

"No. You've already done that. I see no point in doing so again. In fact, I'm taking her off the watch list."

"You're what?!" Marcus asked, surprised.

"Councilors, if she was going to have a problem she would have by now, especially if she's been using it, and she's right. What we've done for the past ten thousand years hasn't worked, and I'd personally prefer to never have to test another child ever again, if we can find better ways to treat psychosis before it becomes a problem. She *is* visibly calmer when she draws. I didn't believe it myself at first, and I watched her draw for several hours without so much as a twitch, even when people were walking by."

Jer sat there shocked. "I'm not going to deny it, I'm relieved, but...why would you take her off the watch list after she sprayed and marked a tree?"

"Because that was a natural response to *your* actions prior, and she remained in control enough not to claw you instead," Kendra replied. "I want her to continue drawing, and doing whatever she feels she needs to do, to help her remain in control, as long as she's not hunting, actively hurting anyone, or having difficulty turning it off, I don't believe there's a problem. I would like a report on anything else she shares with you in that regard though."

"Of course," he replied, stunned that she wanted Marsee to keep drawing.

"I'm not sure how I feel about that," Marcus stated. "Every use of her instinct could make things worse."

Kendra nodded. "Yes it could. Historically, that's been the case too, but then I'm not aware of anyone trying to draw with it before, either. Her physical reaction is unusual. I'm not aware of anyone who gets calmer when they have their instinct on, but she does, and it's worth investigating. If she does start having problems, then we can discuss bringing her into the guard for further training."

Marcus nodded. "Well, if I can save cubs with coloring books, I'll raid the Guild for them."

Kendra chuckled. "I said the exact same thing to Quinn the other day, and have already placed an order."

Jer started to relax, but then froze as Kendra's glare focused hard on him. "Now, what did you mean about not trusting yourself?"

He sighed, realizing Kendra had overheard the entire conversation, which he should have realized was a possibility, and tried to figure out how to explain without giving away what they did with the junior advocates test, as he had no idea if Kendra was aware of the test or not, and glanced up at Marcus, who was looking at him with concern too.

"I was an only cub too, and struggled with my own control issues when I was younger. Marcus worked with me for months to ensure I was fully in control. Marsee knows this, and I've been trying to help her by sharing some of my experiences there, not that it seems to be helping.”

“Have you had issues with your control since then?” she demanded.

He shook his head. “No more than what would be expected for the kind of year we’ve had. I was rather upset when we found the precedent, and terrified that Tabor was going through with it at the trial, but I was able to maintain control.”

“And you didn’t have any problems when Marsee had you pinned, or since?”

He shook his head. “No.”

“I find that hard to believe, Councilor. It didn’t try to save your life?” she asked. “Not even a little?”

Jer sighed and looked up at Marcus again, who nodded slightly. “No,” he finally said. “My instinct recognized her as dominant, and recognized that she just wanted control of the situation, not to hurt or kill me, just like it does with Marcus.”

“Establishing dominance is standard practice for anyone in the Council who has issues during their training,” Marcus replied.

She raised a brow, pursed her lips, and considered. “Have you been tested since that day with Marsee?” she asked him.

“No,” he replied. “I’m guessing you’re going to now?”

“What do you think, Councilor?” she snorted.

He stood and walked around the desk and faced her. At her nod he turned his instinct on and waited patiently for the strike to come. When it did, Kendra hit him so hard and so fast he wasn’t able to fully block the strike. He felt something give and pop in his shoulder from the force of the impact, and he was knocked to the ground. He started scrambling away trying to regain his feet, queasy from the injury, but instantly on alert, trying to determine if Kendra was trying to kill him, test him, or if it had just been an accident. Kendra swung again with a look that terrified him. He ducked and tried to get away, but she struck, hitting him hard in the head, hard enough that he crashed to the ground again. Before he could react, she grabbed him and he went flying through the air, unable to stop her, and found himself pinned under her a moment later. He struggled to get away, but Kendra applied pressure to his injured shoulder, and he realized in that instant if Kendra had wanted him dead he would already be dead, and like with Marsee and Marcus, his instinct calmed and rolled over accepting he'd been thoroughly beaten.

"Kendra, what are you doing?" Marcus yelled.

"Testing him," Kendra replied, and when he didn't struggle, finally let go and helped him up. She looked into his eyes and snorted, as his instinct was already off. "I honestly didn't believe you, Councilor. That was very interesting. Dangerous for your own safety, but interesting. Now, let me take a look at that shoulder."

"Was that necessary," Jer asked as Kendra pulled a scanner off her carry harness. Before she could scan him though he was hit with a wave of dizziness, and sat down in the nearest chair before he fell down, hissing with the pain of the motion.

She just snorted at him. "You were fully prepared, and not the least bit nervous about me striking at you. It wouldn't have been a valid test if you weren't scared, and you know it. I am impressed though. Not many would have managed to block that first strike at all." She scanned him and frowned. "I'm not seeing any signs of a concussion, but as I thought, your shoulder is dislocated." She set the scanner down and grabbed his arm. "This is going to hurt," she replied, and twisted. "A lot."

It hurt so bad he couldn't even scream, but as quickly as the pain started, he felt the joint pop back into place, and the pain calmed down to a dull throb. He swallowed hard trying not to throw up, and leaned back into the chair as Kendra scanned his shoulder again.

"It doesn't look like anything is torn badly enough to need surgery. Nano's should clear it up in a day or two, along with the headache you're likely to have," she said, and she clipped the scanner back onto her carry harness.

He grunted but didn't answer, eyes still closed as he struggled to contain his stomach. A few minutes later it settled, and he opened them again to find Kendra watching him intently.

"We'll talk later about what you did to establish dominance," Kendra said. "But for now, let's get you something for the pain, and since I'm already here, I might as well examine Myra too. It's a little early, but a week or two won't matter all that much."

Jer sighed, instantly worried about his partner, but looked up at his brother. Marcus had his mask on tightly, nodded, and disconnected the call.

"I believe she's at the Trauma Center," he told Kendra.

Kendra nodded, "She is, or was anyway."

They made their way towards Myra's office, after Kendra treated his injuries, but found her in a meeting with Ammond and several others, in Ammond's office. The room went silent as they saw Kendra behind him.

"Myra, a moment of your time please," he said.

"Of course," she replied and left the group. They walked down to her office.

"I'm sure you're aware of why I'm here," Kendra said, once the door was shut and locked.

"I wasn't expecting you for a few weeks, but I have a pretty good idea," Myra said. Five minutes later, Myra had been cleared as well, and sat down hard in her chair, after Kendra nodded to them and left.

"Well, that went better than I expected," Jer replied with a chuckle as his nerves calmed. Myra looked up at him with a frown. "You've been very stressed, which concerned me. The even better news is Kendra removed Marsee from the watch list as well."

"Blessed Moons," Myra whispered, and sagged back in her chair with relief.

"Marsee said you may have found something?" he asked, changing the subject.

"Yes, we're just not sure how to treat it yet," she replied. "But we finally figured out why our other treatments haven't been working. It's a start, and more than I've had to work with since she went into the coma, but speaking of that, I should be getting back before the others start to wonder if I've been executed."

"Before that though, I wanted to talk to you about something," he said, raising a paw to stop her.

She sat back in her seat and raised a brow.

"When I brought Marsee back, she told me that if something happened to Little Flower and you, she wanted custody of Hope. Little Flower left that as one of her preferences, and I don't intend to fight her on it, if she wants that responsibility. I won't be able to care for a cub on my own, not *and* care for Little Flower's people. Anyway, I was thinking that now that Marsee is off the watch list we should make her Hope's primary guardian. It'll help her case if something should happen to both of us before I can do that."

Myra looked up at him in surprise, but then surprised him by nodding. He'd expected an argument at least. "She's been more of a mother to her than any of us. If she wants that responsibility, I won't stop her, and I'm honestly relieved that Hope will have someone that loves her as much as Marsee does, to care for her, if I can't."

He gave her a quick hug and walked back down with her to Ammond's office and listened for a few minutes as they gave him a run down of what they'd found, before returning to his own office, and calling Marcus back.

"She passed," Jer said, the moment Marcus answered.

Marcus sighed with relief. "How's your shoulder?"

"I'll manage," Jer replied. "I'm going to have nightmares, but I'll manage."

Marcus snorted. "You and me, both. I thought she was trying to kill you there for a second."

"Likewise," Jer replied. "How much are we going to tell her?"

"As little as possible. I have no idea if she knows about the junior advocates test, and I don't intend to tell her if she doesn't. Hopefully she'll be more interested in what I did to you than why."

Jer nodded. "What do you think about Marsee drawing?"

"Honestly, I don't like it, but Kendra's the expert on this," Marcus replied. "And if she feels Marsee is safe, who am I to argue?"

"You, not argue? I must be hearing wrong. Maybe I should have Myra check my head out. Kendra must have hit me harder than I thought," Jer teased.

Marcus snorted. "You're lucky Kendra didn't land that first blow or you'd be in a bed next to Little Flower. I've never once seen anyone manage to even partially block a blow from her. Now, you'd better go talk to Marsee. I expect she's panicking by now."

He rolled his eyes at his brother, disconnected the call, grabbed the sketch book, and returned to the tower with it.

Marsee was back in Little Flower's room. Hope was nursing, but Marsee was pacing. She spun when he entered, fear evident on her face, but he smiled at her, handing the sketchbook back, which she took from him with a look of confusion.

"You're not in trouble. I've spoken with both Marcus and Kendra. In fact, Kendra is quite interested in this development, and wants you to keep drawing, and to know what other methods you're using to help you remain in control, and she's taken you and your mother off the watch list."

She just stared at him in shock. "You're serious?"

"I am. I'll be honest, Marcus and I are just as surprised as you are, but if Kendra says you're safe, who are we to disagree?" he said with a wry smile as he repeated Marcus's words. "As long as you aren't hunting, hurting anyone, or having issues shutting it off, we're not going to stop you. It goes against everything we've been taught, but we're willing to give this a chance if it helps you, and perhaps others in the future. If you do have any problems, stop using it immediately, and come see us."

"I promise," Marsee said, but frowned with worry. "Am I going to be in trouble if I do have problems?"

"No. We'll just know that it doesn't work in the long run, and try something different. You might get put back on the watch, but as long as you're not out of control and hurting anyone, I'll keep fighting to find a way to help you. Marsee, I know I've failed you miserably with this whole mess. I promise to do better and listen to you, and try not to let my own fears and insecurities about myself bias what's going on with you. If you've picked up any fear or worry from me, it's only my fear of losing you. I'm not afraid of you. I'm afraid for you. You're not a monster. A monster wouldn't have walked away after what I did and said to you. You are ,and always be, my little kitten, and nothing you ever do will stop me from loving you. Do you think maybe we could start over?"

Marsee sighed but nodded.

Jer grinned with relief. "Thank you!" He tried to give her a hug, but she put up her paw to stop him.

"I'm still mad at you, and a part of me doesn't trust you," she said. "I understand why you did what you did, but I still need time. Perhaps consider yourself on my own personal watch list."

"That's fair, and I completely understand." He was disappointed, but kept that locked behind his mask. "Now, as I promised I would, I've spoken to your mother about making you Hope's *primary* guardian, and she whole-heartedly agreed, and was relieved to know you want custody of Hope. If you still want to become Hope's mother in the future, I can mark that preference down as well, now that you're off the watch list."

Marsee closed her eyes and took a huge shuddering breath before opening them and nodding. "I really do."

Jer grinned. "Now, if something happens to both your mother and I before I can transfer custody, go directly to Marcus. As your senior, and with Little Flower's preferences, he has the authority to make that decision. The Local Council might still appeal it, but I have already had verbal agreement from the other Seniors that they'll vote in your favor, so just fight it if they do."

Marsee grinned, and her tail spiraled in joy, as that worry lifted from her.

"What about Mama?" she asked.

"Clear Seas said he'll vote in her favor, as has Marcus. The others haven't decided yet, but like you, I don't think your sister will live long enough for that to be a concern. I'll have the tie breaking vote at the next meeting, and Clear Seas the one afterwards."

Marsee sighed and looked over with worry at her sister, but nodded. "I suppose that's better than nothing."

"Agreed," he said, and unclipped his tablet. "Now, do you, Marsee Bet Chenzira, promise to care for Hope Chenzira as if she were your own child, until such time as her mother is capable of caring for her again, or advocating her own preferences in that care, with all of the rights and responsibilities that come with being a guardian?"

"I do," she replied, her tail instantly spiraling again.

"Then it is my pleasure and honor to give you the rights of guardianship to Hope Chenzira, and while I hope and pray that your sister recovers, I couldn't think of a better person than you to become Hope's mother, if she doesn't."

"Thanks, Papa," Marsee said, and hugged him.

Jer returned the hug with everything he had, his relief and happiness that she trusted him enough to hug him again far outweighing the pain in his shoulder with the motion. *It was fair, equal, and just for what I did to her,* he decided, and chuckled.

"What's so funny, Papa?" she asked, looking up at him.

"Well, it might not have been your mother's doing, but Kendra decided to test me as well this evening, and I have footage, and a matching injured shoulder." Everything in his office was recorded, in case it was needed for evidence, so he logged into the system, and pulled it up to show her, and then as an act of penance, saved a copy and sent it to her.

Her fur spiked out and then curled as she watched, before she looked up at him. "Fair, equal, and just," she said, with a wicked smile, and then surprised him by hugged him again. "You know, Papa. If you can stay in control through that, maybe you should try to stop fearing the beast inside you too."

He sighed, and caressed the back of her head. "I don't how, Kitten. I really don't."

# CHAPTER 30

# Ellie: Poof

Ellie sat with Myra in what had once been the family room of the ancient tower, watching the emaciated Little Flower nurse her cub. She was honestly surprised that Little Flower was still alive, considering how awful she looked. It was even worse than the last time she'd been here, as all of her head fur had been shaved off to attempt a new treatment the healers had concocted.

She listened in horror as Myra explained the latest treatment they'd tried. They'd actually drilled several tiny holes in Little Flower's skull and injected a modified nano wash directly into her brain in the locations most affected. This treatment had finally shown some improvements on the scans, but Little Flower still hadn't woken. Myra was beyond frustrated, and at a complete loss for what to try next.

Ellie wasn't sure what to do to help, besides offer her support. Officially she was there to review the applications for the latest round of promotions that would be handed out at the Hallowed Eve Festival, but in reality she was mostly there to check on Marsee. She'd expected Marsee to return once Jer returned from his council meeting, but she hadn't, stating she needed to stay and help her mother care for Hope and her sister.

She'd been worried and asked several of Marsee's teachers to let her know if they saw anything concerning, and Master Yellow Tail had reached out to let her know Marsee had missed several classes in a row. When Ellie had questioned her, Marsee had insisted that everything was fine, and that she'd just been busy preparing for the upcoming festival. While it appeared that her relationship with her father had improved, Ellie could still see tension that hadn't been there before, and she had been absolutely horrified to see just how exhausted Marsee looked after barely a month. She was nearly as bad as Myra was. *I need to get her out of here, permanently. It's just not healthy for her here.*

"It's been four months without any change Myra. Isn't it time you let her go?" Ellie gently asked.

"Not you too," Myra growled. "Ellie, I don't care if it takes years, or the rest of my life. As long as she keeps fighting to live, I'm going to fight beside her. It's my fault she's in this situation in the first place, and I will find a way to get her out of it. Please don't ever suggest it again." Myra's tail shivered with emotion at the thought of losing her adopted cub.

Ellie frowned but nodded. "Then you need to take better care of yourself," Ellie chided. "I'm worried about you. You've lost too much weight. Set a reminder to eat your meals. You're not going to be able to help her if you get sick."

"Besides, Hope still needs her," Myra continued, completely ignoring Ellie's comment about her health.

The cub lifted her head at the sound of her name, detached from Little Flower's teat, and began to cry. Myra stood up from her chair, picked the tiny cub up, and began to purr, patting the cub gently on her back. Even though Hope had nearly doubled in weight and size since she was born, she still easily fit in Myra's paws, and was still far smaller than one of their own newborns. She was absolutely adorable, and triggered all of Ellie's maternal instincts, and for the millionth time in her long life, she wished she'd been able to have cubs. After a few moments the tiny cub settled.

"There there," she crooned. "You're all better now. No need to cry."

Marsee stumbled in looking haggard and rundown and let out a huge yawn. "Hope's cry...oh,"

"She's fine," Myra said, as she continued to rock Hope. "Go back to bed. You need your sleep."

"I tried. My brain wouldn't shut up long enough for me to fall asleep," Marsee said, taking Hope from her mother's arms and bringing her over to the large chenzie fur rug.

Marsee placed the cub on her belly, before laying down next to her to play with her, handing her several of the toys that were scattered about the rug. Hope pushed herself up into a sitting position, grabbed one of the crinkly toys, and stuffed it in her mouth.

"Do you need me to give you something to help you sleep?" Myra asked, as she took the opportunity to care for Little Flower.

"I'm okay for now, maybe later, if I still can't sleep," Marsee said, tickling the little cub, who smiled.

With Hope occupied by Marsee, Myra carefully picked up Little Flower and carried her over to the rocking chair Ellie had gifted her. Deliberately tucking her tail in around her side, with an amused smile and knowing glance towards Ellie, Myra carefully sat down and began slowly rocking back and forth, purring and watching the monitors.

Ellie rolled her eyes at the teasing.

"She's still in there Ellie. I know she is. She always knows when Hope is nursing. Her vitals improve while she's nursing and always take a dip afterwards when Hope stops, and she responds to the rocking motion too."

Ellie nodded. She didn't know if it was true or not, or if it was anything more than just Little Flower's body acting instinctively, but she wasn't going to take what little hope her friend had left away from her. She decided to change the subject now that Marsee was in the room.

"So Marsee, how's your latest translation going?" Ellie asked.

Marsee had decided that the Tech Guild wasn't for her, although she'd continued with several classes she'd been interested in, and that she could manage remotely, and then dove into her translation project with a renewed gusto, but had switched to focusing on the books and stories that she was most interested in, which were mainly in the science fiction and fantasy genres, and geared towards the Hue-man cubs. They were typically much shorter, but that meant Marsee could get through them quicker.

"Good. We finished another manuscript this week. That's why I'm so tired. I've been working pretty much non-stop to print and bind enough copies for the Hallowed Eve celebration. They're going to be the treat for the writer's booth," Marsee replied.

They didn't have much in the way of candy to hand out as was the Hue-man's tradition, but they'd decided to use their crafts instead, to showcase what everyone was learning, and everyone had been busy making small gifts to hand out at their booths. Hope tossed the crinkly toy away and reached for a purple ball that was just a little too far away. Hope shifted into a crawling position and made her way over to chase after it.

"What's this one about?" Ellie asked, curious.

"It's a legend about one of their warrior gods. I think. I'm not really sure if he qualifies as a god or not. Anyway, one of the Hue-mans was bitten by some sort of mutated eight-legged crawly and gained the ability to fly by shooting sticky threads out of his wrist. I'm told the sand spinners of Earth used those threads to catch their prey. He uses those powers to defeat the other gods that tried to harm the people he's chosen to protect."

"How very strange. They certainly are a creative species. Although the theme is consistent with the others. Is this one going to be illustrated as well?" Ellie asked.

Marsee nodded. "The cubs have been having all sorts of fun acting out the scenes. It's nowhere near as good as what Little Flower would have drawn, but the cubs seem to be happy with my sketches."

Hope threw the ball and it rolled away. Marsee stopped it and rolled it back. Hope grabbed it with her tiny paws and hit it against the floor several times in a fairly rhythmic pattern.

Ellie wondered if the cub would become a musician some day but then refocused on Marsee. "You're a very talented artist in your own right, and you have a much broader range of skills from what I've seen. It's fine to be critical of your work, to strive to do better with each piece, but you should never judge yourself against what someone else can do, especially when it comes to art, and you should be proud of what you've accomplished," Ellie stated.

"Yes, Senior Guild Master. Thank you," Marsee replied, showing her discomfort at being both chided and praised by Ellie at the same time.

"Pah, enough with the Senior Guild Master already. I've spent the last week stuck in Guild and Council Meetings, and I'm about ready to hand in my tools if I hear that title again."

Marsee's tail curled, as it was a running joke among them now.

"In fact," Ellie scowled at Marsee. "If I hear Senior Guild Master out of you again, outside of a Council Meeting, I'm demoting you to apprentice, and will make you clean my tools by hand for a month."

"Yes, Senior Guild Master," Marsee said with a wicked grin and further curling of her tail.

Ellie mock growled, grabbed a pillow from the couch she was sitting on and threw it at Marsee, careful not to aim anywhere near the tiny cub. "The Impudence! Such disrespect! Disobeying a direct order from your Senior Guild Master! You think I'm not serious, well I am. 'Poof!' There, you're an apprentice now, with all the rights and responsibilities that come with *that* position."

The look of absolute incredulity and horror on Marsee's face, clearly unable to determine if Ellie was serious or not, caused Myra to burst out laughing, which had been Ellie's plan all along. It had been far too long since her friend had had anything to laugh about.

"Are you serious?" Marsee asked.

Between the scowl on Ellie's face and her mother's laughter, it was clear she wasn't sure who to believe. Ellie had noticed that Marsee struggled to read people's intentions, especially when they said one thing but their body said something else, and sarcasm and jokes flew over her head way too often because of it. Marsee had told her once that it was one of the reasons she didn't like being around people all the time. It was just too exhausting to try and figure out what people meant or wanted her to believe, but Ellie had a suspicion that Marsee's struggles came from reading people far too well, and picking up on the things they didn't *want* her to know.

"Completely," Ellie said with all seriousness and the full scowl of disapproval she used when having to deal with unruly apprentices, and the occasional unruly guild master, although she was having a hard time keeping the curl out of her tail. It was times like this that she wished she'd worked harder on the mask of calm the healers and the Council used.

Marsee positively wilted. Her ears drooped and shoulders slumped as she looked away, and almost looked like she was going to cry.

Ellie rolled her eyes in the direction of Myra, whose tail curled in response, and then softened her tone slightly. "But, I might be persuaded to change my mind if you bring that cub over here so I can hold her."

Marsee's ears pricked back up and she dutifully brought the cub over and carefully handed her to Ellie.

"Who's the big girl?" Ellie crooned to Hope who was now trying to stuff her back paw her mouth. Marsee stood there clearly not sure what else to do, and Ellie looked up at her, "Oh fine, Poof! You're a journeyman again with all the rights and blah blah blah..."

Marsee looked at her mother, and then back at the Guild Master and they both burst out laughing at Marsee's look of confusion. The look of relief on Marsee's face when she was sure she was just being teased, made Ellie feel a little guilty for picking on the child, but it had been worth every second, just to hear her friend laugh again.

"I expect I will receive my usual copies?" Ellie asked, bringing the conversation back to their previous topic.

She had a copy of every one of the books Marsee had helped the Hue-mans recreate of their history and legends, and although Marsee didn't know it, she'd sent a copy of each to the Archives in Council City for posterity. Additionally, she'd had the Techs scan them in and Marsee's translations were now the most popular downloads across all five planets. They'd even had to add additional servers just to support the traffic load when the last new release was announced.

Myra and Ellie had decided not to tell her when the first manuscript was released, and had instantly become the top download, for fear that it would overwhelm her, as the initial response to her prints being purchased had done. The work she was doing to preserve the Hue-man's history was too important for her to panic about everyone in the universe seeing her work and her drawings, and she'd made sure that Marsee wouldn't see the books on the top downloads list if she logged into the site herself. Later, when Marsee was more confident in her abilities, she would tell her. Only Little Flower's book remained visible to Marsee, but Marsee didn't see that as her work, and was pleased for her sister's sake. Ellie was trying hard to build up Marsee's self esteem and confidence again without overwhelming her, although from how exhausted and depressed Marsee looked, Ellie wondered if she was taking things too slowly.

"Of course," Marsee said, as she grabbed Hope's favorite rattle out of the play pen, where they kept her during Little Flower's physical therapy sessions, and handed it to Ellie. "I've been focusing on the ones we're handing out first, to make sure we have enough, but if you want copies now I can grab them for you. They wouldn't match the other ones I've done for you though."

"I can wait," Ellie said, and shook the rattle.

Hope grabbed the rattle and promptly tried sticking it in her mouth, but within moments she started to cry, her tiny face going angry and red.

"What's the matter little one? Not as tasty as your mama's milk?" Ellie asked, taking the rattle from the cub and shaking it. Hope hiccuped a few times and then went back to crying.

"She started teething last week," Myra said. "Marsee, get some of that salve for her gums." Marsee did as requested and gently applied it to Hope's sore gums, and the two tiny teeth that were starting to poke through. A few moments later, Hope stopped crying as the salve numbed the pain.

"There, Auntie Marsee made it all better. What do you think, Hope? should I promote your auntie to journeyman level two?" Ellie asked the tiny cub.

Hope burbled and shook the rattle.

"I agree! Poof! Marsee Bet Chenzira, you're now a journeyman level two, with all the rights and blah blah blah…" Ellie said with a dismissive wave of her paw, and went back to tickling the little cub, making her giggle.

Marsee just stood there slack jawed, and turned to look at her mother, who nodded, confirming that Ellie hadn't been joking. As the Senior Guild Master, Ellie had the right to promote or demote anyone within the Guild, at any time, for any reason, although she rarely did, at least not in the lower ranks. She'd learned early on that it rarely went well for the person promoted, even if they were deserving, either because that person had a complete nervous breakdown at being recognized by her, or because it caused jealousy in others who were not promoted, but she had big plans for Marsee, and it was far past time for her to be promoted and earn a mentor. The biggest reason Ellie hadn't allowed it before was because of Marsee's growing signs of psychosis, but now that Marsee was officially cleared and off the watch list, she could.

Marsee started asking the inevitable next question about who her mentor was going to be, not that Ellie had any intention of spoiling the surprise before the promotion ceremony, but before she could, Hope scrunched up her tiny little face and promptly peed on Ellie's leg.

"You, young cub, are never going to make it to journeyman if you keep up that kind of behavior," she gently scolded Hope, and then handed her back to Marsee, who had an absolutely horrified look on her face. "Did you put her up to this?" she teased Marsee. "I can and will take that promotion back, if you did."

Marsee just spluttered, mouth open, unable to respond, as she took the full brunt of the Senior Guild Master's mock anger. It was all Ellie could do to keep up the illusion that she was angry as she walked into the other room to use the sonic shower, because on the other side of the room, her best friend was laughing so hard that she could barely breathe.

# CHAPTER 31

# Infestation

He floated in his ship looking out at the desolate desert landscape around him radiating his disgust. He hated being on land and driving around in those stupid carts, and while he could have stayed in the apartment he'd been given, he'd spent all of about five minutes in there before shuddering at how unnatural the space felt and returning to his personal ship. *After all the money we sent them, they couldn't even make it comfortable? Well, no worries. In a few days, no one is going to remember a thing about the rodent's stupid holiday, or want to come here ever again. I can certainly see why no one wanted to live here before, and why the pussy cats were good with giving it away. This has to be the most desolate landscape in the Consortium and it's not even the worst part of the year.*

He turned when there was a knock on the door of his ship, and swam over to see who it was. Grinning, he opened the door and two of the tiny rodents swam in after he handed them the mask they needed to breathe underwater. He motioned them over to a crate and flipped it open, revealing a stasis unit full of venomous sand spinners. It had taken him weeks to get the order without it tracking back to him. Thankfully he knew the right people to zap when he needed to.

"You should have a few minutes to get away before they wake from stasis," he told them.

"Ugly little monsters," one of the rodents signed.

"Indeed," he replied, although frankly he thought the rodents were far uglier.

"Are you sure this will work?" the other one asked, not entirely convinced.

"Positive. They're venomous enough to cause panic, but easily treatable. Once someone is stung, you swoop in and save them, and your council will be sure to reward you with adulthood. Even if they don't, there will be enough outrage that you aren't rewarded, and eventually someone will come forward and sponsor you."

"You could sponsor us now," the rodent replied.

"I could, but that wouldn't help the others. Plus this way, the Council will see you as honorable, and you'll be able to get more of your agenda items passed in the future."

"True," the first said. "Come on, Danny. We need to get this hidden before the guards show up."

He watched as they closed the lid and carried it out, keeping his emotions firmly locked down, and he wondered just how many of those disgusting rodents would be stung and killed before they dealt with the nest he'd just unleashed, or realized their ability to call for help had been tampered with as well.

*So sorry, Chenzira. Who knew your home was so infested? Shame they showed up the same day every important person on all five worlds was here.*

# CHAPTER 32

# Tranquility or Hope

There was no time here, just the ever rocking sea and the short pauses where the sea settled and stilled and that distant weight returned, but she noticed those moments less and less as she slowly drifted further away from her body.

The tether between her and her body grew steadily thinner as it stretched the further away she drifted. It was now too thin to resist the pull of the sea, and was starting to fray around the edges.

She stayed in that peaceful, tranquil state for eons until one day, the sky above her lightened, not much, but after so long in darkness it was almost blinding.

**It is time to choose. Tranquility or Hope?** a voice boomed through the ether.

*Hope?* What need did she have of hope when she had all of this tranquility?

**Tranquility or Hope?**

*Tranquility of course. This was all that existed. What else could there be?*

And so she continued to drift, the cord connecting her to her body stretched and frayed until it was nothing but the barest hint of a thread.

James slowly paced in his granddaughter's room, trying to soothe his sobbing great granddaughter. Hope had been irritated all day as her teeth continued to poke through, and now, even with Myra's salve, she was refusing to be comforted. "There, there, little one. It'll be okay," he crooned. "You're just becoming a big girl now, with big girl teeth. No reason to cry. You don't want your Halloween pictures to look all poofy-eyed for your mother, now do you?"

Hope hiccuped and rubbed at her eyes.

"That's what I thought. Now dry those little tears so we can show your grandparents and auntie how cute you look in your Halloween costume."

He'd been learning how to craft over the last several months, as it gave him something to do when he watched his grandchildren, and he'd found that the repetitive motion of knitting actually helped him study.

He and Marsee now split the night shift as it worked best with his sleep schedule. With the days now twice as long on Saber as they'd been on earth, and the days brutally hot, he, like most of the others of his species, had become far more nocturnal, sleeping through much of the midday heat and waking during the late evening and early mornings when it was far cooler.

In preparation for Halloween, he'd made Hope a costume that he was itching to show the others. He just hoped they'd find it as funny and cute as he did. He was a little worried that they might take offense, but he was pretty sure he'd figured out their sense of humor in the months he'd lived with them.

Hope currently wore a striped knitted onesie that matched Marsee's colors, if not her pattern, complete with a long fuzzy tail made of chenzie fur and a knitted hat with equally fuzzy ears. He'd then taken a small amount of bandage putty and used that to affix three tiny whiskers to each side of her face. It was the most adorable thing he'd ever seen, but Hope was not at all impressed.

As he tried to calm Hope, he checked the time. Myra still had another hour left to her shift at the Trauma Center. The healers had all adjusted their shifts so that everyone could attend the Halloween

Festival for at least a few hours that evening, and Myra had taken a rare shift so that Brice could come watch Little Flower and Hope, while they all attended Marsee's promotion ceremony later that evening.

Marsee was helping to set up for the festival, and Jer had been sequestered with the other Seniors all day as they prepped for the Full Council meeting that would take place after the celebration.

Hope hiccuped and started screaming again, louder than before. GrandFather sighed and kept pacing. *So much for that idea,* he thought.

Almost as if in response, an alarm started blaring on Little Flower's monitors. He spun to read them and swore. Her heart rate and rate of breathing had dropped below safe levels. Setting Hope down on the bed next to her mother, he grabbed his tablet and called Myra. There was no answer, so he left a quick text for her to get to the tower as fast as she could, and then threw the tablet down on the table beside the bed. He quickly hooked up the oxygen to try and help Little Flower breathe better, and then tried calling again but there was still no response. *Where is she?* he wondered, and tried calling the Trauma Center, but no one answered there either. Frowning with confusion because there should always be someone to pick up, as if no one did it should have automatically re-routed to Command in Council City. He took one more look at the monitors and started running for the clinic as fast as his old legs could take him.

He made it as far as the cafeteria when Myra came barreling around the corner on all fours. Seeing him at a run, she somehow picked up her pace. He stopped and doubled over, gasping for breath, and just pointed back towards the tower. Myra flew past him and disappeared around the corner without stopping to find out what was wrong.

*I'm getting too old for this,* he thought as he took several more deep breaths, and then kept jogging for the Council offices. *If this is the end for Jessica, Marsee and Jer should be there with her too.*

He checked Jer's office first but it was empty and kept running for the Senior's Conference room, figuring Jer was probably still in his meeting. He skidded to a stop, and banged on the door as hard as he could. Jer opened it a moment later.

"What's wrong?" Jer asked, taking in his gasping body.

"Little Flower, she's failing," he signed and doubled over, trying to catch his breath.

Jer swallowed hard and turned back to the room and said something to the others.

"Go," Marcus signed. "This can wait."

Jer turned back to him, and to his surprise scooped him up and took off at a run, cutting through the outer courtyard. It was honestly one of the strangest experiences he'd had since coming to this new world. He'd almost forgotten how much bigger the cats were. He felt more than heard Jer call out to Marsee, but saw her jerk her head over towards them, drop what she had in her paws, her face wracked with the same fear he felt, and start running towards the tower with everything she had.

Just before the tether to her body snapped, she felt something vibrate its way from her body to her. *What was that?* she wondered, pausing her drift to look back. Something was tickling her side, and she felt the distant weight start to return. *Oh, it's just you.* Mystery solved, she turned to settle back down into her tranquil sea, but before she could the weight bit her and pulled on the tether. *Ow! That hurts!* It had been eons since she'd felt pain, and it twanged along the cord, causing choppy waves to form in the once tranquil sea.

### Tranquility or Hope?

*Why am I being asked again? I've already made up my mind,* she wondered. The weight on the other end of the tether pulled harder, yanking her closer to her body. "No!" she yelled. "I chose tranquility! Let me go!" The weight pulled again and she tried to grasp the sea, but there was nothing for her to hold onto, and the sea slipped through her hands. Refusing to give up the tranquility she started swimming. Still, she was pulled closer to her body, the silky sea no longer tranquil as she thrashed.

### Tranquility or Hope?

Her brain, sluggish from eons without thought, tried to remember what was so important about hope. Suddenly the weight was lifted and the pulling stopped with one last jarring and painful twang, but instead of being relieved, she found she missed it, and it left her confused and unsettled, and she didn't understand why.

Myra slid into the room, nearly losing her footing on the stone ramp. She'd known the moment GrandFather's call had come in that it was bad. His expression in the hall had confirmed it. Hope was nursing, but Little Flower's chest was still. She looked up at the monitors, frantic, as Little Flower's heart monitor beat once, then twice, and then stopped.

"Not today!" she screamed. "You're not taking her from me! I won't let you!" she yelled, challenging the Ancient Gods.

She ran to the bed, grabbed Hope, and ripped her from her mother's teat. Hope started screaming, but she didn't have time to worry about an upset cub.

She quickly placed Hope in her play-pen, so she wouldn't get in the way, and then flipped open the cabinet with the shock paddles in them, waited the three eternally long seconds needed to power them on, and applied them to Little Flower's chest.

Little Flower's body arched from the electricity, while Myra waited.

...

*Please don't take her! Not when we're so close!*

...

*Please!*

...

***Tranquility or Hope?***

"Why do you keep asking?" she yelled. "What's so important about hope?"

As if in response, an image played in the ether around her, of a tiny perfect baby nuzzling between the breasts of a woman.

***Tranquility or Hope?***

"What does this have to do with hope?" she asked, trying to understand what the ether was showing her.

Her memories suddenly flooded back into her, as if a dam that had been holding them back had suddenly broken, but more than that, what she'd be missing if stayed. She was completely overwhelmed trying to make sense of the images, both past and future.

"Hope?" she asked the voice, and the first image appeared again, and suddenly she knew.

"I choose Hope!" she screamed to the ether.

Pain, as she'd never experienced it before, traveled from her body through the tether. She stopped treading water and sank, screaming, as she was slammed forcefully back into her body.

Myra counted the eternally long seconds until she could try the shock paddle again, and was poised and ready to try again when Little Flower suddenly let out an audible gasp, and the monitor's started beeping again. *Blessed moons!* She prayed as she watched her daughter's vitals, willing them to stabilize.

Marsee careened into the room, followed by Jer with GrandFather moments later.

"Is she okay?" Jer asked.

Myra shrugged, not really sure. Little Flower's vitals were all over the place. "She wasn't breathing when I arrived and her heart stopped beating for a moment afterwards, but I was able to revive her. She's stabilizing, I think."

Jer set GrandFather down and they all walked over to stand around Little Flowers bed, watching her breathe in and out, wondering if this was just a reprieve. As they stood there in silence, save for Hope's angry hiccups, a haunting melody floated through the open doorway. It sounded like a cub singing, but it was in a language Myra didn't understand. Myra looked over at Jer to see if he heard it too. While she was now starting to hear Hope, she'd never heard their singing this clearly before. It was just too high pitched. He nodded, and they all turned to look outside.

Out in the courtyard, the sun shields had been pulled back to reveal a large crowd that was forming, with people of all species streaming in from everywhere as word spread about Little Flower's condition. They all stood in the beating afternoon sun and faced the tower. All except the Ice Giants who remained in the air conditioned hallways, the afternoon suns far too hot for them. Even the Seniors were there.

At the front of the group stood Henry Curtis. He must have been working on setting up the festival because there was a tool belt strapped to his waist. He'd taken his shirt off and his dark swirling skin glistened in the afternoon sun with his sweat. His beautiful deep voice was just within their upper range of hearing and sounded like a young cub's voice, but far more pure and sweet than any cub she'd ever heard before.

Myra looked over to GrandFather to see tears streaming down his face. "What is he singing?" Myra asked.

"It is a very old hymn from one of the religions on our world called Amazing Grace," he replied, and then began translating the words to them.

Marsee gasped. "Mama!"

"I know. It's beautiful!" she said, *and strangely prophetic. Had their Gods known what was coming and tried to warn them?* she thought to herself.

"No, Mama, look! Her eyes are open!" Marsee exclaimed.

Myra spun to look at Little Flower and stood there, rooted in shock. *Bright blessed full moons! Her eyes are open!*

GrandFather turned to see where they were all looking, and as soon as he saw Little Flower's eyes open, he raced over and grabbed her paw. Little Flower shifted her eyes to follow his motion. *She sees him!* Myra thought. *She's awake!* and then looked at the monitor to confirm. "She's really awake!" she exclaimed, and then rushed to her daughter's side as well.

The song started again, this time with everyone joining in, forming a harmony she felt more than heard, and Myra's heart began to swell with hope. Little Flower's eyes shifted to look at her and her mouth twitched the barest of smiles. She shifted her gaze to look at the others, her smile widening some as she saw Marsee and her father, but then she frowned and looked back to GrandFather and whispered something to him.

"What did she say?" Myra asked.

GrandFather tilted his head and leaned in closer to hear above the sounds of singing and she whispered again. "Hope," he signed. "She's asking for Hope!"

Myra quickly retrieved the angry cub from the play-pen and brought her over, squatting down beside the bed and holding the cub up for her daughter to see.

Little Flower started smiling again, but then she closed her eyes and started to shake.

Myra panicked and looked up at the monitors trying to figure out what was wrong. *Is she having a seizure?* Confused, she read them again, and then again. They said she was okay, better than okay, better than she'd been in months! Looking back at her daughter, confusion and terror still on her face, she slowly realized her daughter wasn't having a seizure, she was laughing!

*What's so funny?* she wondered, and then turned Hope around so she could get a good look at the cub, and realized what she was wearing for the first time.

Myra started chuckling, and then started laughing so hard she had to sit down. They all looked at her in bewilderment, and then they too took a good look at Hope, who glared up at them all with an angry scowl and whiskered face, not impressed at all with the unexpectedly rude treatment she'd experienced, and suddenly the whole room was laughing too.

*Has there ever been a more beautiful sound?* Myra thought as she laughed so hard her tail hurt. The Hue-mans beautiful song filled the room. Her daughter was awake and laughing, and her very soul sang with her joy!

As the song finished, GrandFather walked over to the doorway. Silence greeted his arrival and he called out and signed, "She's awake!" The roar that followed was deafening!

Once Myra stopped laughing long enough to stand up again, she placed Hope back in the bed with her mother and let her resume nursing. Little Flower shifted her head slightly so she could watch Hope, but didn't move her arms or try to hold the cub. This concerned Myra a great deal, but she didn't want the others to know.

"Why don't you all head out and start the Hallowed Eve celebration, now that everyone's already out there," Myra suggested. "I need to give Little Flower an assessment and that should be done in private."

"Myra," GrandFather signed, stopping them. "When I couldn't get a hold of you, I tried calling the Trauma Center, but no one picked up. Has something happened? I thought it should have re-routed to Command."

Myra frowned. "I got your call but couldn't answer. I was in the middle of surgery, but I didn't hear a call come into the Trauma Center." She unclipped her tablet and tried calling but like before, nothing went through, so she called Brice directly. Brice picked up. "Brice, are you able to reach Command?"

Brice leaned over to hit the comms on her desk. "Command, this New Hope Trauma Center, report."

There was no answer.

"I'll take care of it," Jer said, and unclipped his tablet. "Brice, I'm going to have people call you directly for emergencies until we figure out what's going on."

"Yes, sir," she said, and disconnected.

Moments later everyone's tablets blared with the emergency alert.

"Well, that went out at least," Jer said, and left to deal with that issue.

The others soon followed, after spending a few moments with Little Flower. When Myra was finally alone with her daughter, she began her examination.

"Can you understand me?" Myra signed to her daughter.

Little Flower gave her the barest of nods and she breathed a sigh of relief.

"Are you in any pain?" she asked.

Little Flower shook her head.

"Good. I'm going to hold your hand now, and I need you to try to squeeze it for me. Okay?"

Little Flower nodded.

Myra placed two of her much larger fingers against Little Flower's palm and waited. Little Flower scrunched her face with concentration and then her hand twitched ever so slightly. "Very good!" She smiled at her daughter in encouragement. "Now the other paw."

Again a look of intense concentration and the tiniest of movements.

"Excellent!" she signed, and then moved down by her daughter's feet.

"This time, when you feel my touch, I want you to try wiggling your toes," she told her daughter and then ran her finger lightly along the bottom of her foot.

There was no reaction.

Myra struggled to keep her healer's mask firmly in place, and not show her daughter how much that scared her. *Please don't let her be paralyzed,* she prayed to the Ancient Gods. Taking a single claw, she poked it into the middle of her daughter's foot, causing a tiny drop of blood to form.

The foot twitched and Little Flower scowled.

"Felt that did you?" Myra asked.

Little Flower nodded with a hint of a glare.

"Good. Now the other foot."

This time when she lightly brushed the bottom of the foot, the toes curled almost immediately.

"Oh very good, Little Flower!" she signed.

It wasn't much, but the signals were all there and that gave her something to work with. It would probably take months of physical therapy, and far more hard work, but there was a chance her daughter might walk again.

"I'm going to hold up a claw now, and I want you to try to follow it with your eyes for me."

Little Flower nodded, so Myra began the test, moving her claw slowly from side to side, up and down, and then bringing it in to almost touch her daughter's nose, and then back out again. Her eyes were choppy and slow to react, but she followed it.

"Can you blink your eyes twice for me now?" she asked, and Little Flower blinked twice. "Excellent! Now, I'm going to hold up a number of different fingers. I want you to blink to tell me how many you see." She did, and after a slight hesitation Little Flower blinked the appropriate number of times. She was very weak, which wasn't surprising considering how little muscle she had left on her emaciated body, but she was following instructions well, if slowly. It was a very very promising start.

Little Flower looked to Hope, who was still nursing and then back at her, frowning slightly.

"You've been asleep for just over four months now, but your daughter is happy and healthy. We've taken good care of her for you."

Little Flower gasped at the news she'd been out so long, and then her hand twitched and lifted slightly off the bed before falling back down.

"Are you trying to talk?" she asked her daughter.

Little Flower shook her head and looked at Hope and then back at her and then her hand lifted again slightly before dropping back to the bed, a deep scowl of concentration on her face.

"Do you want me to lift your arms so you can hold your daughter?" Myra asked.

This time Little Flower nodded.

"I'm not going to do that." Myra said.

Little Flower glared at her.

"Get mad at me all you want. You need to do this on your own. You have to try hard. You've lost most of your muscle and it's going to take a lot of hard work to rebuild it. You've got a very long fight ahead of you if you're going to fully recover. How much or how little you do depends on how hard you work at it," Myra said, wanting to know how much effort Little Flower would or could put into it. If she truly couldn't do it, she would help, but not before making her daughter at least try first.

Her daughter glared at her again, but she just glared right back, waiting. Finally Little Flower let out an exasperated huff and lifted her hand again, slightly farther than before.

"That's it!" she encouraged. "Keep trying!"

Little Flower tried again, making it the tiniest bit further but let out a growl of frustration as her arm fell back to the bed.

"You can do this, Little Flower, I know you can."

Changing tactics this time, her daughter slowly slid her hand along the bed to her side and used her fingers to climb her leg until it was resting on top of it. Myra grinned. After resting for a moment, she slowly moved her arm up her body until she came in contact with Hope's foot. A huge smile lit up her daughter's face and she continued to crawl her hand up Hope's leg, over her tiny bottom, along her back, and then finally to Hope's head, where she began caressing it. Hope lifted her head up at her touch and stopped nursing, looking into her mother's eyes for the first time. Hope hiccuped, and then went back to nursing.

"There, see! I knew you could do it!"

Little Flower smiled at her, and went back to looking at her daughter. A look of wonder and love in her eyes.

Myra remembered that feeling well with her two litters, and she praised and thanked the Ancient Gods for giving her daughter this moment.

Little Flower's eyelids began to flutter, and she let out a huge yawn.

"You've done very well. Sleep now. I'll take care of your daughter," she signed. Little Flower nodded and closed her eyes.

Myra spun to watch the monitors, praying her daughter wouldn't slip back into her coma again. She did not. Myra let out an enormous sigh of relief as they showed she was entering normal sleep for the first time in months, and not the deep inactivity of coma.

While she waited for the others to return, Myra pulled up the more detailed scans on her tablet and called her mentor. They'd both been in surgery when GrandFather's call had come in, and the moment Ammond had finished a delicate section of the operation, and it was safe for her to move, she'd bolted.

"How is she?" he asked, picking up immediately.

"She's awake or she was anyway. She's sleeping now, actually sleeping, and having one heck of a dream from the looks of it too!" Myra cried with relief.

"Thank the blessed full moons!" Ammond said, closing his eyes and offering a prayer up to the Ancient Gods himself. "How responsive was she?" he asked.

"She was very weak, but she was following my instructions well, if slowly. She has feeling and movement in all four paws, but her right side is significantly weaker. She spoke to GrandFather briefly asking for Hope, but she hasn't signed anything. She might not be able to for a while. Her hands and arms are very weak."

"That's far better than we had any rights to hope for, after all this time," he replied, after she'd given him the full results of her examination. He brought up her scans to review. "There's definitely been improvement in the areas we injected the nano's. Looks like we've hit on a winner there."

"Do we bring her back in for another treatment?" Myra asked.

"Yes, but not right away. I'd rather not risk sedating her now that we've finally managed to wake her up. Let's hold off for a few weeks and see how she does first, and see which areas we need to focus on next. I'd feel a lot better if we could put some weight back on her, and even a little muscle first. She weighs less than she ever did at the Agency."

"You won't get an argument from me there," Myra said.

"That's a first. Speaking of which, when are you planning on getting that tattoo?" he asked.

"Tattoo?" she asked innocently.

"The one that says 'Ammond was right'? You promised to get one on your forehead if I managed to wake her up," he said with a wicked grin.

"You must be remembering wrong," Myra said with a laugh. "I don't remember ever saying you were right, besides, I'm the one that figured out what was wrong with our treatments."

"Impudent cub. I can still demote you, you know," he growled, but then chuckled as she rolled her eyes at him. They discussed physical therapy treatments, and then he left to check on his patient. "Happy Hallowed Eve, Myra"

"You too, Ammond!" she replied, and then sighed with happiness. She was pretty sure this was now her favorite holiday ever!

# CHAPTER 33

# Jeran: Nest of Harbingers

Jer walked down out of the tower to find Kendra already waiting for him. He motioned her into his room and shut the door, as there were far too many people mingling around outside.

"I saw your alert. What's going on?" she asked quietly.

"I'm not sure. GrandFather tried calling the Trauma Center for help, but no one picked up."

"That's not possible," Kendra replied. "It should have gone through to Command."

"That may be, but the impossible has happened twice. Myra just tried again, and Brice couldn't reach Command either. Are you able to contact the Trauma Center or Command?"

Kendra frowned but hit the comms unit on her harness and called the Trauma Center. There was no answer. She tried Command next, again, no answer. She frowned again and tried calling her guards. When there was still no answer, she unclipped her tablet and placed a call. Quinn answered immediately from the guard station in Council City.

"Code Three. The comms are down in New Hope. I can't reach anyone, including Command," Kendra told him.

Quinn frowned and hit his comms. "Command, report."

"This is Command," came the immediate reply.

"Code Three. Comms are down in New Hope. Run a full systems check and re-route trauma calls to Sand Dune," Quinn ordered.

"Yes, sir," came the distant reply.

Kendra frowned as she considered. "This could just be a technical issue since regular communication appears to be working, but the timing is suspect. Place Sand Dune on alert and send a contingent to New Hope."

"Yes, ma'am," Quinn replied.

Kendra hung up and called Avery. "Avery, code three. Check the Command relay first," she ordered. "Regular communication appears to be working. Quinn has been informed."

"Yes, ma'am," he replied and disconnected.

They waited. A few minutes later, Avery called back. "I'm at the relay. You need to see this," he said, scratching the back of his neck. "I'm not sure I would believe me."

Kendra frowned. "On our way," she replied, disconnected, and took off at a fast walk. Jer followed.

A few minutes later they arrived outside the relay tower, which was on the outskirts of New Hope, where Avery and several other guards were waiting for them. Jer wasn't a tech, but even he could see the problem. "Somehow, I have a feeling this is going to take a while to fix," he said dryly.

Kendra and Avery both snorted.

A large flock of the four-winged harbingers were dozing in and around the structure of the tower, and had torn it to shreds. It looked like they had been there for some time. How they'd gotten through the shields he had no idea. He sighed and unclipped his tablet to call for a repair crew, while Kendra and her guards chased the flock off.

Gregory appeared a few minutes later and took in the damage. "This is going to take days to repair," he said. "I'll re-route communications through the main grid until then. It'll slow down regular communications some, but I don't think anyone will notice. We're not big enough yet for that to be a problem."

Jer nodded. "I want to know how they got inside the shields, and your plans to ensure it doesn't happen again."

The builder nodded and went to work. Kendra ordered a few of the guards to stay and help, in case the Harbingers returned and began examining the tower herself.

About ten or fifteen minutes later, Kendra called him over. "I think I found it. It looks like someone got too close to the shield boundary with a cart and hit the power relay."

"Do you think it was an accident, or on purpose?" he asked.

"No idea," she replied. "There are far too many tracks to tell. Probably just an accident. Those Water Sprite carts are not easy to maneuver, especially on sand, which they would not be used to. We've had to unstick at least a dozen people so far." She paused and looked up as a ship approached. "The additional guards I ordered are here. I'll have them run a full sweep of the compound and surrounding area to be sure."

Jer nodded with a frown as he considered. "You're probably right. Most of the Water Sprites here are members of the Council or high up in the Guild anyway. I doubt they're a risk. Keep me informed." She nodded, and he left to deal with his other responsibilities.

# Marsee: Mentor

Marsee walked out onto the landing outside of Little Flower's room, carrying Hope, who was crying again, trying to settle her, only Marsee felt like crying too. Her conflicting emotions were all over the place, ecstatic relief that her sister was awake, nervous excitement about her upcoming mentorship ceremony, and grief and disappointment knowing that she'd soon lose guardianship of Hope. The moment she'd seen Hope in the costume GrandFather had made, it solidified for her instinct that Hope was *their* cub, not Little Flowers, and she was struggling hard to control that feeling. While the past few weeks had been exhausting, they'd also been some of the best of her life, and she'd loved every second she spent caring for Hope.

Her parent's attitudes towards her had changed. They'd spent the past few weeks working with her to make sure she understood all of the legal ramifications and responsibilities that came with being a parent, things that were normally taught during their growth spurt year, and her mother had shifted to work around her schedule, so that she could better manage her responsibilities with the Guild, rather than the other way around. The one positive was that her instinct had settled back down and didn't growl every time her father came around, but she worried it would flare back up once her father removed guardianship.

When Hope failed to settle, she returned to the room and brought her over to see if she'd try nursing. Little Flower didn't wake, but her mother assured her that she was just sleeping, and went back to running through a dozen different things with Brice. Brice's face was the normal calm of a healer, but Marsee could tell she was amused. Her mother was treating her like a brand new apprentice, and considering that Brice had far more experience treating Hue-mans than her mother at this point, even Marsee found it amusing.

"Mama, please, come on! I don't want to be late!" Marsee said after another ten minutes of pacing anxiously by the door.

"She'll be fine Myra, I promise. The comms have been restored, and I'll call you if there's even the slightest flicker of change in her vitals. Go spend some time with Marsee on her special day. Take your time exploring the festival too. You both need a holiday. It's been a very long four months," Brice said, shooing her out the door. With one last worried look towards Little Flower, her mother nodded, and followed Marsee to the festival.

Marsee was bouncing with nervous excitement, and it was all she could do to keep to her mother's pace as they made their way through the crowd. The outer courtyard had been transformed over the past few days. The hydroponics units had all been disconnected and moved to the brand new greenhouse, so that there was space for activities and booths. While she wanted to run to the grand stage, she was also fascinated by what the Hue-mans had accomplished, and intended to come back and explore each and every booth with her family after the ceremony.

Her translations would be on display in the writers booth, but it was the authors that would be celebrated tonight. Ellie had brought copies of all of the other translations she'd worked on, but Marsee had worked hard to personally print and bind enough copies of 'The Adventures of Crawly Man' in five of the six languages for everyone that was expected to attend, as it hadn't been released to the public yet, and it was their agreed upon 'treat' for the booth.

She didn't have any of the special ink and material used for the Water World books ,but Guild Master Agate from Council Platform, had arrived earlier in the day and dropped off the copies her guild had helped bind. She hadn't had a chance to check them out, or thank the Guild Master yet though, as her ship had arrived only moments before GrandFather had come to find them, and then afterwards she'd been asked to help finish setting up some of the other booths.

There were booths handing out samples of strange foods that smelled absolutely glorious, and rumor had it that Jordan was debuting something new tonight. *Maybe I should translate Jordan's cookbook next, Marsee thought as they approached Jordan's booth. Maybe then I could get samples of everything, hmmm, an illustrated translation perhaps?* The crowd was so thick around Jordan's booth that they ended up having to backtrack and go around.

They walked past several rows of booths with all sorts of games of skill set up, but stopped for a moment to watch one that was particularly popular. One of the Hue-mans was dressed in a vibrant costume, with frills and bells, and had even covered their face in paint, and was sitting on a ledge above a large bucket of water. For a credit each player would have two chances to throw a ball at a target, and if they hit it, the person would fall into a large bucket of water, and the player would win a small prize. She wished her sister could see this one, as the Hue-man above the water would call out and sign insults trying to distract the player. It reminded her of when they used to play games in the family room, before it had been demolished to make room for the cafeteria.

Her species was horrible at throwing things, but apparently this was very popular with the guards that were in attendance. She took out her tablet to record a bit to show her sister later, when none other than the Senior Honor Guard walked up for her turn, after teasing one of the other guards who had missed both of their throws, and was now being challenged back. Side bets were running rampant.

"Oh look, yet another member of the fur-ball guard, coming to show just how horrible their aim is," taunted the Hue-man.

"Not just any fur-ball," someone called out, "That's the Senior Honor Guard."

"Is that so? Well, I can't say I'm all that impressed with your guards after their abysmal performance today. It's been so bad, I'm starting to overheat."

Kendra glared at the Hue-man. "Trust me, that will be rectified, on *both* accounts," she both growled and signed, to the groans of the guards in attendance, and the laughter of everyone else. She tossed the ball in the air a few times to get a feel for the weight, and threw. It went wide of the target, to the hoots and jeers of everyone in the crowd.

"Looks like we have another storm trooper, folks. They couldn't hit the broad side of a barn if they were standing two feet in front of it either. Do you need to move forward and use the cub's line?" the Hue-man jeered.

In response, Kendra took two large steps back and glared at the target, her entire body going still and calm, then faster than Marsee could follow, the ball flew out and hit the target with a loud clang. The platform collapsed, and the Hue-man fell with a yelp and a large splash. Cheers rang out, and laughing, the Hue-man stood, wiped water off his face, and handed Kendra her prize, a small pin in the shape of the hat the Hue-man was wearing. Kendra took the pin and attached it to her harness with pride, before glaring at the throng of guards around her. "One hundred laps to any guard who does *not* hit the target before the end of the festival," she said, and walked away to the laughter of the crowd, and the further groans of her guards.

All of the Hue-mans were wearing strange costumes as well, most of which she had no idea what they represented. Some were vaguely animalistic, like the costume GrandFather had made for Hope, while others were just baffling. One person had just wrapped themselves in strips of fabric. She knew this was part of the tradition, but she still didn't fully understand the purpose. She hoped GrandFather would be able to explain it all to her later.

They continued on and slowly weaved their way through the packed crowd. Just about the entire Full Council was in attendance, along with any guild master or healer that had helped in setting up, provisioning, and running New Hope or the Agency, and other special guests. The event was by invite only, due to the limited space they had for visitors, and even then most were staying in Sand Dune, or on their ships rather than here. The fields surrounding the compound were packed full of shuttles and transport ships.

Everyone was curious about the event, the first formal Earth celebration the Hue-mans had observed, so several reporters and historians were also in attendance, both recording the event and interviewing people, so that it could be shared with all five worlds in a live broadcast.

They stopped periodically to greet various officials and dignitaries, and thank people for their well-wishes on behalf of her sister, and it was all Marsee could do to remain polite when she really just wanted to bolt to the stage. She was terrified she'd be late to her own promotion. She didn't even know who half of the people were, but if they were here, they were high ranking and important. Several of her instructors were here as well, and she wondered which one was going to be her mentor, or if Ellie was going to assign several since she had her journeyman's rank in more than one discipline. Ellie had refused to say or even tell her which discipline she was being promoted in either, and had then threatened to demote her if she asked again.

Eventually they made it to the grand stage, a large raised platform that had been built just for the occasion. After the promotions, various Hue-man performers would showcase their skills, and there would be music, dancing, and even a play by the cubs. Then when it was dark out, there was going to be a haunted forest in the garden, which she was really looking forward to as well. Apparently it was a joint effort between the Hue-man and Flyer Councils, and the garden had been closed off for days while they prepared.

Her Papa and GrandFather were already up by the front of the stage, and must have been waiting for them, as when they saw that they'd finally arrived, they waved and took the stage. Marsee blew out a sigh of relief. They'd made it in time!

"Good evening, everyone! May I please have your attention at the grand stage?" her father called out. His voice echoed on speakers planted around the courtyard making Marsee's ears twitch. GrandFather did the same in his language. After the crowds stopped what they were doing and filled in around the stage, he continued in both Saber and sign.

"Welcome everyone to our very first Hallowed Eve Celebration! I hope you all have a wonderful time this evening! I don't want to take up too much of your time tonight, so I'm going to try to keep this short. First, as everyone has been asking, Little Flower did indeed wake up this afternoon."

The crowd cheered their happiness at this news.

"My partner indicates that she still has a long recovery ahead of her, but she was alert and spoke briefly. Your show of support over these past few months, and again this afternoon is greatly appreciated by our family. Henry, I'd especially like to thank you for that beautiful song. Secondly, I would like to welcome two new additions to our community. Mary Shephard gave birth to twin girls early this morning. Mother and cubs are doing just fine!"

Her father paused for the next round of cheers.

"Next, I have the announcements many of you have been waiting for. I've been informed by each of the guilds that promotions are in order for all of your hard work and study. Congratulations and well done! I'm going to read out the promotions, but your certificates can be picked up in the guild hall at your convenience. We didn't want you to have to worry about them while you celebrated tonight. From the Agricultural Guild we have an entirely new sub-specialty and welcome our first journeyman chef, Jordan Ross." Loud cheers and whistles followed this announcement. Jordan's food was very popular amongst all of the resident species, as her booth and the cheers proved.

"Additionally we have several new agricultural apprentice level four members..." Jer continued with the announcements, which went on for some time. Marsee couldn't keep herself from bouncing with nerves as she waited, and waited. It appeared that most of the Hue-mans were being promoted in one guild or another.

GrandFather was promoted to journeyman healer level one *and* master animal healer about halfway through the list, which Marsee cheered hard for. There was a fairly significant applause from the Huemans and healers present as well, which seemed to surprise him. It wasn't quite as loud as Jordan's reaction had been, but it was close.

"And finally, it is my personal honor to announce that my daughter, Marsee Bet Chenzira has been promoted to journeyman level two."

Marsee looked at her mother in confusion. "Mama, he didn't say which guild," but before her mother could answer, her father continued.

"It is the tradition of the Guild to gain a mentor at this rank. A mentor is not just another teacher or sponsor, but someone who has promised to dedicate significant time and effort to their protege, to help them obtain mastery in their chosen skill, and provide guidance and support through all of life's challenges. It's as important to us as gaining adoptive parents or guardians, and comes with many of the same legal responsibilities. Normally the mentorship ceremony is performed by the person's guild master, but I've been given this honor today, since our guild hall does not have an official guild master yet. Marsee, would you please come up on the stage?"

Marsee took a deep breath and weaved her way through the crowd and up onto the stage to stand beside her father.

"I have been informed that the person you see before you, Marsee Bet Chenzira has completed all of the work required to obtain the rank of journeyman level two, and that this work has been completed with excellence. Who here has claimed the right to become Marsee's mentor, to vouch for her skills as a journeyman, and to guide her on her journey to masters and beyond?"

There was a dramatic pause, while everyone waited.

"I do!" a voice rang out from the back of the crowd.

As one, the crowd turned to see who had answered. "I, Elliana Reighly Khihar, Senior Guild Master, do claim that right and vouch for her skills."

The crowd gasped and murmured. Well at least the members of the non Hue-man species did. The Hue-mans would not know the significance of Ellie's claim. Ellie had not claimed the right of mentorship in nearly a hundred years, and not since she was promoted to Senior Guild Master. The crowd parted, giving Ellie a straight path to the stage.

Marsee's jaw dropped, and it was several moments before she pulled herself together. Thankfully everyone was watching Ellie and not her at that moment.

"I accept your right to vouch for her work, and claim the honor and title of mentor. Come forward, Senior Guild Master, and stand beside your protege," her father commanded in the traditional words of the ceremony.

Ellie nodded, and strode confidently forward, the crowd closing in behind her as she passed.

Marsee's mind was whirring so fast she couldn't even think a coherent thought as Ellie made her way forward and onto the stage. *The Senior Guild Master wants to mentor ME?!* she finally managed to think. Even the voice in her head squeaked in astonishment.

"Please kneel," her father commanded, and Marsee and the Senior Guild Master did, in unison, as if they'd practiced the move. To be fair, Marsee's legs were about to give out if he hadn't said to kneel.

"Journeyman Marsee Bet Chenzira, do you promise to uphold the honor and traditions of the Guild, to always strive to do your best work, and to listen and learn from your mentor?"

"I do," Marsee said, trying hard not to shake from nerves in front of everyone. It had been bad enough knowing her mentorship ceremony would be in front of so many high ranking people, but this? This was more than she could grasp.

"Elliana Reighly Khihar, do you promise to guide Marsee in her journey to masters and beyond, to see that she becomes as good, if not better than you, in her chosen craft?" The implications of that oath floored Marsee. *What does that even mean?*

"I do," Ellie promised.

"And as Marsee has earned the rank of journeyman in more than one discipline, which discipline do you wish to mentor Marsee on?" Jer asked.

It was the tradition that a mentor would focus on one discipline, and that a second mentor would be taken later, should they not have the skills to guide the person in that second discipline. There was another dramatic pause, which was just long enough for Marsee to turn and look at her new mentor in confusion.

"I wish to mentor her in all of them, and more. It is my desire that Marsee someday replace me as Senior Guild Master."

The crowd gasped. Marsee's jaw dropped again, and then quickly recovered, but her paws were starting to shake.

*She wants me to replace her? Me?!* her brain voice squeaked again, several octaves higher than before. *Why me*, she wondered.

"Marsee, do you accept the Senior Guild Master's offer of mentorship?" her father asked.

Marsee's mouth opened to answer but nothing came out, she just continued to stare at the Guild Master.

Ellie broke protocol and reached for Marsee's paw. "Marsee, I promise you this. By the time I'm ready to step down, which won't happen for a very, very, *very* long time, I'm not *that* old yet..." laughter followed this pronouncement, "that you will be ready to fill that role, and no one will believe otherwise, including you. Trust me."

*Accept already!* her instinct yelled at her.

Marsee blinked out of her shock, nodded, and then took a deep breath. "I do!" she said clearly and loudly, or she hoped she did anyway. She was pretty sure she was going to pass out.

"Then it is my honor and privilege to be the first to congratulate you on your promotion to journeyman level two. Please rise!" her father said.

The crowd cheered as Ellie helped Marsee stand, her legs wobbling from the shock. Ellie hugged her tightly and then helped guide her off the stage. Several of the people near the stairs stopped to congratulate her. It was all she could do to say thank you back. Ellie quickly guided her around the back of the stage as her father finished up, and sent everyone on their way. She never even heard what he said.

"Come on, let's go find a quiet place to talk," her new mentor said.

*Her mentor,* Marsee thought. *The Senior Guild Master is my mentor?!* Never in a million years had she expected this. She couldn't even believe what had just happened, and dug her claws into her paw to make sure she wasn't dreaming. It was unusual enough that Ellie had offered to allow her to rent a room, but to take her on as her protege, unheard of. Marsee nodded, still in shock, and started for the Tower and her room. It was the only private place she could think of. Marsee climbed to the top of the Tower, with her mentor following closely behind, and when they arrived, she opened and entered her room. With so many people around, she'd decided to close it up. She didn't want anyone walking in by mistake.

"I'll grab a couple of pillows and we can sit out on the balcony," she said, barely able to form the words.

Rather than waiting outside, Ellie followed her into her room and gasped a moment later. Marsee turned to look back and saw where Ellie was looking. It was Little Flower's painting. Ellie walked over examining it closely.

"Little Flower painted this?" she asked, pointing to the lily in the corner.

"She did. She completed it a few minutes before she went into labor," Marsee said.

"It's astounding!" Ellie said, her eyes fixed on the painting.

*It really was a masterpiece,* Marsee thought, wondering if Little Flower would ever paint again. *She barely moved this afternoon. Oh please don't let her lose her gift too!* she prayed to the Ancient Gods, thankful her sister was awake, but scared for her long term recovery.

"She painted it for you," Marsee finally admitted, her voice barely above a whisper.

Ellie turned and looked at her, head tilted and brow raised.

Marsee sighed. "She wanted to give it to you as a thank you for all of your help, but I just couldn't part with it. I'm sorry. It's just...it was the last thing she ever painted, before..."

Ellie nodded and softened her face in sympathy. "I understand completely. She can give it to me later when she's feeling better, if she still wants to, and I'll pretend I've never seen it." Ellie walked closer and fingered the frame. "Did you carve this, or buy it?"

"I carved it. She asked me to help make it for her. I was over in the guild hall when her labor started." She let out a heavy sigh as her guilt hit her again. "If I'd been here I might have been able to get her to the healers sooner..." Marsee turned and grabbed her two best pillows, unable to look at the painting any longer.

"Marsee, what happened to Little Flower was not your fault," Ellie said softly.

Marsee shrugged and started walking out the door with the pillows.

"Marsee. Stop," Ellie commanded.

Marsee stopped but didn't turn around.

"Look at me." Ellie used 'the voice'.

Marsee sighed and turned around to face her new mentor, trying hard to control the guilt that she felt, that she knew she would always feel for not being there when her sister needed her.

"What happened to Little Flower was *not* your fault. Even if it feels like that to you, it wasn't. It was an unfortunate accident, and you've got to stop blaming yourself for it. You can't change the past. All you can do is learn from it and try to do better next time, and you need to stop pushing yourself to exhaustion to try and make it up to her."

Marsee sighed, but nodded.

"Since this is your Mentorship Day, I'll give you a pass this one time, but if I see or hear you wallowing in pity for something you can't change, I promise I'll thwack you upside your head so hard you'll be sharing a bed with your sister."

Marsee remembered how hard Ellie could hit with her tail and snickered. "Yes, Senior Guild Master."

"Impudent cub! I can and will demote you," she growled, but her tail was curled tightly.

"Yup. I am. Are you sure you still want to be my mentor?" Marsee asked, only half joking. She honestly had no idea why Ellie wanted to be *her* mentor. She didn't feel like she'd done anything to deserve it.

"Absolutely. I need someone new to yell at," Ellie said with a wicked grin, and went back to examining the painting, and then started making her way slowly around the room looking at everything else.

Marsee watched, curious what the Guild Master thought of her creations. Many had been made when she was very young. Surprisingly though, there was none of the normal nervousness she usually felt when Ellie examined her work. *That's because you're still in shock,* she told herself, with a snort.

Ellie stopped at the wall of Little Flower's sketches for a while. "I've seen this before, but I don't remember where. What is it?" she asked, pointing to one.

"That's a saber-toothed tiger," Marsee said, using the Hue-man word for it. "It's in the cubs book."

"A yes. This is the Earth creature Little Flower named our species after?" Ellie asked for confirmation. Marsee nodded and Ellie stared at it for a while longer. "There's something about this creature. I can't quite find the right word for it."

"Primal?" Marsee suggested.

Ellie looked at her, considered, and eventually shook her head. "No, familiar. All I can think of when I see that drawing is 'That's someone worth hunting with.'"

Marsee raised a brow. "My instinct said the same thing about it."

Ellie snorted. "I've always wondered if there was some connection between our two planets. The smaller felines we rescued look far too much like our cubs."

"Mama says we're very different," Marsee replied.

Ellie shrugged. "Well, who knows. Maybe we had an ancestor that looked like that too." She made her way back across the room and gave

Marsee's bed a little swing on the way by, and then grabbed one of the pillows from Marsee and motioned for her to continue on out.

Marsee made her way around the tower to overlook the inner courtyard and the celebration below. She flopped down on her pillow with a heavy sigh, her front paws hanging over the edge of the pillow and the balcony, and rested her head on her arms to better look down at the massive crowd of strangers in her home.

"You really do have quite the view from here," her mentor commented eventually.

Marsee just shrugged. They sat there in silence for a while.

"You know, that painting may be a masterpiece, but the frame you made for it, is too. It's probably the most elegant frame I've ever seen, and it accentuates that painting perfectly. I absolutely detest working with rainbow wood because of how temperamental it is, but I particularly love the small carvings of the Earth creatures you added. That level of detail is not easy, even on other types of wood, and you made excellent use of the burls."

Marsee smiled at the praise. "Thanks. It took me almost two months to complete." They sat there in silence for several more minutes as they watched the suns start to set and a group of musicians take the stage below. "Why me?" Marsee finally asked, looking up at her mentor. "I haven't stuck with a craft for more than a year or two before I ended up switching, and well, frankly, my work this past year has been spotty at best. Why would you want to mentor me?"

"For that very reason," Ellie replied.

"Oh," Marsee said, feeling defeated. Her ears drooped and she rested her head on her arms again. "None of the other masters would have me then?"

"On the contrary, Marsee. They all wanted to be your mentor."

Marsee looked over at her in disbelief, trying to figure out if Ellie was pulling her tail again.

"Marsee, what happened to you was not your fault. You were sick and struggling to contain an illness no one should ever have to face alone, and one that has frankly been a death sentence for as far back as our history goes. You should have been promoted years ago, but I couldn't justify promoting you, not until we were sure you had it contained, and well, now that you're officially off the watch list, I can."

"You knew about that? Back then I mean," Marsee asked, slumping. She hadn't been aware that Ellie had known about her issues before that day in the family room, or anyone for that matter.

"Child, I receive notice of anyone and everyone who has a hunter's instinct flare up. I'm legally required to report it to the Council if the person is over twenty, and on more than one occasion, I have had to deal with situations until the Guard could arrive. I've also read your full report and have shared the important bits with my guild masters, in the hopes that we can help someone before it becomes too late. Nearly half the population is part of the Guild in one fashion or another at this point," Ellie stated.

"Moons, does everyone know?" Marsee asked, burying her face under her tail, thoroughly embarrassed and horrified at the idea. "I thought that was only going to the Senior Council."

"No child, of course not. I wouldn't do that to you." Ellie said, patting the back of Marsee's head. "Your father shared your report with me, after I gave my oath not to inform anyone who it was, and I've spoken to both your parents and your uncle about it at length. I was there that day, remember, and I was worried about you too. That's why I brought the others back that afternoon. I didn't want them to see what was planned the next morning, for your sake."

"Oh. Thank you, I guess." She slumped as she considered what Ellie had said, and then looked up. "Were you really serious about all the masters wanting to mentor me?"

"Well 'all' might be a bit of an exaggeration, but yes. The last few months, I've had hundreds of people requesting to be your mentor. I stopped counting."

"Hundreds?" Marsee squeaked. "But...but...why?"

Ellie smiled and nodded. "Well for one, you're talented and inventive. You're easy to work with. You have direct access to the Hue-mans and everything they bring with them, and you're well known. Being your mentor would come with some prestige."

"Oh, so they only wanted to be my mentor because of Little Flower and her people?" Marsee asked.

Ellie sighed, exasperated. "No. They wanted to be your mentor because you've earned it, and they would have done well by you, but none of them would have been the right fit for you either."

Marsee looked at her confused. "Right fit? What do you mean?"

"Have you been able to pick an area you want to focus on yet?" Ellie asked instead.

Marsee deflated. "No. I still can't decide. I like them all. I'd rather bounce around like I did for those few weeks I stayed at your place. Working with the Hue-mans has been fun too. They have so many unique and interesting ways of looking at the world."

Ellie grinned. "That's exactly what I meant. If I'd paired you up with a mentor or even several, you'd have been bored silly within six months, and neither you or your mentor would have been happy. You're like the Hue-mans in a lot of ways, more interested in developing a wide swath of random bits of knowledge, than focusing on one area and becoming an expert. Take GrandFather for example. He's in the Healer's Guild, the Council, and the Guild, and that frankly, is what makes them and you so special."

Marsee flicked her ears back at that. "You think I'm special?"

Ellie flicked her own ears back, as if surprised Marsee would even ask that question. "Of course I do. I wouldn't have claimed you as my protege if I didn't."

Marsee just shook her head in disbelief. "I'm not special."

"What could possibly give you that idea?" Ellie glared at her.

Marsee shrugged. She didn't know how to explain it. "I'm different. I don't feel like I fit in anywhere, like I'm always on the outside looking in. I've isolated myself for so long, I don't really know how to interact with people, and most of the time they just baffle me. The only group I really have any connection with are the Hue-man cubs. They're so direct that it's easy to understand them, but even then I'm not one of them. I don't have many close friends, outside of Little Flower. Outside of her, you and Petra are the only ones I've ever really been able to open up to."

"I understand why you isolated yourself for so long, and it will take time to break yourself out of that habit, but I assure you, you are well liked, and you fit. But you're right. You *are* different, and that's what makes you special. Don't be ashamed of that, celebrate it."

Marsee snorted and rolled her eyes before she could stop herself. *As if it would be that easy.*

Ellie's expression hardened slightly, just short of a glare. "Marsee, whether accidentally or on purpose, you have accomplished what no one else has ever done, not even me. Rather than focusing on one discipline and working your way up as most people do, you've learned the basics in four of the major guilds, artists, crafters, writers, and tech, enough to earn your journeyman's rank in both the Crafter's Guild and the Artist's Guild, and the only reason you haven't earned your journeyman's rank in the Writer's Guild is because I haven't told you yet, which reminds me. Poof! You're now a journeyman in the Writer's Guild, with all the rights and blah blah blah." Ellie used the same dismissive hand motion as the day before. "And you're about *this* close to earning your journeyman's rank in the Tech Guild as well, even if you didn't officially switch guilds. You also have experience in Builder's, with all your help here, likely enough to qualify you for apprentice level two or three, although I haven't assessed it yet. You're an official translator for the Full Council, and it wouldn't surprise me in the least if you didn't know the charters, as well, if not better than most of the Full Council, likely well enough to qualify as a Junior Councilor, if there weren't time restrictions as a staffer to earn that rank."

Marsee just stared at her mentor. This was all too much. She didn't feel special or even consider her work all that good, certainly not enough to be praised. Only the frame did she feel really good about, and that had been a labor of love and penance. She stood up and walked a few steps away, and looked down at her paws, and then grabbed her tail for comfort.

"Plus, you've completed multiple projects that would have more than qualified you for your masters in several areas," Ellie added.

Marsee turned to look back at her with astonishment. "What?!" she exclaimed. "I have not. You're pulling my tail!"

"I am not. Let's see, you invented both shoes and clothing for Little Flower. There was your work with Sina in translating and expanding sign language into the other languages. You mastered two languages in less than a month and learned to read a third, and I wouldn't be surprised if you aren't at least passible in understanding the Hue-man's spoken language by now either, which would make you the only one to know any of their spoken language. You were instrumental in helping to translate the Charter into the Hue-man's written language and sign language. You helped to restore several ancient manuscripts, which I have personally reviewed and found to be exceptional. You learned to overcome your fears of speaking in front of people, and seamlessly translated for the Council and your sister for days, and as far as I could tell, didn't make a single mistake, most of that while battling the advanced stages of psychosis. Since then, you've been actively engaged in working with the various masters to build a home that is functional for species of radically different sizes and needs. There's your work in translating and illustrating the Hue-man manuscripts into the other languages, not to mention your book binding skills. The copies you send me are all beautiful works of art all on their own. Then there's the furniture you built for your sister's room, on short notice, and frankly even that frame you did for your sister, and while I can't show it to anyone, every single one of those drawings in that sketchbook. I've had report after report after report from the master's who have been teaching here how you've been assisting them with classes, something that most people don't start doing until they've earned their masters, and you've done all of that while still taking on the majority of the daily care for your sister and her cub."

"But...but..." Marsee stammered.

"But nothing. The only reason I'm not promoting you further is because you're too young. You need to stop putting yourself down. You're talented, Marsee, but more importantly, you put in the hard work, and you do it because it needs to be done, without any thought to yourself, and what you might get out of it, and that's why I decided to mentor you. Besides, I've been mentoring you for months now. I figured it was time to make it official. It's not like I'm going to let some other master sink their claws into you, not when I can have you all to myself," Ellie said with a wink.

***She's right. You should listen to her. It's nice to see someone finally recognizing our worth,*** her instinct purred.

Marsee sighed. "Thank you. When you put it like that, I guess it makes sense for you to be my mentor, rather than assigning a bunch of them, but what I don't...I mean..." Marsee took several deep breaths to try to compose her thoughts. "Being my mentor is one thing, but I still don't understand why you chose to make me your replacement. Can you even do that? I thought senior guild master was an elected position. Surely one of the other guild masters would be more qualified. What about Master Nardal? I thought he was going to be your replacement, if anyone," Marsee asked.

"They might be higher in rank, but they are certainly *not* more qualified. Most of the masters only want to spend time making things. They have no interest or ability in bringing people together and...translating," Ellie finally decided, "the needs of one group to another. I have a hard enough time finding people capable of running a local guild hall, much less trying to find someone that can manage the entire Guild. As for Master Nardal, he has all the ambition and enthusiasm needed for the job, and he is absolutely fantastic when it comes to managing all of the administrative needs of the Guild, but he has absolutely no people skills. He couldn't read a person if you wrote on them, but you do that all the time with Little Flower's people. You're good at reading people. "

Marsee shook her head. "No I'm not. I mess up all the time. I can't even tell when you're picking on me half the time."

Ellie shook her head. "Marsee, you're far better than you think you are. You're good at picking up the subtle cues that tell what a person is really thinking. Most people just go with what a person says, but you, you can tell what a person is feeling or really thinking, even when they're trying to hide it. I wouldn't be surprised in the least, that the reason you've been confused over the years, is because what a person said and what they were really thinking were two different things."

Marsee considered that for a while and then shrugged. She'd have to explore that idea later.

Ellie continued. "My job isn't about how well I can make a chair, or whether I can write a book, it's about people. It's about smoothing relationships and getting people to compromise. Being able to read people, really read them, not just take what they say at face value, is invaluable, and not something that can easily be taught, but you're already better than most of my guild masters, after decades of being in that position. As for whether I can do it or not, I just did. Yes, it's an elected position, but by the time I'm done with you everyone else will be just as sure as I am that you deserve it, and I'll be honest with you. I want the Guild to continue after I'm gone, and not disintegrate into the arguing and disgruntled factions it was in when I restructured it, and I want to make sure the right person is leading it when I do."

Marsee walked back over to her pillow and flopped back down. This was all just too much. They sat in silence for a long time as Marsee tried to come to grips with everything Ellie had just told her.

"You really think I'm the right person for this?" Marsee asked.

"I really do. So, what do you say? Ready to start traveling the universe with me? Hobnob with guild masters and councilors? Learn how to make a rocking chair from the universe's best and *only* maker of them?" Ellie asked with a wink.

Marsee looked at Ellie, wanting more than anything to feel like the person Ellie thought she was, and then sighed and shook her head. "I can't. I need to be here and help take care of Little Flower and Hope. I'm still Hope's guardian, for however long that lasts, and she's still nursing, and besides, I promised the Council I would help take care of Little Flower's people," she said finally.

Ellie caressed the side of her face. "Oh child, I would never take you away from your sister in her time of need. We have decades before us. But I think you may have misunderstood. The Council didn't ask you to stay here forever and care for Little Flower's people. That's your mother's burden to bear. You've given up the privacy of your home to make a place for your sister's people, and that's all you agreed to, from the Council's perspective anyway. You are free to leave at any time and live your own life." Ellie said.

Marsee looked up at her and frowned again. Her sister needed her and she needed her sister. She felt lost without her, and Hope might not be her cub, but she loved her as much as if she were.

Ellie looked at her sadly, as if understanding the burden and responsibility that Marsee felt. "But until you feel comfortable leaving your sister, there's plenty for us to work on here. I need you to keep working on those manuscripts. They're very important. They may very well be one of the most important things you ever do. I would also like to have you start teaching some of the Guild classes as well, not just assisting. I know that doesn't usually happen until you've earned your masters, but you need the experience, more than you need more training in those individual crafts. Teaching helps lock in your knowledge, and will help to build your confidence too. When you're ready and your sister is better, then we can talk about having you move to Council City, where I can easily thwack you with my tail, but until then, you can join me on a few shorter trips to the other planets and Guilds, and meet everyone."

Marsee sat and thought for a long time. She was absolutely terrified of the idea, but she trusted the Senior Guild Master. Ellie hadn't steered her wrong yet, and she had taken her from the scared cub that couldn't give an interview in front of one person, to standing in front of the Council for the entire universe to watch as she translated for her sister.

"What's really bothering you?" Ellie finally asked.

"People," she said, and sighed, flopping back down on her paws.

Ellie burst out laughing. "You and me, both!" she said finally when she could talk again. "I can't stop people from being people, but I can help you, and teach you to understand and deal with them better, just like we did in preparing you for the trial."

"Okay," Marsee said finally. "I'll do it. I'm absolutely terrified, but I'll do it."

"That's my brave girl! Now, let's go find your family. I want to check out Jordan's booth before all of her wares are gone. I have it on good authority that chocolate chip cookies are better than fried star fruit."

"Oh they are!" Marsee agreed. "And thank you."

"For what, child?" Ellie asked, as they stood up to put the pillows away.

"For believing in me," Marsee said, looking down at her paws and whispered, "even when I don't."

Ellie crushed her in a hug and then held her firmly by her shoulders. "Marsee, I promise you, I will always be your biggest champion," Ellie said with a serious expression that shifted to a mock glare. "And I promise I'll thwack you upside your head when you need it, but only if and when you need it. Now come on. Let's go find those cookies."

~~~~~

Myra watched her daughter leave the stage with Ellie close behind her. There was no one she trusted more to care for her daughter than her oldest and dearest friend, and she'd seen the transformation that Ellie had done with Marsee during her several weeks away. Not to mention all of the work she'd done with her prior to the trial. Ellie was the best mentor Marsee could have ever ended up with, but she was shocked by Ellie's statement about having Marsee replace her. She'd have words with her friend later about keeping that little surprise from her. Marsee had been nearly comatose with shock at that pronouncement, and Myra wondered how Marsee was going to handle it. She'd honestly been surprised that Marsee hadn't run off of the stage in an absolute panic. She started trying to make her way to the stage, but the crowd was going in the other direction, making it difficult. As she passed she focused on the comments of the people around her.

"Have you seen the books she's put together? Even the binding's are works of art!"

"I can't believe the Guild Master finally picked someone to replace her. I was worried what would happen if she up and died on us. Can
~~~~~

you imagine having to pick someone to replace her? It would take decades to get over the drama of it."

"I wonder what Nardal will have to say about this. I'm pretty sure he thought the position was his."

"Can you imagine Nardal as Senior Guild Master though?"

"Ha, no, not really."

"Do you think Marsee is up to it?"

"The Guild Master seems to think so, which is good enough for me. I couldn't ask for a nicer person to lead the Guild though."

"What right does she have to pick her replacement? Shouldn't that be decided by the other Guild Masters?" Myra tried to find the owner of that voice but couldn't in the shifting crowd.

By the time Myra made it to the front of the crowd, Marsee and Ellie were nowhere to be found, but spotting GrandFather and Jer, she made her way over to them instead.

"I'm guessing Ellie took her somewhere to talk," Jer said once she arrived.

Myra nodded her understanding. "That was a lot to drop on someone."

"Indeed. Did you know she was going to do that?" he asked.

"No. You?"

He shook his head. "I had a feeling something was up when Ellie asked me to perform the ceremony, but since I was reading out all the other announcements, it made sense."

"Huh, well I can't think of a better mentor for her," Myra said and shrugged. "Shall we explore the festival, then?"

"I thought you'd never ask," he replied with a grin.

Holding hands and twining tails they made their way back to explore the booths. She looked up at one point to see Marsee and Ellie sitting out on the balcony and smiled. This was certainly a day she was never going to forget!

# CHAPTER 35

# GrandFather: Buster

James made his way to the barn early the next morning, a large black bag slung over his shoulder. The council meeting wouldn't start for another few hours, and he wanted to spend some time with Buster before the craziness of the day took over. He figured everyone would still be sleeping off the Halloween Festival that had gone on well past midnight. He wasn't sure how the Sabers would feel about what he was planning to do, and he hoped he'd at least have an hour to himself before the feeding crew arrived. The lights flickered on as he entered and he smiled knowing he was alone.

Buster nickered a greeting to him as he approached the stall.

"You're going to have to wait a little longer for your breakfast, old boy," James said, as he grabbed the halter and lead rope off of the stall door where it hung.

Buster walked up and nuzzled James's hand and James quickly put the halter on and gave his friend a pat on the side of the neck before leading the massive draft horse out into the aisle. Several of the other horses nickered in greeting, and Buster nickered back.

James chuckled as he attached the cross ties and grabbed Buster's grooming equipment. "You're going to have to wait to play with your lady friends a little while longer too," Fifteen minutes later, Buster was as clean as he was going to get. He could have run the horse through one of the sonic shower stalls they'd installed, but Buster enjoyed grooming more, and he wanted the horse in a good mood. After putting everything away, James lifted the bag he'd brought with him and unhooked Buster from the cross-ties.

"Come on then, old boy, time to see what you remember."

James led Buster out into the massive indoor arena that they used primarily for turnout during inclement weather. This arena was probably ten times the size of the biggest arena James had ever seen, and Buster snorted and pranced, tail and ears up as they entered.

"Easy boy," James said, as he shut the gate behind him, and carefully set the bag to hang over the sides of the arena door. He swapped out the lead rope for the lunge line that hung on the wall just inside the arena, and noticed as he did that the outer door was open slightly, but not enough to worry about. A cool breeze came through the foot high crack and he smiled. This part of the world had three seasons, Spring, when the rains came and turned the land into a lush paradise, 'Summer' which was blistering hot and sticky with humidity most days, and 'High Summer' which was just shy of the average temperature found in Hell, from his perspective anyway. His ancestors may have come from warm, southern climates, but he never liked the heat much. They were transitioning out of spring and into summer, but there were still many days that were still tolerable, especially in the morning before the suns rose.

He walked out into the arena and gave Buster some slack in the line, clucking him forward. Buster snorted and took off at a trot until he came to the end of the line and started circling. After a few laps, James lifted an arm and Buster turned and trotted in the other direction.

"Woah," he called out. Buster took two steps and stopped. "Good boy!" James said, and clucked him forward again. Buster took off at a trot again. "Walk" James called out after a while. Buster snorted but transitioned down to a walk for a few steps. "Okay boy, trot," James commanded and Buster practically bounced back into the trot. James put his other arm up and Buster turned back in the other direction, tossing his head. "Got some energy this morning, I see. Alright boy, let it out. Canter."

Buster gathered his massive haunches beneath him and leapt forward into a full on gas powered gallop which made James chuckle. *Some things never change.* Buster was a brute of a draft horse, nearly twenty hands high, but well proportioned, and the sweetest and calmest work horse he'd ever met, but give him the chance to run, and he'd fly. He wasn't the fastest of horses, no draft horse was, but Buster could easily outpace many other horses just because of his longer legs. The sound of Buster's powerful hooves digging into the earth made James smile. He always loved to watch horses run, and Buster reveled in his power. James let him run off some steam before calling out 'easy boy,' and Buster settled down into a nice easy canter without a complaint. There was no sign of the injury that had nearly taken the horse's life. The cats had done an incredible job in healing him.

The only time Buster ever refused an order was if something was wrong, and James had learned to trust this horse's instinct out on trail. One time they'd been caught in an unexpected snow squall, and James hadn't been able to see more than two feet in front of him the entire time. He'd let Buster take the lead and had practically laid down on top of Buster to keep warm and protect his face from the biting snow. Buster had made his way right back to the barn where Ben had been pacing and waiting for him to return, and it had been Buster's actions that had likely saved his life the day of the Cataclysm.

He slowed Buster down to a walk and let him cool down for a minute, before turning him in the other direction and having him canter again. This time he didn't take off with a snort, but went into a nice easy lope, head down and relaxed, lower lip chewing. As soon as he did, James called out "woah" and Buster came to an immediate stop.

"Have you been working with him?"

James looked over and smiled, seeing Henry Curtis leaning on the gate. "Nope, first time. Not since before anyway," James called back. He gave a slight tug on the line. Buster spun to face him and walked right up to him. "Good Boy!" he said, giving the old horse a pat.

"Before? You knew this brute?" Henry asked as James walked over to the arena door.

"I did. Buster here belonged to my partner, Ben. I was out riding that day. Buster's lucky in more ways than one. He broke his leg pretty badly, and I was looking for something to put him out of his misery when the Flyer's knocked me out instead."

James watched Henry carefully, wondering what he'd think about his past relationship, but Henry didn't say anything, just nodded and then tilted his head at the covered object on the stall door. "So, you fixin' to ride him then?"

James laughed. "That was the plan, although I wasn't expecting to have witnesses. I figured everyone would still be passed out from the party last night. I'm not sure what the Sabers will think if they see me. Nazari seemed shocked and slightly horrified at the very idea." James dropped the lunge line to ground tie Buster, and the horse stood there content as Henry shifted over and gave him a scratch on the forehead.

"Sun's up, I'm up. As for the Sabers, as far as I can tell there's no law against it, which is about all that matters here," Henry said.

James chuckled, and unzipped the bag to reveal the saddle, saddle pad, and bridle that he'd spent the last several months making. "That's just because they never thought to ride one of their domestic animals. Granted, as far as I can tell, they're one of the biggest creatures on this planet, so that might have had something to do with it."

"Did you make that, or one of the Sabers?" Henry asked.

"I did. It's the whole reason I started taking classes at the Guild, but I've been working on it in secret in my room."

Henry walked over and examined everything closely. The Sabers didn't have leather to work with, but James had found a similar synthetic substitute that he hoped would hold up as well. "Did you ever make a saddle before?"

"No, but I spent far too much time teaching people how to fit their saddles as a vet. I can't tell you how many times I came out to treat a lame horse, just to find out it was nothing more than an ill fitting saddle," James said, as he tossed the saddle pad on Buster's back.

Buster flicked an ear but other than that he didn't seem concerned.

"Good Boy," James said, and turned and lifted the saddle out and carefully heaved it over Buster's back and adjusted it, feeling for uneven pressure points.

"Not bad then. Looks a bit like a cross between an English and Aussie saddle."

"It's based loosely on a custom made endurance saddle my partner had. Not nearly as fancy though, but I figured there was no point in decorating it if it didn't work. I can always do that later," James said, as he tightened the cinch. Buster snorted. "You're fine, boy. I know. We haven't made you do anything for years." James grabbed the bridle and swapped that out for the halter, and made some adjustments to better fit Buster's big head.

"No bit?" Henry asked.

"Nope. Ben told me Buster never liked the bit. My guess is it's because he still has his wolf teeth. That could have caused him pain when he was younger. Still, he responds well to the hackamore, or he used to anyway."

When he was done he checked the cinch again and tightened it up a bit. Buster always held his breath the first time, and then he stared at the stirrups that were nearly head high and looked around the big open arena for something to use as a mounting block. He might be in the best shape of his life, thanks to the Sabers, but flexibility had never been his strong suit.

"Need a leg up?" Henry asked.

"Well unless you've got a mounting block or a pickup truck hiding around here, that would be helpful," James said. "Although I might be able to drag one of the benches in here."

Henry chuckled and entered the arena. "Those monstrous things would take a Saber to move. Count of three?"

James nodded, very aware as Henry approached and grabbed his leg. *Focus James. Now is not the time to get distracted,* he chided himself.

"One...Two...Three!" James jumped and Henry lifted, and he found himself sprawled across Busters wide back, nearly flying over the other side. Henry was a lot stronger than he looked. Swinging a leg around, he sat up and patted the horse. Buster never moved.

"What a good boy, Buster!" James said as Henry backed off.

James started by flexing Buster's neck, making sure Buster responded to the bridle and then asked him to back up. Buster snorted but took several steps back. James relaxed and gave Buster the signal to move forward again. Buster walked forward as nice and easy as if it hadn't been over three years, Earth time, since he'd last been ridden. James gave a slight nudge and Buster moved into a very fast and bouncy trot.

"Easy boy," James said with a half chuckle, and Buster slowed and smoothed out after another snort.

James had Buster perform a couple of loose figure eights and when he managed those without difficulty, he clucked the big horse into a canter. Buster's gate smoothed out and they completed a nice easy loop around the arena before James turned him down the middle, switched leads and cantered in the other direction. When they'd finished the loop, James brought him back down to a walk and patted the horse.

"You've earned your star fruit today, old boy," he told the horse. On the way back, he stopped, tried a few side passes and smaller spins in each direction, and brought him to a stop by the arena door where Henry was still watching.

"Mighty fine horse you've got there, James, to behave that good after three years of inactivity," Henry said.

"That he is. Best horse I've ever worked with anyway, smartest too, but that was all Ben's doing. Ben used him on the farm for just about everything." James swung a leg over and slid off with an oof. Buster was a very tall horse, and it was a long way down. Once sure he wasn't going to fall on his butt, he reached into his pocket and removed a handful of dried star fruit, and handed it to the horse who nickered his appreciation.

"Mind if I ride him sometime?" Henry asked.

"Do you have any experience?" James asked back.

"Yup. Worked as a cow hand for years, and even competed in a few rodeos. Won a couple but that was when I was a lot younger and far stupider. But I always enjoyed being in the saddle."

James looked over at Henry trying to figure out if that was an innuendo, or if he was being serious. Going with serious, he answered. "Buster's been trained in English reigning, not western."

Henry nodded. "Saw that."

James held the reins out to Henry. Henry raised his brows in surprise, but took them, flipped them around and grabbed a fistful of mane. "Need a leg..." Henry leapt and swung himself up onto Buster's back."Guess not."

Henry chuckled, and ran Buster through his paces. Riding had always been a hobby for James, not a profession, and it was clear that Henry knew what he was doing. James watched appreciatively until Buster stopped suddenly, and started snorting loudly.

"What's bothering him?" James called out.

"Not sure," Henry answered, and backed the horse up. Buster calmed almost immediately.

James made his way out into the arena. Buster snorted at him as he approached the spot where he'd been having issues. James didn't see anything but a small stick.

"I'm not seeing anything but a stick. Try having him approach again," James said

Henry clucked the horse forward. Buster moved forward a few steps, and started snorting and pawing at the ground.

"That's not like him. Something's clearly bothering him." Just as he said that, the 'stick' launched out of the ground and stung him on the side of the leg. "Yeouch! What the heck was that!" James yelped, hopping away and rubbing at his leg, but before he could figure out what it was, the pain radiated through his body and he started shaking. Moments later he collapsed on the ground unconscious.

# CHAPTER 36

# Henry: Sand Spinners

Henry slid off of Buster and ran over to James, scanning the ground for whatever crawly had bit or stung him, but he couldn't see anything. Suddenly Buster screamed and reared up, coming down on a spot of ground, not two feet from James, and then did it again. Henry grabbed James under his arms and pulled him away from the rearing horse.

"James!" he yelled, "Wake up!" James didn't so much as flutter his eyes. He checked James's pulse and found one, thankfully, and then went to calm the horse. "Woah boy. Easy there. Good boy," he crooned, grabbed the reins, and pulled the horse away. As soon as he was a few feet from whatever had been there, which he still couldn't see, Buster calmed down. Henry removed his shirt and tossed it down where Buster had been attacking to mark the spot for later.

He considered what to do, and then reached down and picked up James with a grunt and heaved him over the saddle, which was far easier said than done. "You would have to have the world's...tallest...horse, wouldn't you?" he muttered under his breath as he heaved. Once James was in place he made for the arena door and out. It was still far too early for anyone else to be in the barn but he still called out for Nazari, who he knew was capable of hearing him, to see if the healer was in the barn yet. No one answered.

"What under the three moons?" Healer Brice signed, as they walked through the doors of the Trauma Center, stunned by the sight of the horse caring James.

"GrandFather was stung or bit by something in the arena. Not sure what. He started shaking and collapsed almost immediately," Henry signed.

Brice blinked once, and then leapt to her feet, startling Buster who snorted, but didn't move off.

"Easy boy," Henry patted the big horse. "Move slowly around the horse please," Henry signed.

Brice slowed down, walked up, grabbed GrandFather, and then bolted for the ward.

"Well, come on boy, let's get you back to your stall. They'll take good care of your friend," he told the big horse, turned and walked out, hoping they knew what to do.

He met Nazari on the way back. "What are you doing with Buster, and what's that on his back?" Nazari asked.

"Dropping off GrandFather at the Trauma Center. Something stung or bit him in the arena and he collapsed. I couldn't carry him all the way here, so I used Buster, and that's a saddle," Henry explained. "We use it for riding."

Her ears flicked back with concern. "Is GrandFather okay?"

"I don't know. Didn't stay to find out. Figured I'd better block off the Arena, before someone else gets hurt," he replied.

Nazari nodded, "I'll come with you, see if we can figure out what it is."

Once they were back in the barn, Henry put Buster in his stall, quickly removed the bridle and saddle, with the intention of grooming him later, and he and Nazari made their way back to the arena.

"Whatever it was, it was over there by my shirt," Henry signed. "I never saw it. James said he saw a stick, but Buster spooked at it, and then stomped hard at that spot several times."

Nazari pinned her ears back at that, and then considered for a moment and left. She returned a minute later with a manure rake in hand. "Stay there. If this is what I think it is, it's very dangerous."

He was perfectly fine with staying out of harm's reach, and watched as Nazari slowly approached, examining the ground in front of her. Carefully lifted the shirt away with the rake, she set it aside, looked at the ground for a moment, and then dug down in the sand. As she lifted the rake, the sand slid away revealing a large twelve legged spider-like crawly, which Nazari flicked away from her and backed off quickly. Henry gulped. If it scared the big cats, it couldn't be good. Whatever it was didn't move, but Nazari didn't approach, and literally ran out of the arena as fast as she could.

"It's a sand spinner. They're venomous, and where there's one there's usually more. The animals stay in today until we can assess the situation," Nazari told him.

"Just how venomous? Is GrandFather going to be okay?"

"Deadly, for us, if not treated soon enough," Nazari replied, as she unclipped her tablet from her carry harness and called the Trauma Center, and spoke something to the healer that answered. "How long ago was GrandFather stung?"

"Fifteen minutes or so. I brought him right over."

Nazari relayed the information and hung up. "They're giving him the anti-venom now. Hopefully that will work as well on your people as it does on mine," Nazari said, and then peered out at the sand covered arena and the unmoving crawly. "Looks like it's dead. If it were still alive, it'd be digging back into the sand by now. The real question is how to ensure the rest of the arena is safe."

"I suppose we could let Buster back out there and have at it. I'm guessing he's already attacked a few of these beasties before, if he's had that strong of a reaction."

"I don't know how I feel about that. Buster could be injured in the process. We should probably check him over too, and make sure he wasn't stung as well. He might not react as quickly as GrandFather due to his bigger size." Henry agreed so they returned to the stall where they found Buster waiting patiently for them and brought him back out into the aisle. They both looked him over closely and found no sign of a bite wound. Nazari scanned him thoroughly as well. "I'm not seeing any venom in his system, so he's probably fine."

Henry took a few minutes to brush the big horse down and then put him back in his stall. Several of the other horses were getting impatient and kicking at the walls of their stalls, as it was well past their normal breakfast time. While Henry started the hard work of feeding all of the creatures, Nazari left to put a sign up on the arena door to warn anyone else that might want to go out there, and then sent out a general warning about the sand spinners to everyone, along with what they looked like, and how to spot them.

The normal crew that helped care for the various Earth creatures started trickling in, most looking tired from a late night of partying, and Henry and Nazari passed along the information. Several frowned at the news, but shrugged and went to work. Once all the creatures were fed for the morning, a large group of people gathered by the arena gate and peered out at the strange carcass that remained in the center of the arena.

"So how do these crawlies hunt if they're buried in the sand? Do their eyes peek up, or do they react to vibration?" Jenny asked.

"Sound vibration," Nazari replied.

"How do you think Buster knew it was there?" Danny asked.

"That's a very good question. Maybe he heard it," Henry replied.

"I'm not aware that they make any sounds," Nazari countered.

"Yeah well you weren't aware we made sounds either," Danny retorted.

"Fair," Nazari replied.

"How far away do they have to be to strike?" Henry asked. "Grand-Father was only standing a foot or two away from the spinner before it struck him, but Buster reacted quite a bit further away.

"Not far actually," Nazari replied. "They're fairly stationary, relying on a sneak attack to catch their prey."

"Will your scanner pick them up?" Jenny asked.

"Yes but not at a distance I would feel safe at," she replied.

"Well, then I still think the best course of action is to let Buster into the arena and see what he goes after. He seemed to have no problem locating and killing the creature."

Nazari nodded. "I'm going to grab a dose of anti-venom from the Trauma Center first though, just in case. We should probably have some here in the first aid kits as well, if they've found their way into the arena, although I'm not sure how. I wouldn't even expect to see them around here this time of year. They usually show up during high summer after everything has turned to sand." Nazari left and returned a few minutes later with a small case. "GrandFather's not awake yet but seems to be responding to the anti-venom," she informed them.

Henry breathed a sigh of relief, and left to fetch Buster again. Buster nickered in greeting as he approached the stall and led him out, although he appeared to be rather annoyed not to be going outside. "Come on boy, you've got more work to do," he told the big horse.

Henry grabbed the lunge line off the hook rather than the lead rope so he could give the horse some distance if he started rearing again, and then he started leading Buster around the arena in a slowly spiraling circle. Nazari followed behind with the rake, anti-venom kit, and scanner.

It wasn't long before Buster let off another warning snort. Henry gave Buster some added slack in the lead and clucked the horse forward. Buster pinned his ears back at Henry, almost as if asking if Henry was stupid. If a horse could roll its eyes at them, Buster just did.

Apparently Nazari thought the same as her tail curled.

Buster's ears flicked forward again and he let off another warning snort, screamed, and reared, coming down hard on the spot several times before letting off another disgusted snort and backing off. Nazari crept forward with her scanner and then scooped out the sand spinner with the rake.

Henry pulled a small handful of dried star fruit out of his pocket and handed it over to Buster who changed from annoyed to appreciative almost immediately, letting out a soft nicker and nodding his head.

"Good boy, Buster. There's more of this for every one of those nasty beasties you take care of," Henry told the horse, giving him a pat at the same time.

Buster snorted and looked back towards the arena entrance, ears up, so he and Nazari turned to find the watching crowd being parted by a pair of guards who looked completely dumbfounded as they made their careful way into the arena.

"Did that creature seriously just locate and kill a sand spinner?" the first guard asked.

"Twice," Henry replied, pointing to the one in the center of the arena. "We had venomous creatures on Earth as well that had tails that rattled in warning. I've seen horses do the same on several occasions."

The guard flicked an ear back in surprise. "We can sniff them out, but killing them is hard. The sand blocks the stunner and we have to lure them out first."

"Stunner?" Henry asked.

The guard unclipped a device from his harness that looked nothing like a weapon to him, more like a curved remote control, and pointed it at the dead spinner. A ball of blue lightning shot out and struck the dead creature. "Designed to be non lethal. This is how we knocked everyone out during the rescue."

"You were there?" Henry asked.

The guard nodded. "Avery Hunt. I was the senior guard for the diplomatic mission. This is Tamarin Fields, my second."

"Thank you," Henry replied, and turned to look back at the dead sand spinner. "How well can you sniff those beasties out?"

"There are three more in here," Avery replied, pointing in their general direction. "And it looks like they came in through the open door."

Nazari flicked her whiskers back in surprise. "How are you able to sniff that out? You don't have your instinct on."

The guard shrugged. "Training. Sand Spinners have a very distinctive smell."

"Instinct?" Henry asked. "What are you talking about? Or am I mistranslating something?"

The guard frowned but it was Nazari that answered. "Much like the horses know how to walk only hours after we're born, our cubs know how to hunt. Cubs will pounce on everything that moves, especially tails when they're young. I've seen the same behavior with the small felines rescued from your world. It's a skill we no longer need, and for the most part we train it out of our children. Most have it fully under control by the age of three, but in an emergency, we can still call on that ability. Doing so heightens our sense of smell, hearing, and vision in low light, among other things."

"All of the species have that to some extent, but we learn to control it at a young age," Avery said. "Part of the training as a guard is learning to do what we can do by instinct, without using our instinct, as there are...problems that come from overuse."

Henry nodded his understanding. "Adrenalin can do amazing things. I've seen and experienced it a few times myself. The crash afterwards is never fun." Henry turned back to look at the sand spinner again. "Why don't you lead us to the spinners and we'll have Buster squash them. That'll save us the effort of walking the arena to find them."

The guard nodded, taking the rake from Nazari, indicating she should leave, and led them over to the first. Buster let off a warning when they got close, but the moment Henry gave Buster the command to move forward, Buster just flicked an ear at him, reared several times without hesitation, before backing off on his own and turning back to Henry with a sweet nicker and head bob as if to say where's my treat.

Henry chuckled and pulled out another small handful.

When that proved to be highly effective, Avery called the rest of his guards and ordered them to locate nests but not approach as they'd found a better way of dealing with the little monsters. A few hours later, they'd cleared the infestation that surrounded New Hope. Buster had made several new friends, and had been deemed an honorary honor guard by Avery's squad. Buster seemed quite proud of himself, and after the first few, was actively seeking the spinners out before Henry gave the command, but that may have had more to do with the small handful of dried star fruit the horse got with every kill.

# CHAPTER 37

# Little Flower: Pickle Torture

Little Flower woke to a gentle touch on her arm, but struggled to open her eyes. When she finally did it was to see her mother holding Hope. Hope's face was scrunched up, red, and crying. Her mother set Hope down on the bed and pulled back the blanket that was covering her so she could nurse her daughter. Hope stopped crying immediately. *What a strange feeling,* Little Flower thought as she watched her daughter, unable to get over just how much bigger she was.

Her mother sat down next to the bed and watched them both for a few moments, and then reached a paw over and stroked her head. Little Flower looked over at her mother at the touch, and smiled at the love she saw in her mother's face, but then frowned. Her mother looked exhausted and worn, and looked like she'd lost a lot of weight.

At her frown, her mother frowned. "What's wrong?" her mother asked.

She tried to lift her arms to respond but they wouldn't cooperate. Letting out a growl of frustration, she just shook her head and looked away. Her mother had told her she'd been in a coma for four months, or a year of her time, but should she really be this weak? She hadn't been this weak after being stuck in the Agency for nearly twice that time.

*Why can't I move?* she wondered. *What else is wrong with me, and why isn't she telling me?*

Hope shifted and she looked back down at her daughter, and noticed in passing that her mother was no longer by her side. Peering around as far as she could see, it looked like her mother had left the room. A few minutes later her mother returned and moved Hope before gently lifting her upper body and placing a pillow behind her, and then moved Hope over to her other side. The room spun and she closed her eyes until the sensation passed. When she opened them again, her mother was sitting beside her again and then held up a sketchbook. *What does she think I'm going to be able to do with that? I couldn't hold a pencil if I tried,* Little Flower thought bitterly, and looked away again.

Her mother touched her arm, but she didn't look back, so her mother walked over to the other side of the bed and flipped open the book to reveal her old pictionary, which she'd once used to communicate before learning how to sign. Her mother set the book down. "I'll hold the book, point to what you want to say. Blink with your right eye to move a page forward, left to move back."

Little Flower nodded. *I might be able to do that,* she thought, but then frowned. That sketchbook hardly had any words, and she didn't know how to ask what was wrong with her. She blinked forward a few pages, and then struggled to lift her hand to touch 'sick'.

Her mother frowned. "Are you feeling sick? Do you need something for your stomach?"

She was but that wasn't what she wanted right now. She shook her head yes, no, and tried pointing to 'curious' but it was at the top of the page and she couldn't lift her arm that high and ended up selecting 'laugh' instead, which just confused her mother. She shook her head and tried again, and with a groan of effort and shaking arm managed to touch 'curious' briefly before her arm fell back to the bed.

"Do you want to know what is wrong with you?" her mother asked. She nodded her head, and her mother frowned. "Your rib broke again, and it punctured you. You lost a lot of blood before I could cut Hope out and repair the injury. You...you died on the surgery table for five minutes before I could bring you back. Your brain suffered a lot of damage."

She swallowed hard. *Am I going to be stuck like this forever?* she wondered. *I don't want to live like this if I am. Why did she save me? What kind of mother will I be to Hope like this?* She closed her eyes and looked away, trying not to cry. Her mother gently turned her head back to look at her.

"It is going to take a lot of hard work but I promise, you will get better with time," her mother signed.

"Scared."

"I know, but it will be alright. I will always take care of you and Hope, even if you don't get better," her mother said.

*Oh gods, I can't live my life like this! What's the point?* she thought, and shook her head hard.

"You don't want me to take care of you?" her mother asked.

She sighed with frustration, shook her head, and had her mother change the pages until the image she needed showed up. "Knife."

It took her mother several tries to understand what she meant by that. "Die?"

Little Flower nodded her head.

"No, I don't think you're going to die. You're doing so much better," her mother said.

She shook her head and had her flip back. "Want."

Her mother frowned at this and then her ears drooped back in anguish as she deciphered her meaning. "You *want* to die?" her mother signed with shaking arms.

She nodded and her mother positively wilted.

"Oh, Little Flower. I know it seems bad now. Please give it time. Let me try to help you. I know I can. Please?" her mother begged. "There are further treatments we will be able to try, when you're a little stronger. You won't always be like this. I promise."

Little Flower frowned, but nodded, and her mother gave a huge sigh of relief. "Thank you."

By then, Hope had finished nursing, so her mother picked her daughter up, and walked around the room, patting Hope on the back, until she fell back asleep, and then set her down somewhere that she couldn't see from her bed. Her mother returned and set a tray down on a table next to her bed.

"Your turn," her mother said and lifted a bowl. "Jordan made this special for you. She says she calls it chicken soup, but there are no chickens in it. She insists it tastes the same though."

Her mother carefully lifted her out of the bed and carried her over to sit in a giant rocking chair, and propped her up in her arms. The room spun wildly and it was several minutes before she could open her eyes. Her mother started purring, and she did her best to breathe through the dizziness.

"Better?" her mother asked, when she finally opened her eyes.

She nodded and her mother lifted the bowl, and tilted it so she could take a sip. Surprisingly it did taste like chicken soup. Her mouth was dry and it was hard to swallow. She made it through maybe a quarter of the bowl before falling asleep mid sip.

It was morning when she woke next, and the day started off much the same. She nursed her daughter, her mother helped her eat, and she nodded off halfway through breakfast. Only this time, her mother didn't let her sleep for long. She woke as her mother was transferring her back into her bed.

"Oh good, you're awake. We can start your physical therapy. When you're done with that you can take a nap," her mother said.

She shook her head, and glared at her mother, who completely ignored her.

"We'll start with your feet and work your way up. Wiggle your toes for me," her mother signed.

Little Flower continued to glare at her mother. She was tired, dizzy, depressed, and just wanted to sleep. She shook her head no, and tried to look at the sketch book, but her mother didn't understand what she wanted.

"Yes. Wiggle your toes, Little Flower. The sooner you do this, the sooner you can take a nap."

She continued to glare, but sighed, and wiggled her toes a little, which her mother seemed to be happy with, but it frustrated her how hard it was to do even that.

"Good, now can you flex your foot? Try to pull it towards you as much as you can and then see if you can get your toes to the bed."

She tried this with one foot and then the other and was able to move them a little, but not much.

"Okay. That's a good start. Now, can you bend your knee?"

She tried and tried but nothing happened, and she let out a frustrated growl and looked away.

Her mother tapped her on her leg to get her attention. When she didn't look back her mother gently turned her head so that she had to look. "It's okay. You've just lost most of your muscle. It will take time but you will recover. I promise. I'm going to lift your leg now. When I stop and nod my head, I want you to push against my paw as hard as you can, so I can see how much strength you have."

*Isn't it obvious?* Little Flower thought, glaring at her mother. *None, zilch, nada.*

Her mother ignored her glare, and lifted her leg up and bent the knee, bringing it as far up to her chest as it would go. Pain radiated down her body at this motion and she cried out. Her mother stopped the moment she did, and backed off before nodding. Little Flower tried pushing, but she wasn't really sure if she managed it or not. She felt so weak. Her mother lowered her leg several times, nodding, until her leg was back on the bed, and then did the same with the other.

"Okay, I'm going to slide you down so your legs are off the bed now," her mother said before lowering the sides on the bed and shifting her down. "Try straightening your leg."

By this point Little Flower had had enough. She was angry, frustrated, horrified by how little she could do, and she just wanted to go to sleep and forget it all. She shook her head, "no," and looked away. Her mother walked over to the side of the bed where she was looking. She tried to look away again, but her mother stopped her.

"Little Flower, I know this is hard, but you have to try. If you don't try, you won't get better," her mother signed.

She closed her eyes so she couldn't see her mother and shook her head again. "No." *What was the point?* she thought.

She was fully expecting her mother to try and make her open her eyes, but what she did next surprised her, although it shouldn't have. The next thing she knew, she felt her mother's paw behind her leg and the very tips of her claws in warning. *She wouldn't,* Little Flower thought. When she didn't move her leg the claws tightened, such that they were almost breaking her skin, and waited. At first it wasn't bad but the longer she left her leg there, the more it started to hurt. She opened her eyes and glared at her mother. Her mother looked at her as if she was bored and had all day to sit there. Eventually she couldn't take it anymore and shifted her leg away. Her mother's expression changed ever so slightly at her victory, and gave her a second and then applied the pressure again. Little Flower called her every name in the book, not that her mother could hear or understand, but she moved her leg again, sooner this time. Her mother reapplied the pressure, and in a fit of rage, Little Flower grabbed the sheets on the bed below her and tried to kick her mother. She didn't come remotely close to doing so, but her mother's face changed to one of happiness and victory. Her mother made her do the same with the other leg, before pulling her back up onto the bed and letting her have a break.

It was a short break though because her mother made her do the same exercises with her arms as well, and then lifted her into a sitting position. The room spun wildly, and she ended up throwing up all over herself and her mother. Her mother said nothing, just cleaned the both of them up.

Little Flower just wanted to curl up in a ball and sleep, but she couldn't even roll over on her own. She tried. She felt positively horrible, physically and mentally, but her mother had no intention of letting her sleep. She started first by putting something in her mouth. It tasted horrible, but calmed the dizziness some, and then after a few minutes lifted her into a sitting position again. This time slowly, giving her time to adjust to each change in elevation. By the time she'd made it to sitting upright, she was breathing hard and sweating, trying to keep from throwing up again. She could barely even hold her own head up. When her mother relaxed her grip, Little Flower thought the ordeal was finally over, and collapsed gratefully against her mother's arms to lay back down, but instead her mother lifted her back into the sitting position.

She glared at her mother but her mother just flexed her claws back in warning. She tried. She really tried to stay upright when her mother relaxed her grip again, but she couldn't, and ended up falling forward this time. Her mother made her try three more times before Little Flower shook her head no, and tears started streaming down her face at her failure.

Her mother sighed, and *finally* laid her back down, and let her sleep. She was asleep within seconds.

~~~~~

When she woke next, GrandFather was there smiling at her.

"Hey sweetheart. How are you feeling?" he asked.

"Hobble apple," she told him.

"What?" he signed.

"I hobble apple feel," she replied, but he looked just as confused.

"Myra, I think something is wrong. She just said 'I hobble apple feel.'"

"That's not what I said." She frowned as her mother came over with concern on her face, and ran her scanner over her.

"I'm not seeing any changes," Myra said. "Little Flower how many claws am I holding up?"

"Two," she replied.

GrandFather nodded.

"I'm going to sign a bunch of words, I want you to speak those to GrandFather." Her mother went through several words which she repeated, or thought she did, until GrandFather signed something
~~~~~

different. "Okay, say again what you were trying to tell your Grand-Father before."

"I hobble apple feel," she said again.

"This time say it one word at a time."

She huffed, but did as requested. "I...feel...apple booty...hairy bible," she said.

"I think she's trying to say I feel absolutely horrible," GrandFather signed.

"That is what I said," she replied.

"No, what you said was "I feel apple booty hairy bible," he signed back.

"Great, just great, I can't even speak right." Which apparently came out "Just great great, I speak even pencil can't." She followed this up with a long string of curses.

"Well that last bit came out right, although I'm not even sure that's anatomically possible," her grandfather said with a laugh.

"What's wrong with me?" she said, slowly, trying to focus on each word individually.

Apparently this came out correctly because her mother replied. "The speech centers of your brain were affected. This is pretty common with brain injuries, but with speech therapy this should get better too."

"Wonder bull," she muttered. Hope chose that moment to wake, so GrandFather walked over to pick her up out of her crib. "Why limping are you?" she asked.

GrandFather snickered.

She glared at him for laughing at her. "It's not funny!"

"Sorry, you just sounded like Yoda. As for why I'm limping, I had an unfortunate run in with a sand spinner this morning," he signed, after setting Hope on the bed so she could nurse. "I'm fine Myra. Healer Brice took good care of me."

She turned to look at her mother with worry for her GrandFather.

"Sand Spinners are very poisonous, and can be deadly if not treated in the first half hour," her mother explained. Where did you come across a sand spinner? I haven't seen one of those around here in years, and it's the wrong time of year for them anyway."

"In the Arena. Thankfully I was with Henry at the time, and he dragged my sorry butt to the clinic. Brice says I should be as good as new by tomorrow," GrandFather explained.

"Inside? How did they get in there? The Arena was designed specifically to keep them out," Myra replied. "I don't like that at all. Let me know if you start to feel light headed or dizzy."

"I have no idea, but Henry and Nazari are doing a sweep of the grounds, and signs have been posted on all the outside doors, and I had the full lecture from Brice before I left the Trauma Center. If I have so much as an itchy nose, I'll let you know," GrandFather signed back.

"In pain are you?" Little Flower asked.

"No, just stiff," he replied. "Thanks to Henry, I was treated before it got too bad. But, enough about me. I have a surprise for you."

"Oh?" she asked.

"Jordan sent you a care package." He turned and lifted a small cloth wrapped package. "One freshly made chocolate chip cookie!"

"What?!" she asked. "Where chocolate find did they?"

"Not a clue. Not even sure if it is chocolate, but I had one the other day, and it sure tastes like it."

"Physical therapy first, then desert," Myra signed.

Little Flower glared at her mother, and then blew her a raspberry. "First cookie or I won't pickle torture do."

GrandFather snorted.

"What?" she asked, frowning at him and wondering what she'd said.

"Pickle torture?" he asked.

"You know meant what I. Her tell!" she growled at him.

"She says she wants the cookie first or she won't do the pickle torture," GrandFather signed, trying hard to keep a straight face. Myra's tail curled.

"Funny not!" She was getting very angry. Not being able to speak on top of everything else *and* being denied her first cookie in years was too much. "I want my cookie," she glared, focusing hard on every word.

"Fine, half now, half after," her mother signed.

"Prom test?"

GrandFather looked at her oddly.

"Promise?" she tried again.

"I Promise," Myra signed back.

GrandFather broke off exactly half of the cookie and started to feed it to her.

"No. She has to eat it herself," Myra said, stopping GrandFather within smelling distance of the cookie. It smelled devine!

Little Flower swore at her mother.

"I am not repeating that," GrandFather signed with a laugh. "It is interesting that you don't seem to have any problems swearing at us. I wonder if swearing uses a different part of the brain."

GrandFather wrapped the other half of the cookie back up, setting it down on the table next to her bed, picked up Hope, and then placed her half in her hand. It took her nearly ten minutes to get that blasted cookie to her mouth, but it was so worth it when she did. She glared at her mother the entire time, but aside from a curl to her tail, she never once broke the calm of her healer's mask. Little Flower wanted to rip that mask off one piece of fur at a time. The moment she was done eating though, her mother went into full healer mode and began the pickle torture. She was asleep before she could even start eating the second half.

~~~~~

The room was dark when she opened her eyes again. Out the open door, she could see the faint sliver of a moon. A warm breeze blew through the room making the insect screen ripple. She could see Hope sleeping in her crib, knees tucked under her and a thumb stuck in her mouth. Fuzzy, her old stuffed animal along with several others, sat guard around her. She turned her head in the other direction, where a dim light was shining behind her, and found Marsee curled up on the couch by the open window, reading a book. She watched as Marsee's whiskers and tail twitched, as whatever she was reading evoked emotion in her,
~~~~~

and turned a page. When her sister let out a sigh, she decided it might be a good time to interrupt. She had to pee.

"Hey," she called out. Her sister's head snapped up immediately, and she smiled, setting the book aside. She watched as her sister unwound from her curled position, melting off of the seat, and stretched just like a house cat, before padding over to her bed and sitting beside her. With a gentle paw, Marsee caressed the top of her head and side of her face with the back of her furry paw. Little Flower closed her eyes enjoying the feel of the soft fur.

"I'm so happy you're awake! I've missed you so much, and I have so much to tell you!" her sister signed when she opened her eyes again.

"Can it wait? I have to pee," she said, not expecting her sister to understand her, but hoping she'd at least get the book out so she could tell her.

Her sister tilted her head and looked at her. "You have to purple?"

"You can understand me?" Little Flower asked.

"Kind of. Mama said your words were all mixed up. I see what she means. What do you need?"

"How?" she asked instead.

"It's been four months, and I've been spending a lot of time with the cubs and the others at the Guild. I can understand a lot better than I can speak it though. Your words are really hard to say."

"Ahh. Pee," Little Flower said, hoping that the word came out right.

"You need to pee?" Marsee signed for confirmation. "Mama took out your catheter and colostomy bag while you slept. She said it might hurt. If it does, let me know. She left me a large jar of nano cream."

Little Flower nodded, so Marsee carefully picked her up and carried her into the bathroom, and set her on the toilet, but the moment Marsee let go, to give her some privacy, she fell forward as the room spun. Marsee caught her before she could fall off. She swore under her breath, as her sister held her while she went. She gritted through it, as it hurt to go, but then started shaking and crying when her sister had to help her clean herself when she was done.

"Did I hurt you?" Marsee asked, when she was done, wiping a tear away from her face with concern. "I can get the nano cream. I'm sorry if I did. I'll be more careful next time."

"No. This is degrading and I hate being like this, and the last person who touched me there..." she said, swallowing hard as her emotions overcame her. Marsee picked her up and pulled her in for a hug, purring, and then carefully carried her back into the other room, and crawled onto the window seat and held her until she cried herself out.

"Better?" her sister asked with one hand.

She nodded, and Marsee carefully propped her up against several pillows on the other side of the window seat and left, returning with her chenzie fur blanket, and a tray of food. Marsee tucked the blanket in around her to keep her from getting a chill from the night breeze, and poured her a drink. After helping her take a long sip of her favorite star fruit juice, she set it down, and uncovered the tray of food, to reveal her favorite fruits, and the second half of her cookie.

"What would you like first?" her sister asked.

"The cookie," she replied, which caused her sister to laugh.

"Mama said you had to have the other stuff first, but I won't tell if you don't," her sister said with a mischievous glint to her eyes.

"Deal!" she said. Marsee handed her the cookie, and helped her raise her arm to her mouth. Reclinined as she was, she was able to keep her arm there and eat reasonably well on her own. "So what did you want to tell me?" she mumbled through her cookie.

"Oh! I still can't believe it! I was promoted to journeyman level two yesterday at the Hallowed Eve Festival, and you'll *never* guess who my mentor is!"

"It's about time! Congratulations!" she said, and Marsee looked at her funny again. Little Flower sighed and tried again, slower this time. "So who is it?"

"Guess!"

"uhhh...The Senior Guild Master," she guessed.

Marsee looked at her in shock. "How...how did you guess?"

"She's been mentoring you for months hasn't she?" she replied.

"Yeah, but that was all to help you," Marsee signed.

"Pah. You were helping me. She was helping you. Besides, I know her type. The moment she started thwacking you with her tail, I knew you were doomed," Little Flower replied, after finishing the last bite of her cookie. "Hand me some of that star fruit please."

Marsee handed her a few pieces, and groaned. "You aren't wrong. She wants *me* to take over the Guild from her when she retires. Me!" Marsee flopped back in abject horror, and then leaned forward and handed her some more fruit.

"I couldn't think of a better person to take over from her. You'll be amazing after a hundred years of being thwacked in the back of the head. That might be long enough to knock some sense into you."

Marsee mock growled, but then brightened. "Do you really think so?"

"I so know. I...know...so," she said, slower. "Stupid brain," she muttered.

"Mama will fix it. I know it. You're awake and talking. I thought for sure we were going to lose you. Even with the feeding tube in your side, we couldn't keep the weight on you, and none of Mama's treatments were working. A few weeks ago they figured out that the nanos weren't making it past a barrier of some kind in your brain, so Mama and Ammond drilled a bunch of holes in your head, and injected it straight into your brain. That's why your hair is all gone. Anyway, they weren't sure what that would do, so they only targeted the worst areas which included the parts of your brain that controlled your sleep. Once you've recovered some of your weight and strength, I bet they'll do another operation for the other areas since it worked so well. Until then, you'll just have to put up with Mama. Trust me, it's easier to just do what she wants, and get it over with than to argue." Marsee handed her some more fruit.

"So what else has happened?" Little Flower asked, abruptly changing the subject. She didn't want to think about being stuck like this forever.

"Well, let's see. There are at least a dozen new buildings, and there are *so* many new people here. They've run out of places to put everyone and there's a years-long waiting list to visit. Sand Dune has nearly tripled in size as people are moving closer to live here permanently and work with the Hue-mans. We're almost big enough to qualify as an actual town, which they've officially named New Hope. Both the village and the Wilds were transferred to your people and it's officially been designated as a separate planet which your people decided to call "Little Earth".

"GrandFather mentioned that. How do you feel about it? It must be hard having so many strangers in your home."

"You have no idea. It's honestly overwhelming most of the time. I have to wear my hearing aids all the time now. Sometimes even at night when I sleep, but not when I have cub sitting duty. I want to make sure I can hear you and Hope."

"Thank you for taking care of her for me," she said.

"Of course! That's what sisters do. She's awesome now. But for the first few months, all she did was eat, sleep, and poop. She's walking now and even signing a few words. GrandFather says she's starting to say a few of your words too but he's not sure if they are intentional yet or just nonsense sounds. She growls at us but nothing really makes sense yet."

"She can hear you?" Little Flower asked.

"Yup, Ammond tested her when she started responding to her name in Saber. Apparently she and the other babies are all starting to develop the ability to hear us, to some extent, but Hope's been cared for by Sabers pretty much exclusively, except for when GrandFather takes a shift, so her hearing range appears to be the best so far. Ammond thinks she won't have any problem hearing any of us. And get this, Mama can hear Hope!"

"Really?" she asked. "How?"

"Well apparently she's got almost as good of a hearing range as me, but somehow her brain learned to filter it out rather than annoying the fur off of her like it does me. Once she started paying attention to it, she could suddenly start hearing it. I think it helped that she knew there was supposed to be a sound. Papa's heard her a few times recently too, although I don't think he's had his hearing tested. I think Hope is learning to lower her voice."

By that point the star fruit was all gone, so Marsee handed her a piece of yellow fang, one of Little Flower's other favorites.

"Let's see, what else? I took a million pictures and videos of Hope so you can see everything you missed when you're up to it. I've translated another half dozen books while you slept, and we bound up the pictures you drew of the Earth animals, and GrandFather added facts and other fun stuff. Ellie published it and it's on the top downloads list!"

"Really?" Little Flower asked, surprised.

"Really." Marsee leapt off the window seat and ran across the room to grab the book to show her.

She just stared at it. Rather than being excited about it though, she suddenly felt like she was going to cry, wondering if she'd ever be able to draw again.

Marsee picked up her mood and her whiskers and ears drooped, but set the book down and kept talking. "GrandFather went back to healing although he's focusing on healing people now, instead of animals. Nazari's his mentor but GrandFather is mentoring Nazari too on all the earth animals. GrandFather's friend, Henry Curtis, comes over all the time for evening meals now, and the men are all.."

"Woah woah woah. Hold up. GrandFather has a friend? Like just a regular friend or a friend friend?" Little Flower asked, shocked out of her grief by Marsee's comments.

"I'm not sure I understand what you mean," Marsee said.

"Is GrandFather interested in Henry as a partner or mate?" she clarified.

"Ooooohhh. I don't know. Friends I guess," but then she paused and thought. "Then again..."

"What do you know? Tell me!" she insisted. This was juicy gossip and GrandFather hadn't mentioned anything about Henry outside of Henry carrying his sorry butt to the healers when the sand spinner stung him.

"Well, I don't know if it means anything, but GrandFather smells different when Henry is over. I didn't really notice before."

"Like he's wearing a scent? To smell better?" Little Flower asked.

"No, it's his own scent. It's nice though. Then again, you all smell nice, unless you have a poop sack full of poop that is." Marsee's nose crinkled. "Speaking of which, Hope needs changing." Marsee walked over and changed Hope so quickly that Hope never even woke up.

"That was impressive!" Little Flower exclaimed.

"What?" Marsee asked.

"You didn't wake Hope when you changed her," she explained.

Marsee just shrugged. "She sleeps pretty soundly these days. I'm guessing that makes up for the madness the rest of the time. She's surprisingly fast on those little legs of hers. Mama doesn't like using the poop sacks though because they're so small. Oh that reminds me, you should have seen it. Hope peed on Ellie the other day, and I almost got demoted because of it! Mama nearly fell out of her chair laughing."

Little Flower chuckled and then yawned.

"Are you ready to go back to bed?" Marsee asked.

"Can I sleep here with you instead? I hate being on my back."

"Sure." Marsee shrugged, picked up the dishes and the book, and then curled up and helped her into a comfortable position and began purring. Marsee picked up her book and kept reading, but Little Flower was asleep in seconds, securely wrapped in her sister's warm and loving embrace.

# CHAPTER 38

# Marsee: Wild Doba

Marsee purred with happiness to have her sister back and laid there snuggling with her and reading until Hope woke and started fussing. She carefully carried her sister back over to the bed, trying not to wake her, and then checked on Hope.

"Hey there, little kitten. Did you have a bad dream?" Marsee asked, picking Hope up and purring. Hope snuggled into her fur, thumb still stuck in her mouth. She walked over to the rocking chair and began slowly rocking. Hope eventually fell back to sleep, but Marsee didn't stop rocking, enjoying this quiet moment.

She was still rocking when her father appeared nearly an hour later. "Hey, Papa. How did your meeting go?" she asked quietly.

"Long, but we're making progress," he replied, as he walked over to check on Little Flower. "How is she?"

"Okay I guess. She woke and had supper. We spoke for a while before she fell back to sleep, after about half an hour or so. Her words are all mixed up, but I can understand her, most of the time. She didn't seem to have any problems understanding me though. She can't sit up on her own, and was really embarrassed to have me hold her while she went to the waste room, and cried when I cleaned her afterwards. I thought I'd hurt her, but she said it was because it was the first time anyone had touched her there since her rape. I'm not sure how to help her there, but I have some ideas."

He sighed and gently ran a paw over her sister's nearly bald head. After a few moments though, he left her sister's side and came over to sit in front of her. "I came to talk to you actually," he said.

"Me? Why?" Marsee asked, although she guessed as his mask was on tightly. She hugged Hope tighter. Deep inside she felt her instinct growl protectively.

"Now that Little Flower is awake and able to communicate her desires for Hope, I need to remove you as Hope's primary guardian."

Marsee sighed. "I figured as much. I'll still help care for her though. It's going to be a long time before she's going to be able to do that on her own. She couldn't even lift her arm to eat."

He smiled at her for understanding, but there was worry in his eyes too. "She's lucky to have a sister as caring as you are," he said, but after a moment his expression changed to one of humor. "So, now that you've had a chance to recover from yesterday's little surprise, how are you doing with being the *future* Senior Guild Master."

Marsee groaned. "I'm about this close to running off and finding a cave in the Wilds to live in, but somehow I'm guessing Ellie would just track me down and drag me back by my scruff if I did."

He chuckled. "No doubt. She is one of the few people besides your sister that can take on the Senior Council. I'm pretty sure she can handle you, even at your grumpiest. Good luck with that."

"Thanks, I think," she replied, rolling her eyes.

"I was honestly very impressed you didn't run into the wilds yesterday," he said, teasing.

"That's just because my legs wouldn't work," she muttered, to his laughter. "I haven't even dared to look at the news or my messages yet though. How bad is it?" He didn't answer right away which made her sag. "That bad?"

"Honestly, not as bad as I was expecting. She's been mentoring you for a while, even if it hasn't been official. Your arrival in Council City with her was noticed before, and most people were already trying to figure out if she was going to mentor you, since she signed you up for a number of master level classes, or if she was just trying to figure out who the best mentor for you would be. I did speak to a Flyer by the name of Yellow Tail last night, who was very disappointed not to get the position as your mentor, although he said he looked forward to working with you in the future."

Marsee groaned and slid further down in her seat.

Her father looked at her in confusion. "What's that reaction for? Did you want him to be your mentor?"

"Moons no. I'll take Ellie's tail over his horrible puns any day. I groaned because he's my Advanced Flyer language instructor and he's also apparently the reason Uncle Marcus called Wind Rider a smelly fish. The first day I showed up to class with him, he dedicated the class to me and spent the entirety going over words I got wrong in my language dictionary. He's going to be insufferable for weeks now. I might have to talk to Ellie about changing my courses."

He laughed. "Well in that case, you might also want to verify everything he's teaching you, if he managed to pull one over on Marcus."

"Oh trust me, I already am," she replied, to his further laughter, and then squinted her eyes at him. "What aren't you telling me?"

He shrugged. "There's nothing negative towards you, at least not that I've seen, but there are people who are upset by her actions. Some seem to think it gives our family more power than we had before, but your promotion doesn't really change anything. We certainly wouldn't expect any sort of favors from Ellie just because she's your mentor. If anything, she's likely to be far more careful with anything we request, to avoid any semblance of bias, as are we. Plus, you'll still need to be voted into that position and ratified by whatever Senior Council exists at that time, and neither Marcus or I will likely be on the Council when that happens. Marcus has already stated he plans to step down at the end of his term, and I doubt I'll be re-elected once the rest of the males have the vote. As it is, by the rules of their charter I won't even be able to run, since they have limits on the number of terms someone can be on the Council. They'll have to write my name in."

Marsee sighed. "I wondered if people would be upset by that, especially if they wanted the position for themselves."

"If anyone wants the position, they haven't been forthcoming about it. She's run unchallenged for the last several elections, and the last vote was only a few months ago. If they want that position, they'd better start working hard for it, as I imagine Ellie's preferences will weigh heavily on any future vote, and I've not seen Ellie fail at anything she's put her mind to," he replied.

"Well there was that one rocking chair," Marsee replied with a grin.

"Watch it cub, I can still demote you."

Marsee looked over to the doorway to see Ellie glowering at her, arms crossed, and tail thwacking. "Although it's pretty clear you've learned from your mistakes," Marsee added quickly.

Ellie raised a brow and then broke with a grin. "Better. Although, if your sister hadn't requested one, it probably would have been listed as one of my failures, as I never tried again. It took months for my tail to stop hurting."

"So, what brings you here?" Marsee asked, changing the subject, although her own tail curled in amusement.

"Well, since someone apparently wants to keep me locked in council meetings until the middle of the night, *and* leave me with the mess to clean up afterwards," Ellie glared at her father, tail lashing again. "This is the only time I have to thwack my new protege."

"And that's my cue to say goodnight," her father said, and bolted out of the room.

Ellie chuckled at his sudden exit, and turned back to face her with an assessing stare, but didn't say anything for several long moments.

"What have I done now?" Marsee asked.

"Nothing yet, but I intend to change that," Ellie replied.

"Huh?" Marsee asked, thoroughly confused.

"I'm well aware of what courses you've taken over the years to know what you *should* know, the question is what don't you know," Ellie mused.

Marsee raised a brow not even sure how to respond to that. *How would one even define that?* she wondered.

"We'll definitely have to add several tech courses. As Senior Guild Master you'll have to sign off on any senior level code changes before they can be deployed, and we'll need to start your training with the staffers guild, since you've completely avoided that major discipline," Ellie continued without waiting for a response.

Marsee groaned. She had absolutely no interest in any of the staffer disciplines.

Ellie ignored her and kept going. "Math and statistics as well, at a minimum. Your primary school grades were abysmal there, but you'll need to at least be able to understand the reports Nardal creates for the Council. I'd like to get you up to journeyman in each of the major guilds, with at least an apprentice level two rating in all of the major disciplines. The better you understand the requirements of each of the crafts, the better you'll be able to advocate for them. We'll also need to make sure you have a basic understanding of each of the various species, culture, history, and customs, so that you don't make a complete fool of yourself. I'll talk to Marcus about having you audit some of the Council classes in those areas."

As Ellie continued to list off all of the various areas she wanted her to study, Marsee slid lower and lower in the chair. "So just when am I going to be able to do all of the other stuff you want me to do?" Marsee finally asked. "You know, like learning to build rocking chairs?"

Ellie chuckled. "Don't worry. We're not going to do it all at once. This will take decades, and you'll likely be able to breeze through most of the apprentice level training. The big question is where to start. I'm thinking we'll have you finish your current set of classes, since the semester is almost over, and have you start taking some assessments to see where you actually place in the other guilds."

Ellie pulled off her tablet, and a few moments later, Marsee's started dinging. "Once you've worked through these, we'll review and decide which areas you need the most work in first, and start adding those to whatever other courses you want to take."

Marsee sighed but nodded. She'd agreed to this, even if she hadn't known what was involved, and well, now that she wasn't Hope's primary guardian anymore, she would have more time. Marsee gave Hope a careful squeeze, and sighed again, this time with sadness.

Ellie squinted at her. "What's going on in that furry little brain of yours?"

Marsee looked away. "I guess, I'm just all over the place with my emotions right now, and I'm feeling a little overwhelmed," she finally admitted.

Ellie sat down in front of her, shifting from grumpy mentor to compassionate friend. "I wouldn't expect otherwise. You're handling it well though. I fully expected you to run off the stage and go hide under a rock somewhere."

"Trust me I'm considering it," Marsee replied, and then looked over at her sister with another sigh. "Papa just came to let me know he removed me as Hope's guardian, now that Little Flower is awake, and we talked a little about how people are reacting to my promotion."

"Ahh," Ellie replied.

"I don't even know how to process my thoughts around Little Flower. We all thought she was dying, and then she woke up, but Hope is physically more capable than she is right now, even if she still seems to be in there. I'm thrilled she's awake, but I'm also sad I'm losing Hope. Is that wrong of me?"

"No, of course not. You've been carrying for Hope from day one, but it's not like she's going to kick you out. You're still Hope's Auntie, and always will be, and that's actually a much better place to be in. You get to be the fun one now. Of course, you could always talk to her about partnership too."

Marsee looked over at her sister again and shook her head with a sigh. "I'd like that, but..."

"But?" Ellie asked kindly.

"Mama told me that Little Flower reacted poorly to finding out about her injuries, and said she wanted to die, and she had a really hard time tonight. I'm worried that if I even suggested partnership, she would just give me Hope, and then stop fighting to get better. GrandFather says Hope is old enough to be weaned, and we were starting the process before Little Flower woke up, but now, Mama says we should focus on how much Hope needs her mother to survive, to give her a reason to live and fight."

Ellie looked over at her sleeping sister and sighed. "I'm not sure how I would do in her condition, to be healthy one moment and wake up an invalid. The best thing you could do, is just be her friend and sister, and treat her as if she were no different than before."

"That's what Mama said. I'm still worried about her though," Marsee replied.

Ellie nodded. "I'd be more concerned if you weren't. Now, as far as fallout from your promotion, don't even waste a second worrying about it. Their opinions don't matter, and if anyone gives you a hard time about it, send them to me and I'll knock some sense into them. As far as what we focus on with you, we'll work around your schedule. You tell me what you can handle and what interests you, and we'll make sure that's the primary focus of your studies."

Marsee nodded. "Do you think maybe I could skip Master Yellow Tail's class for a few centuries? Papa says he's mad he didn't get to be my mentor."

Ellie laughed. "Oh child, you're not the one that has to worry about him. He'll probably tease you a little, but if you start by telling him how honored you were by finding out he'd offered, he'll leave you alone, mostly. But if you join in on a prank with him, I will demote you, permanently. Poof."

Marsee laughed and looked up at the ceiling, considering what she could do as a prank, and Ellie thwapped her hard with her tail. Marsee laughed, fully expecting that response. Ellie glared at her for a moment longer, before chuckling. "Well as much as I would love to stay here and keep thwacking you with my tail, your father *has* left me with a mess that I need to clean up before tomorrow's meeting. Have a good night, Marsee."

"You too," Marsee replied, and watched Ellie leave. Once she was sure Ellie was out of hearing distance, Marsee sighed and kept rocking as she tried to come to grips with her mixed emotions, and contain the growing panic she was feeling. Most of it was her own insecurities, but some, her instinct's unhappiness with her father.

*We knew this would happen if Little Flower woke up. I'd rather have Little Flower back and be Hope's Auntie, than Hope's mother without Little Flower.*

It grumbled but settled, mostly.

Half an hour later, GrandFather appeared for his shift. Her grumbling instinct flared with protectiveness for Hope, and she had a hard time handing the cub over to him. Even though her father had already changed the guardianship, somehow it felt like it would be final the moment she walked out the door. She forced herself to hand over Hope to GrandFather and bolted out the door, squashing her instinct and feelings down hard.

She climbed the ramp and paced out on her balcony for a while, trying to settle her growing anxiety. The moons were now all out and nearly full, and for all the people in New Hope for the meeting, it was surprisingly quiet, only a few people were out, but she was far too restless to sleep. When the feeling didn't calm, she decided she needed to go for a run. She knew it was dangerous to go out this late at night, as that was when the larger predators came out, but she also knew she wouldn't sleep if she didn't do something, and somehow she knew drawing wouldn't help this time, not when so much of her anxiety was about her future in the Guild.

She padded down the ramp and saw her father's light on as he worked. Her mother was curled up on her bed reading. Marsee frowned, considered, decided she needed to find a way to calm her instinct's feelings about her father too, and then knocked on the door. He answered immediately. "What is it, Kitten?"

"I need to go for a run. Will you come with me?"

Her mother looked up from the bed with a frown. "Are you having issues with your instinct?"

"Not yet. I'm...anxious and out of sorts," she finally decided. "Too much has happened and I need to run before it becomes an issue, and I don't want to go out alone."

Her father nodded with understanding. "Then that's what we'll do."

Her mother frowned with worry, but said nothing as he followed her outside. They walked in silence as they made their way past dozens of ships and shuttles surrounding the compound. Then when they were finally out of sight, she took a deep breath, and let her instinct out. She looked over at her father to let him know it was on. To her surprise, he said nothing, just nodded. A moment later she noticed his eyes dilate and reflect with moonlight as he turned his own instinct on.

Surprised, but pleased, she grinned, and without another word took off, digging deep with everything she had. At first her instinct was worried with the remembered fight, but eventually settled when nothing happened. He kept pace with her, matching her stride for stride. They didn't stop until she stumbled from exhaustion and sat down on the top of a distant hill she'd never seen before, panting hard.

Lit up by the moonlight, the world around them glistened in strange colors. A small herd of wild doba grazed in the valley below, near a small bandala tree. She sniffed deeply but there was no urge to hunt. Her instinct was content with the run they'd just had, and was far more interested in seeing if there were any chocolate chip cookies left than hunting down one of the fast moving doba. She drooled at the memory and decided she'd grab one and something to drink when they returned. In the distance she could smell water dripping from the bandala tree and realized she was thirsty.

She was about to suggest making her way down for a drink when her father spoke first. "How are you doing?"

"Better, thanks. You?" He didn't respond right away and she looked over at him and noticed his instinct was still on. "Papa, are you okay?"

He shrugged. "I don't really know. I've never done this before."

"Done what?" she asked, confused.

"Run for the sake of running or just sit still with my instinct on. My hunt was so long ago it's kind of hard to remember. Mostly, I just remember being horrified by my desire to kill, and the fear of being hunted afterwards. Since that first hunt, I've always feared my instinct, feared a loss of control, even more after I nearly killed someone, and have done everything I could to suppress it. I could never see the beauty in it."

"But you can now?" she asked.

He nodded. "I didn't even know it was a possibility until I saw your drawings. I've never seen the world like I am tonight. I don't even have the words to describe it." He turned to look at her. "But none of it compares to the beauty I see when I look at you. There's a glow around you, blue, vibrant, like the color of joy on a Water Sprite."

She grinned. "I've wondered. I can't see it in a mirror for some reason. You look green to me, with sparkles of gold. It matches your eyes. Mama's bright gold and feels like a warm sunbeam. Hope and Little Flower are the most beautiful shade of indigo I've ever seen before, or were, Hope's color is changing. It has hints of pink in it now, and Little Flower's has been tinged with gray since she woke up. I don't know what that means, but the gray worries me."

He frowned with his own worry, and then his expression shifted to curiosity. "What about Marcus?"

"He's a rich brown, almost the same as my favorite stain, but with speckles of dark green and blue, and smells like old books."

Her father snorted with laughter. "It would."

They sat there again in silence as they each examined the world around them. After a few minutes though, she stood, stretched, and walked over to him, rubbing her face against his like she had that day in the garden with Little Flower. He gasped and pulled away, sniffing hard, and frowning.

"What is it?" she asked, surprised by his reaction, and turned thinking there was something behind her.

His scent radiated confusion and embarrassment, which further confused her. "The last time I felt that way was when your mother was in heat," he finally admitted, "but I can tell you're not, so I don't know why I'm reacting that way. I have the urge to rub all over you, and I'm sorry. I promise I won't."

Marsee shrugged. "There's nothing to be sorry about. I felt the same way with Little Flower that night in the garden. It was like...I needed to mark her as someone trusted. My instinct doesn't trust you, but I want it to. I'm tired of the grumbles every time you come around. I thought maybe this might help."

He reached over and caressed the side of her face and she instantly started purring. He dropped his arm and turned away, smelling of confusion and worry. She sighed, and sat down beside him, rubbing against him as she did. He stiffened, so she stopped and instead, just wrapped her tail around him, and leaned in. He sighed and eventually wrapped an arm around her and hugged her back. They sat there for some time in silence, each lost in their own thoughts. It wasn't quite right, but she didn't push it. Still, it seemed to help some, and she gradually felt her instinct settle. It still didn't fully trust him, but it was respecting her wishes.

"Come on, we should head back before your mother gets worried and calls the guards to hunt us down," he said eventually.

She chuckled, nodded, stretched again as she stood, feeling her back and tail snap and pop with the motion, and turned around. "Too late," she whispered.

Her father spun around to face where she was looking, tense with fear. Kendra was sitting some distance from them, watching. The Senior Honor Guard stood and padded slowly towards them on all fours. Everything about the Senior Honor Guard radiated power and authority. She had the authority to kill if she felt there was just cause, without trial.

Realizing her instinct was still on, Marsee quickly flicked it off and blinked in the sudden darkness. "Am I in trouble?"

Kendra said nothing, just kept walking until she was in front of them, close enough to examine them in the moonlight. She first examined Marsee, tilting her head up to stare into her eyes, before turning to her father and examining him. "Are you having any issues?"

"No, ma'am," he replied. Marsee shook her head no too.

Kendra's attention shifted to behind them, and she snorted with amusement, before turning her attention back to Marsee. "No, child. You're not in trouble. If the two of you can have your instinct on for all that time, and sit here with a herd of doba in front of you without having issues, I don't think I need to worry about you. Either of you."

She heard her father sigh with relief, but before anyone could say anything in response, the doba suddenly squealed with alarm. She turned to look, instantly on alert as they started running straight towards them.

Kendra immediately shoved Marsee behind her, placing herself between them and the herd. The lead buck saw them, squealed another alarm, and swerved away from them.

"Come on, I don't want to wait around for whatever spooked them. Run!" Kendra shoved her hard in the direction of New Hope.

Marsee turned and bolted, but stumbled almost immediately in the dark.

Kendra caught her before she could fall. "Turn your instinct on until we get back."

Marsee didn't waste a second thought, just did as ordered, and surged forward. She dug deep and did her best to keep up, as Kendra pushed the pace hard, while her instinct reveled at the challenge and permission to be free. Even with its help, she was panting hard and dragging her tail by the time they made it safely back to the tower. Kendra examined them both again, once they were inside, to make sure their instincts were off, and bid them a good night.

She turned towards the tower and saw her mother watching from their doorway, a look of astonishment and relief on her face. Marsee grinned at her, and looked up at her father. "Thank you."

"Any time, Kitten." He caressed the side of her face again, before crushing her in a hug. She purred with happiness and just let herself be held. Eventually he pulled away and looked at her closely. "Any issues?"

She shook her head. "No, but I am going to hunt down a cookie or three and something to drink, assuming I can make it to the kitchen. For some reason, my legs are all wobbly and I'm thirsty."

He chuckled. "I'm not surprised. I had a hard time keeping up with Kendra. I'm impressed you managed."

They walked slowly to the kitchen, finding it empty. Her father flicked on the lights and made his way back to the cooler to grab something to drink, while she sniffed out the cookies and grabbed a large plateful. Hunt successful, she made her way out to the cafeteria where her father was waiting with the drinks at the nearest table.

She collapsed into a chair with a groan as her father poured out a glass of star fruit juice. "Thanks," she said as she took the proffered glass and downed it in a single gulp.

He chuckled and filled it back up as she reached for a cookie and bit in with a groan. "Best hunt ever," she mumbled through the cookie.

He grinned at her. "That it is, and in case you're wondering. Chocolate chip cookies taste far better than wild doba."

She raised a brow and grabbed another cookie. "Well I'm just glad they don't have legs, because I'm far too tired to chase them down."

Laughing he grabbed another cookie for himself. "You and me both, Kitten."

After their successful raid of the kitchen, she hugged her father goodnight and dragged herself back up to her room. Feeling far calmer than before, she climbed into her bed and curled around a pillow, but as exhausted as she was, she couldn't fall asleep.

After an hour of tossing and turning, she gave up and padded her way down to her sister's room and sent GrandFather home. Then climbing into her sister's bed, she wrapped herself protectively around Little Flower and Hope. Little Flower woke briefly with the motion, but just smiled back up at her, and snuggled into her warm fur.

With a happy sigh and her family safe in her arms where they belonged, Marsee finally fell asleep with dreams of running through the Wilds under the light of the three moons, hunting wild doba with her father, doba that looked and smelled like chocolate chip cookies.

Sometime in the early morning, her dreams changed. Suddenly they were the ones being hunted. She jerked awake, panting hard from the fear of her night terror, her instinct fully on and alert. Her hackles were raised, and she had the intense feeling of being watched.

She listened hard but there was nothing but the normal sounds of New Hope in the early morning. Turning her instinct off and chalking it up to nerves from her dream and whatever had scared the doba, she wrapped herself protectively around her family again, but it was a long time before she finally fell back to sleep.

~~~~~

Kendra sat, perched lightly on the wall of the inner garden, hidden in the shadows and leaves of the bandala tree, watching Marsee sleep. She wasn't worried about Marsee, not after how well she'd handled her stress and anxiety that evening, but for her.

She'd been on high alert the moment the command relay had been compromised. While it could have just been an accident, she didn't think so. Her guards had been busy dealing with one wild animal or crawly since, and for them to all appear right when the Full Council and every guild senior was in attendance had to be more than a coincidence. She just didn't know who was behind it.

Nearly half the Council was on edge, far more than she'd ever seen them before, and it had only gotten worse since Marsee's promotion. *What was Ellie thinking?! The whole point of this holiday and emergency council was to try to reduce tensions, and she goes and exacerbates them by handing over her power and authority to Chenzira's daughter! Taking her as her protege sure, she's been mentoring the child for months, but saying she wants Marsee to take over for her? She might as well have put a target on the child's head.*

She'd immediately put a watch on Marsee and the tower as a precaution, but had ended up watching the tower herself, unable to sleep, and she was very glad she had. If her nose was right about what or rather who had been hunting the doba, and it usually was, they'd been very lucky tonight. That too could have been a coincidence, as many of the Ice Giants still hunted for their food, and it was a cool enough night for them to go out, but there had been far too many coincidences in one day for her liking.
~~~~~

Kendra froze as Marsee woke with a snort, twanging hard, instantly on alert and focusing hard out her door. She followed Marsee's gaze towards the visitor's apartments, and frowned.

There floating in his window, looking back at the tower, was none other than Senior Councilor Clear Seas.

# CHAPTER 39

# Damon: Snapper Fish

Damon, along with the rest of his group of friends spent most of the Halloween Festival canvasing the various guests, trying to convince them to go along with changes Chenzira was planning to propose at the council meeting, designed to allow them to join before earning their adulthood. Most took the time to listen to him, but he had no idea how any of them would vote. The Guild Masters he spoke to were fairly against it though, stating the same arguments Jer had mentioned that first day. A few of the councilors seemed interested though. He even tried asking the Commander of the Ship's Guild directly, hoping to impress him with the knowledge that he'd learned on his own, but he never managed more than a single sentence explaining who he was, before the Commander told him that he would be more than welcome once he'd earned his adulthood, but not until then, and turned and walked away.

He'd given up after that and stormed off to find a place to sulk.

"That went well," Paul said, sitting down next to him. "I saw your conversation with the Commander."

Damon snorted. "At this point, we'll have better luck trying to convince someone to mentor us, like Henry did."

Paul rolled his eyes. "The only reason Henry got that is because he's been hanging out with GrandFather, and there's no way in the universe GrandFather would hang out with you."

Damon snorted again. "I haven't been able to get close enough to even talk to him in months. He sees me and disappears. Well, at least some of the Councilors seemed interested. Maybe that will be enough."

"I doubt it. They're far too good at hiding what they're really thinking, and were probably just being polite. King Pussycat barely twitches a whisker most days. He says he's trying, but we've seen almost nothing in the way of progress. He's just humoring us. It's the last thing they have on the docket, and more than likely it'll get bumped to the next meeting, and the next, and the next. Mark my words," Paul said.

Damon rolled his eyes. He fully expected the same. He'd done his best to ignore the glares of the others, with the guild classes he'd taken, at Chenzira's suggestion, but it hadn't helped. Even though he'd focused hard to try and impress his instructors, he hadn't even been promoted to apprentice level two, and he was far better than several of the others, in his opinion anyway.

"Well, come on. A few of the guys in the agricultural guild have been...running scientific experiments, and they have something for us to try in the green house," Paul said.

Damon grinned. "Now, I was never very good at science back on Earth, but I'm willing to take another stab at learning."

He followed Paul to the back of one of the greenhouses, where others were slowly gathering, and he was handed a glass. He sniffed cautiously, shrugged, downed it in a single gulp, and gasped. "Good lord! Are you trying to kill me?" he asked when he could breathe again.

Everyone laughed.

"You should have tried the first batch. I'm pretty sure we could have used it to strip paint," Danny said.

"Strip paint? Nah that stuff would have eaten through metal," Paul replied.

Damon chuckled and held his glass out for a refill, although he nursed this one. By the time he staggered back to his room, he was thoroughly drunk, and for the first time since he'd arrived on this inferno of a planet, he didn't cry himself to sleep. Although that was mostly because he had no recollection of even making it back to his bed.

When his alarm went off the next morning he was sure someone was drilling holes in his head, but he had work to do. The last thing he needed was to make the visiting dignitaries think he wasn't up to hard work. Still, he stopped in the trauma center for some pain meds that worked far better than anything he'd ever had before. He was rather amused at the reaction from the healer who scanned him. She looked thoroughly perplexed. *I wonder if the fuzz-balls have alcohol or anything similar,* he thought. Based on her size though, she was young, and by her badge, only a journeyman. She eventually just shrugged, and left to get him something for his headache.

Headache treated, he made his way to the utility closet and activated the cleaning drones before making his way out into the courtyard, which was a mess. He sighed and began work emptying the recyclers, and to his utter annoyance, he didn't see a single person the entire time he worked.

Several days passed as the Council deliberated. He, like most of the men attended, although they weren't allowed to speak, and were delegated to a visitors section that was blocked off behind some sort of shield that prevented the rest of the Council from even hearing them talk. To absolutely no one's surprise though, Jeran ended the meeting before deliberating on the change to adulthood status. Damon got twice as drunk that night, and for the first time since arriving in New Hope, he called out sick. No one, not even his supervisor, called to check on him.

He was sprawled on his couch, trying to decide if he was just going to drink himself into oblivion, as he couldn't see any other way out of this hell hole, when his tablet dinged. Surprised, as almost no one called or texted him, he opened it with curiosity.

"It seems you were right. Chenzira did not bring your motion forward, although that doesn't surprise me. I'd like to hear more about what they've been doing to you, and see if there isn't some way I could help." The message was in Saber, which he could easily read now, but he double checked with the translation to be sure.

Damon sat up. *This is new.*

"Why doesn't that surprise you?" he texted back.

"Because, to allow the rest of your species to vote would take power away from him. None of you are happy with him, and there'd be enough of you to vote him out. Plus, he and Surellis have a choke hold on the Consortium, and now they have somehow convinced the Senior Guild Master to make their brat the heir to her domain. If you think they're going to give up power easily, you're sadly mistaken."

Damon sat back, stunned. He'd never gotten the impression that Jeran was trying to take power. He'd always had the sense that they were trapped behind the laws of the Consortium. He'd watched all of the sentience trial, twice. Once on his own, and again in the required classes he'd had to take on the law and government. Everything he'd been taught said they'd gone into the trial expecting to die. Certainly Myra had come close.

"What makes you think they're trying to take power? Nothing I've seen has shown that," he replied. "No one else even wanted to run against Surellis."

"Because they couldn't. After what Chenzira's daughter had accused the entire council of, if any of them had gone forward stating they wanted the role, they'd have been kicked out immediately. Surellis is shrewd. By turning down the nomination he was able to hide his power grab. Chenzira too. After everything Little Flower said about your people, she couldn't take power either, and who else was there for her to pick but Chenzira? It was a fairly convincing act. Even had me fooled for a bit. Chenzira and Surellis both knew they'd never go through with convicting the Council. By offering himself up as a sacrifice, he made everyone believe he and his brother were honorable and untouchable. I wonder how long they worked on Little Flower's speech. Anyway, regardless of their motives, they have power now, and it's unlikely they'll do anything to risk it."

Damon read the message several times, and then clicked on the profile of the person sending it, and blinked in surprise as it indicated the Water Sprite named Snapper Fish was dead.

"Who are you?" he asked.

"It doesn't matter," Snapper Fish replied. "Let's just say, I'm trying to keep both of us safe. If Chenzira knew who I was, or that I was talking with you, we would both be in danger. Now, tell me, what has Chenzira been doing to you?"

Damon raised a brow and didn't answer for a long time, but then decided to take a chance and sent Snapper Fish his list of grievances. As he wrote, he thought about everything that Jeran and his family had done in this new light, and his anger deepened.

"I had no idea it was this bad," Snapper Fish replied afterwards. "Let me give it some thought."

A few moments after he'd read the message, their conversation disappeared. Damon raised a brow at that and tossed his tablet down. After pouring another drink, he raised the glass to Snapper Fish. "Here's hoping you have better luck."

# CHAPTER 40

# Ellie: Behind Schedule

Nearly two months had passed since the Hallowed Eve festival. Ellie had temporarily moved her primary office to New Hope to better work with Marsee, and now sat in her new office growling at the latest message from Agate.

"I'll come back later."

Ellie looked up to see Marsee, paw poised to knock on the door sill. "Come in. I'm not growling at you. I just received a message from Agate. The new shipyard in the East Sea District is behind schedule *again*, and this time nearly a dozen builders have quit."

"Why?" Marsee asked.

Ellie snorted in disgust. "The Master Builder says they're saying the build is haunted. Tools keep going missing and they keep hearing the sounds of screams, but they can't find anyone or anything to explain it, or so he says."

Marsee raised a brow. "Haunted?"

Ellie shrugged. "So he says. The Sprites are incredibly superstitious, and not everyone has been happy about the new shipyard. They'd rather keep building them on the Ice Planet, even though that's far more expensive. My guess is that some protester has hidden a speaker somewhere, and is snagging tools to make it appear haunted."

"Protesters?" Marsee asked. "I thought the protests had calmed down after the Hallowed Eve celebration. That's what Papa said anyway."

"They have for the most part," Ellie replied with a shrug. "But, it's not uncommon for people to protest new construction. Especially something like this, which is incredibly large and expensive, even though it will end up being far more profitable for their community in the long run. This is one of the most ambitious projects we've taken up on the Water World, outside of the Habitat and landing platforms. It's the first shipyard capable of building the larger transport ships, and it's challenging, as everything needs to be modified to work underwater, and with the Sprites biology in mind. For all that some of our best tech comes from there, they're not a big fan of technology in general, or anything that requires a significant amount of mining, which this will, to support. If it can be done by hand, that's how they'll do it. They loathe factories and prefer everything to be handmade. Their work is exceptional, assuming I can get them to join the Guild," she muttered. "Most people have provisional accounts, like your sister, although that's slowly been changing over the past few decades."

"Why is that?" Marsee asked.

"It has to do with their feudal system. People learn their skills and crafts from their parents or close relatives, and craft secrets are highly guarded, much like it was here between the various disciplines before I restructured the Guild, only at the micro level. Joining the Guild means sharing that information. Most of our members there are fairly young because of it, people who don't want to do what their parents did. They are starting to come around, but it's taken decades to build out and convince older masters to join, and that has required some rather deft political maneuvering. Most people gain a mentor when they join or shortly after, if they're not sure what they want to do, rather than at journeyman level two, like what usually happens on all the other planets, and they stick to one fairly narrow craft, but they learn quickly, and are phenomenal at what they do, so I can't really complain."

"So what do you intend to do about the shipyard?" Marsee asked, curiously.

"I'm not sure. Agate wants me to come for a visit. I haven't been there since before the Cataclysm, so it's overdue for sure. I usually only go for council meetings, or when I have to be there for physical upgrades to their server hardware."

Marsee frowned. "Why do you have to go there for the upgrades? Don't you have techs there that can do that?"

"You'd think, but for some strange reason I've never been able to get out of Clear Seas, the Council Servers are in a dry room in the depths of their archives. I'm guessing it's because we didn't have waterproof servers at the time they were first installed. I've tried for decades to get Clear Seas to let me move them, but he's denied it on several occasions, and based on where they are, I or one of the other land based Seniors has to escort them in. The carts don't even fit." Ellie snorted and shook her head. "The last time I asked, he said he liked having an excuse for me to come visit regularly."

Marsee grinned. "Well, sounds like a visit is in order. Do they need any upgrades?"

"Not that I'm aware of, but you're probably right. The Council meeting is coming up soon anyway. Ready for a trip? We'll probably be gone for several weeks."

"Me?" Marsee asked.

"No, I was asking Nardal," Ellie snorted, rolling her eyes. "Of course you."

"I don't know. I've never been off-world. Don't get me wrong, I want to, but I'm not sure about being gone for weeks yet. I need to talk with my parents and Little Flower first. She's better but still needs a lot of help, and I'm still having to translate for her most of the time."

"That's fair. I'll start making arrangements, and you can talk to your parents later. If you can make it, great, if not, I'll expect at least three more translations done before I get back."

Marsee groaned.

Ellie chuckled to herself, knowing that Marsee just needed incentive to get over her fear of leaving. "Watch the attitude or I'll make it four and demote you back to apprentice."

Marsee just rolled her eyes. "Yes, Senior Guild Master."

Ellie glared at her for a moment before letting her own tail curl. "Impudent cub. Now what were you coming to see me for? I'm guessing it wasn't just to be growled at, but I'm more than willing to oblige."

Marsee grinned. "I suppose I should wait now, so I can count this towards one of my four translations. The sketches are still pretty rough, but Little Flower told me the story last night when she couldn't sleep, and I wanted to get it down before I forgot it. The closest translation we could come up with was the Night Flyer."

Ellie's glare turned to a grin and she held her paw out, with greedy grabbing motions. Little Flower had flat out refused to try drawing, but Ellie had finally convinced her to tell some of her stories for Marsee to translate. "Let me see!"

Marsee handed over her drawing tablet and Ellie started swiping through the drawings.

*Oh this is fantastic!* Ellie thought. "I honestly don't think you should change anything. I really like the different style. It fits the mood of the character. A few touch-ups here or there, but that's about it."

"Seriously?" Marsee asked. "I didn't spend all that much time on the drawings. I just wanted to get the general idea down."

Ellie looked up at Marsee. "Do you remember the day I first came to your home and the sketches your sister did?"

"How could I forget? I was a complete blubbering mess the entire day," Marsee replied. "It was one of the most exciting and terrifying days of my life, but then that seems to be par for the course around you."

Ellie chuckled. "I tend to have that effect on people. Anyway, these are like your sister's drawings that day. She didn't spend all that much time on them either, but their simplicity was powerful in conveying the emotion of the scene. I honestly like those original sketches far more than the finished ones she did later. Good work doesn't have to be labor intensive, or take months to complete. Artwork just needs to speak to the soul. What one person loves another person might hate, and I've seen many beautiful pieces of artwork destroyed by overthinking."

Ellie handed the table tablet back and then glared at Marsee. "Be honest with yourself. You like them too, or you wouldn't have come here to show me."

Marsee looked away, flustered and embarrassed, but nodded. "I wasn't sure though, because they feel so unfinished compared to everything else I've ever seen, or been expected to do."

"Well that's where you excel, and likely where your instructors have gone wrong with you in the past," Ellie said.

Marsee frowned at her. "How so?"

"Our job is to teach you the techniques to do the work, but that doesn't leave a lot of room for creativity. You do well under pressure, take the stuff you created to help your sister. I'm guessing the expected coursework felt constrictive to you over the years, and probably one of the reasons why you jumped guilds so much."

Marsee shrugged. "I guess that's part of it. Once I got to journeyman the courses changed. I like the variety of being an apprentice, and I often didn't have the patience for going over the forty three different uses for some wood stain."

"Part of it?" Ellie asked and frowned. Something about Marsee's body language bothered her.

Marsee didn't answer for a while.

"What happened?" Ellie demanded.

Marsee looked away, unable to make eye contact and sighed. "When no one would mentor me or tell me why, I figured I just wasn't good enough, and switched disciplines trying to find something I was good at."

"That's not true and you know it. You would have been promoted years ago if it weren't for your instinct," Ellie growled.

"I know that now, but I didn't then. Plus, if I did what was expected of me, which was downright boring most of the time, my instructors seemed disappointed in me, but if I put effort into my projects to try and impress them, all I ever got was 'that's...inventive' or something similar, and they'd walk away and work with someone else. I switched to the Artist's Guild hoping that if I could embellish my work better, that it might impress someone, and a big part of the reason I switched to the Writer's Guild was because I just gave up, figuring no one would ever mentor me. My uncle had a Flyer come work on one of his old books when I was at his home one day, and I realized I could do that work and be seen as good at it, even if I wasn't necessarily enthusiastic about doing that work for the rest of my life, outside of getting to see and read all those ancient books. When I spoke to admissions in the Writers Guild about it, they were positively giddy over my application, and it was the first time I felt appreciated and good about my work. I only focused on learning the other languages at first so I could read the books I was fixing."

Ellie snorted and shook her head. "Those idiots. You too for that matter."

"Me? What did I do wrong this time?" Marsee asked, thoroughly confused.

"Your instructors likely didn't know how to handle your creativity, and should have been encouraging and challenging you, but weren't, or at least not in a way you understood or needed. As an instructor, it's usually the student who needs the most help that gets the most attention, and as I've learned from working with Hue-mans, we are not an inventive species, not unless we have a real problem to solve. It's not surprising that your instructors in the Writer's Guild were giddy over your application. I know I heard from several how excited they were to have you there, and how disappointed they were that I stole you from them, because very few people have your level of skill in the multiple areas needed for that craft, and actually *want* to work with old musty books. I'll probably have to have you work on a few just to keep them from staging a coup to get you back."

"Seriously?" Marsee asked, thoroughly surprised.

Ellie rolled her eyes. "Let me be perfectly clear with you, I *want* you to explore anything and everything that interests you. If you want to try something new, do so. I don't care if it's a complete failure, like my rocking chair. In fact, if you so much as deliver something normal and standard, I'll deny it. I have enough of that from other crafters, who like doing that kind of thing. People want new and different. That," she said, pointing to the drawing tablet, "will be a success. I guarantee it. Now go on. Talk to your family about the trip, and finish that book. I expect my copies to be bound completely differently than before."

Marsee blinked at her and nodded. "Yes, ma'am."

Ellie chuckled after Marsee left, shook her head that someone as talented as Marsee was, still couldn't see it. *Well, I suppose it's better than her being arrogant about it like some of my Guild Masters,* she thought, and then with a heavy sigh, returned to her problems on the Water World.

# CHAPTER 41

# Feral Kitten

He set his tablet down and chuckled over the latest message from Damon. *He's far too easy to manipulate. I wonder if he'll actually follow through with it though. Well if nothing else it'll cause a distraction, but if he does, Chenzira's rodent of a daughter will be dead soon, killed by her own people. Chenzira too, if I'm lucky. Once the rest of the Consortium realizes just how dangerous those rodents are, all of Chenzira's popularity will vanish along with them.*

His efforts at stirring up unrest with the people had been going well, until that stupid festival had caused Layton to become enamored with the rodents, and those stupid cookies. *I do have to admit they were tasty, but they're far too expensive to import. I can't believe how much Chenzira's getting away with charging for them. I need to redirect Layton. The question is how?*

His thoughts drifted back to that awful trip to New Hope. *How convenient that that little rodent wakes up the same day everyone shows up at Prince Pussycat's castle. He couldn't have planned more sympathy with that vigil if he'd tried, or more of a distraction from his real plans. Having a third of the Council wasn't good enough, he had to go and take over the Guild too? That can't be allowed to stand. The Guild has far too much power as it is, and the Translator is far too popular to be allowed to take over.*

He snorted in disgust at the title his people were calling the furry little princess these days. *It would have been poetic justice if those sand spinners had stung her,* he thought, remembering that awful book she'd translated. He frowned, as that made him remember that all of his efforts to cause chaos in New Hope had failed disastrously, but then he shrugged. *That's what I get for letting someone else do the dirty work.* The other two rodents had failed to live up to his expectations, and would soon die for their failure, after he had them cause a little more chaos. *Damon is proving to be a much better pawn anyway. Shame he'll have to die too.*

He pulled himself out of his thoughts and picked up the letter that had been delivered to his home earlier, just as he was leaving to go play with his toys. The letter was unmarked, but he recognized the hand writing and envelope which his informant in the guard always used. He opened it and read the message.

"The trip has been finalized. The brat leaves in two days. Just her and her mentor," was all it said, along with a number.

*Took them long enough,* he thought.

When the other protests had died off and his original plans had gone awry, he'd changed tactics, deciding he needed to take a more active role. It was hard to do that off planet, so he'd decided to lure them to his domain. He grinned as the first of his prey was swimming right into his trap. The trip to New Hope hadn't been entirely a waste. He'd managed to overhear what turned out to be two of Ellie's pilots grumbling about Ellie and the promotion, and had found out her third pilot was none other than Wind Rider's daughter.

He chuckled at his plans there and refocused on the letter, wondering what the numbers were. He wasn't sure, but he had an idea. He picked up his tablet again, and logged back into Snapper Fish's old account to avoid being tracked, and pulled up the Council records, but found nothing, so he switched into the Guard's queue and tried there. *Oh ho! What have we here? Someone's been a very naughty kitten.*

He read through the ticket which had already been closed and signed off on, by none other than the Senior Honor Kitten herself, detailing some lovely injuries on the brat's medical record. *If he's been abusing his kitten, I'll be able to destroy him with this information.*

He pulled up the attached document and began reading, his skin rippling with giddiness as he realized just what he had. It took him several hours to finish reading. It was by far the most captivating thing the Translator had ever written. He frowned when he realized the journal was nearly two months old, so he switched into her account and quickly located the original. When he was done he logged into the Healer's Guild and pulled up everything he could find on the illness, and then switched back into the guard records to see just how prevalent this particular illness was.

He'd dismissed Marsee's illness when he'd first learned of it, since they seemed to have found a cure, or at least a treatment for it, but this illness was far more than he'd been led to believe, if her journal was accurate. He saw no reason why it wouldn't be.

He sat there stunned when he realized what was really going on. *Oh this is even better,* he thought. *I'll be able to destroy all of Saber with this information. Seems our kitty cats have been hiding a little secret. Yes, everything is going according to plan. By the end of the week the entire Senior Council will be mine, and none will be the wiser. With this information, every last kitty cat will be stripped of their claws, if not kicked out of the Consortium entirely.*

He chuckled, deciding his informant had just secured a place as his Senior Honor Guard, and tossed the letter and tablet in his desk before turning to examine his collection of toys.

*I suppose I should get some practice in before the brat arrives. I can't have her going all feral on me before I'm ready to spring my trap.* He frowned as a thought occurred. *They're not going to go down without a fight. I'd better make some contingency plans. Now the real question is, who haven't I heard scream in a while?*

His skin rippling with anticipation, he unlocked the cage and swam in.

LAURA NAPOLI

Laura Napoli was born and raised in northern Vermont and continues to make the area her home. When not spending her time on the warm clicky box (computer), she is the caregiver to four heating cats who provide her with heat, massage, acu-paw-ture, and purr-therapy in exchange for pets and catnip treaties. For more information, visit https://www.heatingcats.com

*Publications*

Book 1: The Tails of Little Flower

Book 2: The Pride of Little Flower

Book 3: The Whiskers of Hope

*Coming Soon*

Book 4: The Paws of Hope

# CHARACTER REFERENCE

HUE-MAN (LITTLE EARTH)

- **2A84**
  - ◦ Alias: Nazari's Cub
- **Aaron Delaney**
- **Anne Harding**
  - ◦ *Rank:* Councilor
- **Ben**
- **Danny Shuto**
- **Damon Minor**
  - ◦ *Partner:* Amanda Minor *
  - ◦ *Children:* Sarah Minor *
- **Ezra Borovik**
- **Henry Curtis**
- **Irene**
  - ◦ *Rank:* Councilor
- **James O'Neil**
  - ◦ *Rank:* Councilor
  - ◦ *Partner:* Ben O'Neil *
  - ◦ *Grandchildren:* Jessica O'Neil
  - ◦ *Aliases:* GrandFather, Uncle James
- **Janet**
  - ◦ *Rank:* Councilor
  - ◦ *Alias:* 1A102
- **Jenny Rousseau**
  - ◦ *Rank:* Councilor

- **Jeran Frederick Chenzira**
    - *Rank:* Senior Councilor
    - *Mentor:* Marcus Surellis
    - *Partner:* Myra Chenzira
    - *Parents:* Frederick Surellis, Grammy Surellis
    - *Children:* Marsee, Jenny, Thomas, three others
- **Jordan Ross**
    - *Rank:* Councilor
- **Kai Nez**
    - *Rank:* Councilor
- **Little Flower Chenzira**
    - *Rank:* Councilor
    - *Parents:* Jeran Chenzira, Myra Chenzira, Alice O'Neil *, David O'Neil *
    - *Grandparents:* Frederick Chenzira, Grammy Chenzira, James O'Neil, Ben O'Neil *
    - *Aliases:* Jessica O'Neil, 1A1
- **Margaret**
    - *Rank:* Councilor
    - *Alias:* 4A35
- **Mary Shepard**
    - *Rank:* Councilor
- **Mitch ***
    - Alias: 3A236
- **Paul Markson**
- **Rachael Hoffsteader**
    - *Rank:* Councilor
- **Vera Scott**
    - *Rank:* Councilor

## SABER

- **Ammond Greyfoot**
    - *Rank:* Master Healer - Hearing Specialist
    - *Partner:* Theresa Greyfoot
- **Avery Hunt**
    - *Rank:* Honor Guard
    - *Mentor:* Kendra Hunt
- **Brice Morningstar**
    - *Rank:* Senior Healer - Agency
    - *Mentor:* Myra Chenzira
- **Cynthia Lowell**
    - *Rank:* Master Tech - Tech Guild
- **Elliana Reighly Khihar**
    - *Rank:* Senior Guild Master
- **Gregory**
    - *Rank:* Master - Builder's Guild
- **Gentry Fartooth**
    - *Rank:* Master - Writer's Guild
- **Jennette Tabor**
    - *Rank:* Senior Councilor
- **Kendra Hunt**
    - *Rank:* Senior Honor Guard
- **Kelly Goodwind**
    - *Rank:* Master Healer
    - *Mentor:* Myra Chenzira
- **Layton Reheem**
    - *Rank:* Broadcaster - Press Guild
- **Maggie Chenzira**
    - *Parents:* Thomas Chenzira, Jenny Chenzira
- **Marcus Surellis**
    - *Rank:* Councilor - South Plains District
    - *Parents:* Frederick Surellis, Grammy Surellis

- **Marsee Bet Chenzira**
    - *Rank:* Journeyman - Artist's Guild, Journeyman - Crafter's Guild, Apprentice - Writer's Guild, Translator - Council
    - *Parents:* Myra Chenzira, Jeran Chenzira
- **Mattis Lawson**
    - *Rank:* Guild Senior - Primary School Guild
- **Myra Beth Chenzira**
    - *Rank:* Master Healer, Master Animal Healer
    - *Partner:* Jeran Chenzira
    - *Mentors:* Ammond Greyfoot, Nazari Jabri
    - *Children:* Marsee, Jenny, Thomas, three others
- **Nazari Jabri**
    - *Rank:* Master Healer, Master Animal Healer
- **Ned Griffith**
    - *Rank:* Councilor - North Plains District
- **Nerissa Witherspoon**
    - *Rank:* Senior Guild Healer
- **Nichola Sampson**
    - *Rank:* Oscar Rynhold
    - *Mentor: Oscar Rynhold*
- **Paxton Parner**
    - *Rank:* Councilor - Jandolf Square District
- **Oscar Rynhold**
    - *Rank:* Commander - Ship's Guild
- **Quinn Bluestone**
    - *Rank:* District Senior - Council City - Honor Guard
    - *Mentor:* Kendra Hunt
- **Rowan**
    - *Rank:* Journeyman Healer
- **Tamarin Fields**
    - *Rank:* Honor Guard
- **Theresa Greyfoot**
    - *Partner:* Ammond Greyfoot
- **Thomas Chenzira**

    ◦ *Rank:* Master - Musician's Guild

## WATER SPRITE (WATER WORLD)

- **Agate**
  - *Rank:* Guild Master
- **Clear Seas**
  - *Rank:* Senior Councilor
- **Rip Current**
  - *Rank:* Councilor - East Sea District
- **Rainbow Scales**
  - *Rank:* Translator

## DIGGER

- **Sammianna**
  - *Rank:* Senior Councilor
- **Nardal**
  - *Rank:* Guild Master - Staffer's Guild

## FLYER

- **Petra**
  - *Rank:* Ship Master
  - *Parents:* Wind Rider
- **Wind Rider**
  - *Rank:* Senior Councilor
- **Yellow Tail**
  - *Rank:* Master - Writer's Guild

## ICE GIANT (ICE PLANET)

- **Apakna**
  - *Rank:* Senior Councilor

## HUMAN (EARTH)

- **Alice O'Neil** *
  - *Occupation:* Baker, Business Owner
  - *Partner:* David O'Neil
  - *Children:* Jessica O'Neil
- **Amanda Minor** *
  - *Occupation:* Social Worker
  - *Partner:* Damon Minor
  - *Children:* Sarah Minor
- **Ben O'Neil** *
  - *Occupation:* Farmer
  - *Partner:* James O'Neil
  - *Children:* David O'Neil
  - *Grandchildren:* Jessica O'Neil
- **David O'Neil** *
  - *Occupation:* Lieutenant Marines - Retired, Business Owner
  - *Partner:* Alice O'Neil
  - *Children:* Jessica O'Neil
- **Ms. Walters** *
  - *Occupation:* High school Spanish Teacher
- **Susie Thomson** *
- **Joey** *
- **Mark** *
- **Sarah Minor** *
  - *Parents:* Amanda Minor, Damon Minor

* Deceased

Note: All ranks, species, and guild affiliations listed are those at the time they were first introduced in this book or at the time of their death.

www.ingramcontent.com/pod-product-compliance
Lightning Source LLC
Chambersburg PA
CBHW062107290726
48975CB00001B/136